PHARCEL

To: Monice
From: Berty & family
October, 2008

467 1813

PHARCEL

RUNAWAY SLAVE

A NOVEL BY

ALICK LAZARE

iUniverse, Inc.
New York Lincoln Shanghai

Pharcel
Runaway Slave

iUniverse books may be ordered through booksellers or by contacting:

iUniverse
2021 Pine Lake Road, Suite 100
Lincoln, NE 68512
www.iuniverse.com
1-800-Authors (1-800-288-4677)

This is a work of fiction. All of the characters, names, incidents, organizations and dialogue in this novel are either the products of the author's imagination or are used fictitiously.

ISBN-13: 978-0-595-39578-1 (pbk)
ISBN-13: 978-0-595-83981-0 (ebk)
ISBN-10: 0-595-39578-3 (pbk)
ISBN-10: 0-595-83981-9 (ebk)

Printed in the United States of America

PREFACE

The story in this book is fictional although the names of most of the characters and the events described are drawn from various sources in the history of runaway slaves in Dominica.

The author is pleased to acknowledge the works of Lennox Honychurch and CLR James as well as the published notes and sermons of Rev. Charles Peters, from which he has drawn substantially. Most of the historical data on the condition of slaves in Dominica and the exploits of the runaways during the period 1786 to 1800 have been taken from Honychurch's *The Dominica Story* and from Rev. Peter's *Anecdotes: Description of the Temper and the Habits Which Generally Characterized the White Inhabitants of Dominica in Respect of the Negro Race in the Years 1799 and 1800* and *Two Sermons Preached At Dominica On the 11th. and 12th. Of April, 1800*. CLR James' *The Black Jacobins* provided an invaluable insight into the nature of the Negro revolt in San Domingo and its effect on the colonies in the rest of the Caribbean; and Thomas Atwood's *The History of the Island of Dominica* also served as a useful source of reference.

The author was fortunate to have on hand extracts from Dominica Court Sessions and Council Minutes covering the period 1786 to 1803 which gave the names of the runaway chiefs and many of those of their followers who had been captured and brought to trial.

Since this is a work of fiction, the author has had to take considerable license in his descriptions of the characters in the book and in the sequencing and placement of historical events. Although actual names were used, the portrayal of the characters are pure inventions and do not relate in any particular to persons, alive or dead.

The author accepts full responsibility for any deviations from historical fact.

CHAPTER 1

The boy sat on the bare ground, frozen in wonder, his mouth opened wide, eyes staring intently. His breath caught in his throat as he looked fixedly on the little white girl squatting in the bush. Unaware of his presence, she lifted her rose-colored dress and squirted in the dry dust. Head down, she gazed at her water as it spread almost to her slippers before it was soaked up by the parched ground. She was no more than twelve years old, with russet hair and pink-shaded cheeks lightly sprinkled with pale brown freckles. Her face was full, almost square with a pronounced jut to her chin. Her full lips turned down sharply at their extremities, giving them a petulant turn. She lifted her head and stared straight into the boy's curious eyes. Startled, she leapt up from her squatting position, her face a flaming red, her freckles seeming to burn a darker brown. Hastily, she drew her dress close between her legs and opened her mouth to scream.

"Sorry!" The boy pleaded with his eyes. Panic furrowed his brow and twisted the generous curvature of his lips. "I didn't mean to look. I didn't see anything."

"Yes, you did. You saw me!"

"I didn't mean to. I was just......I wasn't looking."

He was tall for his age at seventeen. His chocolate-colored skin glowed with vitality, and the short golden hairs on his arms and legs gave his body a sultry look. He had the face of a young warrior; short, matted hair, deep brown with streaks of gold, curling tightly over a wide, low brow; a somewhat high nose flaring suddenly over thick, firm lips. His chin, squared and resolute, gave strength to his otherwise gentle features. Deep below his brow, his eyes sparkled, a liquid brown that seemed to dance continuously in its pure white field. His body was robust, not yet knotted with muscles, but showing well-defined proportions. He wore only pantaloons, frayed and torn; a bit too large, and hardly concealing his nakedness. They were held to his waist with a piece of rope.

He had come to the bush to get away from the heat that turned the small kitchen, where he helped with the cooking and cleaning, into a veritable oven. There were shrubs of all kinds growing in a semi-circular patch at the back of the house. Beyond the shrubs, and on both sides of the house, stretches of lawn sloped down to a profusion of fruit trees. Red cedar trees leaned over the bush, throwing deep shade over most of it. The bush itself grew in patches, leaving almost bare the ash-colored ground between. It was a warm day. The air was still. Dark clouds hovered over the trees, but there was no sign of rain.

He was sitting there on the warm earth amidst the bushes, whittling away at a length of twig, when the girl appeared suddenly and squatted before him. He was too shocked to move or say anything. He just stared, fascinated by what he saw. He had seen her many times before, running about the yard, or drifting from room to room in the house, but he had never come close to her. He had often heard the slaves speak of her vile temper and provoking ways. They all knew that she was spoilt and rather neglected by her too indulgent father. Up to this moment, he had succeeded in staying out of her way. Now she stood before him, storm-dark in fury; and he was afraid. He sensed that she was frightened, too. She turned to face him, a menacing look on her eyes.

"You did, too. You saw!"

All of a sudden, her countenance changed from fury to willful curiosity. She hesitated only for a moment; then strode purposely to him and grabbed at his flimsy trousers. He leapt backwards, almost tumbling into the thick, prickly growth. She followed him, her chin upturned at a determined angle.

"I will, too. I will see!" she said keeping a firm hold on him.

He stood there in the bush, shivering with fright. Beads of sweat formed on his forehead and ran down into his eyes. At the same time he felt a growing warmth and strength in his loins. He tried to conceal himself; but, to his dismay, his nakedness rose to the sun, golden-brown and gleaming.

A loud gasp came from the clearing. Just a few feet away, a look of horror in her eyes and in her gaping mouth, the child's mother stood. She screamed again and again; then leapt towards her daughter and dragged her away from him towards the house. She enfolded the girl in her arms, her hands over the girl's eyes shutting out the sight of the slave boy's nakedness; but her gaze remained riveted to him, unable to escape the fascination of his vibrant manhood.

The little girl whimpered and held on tightly as she buried her face in the folds of her mother's dress.

"Did he do anything to you? Tell me, Georgette, did he hurt you?"

"Oh, Mama!" Georgette snuffled, and pressed her face onto her mother's stomach.

"Did he?" The woman was hysterical.

The boy stood there, unable to decide what he should do or say. Sweat poured down his face and onto his chest and belly. He sensed shadows gathering around him, and suddenly there were many faces looking at him with dismay and bewilderment. They crept out of the bushes in all directions, their eyes showing various stages of trepidation and concern.

Alexis stepped forward, his stocky frame taut and ready. His black skin shone with sweat and tension, the muscles in his arms and abdomen rippling as he moved. His face was creased and twisted like a dried prune; his eyes small and close; his nose short and thick, and his lips fat and compressed into a permanent pout. Hair stuck to his head in tiny curls like a mass of clockwork springs. He wore gardeners' stained and patched trousers of a coarse calico, the original texture of which was no longer identifiable. Beneath his frayed trousers, his legs were a thin column of tight tendons and bulging veins down to his short, splayed feet.

He stood before the boy, a puzzled and dreadful look on his face. His right arm was held rigidly downwards, holding a cutlass horizontally erect.

"Pharcel! What have you done, boy?" he asked softly.

Toma was standing near the white woman and Georgette. He bent solicitously forward.

"Mde. Lyonnais, what did that boy do? Did he molest the child?"

Mde. Lyonnais, pale and horrified, pointed an accusing finger at Pharcel.

"Take him away!" she gasped. "Lock him in the pen"

She clutched Georgette firmly to her bosom.

Mde. Elise Lyonnais was a lean white woman, with homely features and sun-bleached complexion. After many years in the sun and the rain, her skin had settled into the color of parchment. There were thin, delicate lines at the corners of her eyes, above her upper lips, and at the edges of her mouth. Her hair hung about her face in desultory strands, like straw. But the broad expanse of her forehead and cheeks, the decided arch of her brow, the cool clearness of her grey eyes, the cheerful turn of her nose and her plump lips, gave the appearance of ease and confidence. Lean as she was, her hips curved from a narrow waist down to muscular thighs and shapely legs. Unlike most white women, her rump was full and rounded. When she walked, her stride was straight, long and firm; and her abdomen tended to push forward with every step. She wore a plain, low-cut, white linen dress, ruffled at the front, with mid-arm sleeves, which flared and swirled at her feet; but its folds hardly concealed the sensuousness of her limbs. Her feet, comfortably encased in short, laced boots, were large for a woman, though in delicate proportion to the strength of her legs.

The fright in her added to the paleness of her face, and turned her usual placid countenance to a defensive scowl. She turned to Toma, hovering at her elbow.

"Now, Toma. Take him away. Keep him locked until M. Lyonnais returns."

Toma was the house servant, shabbily elegant in M. Lyonnais' cast-off field suit. He was of medium height, with drooping shoulders, and slightly stooped. A round head with small, alert ears; bulbous eyes staring out beneath patchy eyebrows; flat nose with cavernous nostrils, and a lower lip that jutted out aggressively, gave him the look of a habitual eavesdropper. He had a shuffling, bent-at-the-knees walk, either cultivated as an air of caution or caused by the rheumatism that afflicts house slaves after years of constantly pandering to the night and day wishes of their masters. He spoke in low, respectful tones to all white persons; but to his fellow slaves, he adopted a sharp, commanding voice, somehow arrogant in inflection.

He turned to the small group that had gathered around Pharcel.

"Bring him along," he ordered.

They took hold of Pharcel who reflexively braced himself to resist; but they nudged him gently onward. Bessie, the cook, ample breasts filled with concern, stepped forward; straightened his torn pantaloons, and made him decent. They took him to the pen, pushed him in, and secured its single door and window.

The dark cloud that hung over the trees spread in thick folds towards the sunset, leaving a grey pall over the narrow valley and the dark, dappled sea beyond. A melancholy silence filled the little valley with dreadful foreboding. This had been a quiet, well regulated community. There was M. Lyonnais with his wife and his daughter, who were white; and there was the small group of slaves, no more than twenty, who labored day after day on the hundred acre estate. Occasionally, other white persons came from the neighboring estates at Geneva and at Stowe, mostly men. More frequently, slaves from those estates and from as far as Bagatelle and Pichelin, came secretly to visit friends and relatives, or to court the few female slaves on the estate. No major disruption to this quiet life had occurred for a very long time; not since Alexis had been brought back from the forest trussed like a pig, and whipped near death by the burly overseer who had been summoned from Geneva Estate. Alexis carried the scars of this punishment like a badge of shame on his back and buttocks.

M. Lyonnais returned home just before sunset. As he rode through the fruit trees into the clearing that surrounded the house on three sides, the silence pervading the place struck him with a sense of uneasiness. He was hot and sweaty; and he longed to be out of his field clothes and washed. He rode up to the house, tethered his horse to a calabash tree in the front yard, and ambled stiffly up the steps and into the verandah. Toma came out bearing a goblet of water and a short glass half filled with rum.

"Afternoon, Master Jean," he said somberly.

"Afternoon, Toma," M. Lyonnais replied, giving Toma a quizzical look.

Toma bent his head.

"Madam is in the pantry," he ventured respectfully.

M. Lyonnais downed the rum in one swallow, held out the glass to be filled with water, and drank in satisfying gulps. He cleared his throat and spat over the verandah rails. He gave Toma another questioning look; then turned and strode into the house.

Elise, her two arms tense at her sides, sat in the narrow pantry. Arched brow raised, eyes clouded with worry, she lifted her face as he came in and gripped the edges of the sofa on which she was sitting.

"What is it, Elise?" he asked nervously.

She hesitated just for a moment.

"It is Georgette," she answered.

"What about her?"

"It is that boy, Pharcel."

"What happened?"

"We have to send her away."

"Did he....?"

He was unable to complete the thought. He knew that strange and unexpected things happened on a plantation. There were many stories of white men cohabiting with their slaves, and even of white women physically exploiting them. Recently, there had been a few scandals which had been efficiently suppressed. Many of those white women involved quietly disappeared; returned to Europe; or sent out to larger colonies like Trinidad or Jamaica. But here at Dubique things were different. There was only his wife, and his daughter, and his twenty slaves. They were a small community, virtually isolated from the more populous centers at Grandbay and the surrounding larger estates.

"Did he........?"

Again he hesitated to express what he was thinking. He could not complete the thought because it looked so improbable.

Elise shook her head from side to side. Her eyes were veiled as if concealing her own emotions.

"I don't know. I found them in the bushes at the back." She faltered for a while, and then spoke rapidly. "He was very aroused."

Patches of blood suffused her cheeks, giving a bruised look to her pale face.

Haltingly, she recounted the events of the afternoon as she had seen them—Georgette's eager hand at the slave's torn trousers, and the compelling and menacing sight of his manhood, so alive and captivating. She tried not to dwell too much on this; but the sight of him, so vibrant and beautiful, had put her mind in a fever of excitement that was, to her, strange and incomprehensible. There was nothing much to tell, really; only the threat of his black potency glistening in the afternoon sun; and Georgette's zestful attempt to unclothe him. Elise could hardly admit to this about her daughter and merely said lamely, "Her hand was on him."

Jean knew his daughter. He was aware that she was unseemly daring, and sometimes rambunctious; but he didn't think she could be so bold as to provoke advances from a slave.

"Where is he?"

"In the pen. I told them to lock him in."

"I will deal with it in the morning." He took a step towards the bedroom, and then stopped. "Where is Georgette?"

"She is asleep. She was frightened."

He turned to go, paused, looked over his shoulder and said, "Tell Toma to send over to Geneva and ask Brent to come in early tomorrow morning. He must come prepared."

Jean entered the bedroom where his daughter slept curled in a foetal position. Deep sleep covered the lively boldness that normally brightened her face. She looked innocent and vulnerable asleep; but he knew very well that she had an irrepressible tendency to mischief. In the confines of Dubique there was so little to absorb her enormous energy and challenge her spirited imagination. He had planned to send her away to boarding school when she had attained her fourteenth birthday. Now, he couldn't wait any longer. He had to do it immediately. Elise would have to be persuaded because Georgette gave meaning to her life on the estate, a life which was otherwise dreary and uneventful. But he would have to be firm about this.

At twelve, Georgette had developed a reckless precociousness that was well-nigh uncontrollable. The other estates were too far for her to mingle with her kind and her own age, so she ventured among the slaves, assuming an aggressive loftiness which was at once comical and provoking. She was in no great danger since everyone on the estate regarded her simply as a harmless, though unruly child. Elise protected her as much as she could but she was unable to contain her occasional willfulness and boisterous escapades.

After a cool wash in the stone bath, barefoot and wearing a light linen shirt and white drill pants, Jean ate a warm supper of baked yams and corned pork.

The heat had abated and the still evening stirred with puffs of cool air. Elise had already retired to their bedroom and should soon be asleep. He sat on a rocker on the back porch, staring at the deepening dark, and listening to the sounds of night creeping in—the crack-crack of crickets and the sharp screech of tree lizards. He reached for the glass and the bottle of rum which Toma had placed on the verandah floor, ready for his convenience. As he sipped the burning liquid, he thought of the slave locked in the pen and the unpleasant task that awaited him next morning. He had seen Pharcel grow up into a sturdy and handsome young man, quite intelligent, although untaught. He dismissed the thought that the boy had any malice in him, or that he could willfully provoke an encounter with his daughter. The boy had proved himself reliable and loyal, as any slave could be expected to be reliable and loyal. At least there was no sign in him of the truculence so often betrayed by the field slaves.

Jean Lyonnais had a reputation for treating his slaves with benevolent indifference. As far as he was concerned, his obligation was to feed them well, and clothe and shelter them. Theirs was to give a twelve hour a day work. He never took part in those philosophical debates as to whether slaves were fully human, or were inferior beings, or whatever else the clergy and the abolitionists spoke so much about in recent tracts and sermons. On the field, he ate and worked with them; and he sweated as much as they did in the burning sun as together they planted and reaped the sugar cane that filled the upper valley and hill slopes of the small estate. He was stern, but never employed the constant and harsh punishment that other plantations were known to do. Only once had he to resort to actually whipping one of his slaves. That was the time Alexis had been found wandering in the forest and had been returned to him by the white men who had caught him. It was at their insistence that he had reluctantly agreed to punish the slave. He himself had felt that the penalty recommended was too severe, but he desisted from protesting to his white neighbors about this. In any event, that had discouraged Alexis and any other slaves on the estate from further attempts at running away.

He had heard many stories of atrocities committed against their slaves by estate owners in other parts of the island, and he could not understand why men who cherished their horses and dogs so wonderfully could treat their slaves with such cruelty. On one of his rare visits to the plantation of one of his acquaintances, he had observed much that was reprehensible. He remembered what he had seen when, walking about the estate compound, he had come across a slave boy almost starved to death, chained to a wooden hutch no bigger than a kennel. The boy had been kept in that condition for weeks. His owner, M. Grenault, had explained sourly that the boy was of no use. He suffered from an infected leg, and was unable to work. The sight of the boy's emaciated body and swollen, purulent leg had repelled him. After that, he had shortened his visit and he had never returned to that place.

And now he had to decide what punishment to mete out to Pharcel. The boy had been good, a steady and unobtrusive worker, an ideal house and kitchen attendant. He was neat in appearance even with the faded and torn cast-offs that he wore. He carried himself with an air of quiet assurance. Often, Jean would find him standing in the shade of the calabash tree, deep in thought, his chin slightly raised and inclining towards his right shoulder, his eyes somber and his broad lips set tight. He thought of the afternoon's event with disquiet. He did not believe that the boy had willfully or otherwise assaulted his daughter, but he had to take firm action. His wife and his daughter were compromised in some way or other; and the boy had to be punished.

He poured himself another shot of rum.

Elise lay in the four poster, canopied bed, warm in the folds of her voluminous nightgown. Her eyes were tightly shut, but she was not asleep. Tonight she lay there not waiting for her husband, because she knew that he would not be retiring soon. In any case, the tiredness in his face when he came home was a sure sign that he would not look to her for comfort on this night. She had learned to anticipate his needs, knowing when to prepare herself for his increasingly infrequent bouts of passion. They had been married thirteen years, and they were thirteen years of a desultory union that produced just one daughter and enough sugar cane to keep the bankers at bay. Her husband was a good planter; otherwise he could not have eked out enough to keep them from penury, from the stony hillsides in which he had so imprudently invested.

Jean was a steady and frugal man, intelligent in his own way; but intellectually lazy. He possessed few social graces, but he had that rustic respectability that most farmers had. He worked. He rested. On the few occasions when they entertained, he was lavish in the simple country fare that he always provided for his guests; and he managed, albeit with a great deal of awkwardness, to keep up a faltering conversation for the greater part of the night. He and Elise received few invitations to social gatherings from their neighbors and even fewer from acquaintances in Roseau.

Elise was naturally sociable, and she enjoyed the wit and humor of good conversation; however, she always felt uneasy when she attended the few grand dinners and balls in the company of her husband, not because she was ashamed of his gaucheness, but out of concern for his open discomfort in the company of his peers. In the midst of animated conversation all around, he always managed to slip to the fringes of lively groups, roaming with vacant eyes and hesitant steps as if searching for a way out. She had met some interesting people at many of these gatherings—men who were able to converse endlessly about nothing in particular, and to spice the paucity of their ideas with titillating wit and humor; and women who turned the most vicious gossiping into a fine conversational art.

She remembered the first time she had met Captain Marshall of the 15th Regiment. He had been sent to Grandbay to scout the location of runaways in the heights of Geneva, and had spent a great amount of time carousing from plantation to plantation. It had got so noticeable that the wags in the area began to speak of him as the runaway Captain. One Sunday morning, he had come to the house at Dubique, wearing rumpled white trousers and scarlet tunic, hair tousled and a two day growth of beard on his face. He sat on the front verandah with Jean, drinking rum; and his conversation flowed endlessly in a series of anecdotes and reminiscences of his public school days and his exploits in the army, sometimes provocative, but more often quite risqué; though when Elise and Georgette sat with them his more daring stories were told with delicacy and charm.

She had been captivated by him and his pleasant humor which had lightened the dreary days on the estate; and she had listened to his every word with an excitement that seemed to stir her mysteriously. She had felt herself drawn to him in a most disturbing way whenever he turned his lazy, far away look on her; and she had felt herself losing control, caught up in a breathless, panting excitement that she had never experienced before, as if he had taken possession of her spirit.

And so it was when he came again the following afternoon. Jean was up in the hills; the yard was quiet and deserted; Toma and Bessie were clearing up after lunch; and Georgette was asleep. Elise was walking among the fruit trees in the shade of the dark, lush foliage of the spreading mango trees. She sensed him before she saw him standing there among the trees. He had the same lazy, distant look in his eyes. He was clean-shaven this time; and his clothes were newly pressed, his brown hair still fell in rumpled curls over his forehead and he smelled of bay cologne. Instantly, she felt breathless, and there was a strange stirring in her loins.

In the deep shade of a mango tree he stood over her, a tentative smile flashing across his lips. He drew her to him, leaned her over the low-slung cleavage of the mango tree, and kissed her. She was too shocked and bewildered to say anything, or to resist as he lifted her skirt and entered her. Elise felt a tremor in her legs and a liquid quivering of her loins as he moved quickly into her; and her body responded with a life of its own as spasm after spasm washed over her belly and thighs. Her eyes were tightly shut and she clutched his arms, wanting to hold him to her. Then in desperation, with a furious, violent onset of denial, she pushed him away from her. The move took him by surprise, and he just stood there, unable to understand the sudden and unexpected change in her. His passion suddenly faded, and he stood before her limp and crestfallen. Collecting himself, he slowly righted his clothes, smiled feebly, strode out of the shade, and walked down the sloping lawn to the river where his horse had been tethered.

Elise remained there under the tree for a long time, wondering what it had all been about. It finally dawned on her that her sudden passion had not been physical; rather it was an inexplicable upsurge of emotion and need that had been buried for so long deep within her. She had not realized how pent-up her hidden desires had been or how intense had been her need for emotional release. The Captain was by no means more virile than her husband, and his physical attributes were certainly less generous. What happened between them had been an emotional upheaval and an inexplicable need for deliverance, nothing more. She wondered at the suddenness and intensity of the feeling. It was the first time she had been unfaithful to her husband. She did not think there could be another.

The incident had been quick and secret. Or so she thought. Neither the Captain nor Elise had seen the boy perched high in the tree, terrified and fearful to reveal his presence.

That had happened two years ago. Tonight, as she lay in bed alone and awake, it was not the Captain that occupied her thoughts; neither was it her daughter fast asleep in the room next door, nor her husband swigging rum on the back verandah. The image that occupied her mind was the chocolate-skinned, well-proportioned slave boy in his torn pantaloons, his golden-brown manhood glistening in the sun.

Pharcel lay in the dark, hugging his knees. The night had settled in, and small creatures scuttled in the grass and among the trees. Through the chinks in the walls, he could see flashes of fireflies darting amidst the branches. The night was a cacophony of sound—the croak of frogs, the screech of owls, the sharp whistle of tree lizards and the clack of crickets; sounds that on other nights he had found soothing; sounds that in other circumstances induced comfort and gentle sleep. But tonight sleep would not come to him. He knew what awaited him next day. He had been only a child then, but he remembered the horror of the whipping at the time when Alexis had been captured.

He had not meant to frighten the little white girl. He certainly had not intended to peep at her nakedness. But there she had been, opened out before him; and the fascination of her open nakedness had held him to a stupor. At his age, he was not an innocent as far as sex was concerned. In a slave camp sex could not be hidden. It was everywhere in the bushes and on the other side of the thin partitions that separated the tiny rooms of the slave huts. Even at an early age, the men had begun to tease him about his virility; and it had not been long before the older girls, and even the younger women, began to notice him. He remembered, too, the brief copulation he had witnessed when the Captain had so unceremoniously taken Elise. That had left him mystified about white people's way with sex and loving. They were a race apart, far distant from the simple purity of black people's way with each other. As far as the little white girl was concerned, he had watched her with a total lack of emotion, more stupefied by her sudden exposure before him than he was in any way curious about her nakedness. His emotion had been only aroused when she taken hold of him.

All night long he tossed restlessly in the confines of the pen. It was a tiny, flat-roofed hut, made to accommodate a single person at a time; a timber frame boarded over with uneven planks that left chinks through which a prisoner could be observed. It was too short in length, and he could not stretch out fully. The floor was also uneven as the boards were warped from the ground moisture. There were gaps between the boards that admitted all sorts of insects and bugs that infested the night. The roof was plastered with shingles which the sun and the rain had twisted into grey scallops. During the day it was a veritable furnace, but at night the chill crept in with the myriad insects and bugs.

Pharcel shivered, not only from the night's coolness, but more so from the dread of being shackled and beaten as he had seen them do to Alexis. He had done nothing wrong. He had only just seen a little white girl's nakedness. He thought of Mde. Lyonnais and the time she had been so brutishly ravaged by the Captain. In his black world, the woman should have been stoned or drowned in the river for her betrayal of her husband; and the Captain spayed and left to die somewhere in the forest. Now he was to be punished merely for being there while the little white girl had indecorously exposed herself in the scant cover of the bushes.

He felt deeply the injustice of his situation, but he knew he was helpless to stand against it. The slaves at Dubique were naturally resentful at being slaves; however, they had become conditioned to living from day to day, hoping that some day the struggle out in the hills beyond would bring deliverance at last. Remote as the estate was, word had filtered through about the valiant struggle of Coree Greg, Bala, Mabouya and their bands of warriors; and about their dream that some day the white planters and their servants would be driven from the island, and all Africans would return to their homeland free once more.

He could easily have escaped the pen. The structure was fragile, and he was certain that with little effort he could break down the walls. He could run. He was familiar with the tracks that led to the boundaries of the estate; but, beyond that, the impenetrable forest was a barrier he did not know how to penetrate. There were tracks that traversed the forest to the camps in the heights of Grandbay, to Grand Fond, and to Belles; but they were so camouflaged that only those who had help and who were guided there could find them. He had heard that Jacques, who had escaped from the Lavenier estate and who was still in the woods nearby, helped those who wanted to join a camp. Jacques had run away because he had lost one of Mr. Lavenier's sheep, for which crime he had been tied to a tree all night to be punished next day. He had managed to free himself, ran away, and kept to the woods bordering the estate for several years before he was finally recaptured. He never stayed in the camps, but he was a trusted guide for any slave that wanted to join one of the three camps in the vicinity of the lakes. Pharcel had also heard that life in the camps was rough and dangerous. At least, here he was fed and sheltered and safe from being shot at by the militia. Out there, life was uncertain, and living conditions were said to be vile.

Alexis had whispered darkly to him that Brent, the overseer at Geneva, had been sent for with his instruments. He knew what that meant. There were two of these instruments he dreaded most—the cat o' nine tails and the bull pistle. The latter was the dried penis of a bull, stretched out to a pliable thinness. It was said that it would cut deeply into the flesh with surgical precision, leaving only thin scars after the cuts healed. He had no notion which of the two was most dreadful, but he was filled with a deep and agonizing fear at the mere contemplation of any of these instruments lacerating his flesh. Despite the chill, he felt sweat coursing down his face and neck; and he shuddered in fear, and curled his body, knees to forehead, as if to hide away from the very thought of his impending ordeal. He remained that way while the night and all its creatures crept slowly over him. He sensed the beginning of dawn when the night sounds began to fade and the first grey light lifted the dark curtain from the trees and from the slowly rising hills beyond.

CHAPTER 2

The sun was still behind the hills when Elise and Georgette left for the two mile walk from the estate to Grandbay. They were to leave Grandbay by row boat to Roseau where they would remain a week until Georgette could be placed in boarding school and Elise return to Dubique. Jean saw them walk down the narrow path and across the stream until they disappeared in the still grey light around the foot of the hill to the North overlooking the sea.

The house rested on the breast of a hill in a flat meadow that gleamed wet in the dim light. As the sun crept to the brim of the hills behind, streaks of light flashed downwards to the sea, revealing the furrowed sides of the hills and the narrow clearing where the house snuggly nestled. Behind the house, the land arched backwards in fields of sugar cane before rising sharply to a dark patch of forest at the top of a hill. The fields were intercepted by irregular lines of fruit trees planted to shield the cane from the blasts of salt wind that blew from the sea. At the southern side of the house, the meadow dipped to a hollow formed by a brook which cascaded among rocks; and just beside the house, the brook plunged in a tiny waterfall to a shallow basin, surrounded by raspberry bushes and other low vegetation, before it continued downhill to the shore. Towards the North, the meadow sloped to a strip of land cultivated in garden crops, down to the steep banks of a shallow stream. On the other side, on a sharply rising incline, slave huts huddled in the shade of a grove of mango, breadfruit and avocado trees stretching downwards towards the sea. At the bottom of the hill, the brook joined the stream, and the land flattened in a narrow stretch of grass to the rocky shore. A compact stone building stood squarely at the upper end of the flat, and attached to it was an open shed where tools were stored and bullock carts were sheltered. During harvest, stacks of cane were piled on the ground in front of the building, waiting to be hauled to the mill at Geneva.

In the early morning sunlight, the estate house sat dour and wet in its clearing. It was a wooden frame house boarded on all sides with rough planks. The main roof extended on all sides to form a verandah. From the back, narrow steps led to a bare, open patch of earth; to a low bush, and then to a cluster of low hanging trees. At the front, broader steps dropped to an open lawn beyond which was the orchard; and further still, the meadow, where small stock and a few cattle grazed. The house was topped by a hip roof rising steeply to a short ridge and covered with shingles, warped and grey from seasons of sun and rain. Beside the house, the brook gurgled and splashed in a soothing continuity of sound that harmonized with the sound of the wakening day.

To the side and back of the house closer to the brook was the kitchen where Bessie was already stirring and the smell of brewing coffee was rising from the crude percolator on the fireplace. Toma was in the sitting room to the side adjoining the kitchen, opening the wooden door and windows that were held shut by wooden bars bolted in the middle. He had already opened out the main door in the pantry where he had stood somberly while Elise and Georgette had left in the lightening dark. Behind the pantry was the dining room. There were only two other rooms. To the front next to the pantry was the bedroom where Jean and Elise slept, and across a narrow corridor behind this, another bedroom which served as the nursery where Georgette slept. On the few occasions when there were visitors, the other bedroom where Georgette slept was used as a guest room.

Jean was still standing on the front verandah, staring down the slope to the shore where he had last seen his wife and daughter walking away in the low morning light. To his left, overlooking the brook, a calabash tree spread its branches just a few paces from the verandah, its green canon ball fruit glistening in the rising sunlight. A few yards beyond downhill, almost smothered by small trees and prickly bushes, was the pen where he knew Pharcel was awake and awaiting his fate. From where he stood, he could see the slave huts already stirring to life. Wisps of smoke rose from them, and there was the muted sound of morning calls as the slaves awoke to the new day.

He noticed that activity was more subdued than usual, and sensed that there would be resentment at Pharcel's confinement and the punishment he was about to receive. He himself felt a disturbing uncertainty about his action. Had he not already summoned Brent, he might have relented and allowed the incident to fade into insignificance; but now he had to go through with it to save face. He rarely ever meted out physical punishment to his slaves except in the most extreme circumstances, and he never personally administered it. In the present situation, he was in doubt about the boy's guilt; but he had seen the look of near panic in Elise's eyes, a look of fear and insecurity that he had never seen in her before. The boy had to be whipped if only to assuage his wife's distress.

Because of his inner disquiet, he would not make a public spectacle of the whipping. The slaves would not be gathered about the calabash tree to witness the flogging as was commonly done on other plantations. Soon, the slaves would be coming out of their huts in gangs, filing out through the narrow path to the fields above the house. Brent might be less assiduous in his task if he did not have spectators to witness his notorious prowess with the whip.

Pharcel lay on his back in the pen, his legs folded at his hips and knees, arms pressing his thighs to his chest. All night long he had turned to one side and then to the other, seeking relief from the insect bites and the cramps in his thighs and calves. He itched all over his back and sides, and there were already burning sores on his legs right down to his feet where ants and beetles had crawled over him and stung his flesh. It had been the most miserable night of his life and he felt a burning resentment at the torture he had been through. He thought again and again of the little white girl carelessly stooping uncovered before him, and he could not understand how events following this simple encounter could have turned so dreadfully against him. He had done nothing wrong except be there. Now he was caged like a rogue animal waiting to be flogged.

He had spent seventeen years of his life on the estate serving the white man and his wife, doing what he was told to do, keeping to his own kind. He had never given much thought to his condition as a slave; that was the only life he knew, growing up among the slave huts and in the fields until he was old enough to serve as a house slave. His life among the black men, women and children in the huts was secure and uncomplicated. He ate what he was given, drank the cool water from the stream and coconuts that grew among the huts, partook of the abundant fruit on the estate, slept during the afternoons in the shade under the trees bordering the fields, and gave no thought to what other life there was or could be.

His life in the estate house had also been uncomplicated; his chores were simple—to clean up after cooking was done, and to do Bessie's bidding. The rest of the time he spent around the yard or in the shade of the low trees at the back of the house. He had his favorite spot among the trees where he thought no one came. It was a tree with thickly-leaved and low-hanging branches that formed a tent-like hollow. The earth beneath was always dry except after heavy rains; it was close enough to the house that he could hear whenever Bessie called, but it was so private he could loiter there without fear of discovery.

Now he lay there in the pen, itching and burning all over, brooding darkly at his misfortune. He knew he did not deserve to be flogged; he had done nothing wrong, just unwittingly watched the little girl stooping naked under her pink dress. Little black children squatted naked among the huts and nobody cared. What had he done wrong to merit punishment? It was the little girl who should be punished. She it was who had come at him to uncover his nakedness. What had the woman witnessed? Surely, she had seen it all. Was the thought of her innocent daughter wantonly seizing upon a slave too much for her sensibilities? And was he to be punished for that? These questions tormented his mind and a sense of injustice burned in his heart.

He thought that he could run away, and he wondered why nobody else did. Alexis had tried; but he was brought back soon after and whipped into submission. Pharcel had heard among the older men murmurs about the lure of freedom. Those were the men who had been brought on the slave ships from Africa and who were constantly whispering among themselves about a coming insurrection that would deliver them from bondage and return them to their cherished homeland. They knew about the runaway slave camps nearby in the mountains. Two of these runaways had actually visited the huts one night and sat with them till dawn, telling stories about their exploits. One of them was Cicero who had been gun-bearer to Congoree before he joined Bala's camp. He was a short, wiry man who seemed forever on the move; his eyes shifted from side to side as he spoke; and he had the nervous habit of darting in and out of places as if always on the run.

That night the two runaways had recounted how they had raided many estates in the East and on the West coast, burning storehouses, stealing cattle and liberating female slaves. They had boldly attacked some of the planters in their own houses and one planter had died after being slashed across his breast when he attempted to intercept them. There were warriors everywhere in the hills and on the highways armed with cutlasses, spears and even pistols. The white planters were terrorized, and some of them had already abandoned their estates and returned to England.

Recently, the militia had been mobilized and was on the march, invading some of the camps on the west coast. Fierce battles were being fought in the woods. The runaways lured the white soldiers into the dense forest and attacked them there, but there were traitors among the slaves who guided the militia to some of the less well guarded camps. There had been a raid on one of the camps above Mahaut that took the runaways by surprise; many had been killed and others scattered in the woods; some were later captured, but many crossed the hills to join a small camp near Belles in the center of the island.

That night, the slaves had huddled around the two runaways and listened with fascination to their accounts of heroic deeds and dastardly betrayals. Bala, the leader of the camp at Morne Rosae near the Fresh Water Lake, had pronounced death on two slaves on the Rosalie estate for plotting with the militia to raid his camp. The men would be killed on sight by anyone of the warriors any day now. The slaves were fired up by these accounts of the bravery and bold resolution of the leaders of the camps, especially of Bala, Mabouya and Coree Greg who commanded the Eastern forests; but they had also heard of the privation, disease and death in those camps, and were unwilling to leave the security of the estate to venture into those unknown and formidable woods.

All this Pharcel remembered as the night slowly crept towards dawn. Grey light filtered through the gaps in the sides of the pen, and the night creatures vanished with the dark. He groaned as the cramps seized the muscles of his legs; he sat up and stretched them as far as they would go in the short space between the walls of the pen; his back ached and itched at the same time; he tried rubbing himself on the side of the pen to relieve the itch, but his flesh rubbed raw and burning against the rough wood. In frustration, he bent his head between his knees and wondered if this was a deliberate prelude to the greater torment he was soon to endure.

The sounds of early morning began like an overture from a barnyard orchestra. A cock crowed in the distance and provoked lusty responses from more than a dozen chanticleers all over the estate. A donkey brayed mockingly, and the low moan of oxen in the pasture nearby sent a sobering signal that the day's work was soon to begin. The air was soon filled with the chirping of birds and the cackle of hens. Dogs barked to no purpose except to proclaim their watchfulness. The creeping light of day swept away the vestiges of the dark and the heat of the sun quickly dried the wetness on the trees and on the grass.

Pharcel stirred uneasily in the warming light, musing on the terrors of the night he had come through, the phantoms of his warrior ancestors that had filled his wakefulness with brave thoughts and glorious imaginings, and on the reasons why they had not come for him with the opening of day. He thought in dread of the pain and humiliation he had to undergo, and his fevered mind invoked the spirit of Cicero and the warriors in the woods as he prepared to face the day. He wondered if he could be brave like them and defy the white man's injustice, helpless and alone as he was. He had heard the field slaves' subdued march through the meadow and up to the fields, so there would be none to even look at him with sympathy, not even Bessie whose great act of kindness would be to prepare the herbal salve that would cleanse his wounds and keep down the fever that was bound to follow his flogging. Bessie would be too soft-hearted to attend a flogging. Somehow he sensed that the sound of every stroke of the whip would sear her very soul.

Footsteps broke in on his thoughts. The latch was swung upwards and the door creaked on its hinges as it swung outwards. Pharcel sat upright, hugging his knees, eyes wide with fright. Toma reached in and grabbed his forearm, dragging him over the uneven floor. Pharcel unfolded his arms, stood bending double in the low pen and shuffled out. For a moment he stood at the door of the pen, raised his eyes to the sun, and stretched his muscles as if preparing himself for flight. Toma reached out to him again, but Pharcel strode out of his reach, head high, shoulders squared, and eyes fixed upwards to the brightening sky. He walked purposefully right up to the calabash tree where Jean and Brent were already waiting.

Jean watched him approach, somewhat perplexed at his composure and lack of concern. He expected the boy would be subdued and cringing with fear; but here he was striding towards him as brave as a man would be who had been summoned to receive an award for gallantry. The boy's bravado made him angry, as if it was an act of defiance.

He turned to Toma. "Tie him up, Toma. Both arms and legs."

Toma hesitated. "His clothes……" he began.

"Take them off. We do not want them torn more than they are already."

Pharcel looked over his shoulder at the white man standing beside Jean and saw his eyes, mean and widely set; nose, blunt and short; fleshy lips set in a dour droop, and cheeks and jowls, ragged, scarred and furrowed by pox. He was tall and lean, and the tendons of his arms and legs tensed with every movement. He seemed as pliant as the whip which he flexed in his right hand. In his left, he held a cat-o-nine tails, the strands of which were punctuated by barbs of metal.

"Use only the bull pistle", Jean instructed.

"Damn! You are too soft!" Brent said gruffly.

He dropped the cat-o-nine tails and took a few steps toward the tree. Toma saw him approach and quickly tied the last knot securing Pharcel's arms. He scuttled away from the tree and stood behind Jean, a few steps from the front verandah. Brent flexed the bull pistle between his hands, looking appreciatively at the slender form of the boy he was about to flog. He took in the delicate, chocolate brown skin and high, rounded buttocks. The boy's body tensed in anticipation, but Brent was in no hurry. He walked slowly with a sideways look as if stalking a prey. As he came within arms length, his arm suddenly arched upwards and swung in a downward sweep across the boy's body. Pharcel jerked upward, standing on his toes. His back twisted with the agony of pain as the bull pistle cut into his flesh, and his head fell back in a stifled scream. The next blow caught him in the opposite direction forming a cross in the center of his back. He dropped his head against the tree and emitted a snort, like an embattled bull beginning to feel the barbs of torment. Brent's arms rose and fell again and again; and Pharcel dropped lower and lower against the tree, each blow cutting deeper into his flesh. His snorts came fiercer and fiercer, but no cry escaped his lips again.

"Enough!" Jean called out in exasperation. "I don't want him killed."

But Brent was as if incensed by the boy's defiant silence. "He will cry! You will cry, damn you!" he shouted, his fat lips foaming at the corners, his eyes wild with anger and frustration.

Jean rushed up to him. Toma followed. Together they took hold of him and dragged him away from the boy's now limp body. Brent threw the whip away from him in disgust. He shook himself free and strode across the lawn and down the hill towards the shore.

Jean and Toma came quietly and released the bonds that tied Pharcel to the tree. Blood oozed from the deep lacerations on his back. The boy slowly settled at the foot of the tree and curled on the ground. He had that vacant look in his eyes as if he had withdrawn his spirit. Toma shuddered at the pitiful wounds and torn flesh, but more so at the baleful look in the boy's eyes. He hurried away from the tree and followed Jean into the house.

In a moment, Bessie came out of the kitchen with a basin and cloth in one hand and a gourd in the other. She set them down on the ground and began to dab at his wounds with the wet cloth. She said not a word, but soon a low humming came from her mouth, a sound as of some kind of lamentation or incantation. She continued with her low humming while she spread a green salve which she poured from the gourd onto his back. He cringed as the salve sank into the deep cuts. But soon he rested easily, still curled on the ground beneath the calabash tree. Bessie left him there, knowing that he would not want food or drink just yet; knowing, too, that his spirit was wandering among the ghosts of his past, seeking comfort and courage to some day make things right.

He lay there under the calabash tree for many hours until his spirit returned to his vacant eyes; then, slowly, he rose and walked painfully to the slave huts down by the stream.

Bessie came to him every morning after breakfast, tending his wounds and feeding him nourishing frog leg broth. She forced a bitter brew down his throat to keep down the fever which burned in him while his cuts oozed and became inflamed before they began to heal. Bessie's hands were tough from constant cleaning, scrubbing and exposure to the heat of fire; but her touch was gentle as she applied the green and slimy salve to his back. She carried her rotund form on thick sturdy legs, her short, firm arms reaching just below her breast where her belly protruded and fell in a bulging decline to her massive thighs. She had a large, round head which sat on her shoulders and swiveled only part way when she glanced from side to side, and a round face that gleamed with an ebony brightness. With deep-set eyes, pug nose and thick, black lips, she was the picture of composure and impregnable dignity.

"Madam is back," Bessie said one morning.

Pharcel merely grunted, a silent resentment boiling in his heart.

"She asked for you."

He maintained a sullen silence.

"Your cuts are almost dry. You can come back to work now."

He lifted his eyes to her and nodded. She left, marveling at his indifference. She could not see the darkness seething within him; not the darkness of hate, but one compounded of scorn, outrage, reproach and a burning desire for some way to vindicate the wrong that he had suffered. All his life he had lived with the consciousness of being different. He had remained separate and aloof from the white world on the margins of which he had learned to survive. He did not feel himself inferior in any way; though he understood the disadvantage of his being born black and a slave; but now the injustice of his condition rankled in his breast, and he felt betrayed.

Elise found him one afternoon lying beneath the bower. It was late, and the sun had already gone over the sea. The heat of the day barely penetrated the thick foliage of the trees. He was curled on his side, eyes shut in a half sleep. The weals on his back were still tender, and he had found it painful to lean against the trunk of the tree; so he lay on his side, curled up on the ground. She came to him and stooped at his back, the fingers of her right hand stretched out hesitantly towards him. Pharcel felt her fingers gently trace a delicate line down the scars on his back. He raised himself quickly on an elbow, looking wild-eyed at her. There was a far-away look on her face as her fingers shifted downwards to his thighs and rested there in suspended motion; then quickly she took hold of him. Her lips fell apart, her bosom heaved, and her glazed eyes rested on him for a moment as he grew in her grasp.

They both sprang apart at the same time. She rose to her feet, momentarily confused, a flicker of guilt in her eyes; wiped her hand in the folds of her dress, and then quickly bolted from the dark interior of the bower through the low bush beyond.

Pharcel was dumbfounded. He could not understand what it was that drove the white woman, the planter's wife, to lose control in this way. He could understand the prurient curiosity of the little girl, but he was mystified at the trancelike and almost disembodied way Elise had stroked his body. A week ago he had been severely flogged for unintentionally witnessing a little white girl carelessly exposing herself in an act of nature. Today this white woman, the wife of the man whose slave he was, had come to him as if in a dream, gently caressing his manhood. His mind was confused all afternoon. As he lay in his bed later that night, unable to sleep, he could feel her hand on him, warm and soft, as if begging for forgiveness. Only the lost look in her eyes, the parting of her lips and the breathless heaving of her breasts betrayed the passion that raged deep in her bosom. Despite his arousal, he had no inclination to return whatever sentiments had drawn the woman to him. The dream-like encounter in the deep, cool shade of the trees possessed the quality of magical enchantment that was alien to his world. He wanted to keep away from her. He wanted to run. But the magic of that moment in the deep-shaded arbor haunted him for many days.

He did not return there for a long time. Though his spirit invoked the shades of the enchantment that dwelled in the seclusion of the trees, he tore his mind away from any thoughts of desire. He knew that giving in to the obsessive urge that impelled him towards the hidden place would be the ultimate act of defiance—an act which could lead to a fate worse than he could ever imagine. Her image haunted him every day, and he thought he could smell the natural fragrance of her body wherever he went. At night the softness of her hands filled his dreams. He began to loiter in the far away fields during the afternoons when he thought his work was done, appearing among the gangs at work as if he had suddenly discovered the wonders of physical labor. Sometimes he joined the gangs at work, eagerly sweating in the declining sun, and hoping for an exorcism of the fatal magic which had so taken hold of him; but such release never came.

He had seen Elise about the house, looking sedate and languid; and at those times she had regarded him with that vapid look and a frown which slowly darkened her face. Sometimes, an expression of sudden fright whitened her countenance, and she would move nervously away. He thought she scorned him, and he stayed out of the house as much as he could. Still he wondered why she had come to him that day. He had seen Captain Marshall come to the house on several occasions, but she never gave him any opportunity for intimacy after that first time when he had overcome her virtue, and he always left somewhat crestfallen after each such visit. Pharcel's mind dwelled on this inconsistency, and sometimes he thought that what had happened beneath the tree had been only a dream.

Bessie sensed the disturbance in him and sat with him one afternoon in the shade below the back verandah.

"The pain will go away," she said, thinking that he was still hurt by the flogging that he had suffered. "It always does."

"It is not the pain," he replied, the dreamy look covering his face.

"Don't worry. It will not happen again as long as you keep out of their way," she assured him.

He looked at her with his haunted eyes, but he remained silent; he could not tell her of the torment and the conflict in his soul; he could not reveal the nightly, wide-awake dreams and the dark feeling that urged him towards the trees every day.

She thought she understood.

"Now, don't think of running away," she cautioned. "If they catch you, it will be ten times worse. Even if you get away, you will die in the woods. Those runaways, they die of disease and starvation. Better you stay here and wait for the day!"

"Yes, ma'am," he murmured, that distant look in his eyes.

She was not convinced that he accepted her warning. That boy was up to something, she thought. Bessie feared for him, and would have done everything to protect him. She left him sitting in the shade and returned to the kitchen.

As if responding to that hypnotic urge, he rose and walked slowly through the bush and into the trees. He lay there brooding for a moment; then his thoughts began to conjure the image of the woman, and his heart was filled with the enchantment that she had caused by her mere touch on his flesh. He thought he smelled her fragrance in the leaves above him, and his awareness was filled with the sense of her presence right there beside him. He thought he heard a whisper of sound as her skirt brushed through the bush. He raised his head and looked anxiously at the sheltering branches.

She was standing there, the same vapid look in her eyes, her lips parted in an almost painful expression. She came to him with a slow hesitant walk; then sitting beside him, she rested her hand on his thigh. Her movements were slow and deliberate, as if willed by an irresistible force deep within her. She took him in her hand and gave a slight start as he rose to her. Her breath came quickly, and a rosy tint spread over her cheeks and neck. Wordlessly, she stood over him, her wide skirt forming a tent as she lowered herself. She gasped and gave a stifled cry as she settled onto him.

Pharcel felt her warm wetness as she slid down on him. He lay there with only the slightest movement; eyes tightly shut, hands scratching the ground beside him. His soul flowed down to his abdomen as he felt the soft fluttering of her insides and a warm wetness such as he had never felt before. He heard far away her low moans, and felt the bruising grip of her hands on his shoulders as she fell forward over him. His body came alive with a sudden hunger; then suddenly he was alone in the silence of the trees. He opened his eyes to see the grey swirls of her skirt disappearing beneath the dark folds of the low branches.

He remained there in an indescribable emptiness as the light slowly faded and darkness began to settle.

He did not see her for many days after that. It was as if she was entombed somewhere in the dusky chambers of the house. He went about his tasks as one possessed of a dark spell. Without spirit. Without will. Bessie regarded him questioningly. She sat beside him in the afternoons, but she made no further attempts to draw from him the cause of his agony. She felt that he suffered inwardly, and she wondered why it was that his sensitivity could have affected him so badly. For many days he waited expectantly in the dark under the trees, and for many nights he was tormented with dreams of emptiness and dreadful desolation.

Alexis came to him late one afternoon and took him down by the stream.

"I know," he said solemnly. "I saw."

Pharcel started, a deep fear filling his heart.

"You must run," Alexis said. "If you stay, they will kill you this time."

Startled and bewildered, Pharcel stared at him, fear and confusion in his eyes. Alexis grabbed his shoulders, his eyes wild with fright. He shook him violently.

"Run, Pharcel!" he exploded. "You must run!"

CHAPTER 3

Coree Greg, smoking a bamboo pipe, sat on a crude bench fixed to the side of his hut. His mouth puckered and slurped as he pulled on the thin stem of the pipe, letting out puffs of pale blue smoke. His grey hair stood in tufts on his round head; his elongated face had the look of ebony carving with a long nose that broadened at the base, popping eyes yellowed with time and the ravages of sickness, and lips twisted in a cynical smile. He was an old tribesman of the Kongo nation, and he commanded a small camp of runaways deep in the mountains just beyond Grandbay.

It was late afternoon, and the sun filtered in slanted rays through the trees that bordered the camp. As usual, he had an audience at his feet as, between puffs of tobacco smoke, he told of the wonders of his homeland. He loved to tell stories of his village and to speak of the history of the people of Africa because that was what kept him connected to his past. He could not be a slave if he lived his own past. Only those who lost their past can be truly enslaved. So he spent his days retelling the annals of his homeland to all those who sat with him and listened.

He spoke softly in measured cadences as he told them of the Great Kingdom of Kongo that was a prosperous trading nation even before the Portuguese came. He related how, by a process of enculturation, the invaders had divided the Kongolese people and then waged war on them. He told the story of Queen Nzinga, the greatest woman warrior in African history, who had led her people in revolt, outwitting the white invaders with diplomacy, defeating them in war and wasting their bodies in the forests and plains. He spoke of the Great Mutota who was king when Kongo and other Middle African kingdoms were on the brink of extermination. How he gathered the nations together, seized the engines of trade from the Arabs and fought the mighty armies of Portugal, Germany and England to unite the vastest region in the history of the continent.

"Our nation was a true democracy," he proclaimed. "The nation was its people. Kings and chiefs did not rule, but were merely leaders by virtue of birth or the special talent they possessed. Ours was a civilization greater than those of our invaders—in courtly protocol, respect for authority, reverence for our elders and refinement of social intercourse. I tell you, African people have within them a gentility of breeding which all the years of white brutality will never eradicate."

Pharcel sat on a tree stump in the shadows, listening avidly. His heart swelled within him as he understood that he came of a people great in war, commerce and diplomacy. He did not know what African nation he came from. Still, he felt the blood of warriors coursing through his veins. The tales that Coree Greg told uplifted his spirit and raised a mighty surge of valor within him.

He had come to the camp after wandering many days in the woods, and was almost killed when, breaking through a clearing, he came face to face with Jacko and Hall. Jacko's cutlass had flashed above him, but Hall had arrested his arm and intercepted a blow which would have meant certain death. They had looked at him and seen the drawn and pitiful expression in his face as one who was lost and on the point of collapse. He had wavered on his legs and leaned against a tree. After that, the two men had led him through a faint trace and into the camp. That was nearly three weeks ago. No one had paid much attention to him after that. He had slept under the trees the first night.

One of the women, robust but unkempt, her full breasts and voluptuous frame thrusting under the thin cotton shift that she wore, brought him cooked wild yam and the bitter meat of a wild pigeon in a calabash dish. He understood from her looks that he had to fend for himself, so he set about erecting a shelter to one side of open ground under the trees. By and by, the others came and helped him gather posts and twigs and palm fronds. By the evening of the second day, he slept in the shelter of a crude hut on the bare earth and dreamed of the bower where his manhood really began.

The camp was set in a narrow wooded valley. On three sides, the land rose steeply to hills so rugged as if the land had been crumpled by gigantic hands. The narrow gorges between the hills were thickly forested, forming an impenetrable barrier behind and to the sides of the small camp. To the West, the land rose less steeply on either side of a narrow ravine overhung with clusters of bamboo and red cedar trees. The site of the camp was slightly elevated, giving a clear view of the ravine and the hills beside it. Thatched huts were scattered under towering trees that allowed just enough sunlight to keep the area dry. From the hills on either side of the ravine, the dark green foliage of the trees hid the huts from view. Root crops and a scattering of fruit trees, mostly apricot and soursop, grew in discrete clearings at the back of the camp.

Coree Greg had chosen the location because of its formidable defenses. Only once had the militia approached his camp. His men had quickly caught the gleam of their guns and the bright flash of their uniforms on the open side of the incline beyond the ravine. They had hastily formed themselves into small groups and waited for them above the ravine. The ambush was quick and savage. Five of the soldiers lay bleeding beside the stream. The lieutenant and the rest of his patrol fled in the direction from which they had come.

The camp was small in number, just twenty men and women in a pristine setting, living a life of ease and simplicity. There were only five women in the camp. Besides Claire, who slept with Coree Greg in his hut with her baby son, Joseph, there were only Marie Claire, Genevieve and her baby daughter, Charlotte, and Betty. Marie Claire and Betty lived together in a tiny hut somewhat removed from the others. The other two women partnered with Tom and Hall. Claire was a lean, angular woman with a deep ebony complexion and sharply drawn features. She walked with firm steps like a man, and was known to be physically strong and ferocious in a fight. Marie Claire's ample figure was once seductive, but years of neglect and promiscuity had brought a gross appearance to her looks and body. She guarded Betty with a maternal fierceness that kept the men at bay.

Betty had been found wandering in the woods by Jacques and taken to the camp many months ago. She was a scrawny, fifteen year old girl with tiny breasts and hardly any curvature about her thin frame except for prominently rounded buttocks. She had large, shy eyes under a jutting forehead; a flat, spreading nose; small but plump lips, and a pointed chin. She glided among the huts with tentative steps as she went about collecting herbs and vegetables or doing the simple but important tasks of a woman in a bush camp. She seldom spoke to anyone, and when she did, it was with a halting uncertainty, as if she picked her thoughts from some deep recess within her head.

The women wore shifts of a cloth which had become uniformly grey from use and constant washing. A square of the same material wrapped their hair in an elaborate design; although Betty wore hers tied in a simple knot that left two ends hanging down her back.

The men wore short trousers made from a coarse cloth of the kind given to slaves by the plantation owners, and were mostly bareback. Even Coree Greg was clad only in this rough garment, except for a fold of dyed ochre-red cloth which he sometimes wore over his left shoulder. They were all mature men bordering on middle age, but sturdy and agile in their movements. Pharcel's youthfulness contrasted sharply with the advanced age of the rest of the men. He knew that they were seasoned fighters, and sat respectfully at their feet.

It was evening. The sun had fallen behind the hills, and shadows crept slowly up the forested incline past the ravine. In the cool graying light, Pharcel and

Betty sat under a giant gommier tree. He leaned towards her, his hands clasped around his knees.

"I ran away because of a little white girl," he said. "I saw her naked."

She regarded him curiously.

"Did you touch her?"

"No. I merely saw."

"Is that all?"

"Yes."

Betty giggled.

"What happened then?" she asked, a smile of amusement still lingering on her face.

He showed her his back with the grey scars still peeling around the edges. She let her fingers run down one of the scars. A soft, tender touch.

"You got that only for seeing?" she asked, her eyes turned to him doubtfully.

"Well, the little girl touched me," he said smiling, with a downward glance.

She giggled again, uncontrollably.

"Then why did you run?"

"The mistress touched me too. I was afraid this time they would hang me."

"She touched you there?"

"Yes. And did it to me!"

She cast her eyes down shyly.

"The white lady did it to you?" She asked wonderingly.

He nodded, smiling.

She frowned, looking downcast.

"And you let her?"

He shrugged. She lowered her eyes, a bemused expression on her face. They remained in silence as if they had come to the end of their thoughts.

"Why did you run?" he asked after several moments.

There was a startled look on her face. Then she turned away from him.

"They did it to me too," she said softly.

"They?"

"Yes. The overseer and all his white friends."

She paused briefly, lifted her eyes to him and continued.

"Day after day. Night after night."

He stiffened all over. He felt the pain in her eyes. His jaw clenched with a sudden rage that blackened his vision. After a while his anger cleared and he reached out to touch her hand. She drew it from him quickly, rose and walked away.

He remained sitting there on the dampening ground, still shaken by her revelation, until the dark and the mosquitoes drove him to the shelter of his little hut.

One afternoon, as he sat on a moss green stone in the shade of the gommier
tree, Coree Greg came and squatted beside him.

"You are from the Guinea coast," he remarked. "Your face and your color tell
me that."

Pharcel was intrigued, wanting to know more of his origin. Coree Greg sucked
at the gaps between his few remaining teeth. He paused as if recalling something
dreadful in his past.

"The men of Guinea are brave and intelligent."

He lapsed into a prolonged silence. Then, reluctantly he continued.

"But they lack constancy. They are a divided people."

He peered closely at Pharcel, his bulging eyes seeming to bore into his mind.

"You are strong," he said, "and not lacking in courage. My men are few and
no longer young; but they are loyal to their past. It is important that you be loyal
to your past."

He stayed there squatting in the shade for several moments, his long face somber in thought. Then he stood and quietly walked towards his hut.

The days seemed to go by drearily in the camp. The men went daily to clear
traps in the bushes or to hunt for small game. Sometimes, they returned with
sacks of wild yam. The women tended the plots of vegetables and ground provisions, and swept among the huts. Occasionally, Betty disappeared for two or
three days, returning with a pannier load of salt and oil and other commodities.
He learned from her that she visited the plantations near Grandbay, sometimes
entering Grandbay itself which was densely populated with whites and slaves
employed in working the Geneva sugar mills. There she would trade wild pigeons
and venison for salt and other goods. She knew which plantations were safe and
which of the free Africans in Grandbay she could trust.

One day, he accompanied her to the ridge overlooking Geneva estate. They
spent all afternoon in the woods, whispering to each other, listening to every
sound in the dense bushes—the sudden flutter of birds lifting from the branches,
the swish of grass in a swirl of wind, the crack of a dry limb falling from the trees.
When night came she crept through the boundary of the estate down to the slave
huts. Pharcel went in the opposite direction, skirting the ridge over the narrow
valley where Dubique rested silent in the gathering gloom. He came down the
valley through the fields of cane to the dark patch of wood at the back of the
house and hid in one of the taller trees all night, and when the day brightened, he
lay along a high branch peering through the thick foliage towards the back veran-

dah. He saw Bessie bustling in the kitchen, and Toma walking stiffly around the wide verandah to the back, as if inspecting the world to see if anything had changed overnight. For a while, Toma stared fixedly at the clump of trees. Pharcel shifted uneasily on the branch until Toma turned and entered the kitchen through the back door.

It was not until mid-morning that Elise emerged through the front verandah, walked across the patch of lawn and down to the tiny waterfall. He knew she would be bathing behind the raspberry screen in the warm morning sun. His mind wandered to the small enclosure where he imagined she was lying naked with no fear of intrusion at this time of day. His mind returned to the time when she had come to him, and he thought he could feel again her soft fluttering warmth around his manhood. He must have dozed for a while because when he came awake there was a soft rustling of dry leaves below him. She was sitting against the tree where she had found him that day, brushing the leaves and twigs on the ground around her. She raised her head in a dreamy, wistful look as of one conjuring the past into her presence. She remained that way for what seemed an interminable moment. Then she stood and, with downcast eyes, walked slowly out of the trees into the sunlight.

He stayed hidden in the branches all day until the gangs of slaves trooped by and the estate gradually settled into night.

He never told Betty what he had done when she returned.

Betty brought news of a great panic in the capital town of Roseau. She told them that Sandy and Jacco, from their camps near Colihaut and Belles, had terrorized several plantations on the West coast, plundering estates and their mansions, and threatening destruction to all whites. Sandy's men, in particular, ventured boldly on the roads between Colihaut and the Mahaut valley, making commerce with the capital and the villages between, difficult and dangerous. Many of the white planters and their families had abandoned their estates and were lodging in the town, waiting for the first vessel to return to England. The French planters at Colihaut were especially clamorous since they were forbidden by Council to bear arms and so were unable to defend themselves and their families. The Council had been forced to vote a considerable sum to arm the militia and get them on the move to destroy the camps in the woods. To add to the sense of fear among the white population, the French in Martinique and Guadeloupe were caught up in the heat of their Revolution, and already the cries for liberty, fraternity and equality were resounding among the middle and lower classes of whites and free mulattos.

Coree Greg heard the news with mounting despair. He was an old warrior, wise in the ways of politics. He knew the time had not yet come for aggression. Most of the camps were undermanned, a motley gathering of half-starved men and their drained-out women. His camp was the most secure and best organized, with strong natural defenses and ready supplies of clean water, ground provision and fruits. Most of the other camps depended on frequent raids on plantation supplies and livestock for their survival; and they spent most of their time planning minor assaults on the nearby plantations. As a tested and seasoned warrior, he believed in maintaining peace until war was unavoidable, either in defense of unprovoked attacks or in pre-emptive strikes to avoid enemy aggression. Furthermore, he understood that his warriors and the men of the other camps were poorly armed with only machetes and wooden spears and clubs and a few rusted muskets and pistols. Only a few camps had a good store of weapons which they had stolen from estate houses. Now that the militia was being fully armed and equipped to wage a prolonged war on them, he feared that the rash action of Sandy and Jacco had unleashed a force that they could hardly contend with in their present state of unpreparedness.

Coree Greg scratched at the tufts of grey hair on his round head. He cursed the hot-headedness of the likes of Jacco, Bala and especially Sandy.

"The French mulattos are always in and out of Grandbay," Pharcel ventured timidly. "Why don't we get guns from them?"

Coree Greg gave him a withering look.

"Never!" he growled. "Never treat with mulattos and white men. We are Africans. Our interests are not with whites or mulattos!"

With that, he entered his hut and left the shaken crowd to ponder his dictum.

It was not long after that that Petit Jacques came running one morning with word that Bala had entered the narrow ravine and was on his way to the camp. Bala came striding into the tree-shaded clearing with a retinue of five. Cicero, his gun-bearer, walked a few paces behind him. The others followed unceremoniously, looking curiously at the order and cleanliness about them.

Coree Greg came out of his hut and stood before Bala.

"You have come unannounced," he said simply.

"At a time of war, old man, there is no time for good manners!" Bala replied.

"There is always time for good manners among friends," Coree Greg said frostily.

Bala stood six feet tall and looked down at the wizened frame of the old warrior. Bala was powerfully built, with wide shoulders, brawny arms and firm, muscled legs. His face was broad, with wide overhanging forehead, deep-set eyes, nose that ran like a massive ridge straight down from his eyebrows, fat lips that stretched into a permanent sneer, and squared jaw; a combination which gave him a somewhat loutish appearance. Cicero stood at his elbow, short and sturdy, his furtive eyes darting from one corner of the camp to another. He fidgeted on his feet, restless and seemingly unaccustomed to standing too long in the same place. Bala had found Cicero in Congoree's camp where he served as gun-bearer to that chief, and had simply commanded him to follow and become his gun-bearer instead. That was the nature of the man. His arrogance and imperiousness were legend. So was his bravery and brutality in war.

Unlike the warriors in Coree Greg's camp, Bala's men were clothed in European garb, albeit stained and torn in places. Bala himself affected sophistication in his choice of garments, and his frilled shirts and tailored trousers looked at odds with his uncouth appearance. He wore tight grey breeches favored by the militia, which emphasized the grossness of his genitals. His upper body was squeezed into a white cotton shirt and brown tweed coat that puckered at his armpits and left his broad, deep chest almost completely exposed. A wide straw hat of the kind worn by planters sat grotesquely on his head. His feet were packed into boots that were too small, so that his spread toes jutted out of cut-off ends.

Cicero and all the other men wore simple but well cut clothes, and went about barefooted.

"I have come in a hurry," Bala declared. "It is time for a war conference. Mabouya and Sandy are anxious to meet and talk"

"But why the talk of war?" Coree Greg spoke in a calm voice. "Surely, the time has not yet come?"

"The time has come, indeed. When the white man beats the drums of war, we should not wait like sheep to be slaughtered. Even the lazy possum will snarl when provoked."

"We are not possum," Coree Greg replied. "We should be wise and wait until the time is right."

Bala sneered.

"Freedom will not come from getting old under the trees," he said, not bothering to hide the disdain with which he always treated any counsel that did not favor bold action.

They sat and spoke all night until the dark lightened into grey and the earth began to stir into awakening

Bala spoke of the raids carried out by Sandy and Jacco in the West, and how the white planters were virtually driven out of their estates. The camps in the South and East should now come together and join forces with the Western groups and take over the entire island. The time was opportune since the ever present threat of war from the French and the stirrings of the Revolution in Guadeloupe and Martinique created diversions that occupied the minds of the Council and the English planters. Never mind the scarcity of arms. They would eventually arm themselves from breaking into the estate houses, killing the planters, and seizing whatever muskets and pistols they could find. As for the militia, they would easily slaughter them as they ventured into the unfamiliar woods. That should provide all the weapons they needed.

In the end, Coree Greg remained skeptical.

"I will think on what you say," he wavered. "In a few days I will send you my decision."

Later that morning, Pharcel stood with Zombie and Juba, two of Bala's men, and listened to them intently as they spoke of their brave incursions on the estates in the East, a tale of destruction and rape and persistent harassment of the white planters. Pharcel was struck with the difference between Coree Greg's camp and the adventurous gangs that formed the camps of Bala, Mabouya, Sandy and Jacco. He was not sure if he approved of Coree Greg's pacifist approach to the question of liberation. He found Bala's militancy far more appealing. He told them that he had escaped from the Dubique estate, and they exclaimed that there was another in their camp who called himself Alexis and who was from the same place. Pharcel could hardly suppress his astonishment. He thought he should visit Bala's camp as soon as possible to find Alexis, and to be part of the wonderful adventure that they lived there day by day.

It was late evening when Bala came out of one of the huts which had been assigned to his use during his stay in the camp. Pharcel was sitting with Betty on a log set against the outer wall of Marie Claire's hut. Bala glanced at him briefly, wondering that such a sturdy youth should find a home among the old veterans of Coree Greg's camp. His eyes lingered on Betty and he bit on his lower fleshy lip as he took in her slight figure and piquant face.

"That your place?" he asked brusquely.

"Yes," she answered, her eyes dropping shyly, her hands nervously folded on her lap.

"Good to know," he remarked. "I hope I can visit."

He walked on without a backward glance.

Inside the hut, Marie Claire heard and was worried. She understood fully what Bala intended and decided there and then that she would protect Betty from the clutches of the barbarous chief even if she had to sacrifice her own person. Pharcel looked in admiration at the heroic figure of the man whose deeds had already become legendary. He did not understand the intent and significance behind Bala's words. He and Betty continued their idle converse.

It was much later in the night that the door to Marie Claire's hut was pulled roughly apart and Bala stood there, his great bulk silhouetted against the faint light coming through the door. He stood there for a long time while his eyes adjusted to the dark. He peered at Marie Claire's rotund figure stretched out on the floor and turned to look more closely at the further corner of the little hut. He gave a snort of impatience as he turned again to Marie Claire.

"Where is the girl?" he demanded sharply.

She raised herself on one elbow, looking bewildered as if she had just been awakened from a deep sleep.

"Which girl?" she responded.

"The one who was here this afternoon."

"Oh, she? She is gone away for the night."

"Where has she gone?"

"To Geneva. She fetches our provender from the nearby plantations."

He stood in the dark uncertain what to do. He had seen only the five women in the camp. The girl was the only one that he had found worthy of his attention. He felt deprived and cheated.

After a while Marie Claire sat upright, her nakedness wide open even in the dark.

"Can I be of service to you?" she enquired hesitantly.

She was surrounded by the smell of rancid flesh, but over this floated to his nostrils the pungent muskiness of her sex. As if drawn by an atavistic urge stronger than his will, he moved closer to the dark bulk of her body, sat beside her and reached out for the great mound of her belly.

"I hope you can," he said, as he leaned onto her.

She felt him as he lowered himself over her and was thankful that she had thought to send Betty away out of her hut. That poor girl could not have withstood this giant of a man. It was better that she find shelter with the boy. At least she wouldn't be brutalized again, vulnerable as she was.

All night long, the little hut rumbled with groans and animal grunts, with thrashing and heaving as of two great beasts coupling in the wild. The groans and the cries filled the night with blood-red passion rising to unbelievable heights. It went on interminably, each wave seeming to crest higher than the last.

Pharcel and Betty lay in each other's arms in his small shack. Across the clearing, they heard the first rumble coming from Marie Claire's hut. Betty clutched his arm and sniffled in his chest. He held her closely, stroking the fear out of her. She clung to him in a panic of remembering those many days and nights when she was held in the stables at Geneva, chained like a beast, having to endure the brutal onslaughts of men devoid of any sensibility, men who stank of rum and garlic, whose animal lust drove them to acts of cruelty and perversion that no savage would even contemplate.

The night quivered with myriad fantasies that fired the two young lives snuggling in the dark in Pharcel's hut, and drew them to each other like delicate insects to the fragrance of a newly opened flower. Finally, they slept in a close embrace, like siblings seeking mutual comforting.

In the morning, the camp was deathly quiet.

Bala emerged from the reeking inside of the close hovel that was Marie Claire's abode and stood grandly in the crisp morning air. He glanced briefly at the periphery of the clearing where the furthest shack stood in near isolation, and thought he caught a fleeting glimpse of the little girl with the piquant face that he had seen the evening before, darting quickly behind the shack. In another moment, Pharcel came out from the shack and walked towards him. Bala scowled, a look of deep suspicion darkening his face. Pharcel, unaware of the reasons for his resentment, smiled amicably; but Bala looked away and made as if to rush to the spot where the girl had disappeared, halted his steps as the night's weariness suddenly came upon him and impelled him towards his own quarters.

After a short distance, he turned again towards Pharcel, a look of intense animosity on his face.

CHAPTER 4

Captain Marshall, sipping planter's punch, sat on a tiny portico on the main street of the town. In his left hand he held a copy of the *Journal or Weekly Intelligencer* dated 7th February, 1785, a local newspaper that circulated among the officials and the more enlightened of the planter class of the island. It was already mid-morning, and the white merchants and petty officials were already gathering in various parts of the town center for their pre-lunch drink. The house where he sat had a narrow frontage, but it extended deep to a short, close lane at the back where stables were kept. It was a wooden house finely constructed with jalousie windows and doors and a steep gable roof that was covered with shingles—the private residence of Charles Winston, a member of Council; but the little portico served as the daily gathering place for a select group from the military, senior officials and other members of Council. A few of the more affluent planters dropped by occasionally whenever they visited the town. Sometimes the rector of the Anglican Church graced the gathering with a brief visit, mostly on Wednesdays when the pressure of his clerical duties was not so urgent.

From where he sat, Captain Marshall could see the main street stretching eastward no more than a quarter of a mile to the wide valley beyond. Surrounding the town was a semi-circle of hills; and through a narrow gorge in the middle, the cool, clear waters of a river flowed past its northern boundary. The hills on both sides of the gorge fell in perpendicular walls, and at the summit of the one on the right was a battery of cannons that commanded the harbor in all directions. A bright white cross, several feet tall, stood prominently among the cannons as if to cast a benediction on the devastation they were placed there to inflict on any enemy ships that encroached upon the wide harbor. The vegetation on these surrounding hills was spectacular. Myriad shades of green interspersed with the red and orange of flamboyant trees, frangipani yellows and the bright scarlet of the bois caraibe. Past the circle of hills, the land uplifted in row upon row of mountains rising up to great heights and clothed in progressively darkening shades of green to a blue grey where they met the sky.

There were just over five hundred houses in the town. Most of the large residences and merchants' houses faced on the main street—a wide, cobbled road with a storm drain down its middle—which ran directly from the loading jetty on the shore across the town to the opening of the valley beyond. Other narrower streets ran in irregular patterns on both sides of it, sometimes joining at acute angles and forming a warren of by-ways that led in a disorderly fashion to the river on the north of the town. Smaller wooden houses nestled along the narrow streets and lanes and beneath overhanging trees on both sides of the main thoroughfare to the river in the North and Charlotte Ville in the South. The Catholic Cathedral, an expansive wooden structure with twin steeples, stood on a high prominence overlooking the flat river plain on which the town was built. Beside it, the sharp steeple of the Anglican Church penetrated a barrier of trees that screened it from the rest of the town. Behind was the Governor's residence; and further beyond, the public buildings. Opposite the Anglican Church on a bluff that descended perpendicularly to the sea, stood the massive bulk of the Fort where Captain Marshall and the officers and men of the 15th Regiment were quartered, its dark grey walls punctuated with small, apertures for gun placements. On its stout parapet overlooking the sea, brightly polished canons faced the entrance to the harbor northwards and southwards. All together, the town was pleasantly situated. Its well-paved streets were clean and lively with commerce at this time of day. The abundance of trees of many tropical varieties rising in lush splendor among the mainly wooden houses gave it a cool and restful appearance.

Captain Marshall raised his eyes from the journal and turned to Captain Urquhart.

"See here!" he said. "The paper is filled with notices of escaped slaves, and here we are stuck in this town while the beastly marauders do what they like."

"Council has just voted 1,000 Johannes for a fresh assault on their camps," replied Captain Urquhart.

"And about time, too."

Captain Marshall waved the journal impatiently.

"One good assault and we can wipe them from the face of the earth," he boasted.

"Don't be so sure," cautioned McPherson, a burly Scot whose lands in the Mahaut heights had been a favorite haunt of the runaways in that area. "Their chiefs are cunning and bold, and as elusive as the mountain doves. When they are in the woods they move like shadows. They can traverse the island from camp to camp without leaving a trace."

"Nonsense!" shouted Captain Marshall. "You can't be serious! A well trained regiment like the Fifteenth can't deal with a bunch of savages?"

"You should not be complacent about this," said Winston, walking in from the spacious drawing room inside. "The woods are difficult to penetrate and some of the camps are unapproachable. Council has now voted a generous budget. Let us see what your regiment can do."

"Oh, we will manage just fine," assured Captain Urquhart. "Just give us the men and equipment."

Captain Marshall laughed. He was already slightly drunk, his face florid with the potent drink.

"In just two weeks we will have them running, you'll see," he crowed.

Captain Urquhart turned towards the lane leading up to the Cathedral. His eyes suddenly widened with astonishment.

"Now, look at that!" he exclaimed, indicating a lissome girl across the street.

She was naked and held herself erect as she balanced a pail on her bare head, her pert breasts jiggling with every step. Her limbs were long but of a satisfying fullness; her hips curved gracefully from a narrow waist to firm, rounded thighs, and her haunches stood proud and firm. She had that saucy look that came from accustomed ogling by the men of the town. Although she looked to be only fourteen years old; she had all the attributes of an older woman.

McPherson guffawed.

"That is Stewart's girl," he said. "He is too much of a niggard to spend money on clothes."

"Is he, though?" said Marshall. "Good for him, then."

"But surely, she is too old for this," protested Urquhart. "She can't be allowed to walk around naked in the middle of the town."

"But she is a wonderful sight," Marshall commented. "Just look at those legs!"

"Why should that impress you so?" McPherson grinned, his face glowing with merriment. "We see that everyday on the plantations."

"Oh, not like that," Captain Marshall replied. "The plantation girls are mostly ungraceful, with splayed feet and hardened legs."

"That's Stewart's contribution to entertainment in the town," Winston commented dryly. "But I agree. It is gone far enough."

"Well", said McPherson, "Reverend Peters preached against it in last Sunday's sermon; and against all the alleged atrocities to slaves in general. Since he arrived here, he has been on a campaign to reform us planters."

"That Oxford radical?" Marshall sneered. "He should be watched, is what I say."

"He is to replace Rector Johnson who is about to retire," explained Winston. "In fact he should be sailing next week. I don't know how Peters will fit in, though. We should give him time, I suppose."

Winston made excuses and left them there. He had an appointment with the Governor. It was a short walk up the incline past the Cathedral to the back entrance to the governor's residence. He was a bit early, but he wanted to have a private word about the state of the official church now that a new rector would soon be installed.

"Never mind me," he said cordially to his guests. "Joseph will take care of drinks. Just call on him."

The girl had long since disappeared down the street towards the shore; but Captain Marshall, as if bemused, continued to gaze in that direction.

"Why should that bookish priest be concerned about a naked slave?" he asked pensively. "Naked or not she is just property to be used."

"But not abused," Urquhart reminded him.

"Well," said McPherson, "he will have quite a job ahead of him, especially on the plantations. I once visited an estate in the North—a sprawling place with vast stretches of flat land belonging to a chap called Ferrol. You wouldn't believe he had a bunch of wonderfully nubile female slaves, absolutely nude, serving us dinner. He said it was cleaner to have them naked than wearing their muddy garments around a dinner table. Personally, I thought he just wanted to provide a bit of amusement to his guests."

"Anyway," joined Urquhart, "some owners are given to really cruel acts, even some of the most respectable ladies of the town. I heard the other day a story concerning the wife of a petty merchant, not too far from here, who punished her slave in a most abominable way for just being incontinent at night. The poor slave was quite emaciated, probably from some disease of the kidney, and was half demented besides. Her owner had plates of tin hung around her front and back, and had her paraded half naked around the streets, with children beating on the plates everywhere she passed."

"Urgh!" Captain Marshall grimaced in disgust. "That is absolutely repulsive. Not as fascinating a sight as the creature that just went by."

Captain Urquhart and McPherson chuckled. It was nearing the lunch hour and they would soon be moving along to their respective houses or dining places.

"I think I should have another," McPherson suggested.

"So will I," Captain Urquhart agreed. "Shall we call Joseph?"

As if on cue, Joseph came with a decanter filled with the gold colored liquid. He poured into each glass and quietly returned indoors.

"Did you ever return to Grandbay since our last sortie there?" Captain Urquhart asked, turning to Captain Marshall.

"Well, yes," Captain Marshall replied. "I have been a few times since. There is this small estate at a place called Dubique owned by a French planter."

"Ah!" exclaimed McPherson. "You mean Lyonnais!"

"You know him?" Captain Marshall asked in astonishment.

"Of course! I met him a few times on his rare visits to town. Quite a decent chap, but socially gauche. He has a most charming wife."

"Oh, yes. She is charming." Captain Marshall said, his enthusiasm bubbling in the warmth of his expression. "A most captivating and mysterious woman."

"Hey!" interposed Captain Urquhart. "I smell some sordid and illicit affair here. Is that another conquest, Marshall?"

Captain Marshall smiled suggestively.

"By the way," McPherson said casually, "she was in town not too long ago."

"Elise in town?" Captain Marshall was obviously flustered.

"Just for a few days. It's been several weeks now."

"I was not aware of that. Pity."

"She came with her daughter to place her in boarding school."

"Oh? That rambunctious brat? Where is she?"

"Over at old Miss Morson. On the hill. Just past the Cathedral."

Captain Marshall mused on this for a moment.

"Hm!" he murmured abstractly. "I must see her, I suppose."

"Gentlemen?" Captain Urquhart rose unsteadily on his feet. "Time for lunch."

They left. Captain Marshall and his companion followed the slight incline towards the Fort. They would dine in the officer's mess.

A few days later, towards evening, Captain Marshall trudged the incline to the lane that passed in front of the Cathedral and then to a row of houses where the Morson establishment stood. It was a low building with a wide frontage that was a school for girls and a boarding house for those out-of-town pupils. The wide front room served as the single classroom. At its back were the dining room and kitchen, and beyond, closely partitioned rooms where the girls slept. On one side of the building was a kind of cloister where the girls gathered after classes—the only part of the establishment reserved for recreation.

The classroom was deserted, but there was a subdued sound of chatter coming from within. Captain Marshall knocked on the thick wooden door and stood waiting for what seemed a long time before he heard the muffled sound of footsteps approaching. The door opened cautiously and the grey covered head of a wrinkled black woman peered at him curiously.

"Fetch Miss Morson," he demanded shortly.

The grey head bobbed for a moment and disappeared again behind the closed door. He stood uncertainly, waiting, until firm steps marched towards him and the door opened wide. The woman who stood before him was formidable. She must have been six feet tall with a massive head set upon a thick columnar neck. Her breasts hung like ramparts on her chest, the rest of her body tapering to thick legs that were discernible even beneath her dark, austere clothing that reached down to her toes. She held her head erect, and from her unusual height she looked down at the rest of the world as if with loathing. She had a commanding face with large bulging eyes; a high, thin nose, and firm lips.

She looked down at Captain Marshall.

"Yes?" she enquired.

Captain Marshall quailed before her withering look; then he braced his shoulders and smiled cheerfully.

"I've come to see Miss Lyonnais."

The woman continued to regard him with distaste.

"I have brought her some things," he stammered.

The woman remained silent, scowling darkly.

"From her mother," he ended lamely.

"Who are you?" she enquired at last.

"Captain Marshall of the 15th Regiment at you service, Madam," he replied gallantly.

"I have not asked for your service, have I?" she growled. "What do you want?"

"I have come to see Miss Lyonnais. Georgette."

"We do not admit visitors," she said brusquely.

"Can I just give her the things, then?" he asked quietly.

"What things?"

"Sweets…and…other things," he stuttered; then added, "From her mother"

"Do you know her parents?"

"I am a friend…. of the family."

He shuffled uneasily.

"I just came from there. From Dubique."

"Hand them over. I will take them to her."

"Well, yes. But I was asked to see her."

He smiled his most engaging smile. She scowled at him, not liking his roguish looks.

"Madam, I am a gentleman officer of the 15th Regiment," he assured her.

"I don't care. We don't admit visitors."

"Then take this to her with my compliments."

She seized the package from his outstretched hands and turned to go; then she paused, looked over her shoulder and regarded him closely. The stern look on her face barely softened.

"Wait here," she instructed him.

He stood at the door shuffling his feet nervously. A small wicket gate opened on the side close to the cloister. She beckoned to him and held open the gate.

"She will be with you presently," she said sharply. "But only for a minute."

She brought him through a latticed door into the cloister and left him standing there. In a moment Georgette appeared wearing a dark grey dress that fell almost to her ankles. Behind her stood another girl wearing the same mode of garment, shyly hovering at the door of the classroom.

"I am Captain Marshall," he introduced himself. "You remember me?"

"Yes," she muttered. "You came to our home a few times."

He had hardly noticed her then. She must have been rather curious about him to remember him so well. What he recalled about her was her stout legs flashing under short, flimsy skirt as she ran from one side to the other of their rustic house to peer at him as he sat with her mother, exchanging the best of his wit and trying desperately to lure Elise one more time to the cover of the trees or to her husband's chamber. Elise had managed with considerable aplomb to keep their conversation impersonal and to keep his roving hands always at a distance. The child he saw before him was a considerable distance from the boisterous estate girl that ran with abandon all over the open spaces around their house. He could hardly recognize the pitiful waif standing there.

"I brought you some things," he said to her, smiling uncertainly.

She merely nodded.

"Are you all right?" he asked as brightly as he could.

"I hate it," she replied vehemently. "I want to go home."

He was silent, uncertain how to proceed. After a while he braced himself as if coming to attention.

"I will come again soon," he said smiling.

She turned away from him and marched stiffly into the house.

He returned many times to see her. Each time Miss Morson seemed to soften a little more, and each time Georgette turned away from him less stiffly. He brought her little cakes and sweets and handed them over to Miss Morson before he would be admitted through the wicket gate. Georgette never mentioned receiving them and he never enquired. Soon he noticed that she had dropped her sulky mien and even appeared content that he was there with her. She began to pay more attention to his attempts at conversation, looking at him with a curiosity that was disturbing to him.

It was close to Christmas and soon she would return to the estate for the holidays. Her gloom was lifting gradually and the mischievous glimmer in her eyes began to reappear.

One day she came alone, her usual companion nowhere in the background. She stood close to him and suddenly whispered.

"You want my mother, don't you?"

He almost reeled with shock.

"My father won't approve," she said decisively. "He won't at all."

"What put that silly notion in your head?" he asked, wanting to cut short this line of conversation.

"Oh, I know. I've seen you with her."

"Your mother and me, we are friends. As I am with your father," he added.

"Don't worry," she said mockingly. "You won't get her."

He was upset by her sudden boldness and turned to go.

"But you can come to see me at home," she whispered at his back as he rushed out of the gate.

It was several weeks later in the middle of the week that Captain Marshall sat again on the portico of Winston's house. A few councilors had gathered there before lunch.

The talk that morning was all about the latest assaults by the runaways and the defiance with which they had met the measures taken by Council to suppress them. Despite the disposition of legions from the militia in three separate encampments at Laudat, Layou and Grandbay, virtually encircling the main camps, the runaways continued to carry out raids on estate properties with impunity. In fact Bala had sent a mocking message to the Lieutenant Governor at Castle Bruce deriding the weakness and uselessness of the legions, and threatening to intensify his assaults unless the legions were promptly disbanded and the runaways left to their own security in the woods.

Only a week before, the estate of Thomas Osborne above Layou was attacked and pillaged and, whether by accident or design, the estate house and other adjoining property were completely burnt down. Osborne himself had barely escaped and had to take refuge with friends at Colihaut.

Captains Marshall and Urquhart were subjected to intense chaffing by Winston and Shaw for their idleness in not being able to challenge the forces of the runaways.

"I warned you," Winston said teasingly, "that it was not going to be easy."

"We know that was the work of Sandy," Captain Marshall said quietly. "He and Bala are hotheads. We have a plan to entrap them."

"Not all the chiefs are as impetuous as those two," warned Shaw. "Coree Greg is as wily as he is brave. He is known to be a seasoned fighter. His record shows that he comes of Kongo stock and they are known to have a genius for military strategy."

"Coree Greg is in my area," Captain Marshall retorted. "I know how to deal with him. That is why I have stationed my men at Grandbay. Urquhart here will take care of Sandy, Jacco and Congoree. There will be time for me to deal with Bala and Mabouya on the eastern side."

Winston snorted, not convinced that the two captains had as yet found the measure of their opponents.

"Well, gentlemen, the council has entrusted you with a large budget to bring peace and stability to the colony," Grove spoke ponderously. "We look forward to early results."

"Early?" chided Shaw. "Nearly two months have already gone by"

"I promise," insisted Captain Marshall, "by Christmas, the woods and the highways will be safe again."

"We have developed a plan," Captain Urquhart said thoughtfully. "It is simple, but effective"

The group crowded together around the decanter of punch as Captain Urquhart, speaking in hushed tones, meticulously outlined the basic strategy that would be employed in entrapping the leaders of the several camps. There was a satisfied murmur coming from the few councilors present. Hatton, an overseer on the Castle Bruce estate, had listened intently, and said nothing; but his face reflected skepticism.

"I think the Council will be pleased to hear these details," said Winston. "I will convey this to them. Now, gentlemen, our decanter is......"

Joseph came in silently with a filled decanter, placed it on the low table, and as silently disappeared.

CHAPTER 5

Pharcel lay flat on a high branch all night waiting. A chill had set in and dew had formed on the leaves of the trees. He could smell the tree ants on the rough bark and feel them crawling on his bare chest. An occasional mosquito buzzed in his ears or stung his back, but he lay there unmoving. After months of engagement in Coree Greg's camp, he had learned to endure hardship and such irritations with supreme stoicism. He had become a stalker in the forest, able to move where no trail or track existed without a sound or a trace of his footsteps. He stayed there on the bough motionless as the morning lightened, his eyes riveted to the back of the house.

Months had gone by since the last time he saw Elise sitting under this same tree with that empty, lost look on her face. He had been tempted then to drop down beside her, but he had restrained himself, not certain what her true feelings towards him were. What if she detested him or, driven by guilt of her own inward weakness, held him culpable for the brief, lustful encounter so many months ago? White women, he had been told, were a contradiction in themselves—feeling guilt and shame for what was instinctive and natural among black society, bringing them to a state of denial of the natural concupiscence that simmered deep within them. At the same time, they maintained a callous disregard for the feelings and human dignity of their servants and slaves. Black people gave expression to their feelings without guilt or regret, without inhibitions or false prejudices. In the ancient culture of Africa, he had learned, slaves were not abused and dehumanized, but were accepted as part of a family and household, subservient, but valued as human possessions.

He thought of the last time she had come to him, the quick and sudden spasms that had shaken her, her stunned awakening and hasty, silent retreat. He thought of her all these months as of a desire half fulfilled. He had welcomed the gentle solace of Betty in his shack. Since the time of Bala's tumultuous rutting in Marie Claire's hut, she had stayed with him every night; and Marie Claire had quietly left them alone. At first, he could not understand the violent agitation that seized her every time he held her in an intimate embrace; but gradually he recognized the deep revulsion that lingered in her for any semblance of the violation of her person that she had been made to suffer for so long. He spent many nights gentling her, quieting the demons of hate and loathing for any act of sexuality that abided within her until by and by, like a lost and wounded animal seeking a place to hide, she came to rest calmly in his protective arms. Even so, she often received him with a bashful reluctance, and her painful sufferance always elicited from him a careful tenderness.

The months away from Dubique had awakened in him a consciousness of his own manhood. He found life in the camp exciting and instructive, and he savored his new independence and maturity. Being in Coree Greg's camp did not require the strict military discipline that obtained in Bala's camp, except in matters of common survival. Coree Greg's main concern was the protection of his small community, and so he maintained careful watch of all the approaches to his camp. He taught his men and women how to walk the forests without leaving trace of their passage and how to blend with the trunks of trees or the fallen logs that strewed the forest floor. There was no hierarchical order in his camp. His men obeyed him because they recognized him as their chosen chief. There was no identifiable command structure, and men and women went about their daily occupations in voluntary cooperation and with no strict adherence to rules except in matters of defense.

Pharcel had found acceptance in Coree Greg's camp as a foundling would, just by being there. He would often sit outside the old man's hut listening to his stories of how he had been betrayed by the Lendu tribe and sold to the Arabs with an entire village of his own people. He vowed that someday he would return to Africa and seek vengeance on those who had so treacherously destroyed his family and his village. Coree Greg's life had been one of continuous struggle for freedom since he was brought to this island. He had bided his time on an estate not too far from the capital town, and managed to escape one dark and rainy night into the woods. His tribe, the Hema people, had always lived on the hills of the Ituri district of the Kongo, and he found habitation in the close fastnesses of the mountain gorges quite conducive to his own accustomed way of living. There were many wanderers in the forest then, and he had brought them to this secure place where they had lived away from danger. Many had died of disease and old age, but none had been captured. But now they were constantly threatened by the presence of the legions on the borders of the woods. He blamed Sandy, Jacco and Bala for rousing terror among the white planters and for the dire consequences which could follow. Now the militia had been sent out against them, and a bitter struggle of attrition was inevitable. Only recently, Joseph had sent word of the disposition of the three legions at strategic points around the island.

Coree Greg had scoffed at the positioning of the militia. Obviously, they thought they had the runaway camps surrounded from South, West and East, but as an old war campaigner he knew that the encampments would have extreme difficulty communicating with each other because of the vast, rugged and virtually impassable terrain between them. On the other hand, his men and the men of the several other camps knew the intricate routes through the mountains and gorges extending from North to South and East to West like the backs of their hands, and could easily circumvent the encampments of the legions, even if they had to travel longer routes. He had no fears for himself and his men, but he dreaded what he thought would be the inevitable outcome of a prolonged struggle in view of the rashness and recklessness of the other camp leaders. Nonetheless, he warned Pharcel about leaving the camp whilst the militia continued to patrol Grandbay and the surrounding hills, and he had even suspended Betty's weekly visits for a time until the danger had abated.

On those serene and listless days lying in the shade beneath the giant trees, with the nearby stream gurgling its way to the ravine beyond, Pharcel's thoughts often drifted to the shady copse at the back of the house in Dubique where Elise had awakened in him a desire that had lingered those many months, a desire the like of which he had never experienced before. Even at night, lying beside Betty, sated with but unfulfilled by her tender but still repressed giving of herself, his mind would wander to the white woman who had opened out herself to him with such abandon in the waning hours of one still afternoon; and he thought he could smell again the soft, sweet muskiness of her body, and feel the warm, wet flutter of her inner flesh.

He had been lying in the tree for hours. Time had crept agonizingly to late afternoon, and the shadows were already darkening the valley; and still she had not appeared. He had lain there on the coarse-barked limb conjuring her image, still chaste in that grey long dress, still uprightly moving with slow dignified steps, face in serene composure and hands folded at her waist. Even if he had once seen her face suffused with pleasurable tension, the image that stayed with him was the ordinariness of her daily appearance. He could not understand what it was that drove him here to her except the memory of the enchanted hour right there beneath him.

He had watched the many colors of the grass, the flowers and the leaves ever brightening in the morning light and fading again as the sun arched its way over the hills and down to the sea; and the splendor and beauty of the light and the colors stirred in him a wonder at the world around him. He could not reconcile then the baseness of the passions that filled the hearts of white men and black men even in his own camp, with the glorious manifestations of beauty and peace that flowed before his eyes all day long. As the light dwindled, the colors began to fade into somber grey and black. The sound of approaching night crept in. He heard the gangs moving slowly from the field across the pasture and down to the huts by the stream. He saw Bessie and Toma moving briskly about their separate chores. Soon the smell of cooking wafted on the wind in his direction, and he felt the emptiness in his stomach, suddenly realizing the hunger and thirst of a day with neither food nor water.

Pharcel stayed unmoving on the branch, thinking that he would wait until dark and slip out of the trees and through the fields to the deep woods beyond. He saw the windows shut and the lights dimmed and he knew that Bessie and Toma would be leaving for the short walk towards the edge of the stream where they lived in separate huts. Another hour passed by and still she had not appeared. He felt an emptiness and a blackness settling on him as the thought of not seeing her grew stronger and stronger. He was about to slide down the tree when he caught a flash of grey against the back of the house. He dropped from the tree and scurried towards her. She was standing there in the night looking intently at the dark, shifting shadows beyond the bush. He moved silently and was standing close to her shoulder before she saw him. A short scream held suspended in her throat and her breasts heaved and fell as her breath caught and came again in silent gasps. He stretched his arm toward her and she recoiled instinctively, but he stepped forward and pulled her roughly to him. She clutched his shoulder, searching his eyes frantically as he drew her to the deeper shadows against the house.

Wordlessly, he pressed her against the weathered balustrade of the back verandah and wrapped his arms around her slim waist. She clung to him, her breath coming in short gasps, her fingers tightening on his bare flesh as he raised her skirt and pressed her to him. He felt again the wet fluttering of her soft flesh, and held her closely as her breath came in gasps and low cries escaped her lips. Yet she opened out to him in that soft, warm embrace that suddenly folded and opened again and again in surge upon surge of a rapture that was complete and overwhelming. Weakly, she placed both hands on his chest and made as if to push him away from her, but he gathered her unsteady legs around his waist and held her closer. She held tightly to him and whimpered softly as he settled her on her feet. For a moment they stood there still locked together. Then he saw the paleness creeping back to her face and the look of fright and incomprehension filling her eyes. She would have slipped from his embrace if he had not caught at her wrist and held her fast.

"I will come again." His voice sounded harsh in the dark silence of the night.

She did not respond, but quickly stepped out of his grasp and was gone. He remained leaning against the back verandah for several minutes, then gathered himself and vanished through the bushes.

Pharcel returned many times and each time she came out in the dark searching the night with breathless expectation. Twice he had lain silently in the trees and seen Captain Marshall arrive. The first time she had barely paid any attention to the Captain and Toma had solicitously brought him drinks while he sat alone on the front verandah. The second time she did not come out, but remained in her chamber all day. Toma had served him lunch and he remained sitting there all afternoon until the shadows crept past the clearing where the house stood and began to darken the hills above. Then he strode disconsolately down the path to the stream at the bottom where he had left his horse.

One night she came out searching the dark in nervous agitation. Pharcel came to her and found her in a state of near panic. Her hands shook as she clutched his arm and whispered urgently.

"Georgette is back!"

He was startled for a moment and looked desperately about searching for a place deeper than the dark of the night to creep into. He took her quickly and silently away from the open space at the back of house and into the cover of the trees.

Captain Marshall had chosen the posting to Grandbay ostensibly because he was already familiar with the territory. Captain Urquhart thought otherwise, but he kept silent about it, except when he sometimes chided him mildly for mixing business with pleasure. Amid jocular protestations, Captain Marshall would dwell on the difficulties of his post—the legendary reputation of Coree Greg as a valiant and wily fighter and the formidable defenses of his camp, the almost impassable trail leading to the east coast which he had to patrol regularly, and the settlement of Caribs (the remnants of a tribe of native Indians that occupied parts of the interior of the island) nearby which habitually gave shelter to the runaways. To add to these difficulties, Paulinaire, a free mulatto, was known to frequent the hidden coves in the vicinity of Grandbay, and to make journeys to and from Martinique, smuggling arms and supplies. He thought the presence of his legion there had already considerably reduced this traffic.

Despite his onerous duties, Captain Marshall found time enough to visit Dubique Estate at least once every week. Elise continued to elude him, but now that she was back, Georgette sat with him and sometimes led him to the clump of

trees where they sat in the shade conversing for hours. He regarded Elise's continuing rebuff as mere feminine coquetry, and he accepted it as a challenge to one
day breaking through her cold reserve. The few months in Roseau had not broken Georgette's propensity for unruliness. She had shed the austere drab grey
uniform of the school for the short, swirling skirts that she had taken to wearing
on the estate. Free and without the restraining hand of Miss Morson, she ran
about the pasture and the fields, her natural vivacity leading her to outrageous
escapades in the most unlikely places, even in the miserable slave huts. Captain
Marshall found her vivaciousness refreshing and spent much time in childish
conversation with her.

"Will you be returning to school?" he asked her one day.

"Oh no!" she answered. "I am not going back there."

"Why not?"

"It's an awful place," she said pensively. "There is nothing for me to learn
there."

"But surely," he persisted, "they taught you lady-like things."

"Oh, that's not for me," she said dismissively. "I learn more interesting things
on this estate than I will ever learn in that place."

"You ever received the sweets I brought you?" he asked, turning the subject.

"Sweets? No, she kept them all. Not good for our health she would say"

"I wonder what she did with them."

"What do you think? Ate them all, I'm sure. That is why she is so gross"

"You don't like her, do you?"

"Certainly not!"

"But why? She kept you all too well disciplined?"

"That was only pretence. She had no time for us when her sergeant came."

"A sergeant?"

"He came every Friday. We could hear her caterwauling all night. We knew
enough to keep out of the way the following day so we would not be the object of
her atonement for her night's debauchery."

He laughed, wondering at her precociousness.

They had wandered to the cluster of trees late one morning, bending as they
crept under the low, thickly-leaved branches that formed a tent over the cool
ground beneath. Dry leaves and branches crackled under their feet as they
entered the shady bower. Suddenly, he stopped and placed his hand companion-
ably on her shoulder.

"Why does your mother avoid me so?" he asked miserably. "She will not even
give me the normal courtesy of a guest."

"I told you she would not have you," she answered truculently.

"Have me?" he queried, giving her a nervous glance.

"You want her, don't you?" she challenged.

"Well..... I never said...."

"She will not have you," she repeated assertively.

He stood transfixed where he was, a look of utter consternation on his face. He reached nervously for one end of his moustache, twisting that in his fingers.

"What makes you think...?" he stuttered.

"Oh. I know these things," she answered archly. "I have seen you two together and I know."

He stood there dumbfounded. After a brief silence, she turned to him.

"Why don't you have me?" she asked abruptly.

He almost staggered with the shock of her words. An amused smile played around his lips and the flesh around his eyes creased with merriment.

"You silly, mischievous brat," he exclaimed. "You were joking, weren't you?"

She turned her face up to him, an impish twinkle in her eyes.

"Was I?" She dropped her head demurely and walked out of the trees.

He stood completely abashed in the dark coolness of the bower and watched her go. For the first time he began to see her other than as a child. He caught the firm lines of her haunches and legs, the thrust of her vernal bosom and the proud lift of her head. Hitherto, he had noticed only the brown freckles on her face and the plump roundness of her limbs. Now beneath the childish garment that she wore he discerned the mind and body of a woman. He shook his head violently, trying to discard the thought. Without returning to the house to announce his departure, he sauntered, deep in contemplation, down the hill and rode away to where his legion was encamped.

It was many days before he returned to Dubique. This last encounter with Georgette consumed his mind day after day. His nights were filled with her image, suddenly blossomed to full and seductive womanhood. He no longer saw in her the plump, gold-freckled little vixen that provided him with such amusement and distraction in his frustrated pursuit of her mother. Now his mind conjured the picture of a woman still virginal in the purity of her gaze, but whose body had all the allure of a seasoned temptress. He was by any standard quite experienced in matters of seduction. Even before he had joined the army, he had earned the reputation of a successful libertine. As an officer and a gentleman, he had honed the art of seduction to a level of sophistication that made him the envy of many of his fellow officers. This was necessarily so in view of the few attractive women that could be found in the ungracious and sometimes vulgar social circles of the colonies. He was proud of his accomplishments in that regard.

Experienced though he was, however, he had never met the challenge of the flower of innocence beckoning him to its petals with such flagrant enticement. He remembered that last coy look she had cast on him, as if knowing that he could not possibly resist picking up the scarf that she had thrown so boldly at his feet. He felt within himself a disconcerting helplessness as if he was no longer in control. He was used to romantic intrigues of many sorts and had frequently encountered various stages of infatuation among the young, gawky young ladies in the homes that he frequented. But this he knew instinctively was no calf love, no passing fancy that would never get to maturation. Georgette was decidedly of a different sort. She was young, but she was already a woman of resolution; not one that would be given to simpering flirtation and that would baulk at the final moment of consummation. He had to tread carefully in this new situation.

He had spent many hours examining his deep-down feelings for Elise. His brief, frustrated liaison with her had left with him a restrained infatuation that was more psychological than emotional. It was as if some mystery deep within her had taken hold of him, and his mind had become obsessed with the need to get to the bottom of it. That short, breathless moment in what seemed so long ago, when her passion had flared so ardently and then subsided with such abruptness to a cold, almost disdainful withdrawal, had left him bewitched and in a sense bewildered. He did not believe he was truly enamored of her in any way. She was just a plain country woman with a sinuous body that was more distinctive in its earthiness and natural allure than in any measure of refinement. More than anything in the totality of her features, it was that serene look on her face and the hidden promise of unplumbed sensuality in the faint lines around her lips and eyes that had kept him captivated for so long.

And now he had discovered in Georgette a springtime of passion that he knew he would never be able to resist. For many days he kept about his camp attending to his military duties. Coree Greg and his followers, who he knew were somewhere deep in the woods of the mountains that rose so high and forbiddingly above their encampment, were securely contained. There were no signs or immediate threats of incursions anywhere in the vicinity of Grandbay and Geneva. Over on the eastern coast, Congoree and his men seemed to have gone underground, and the estates at Delices and La Plaine sustained no plundering or attack of any kind. Even Paulinaire had ceased his trafficking in that area and was reported to be quietly conspiring in the town for some treasonous act or another.

The Council was just biding its time until there was sufficient evidence to seize and imprison him.

Elsewhere around the island, even with Captain Urquhart's legion stationed at Laudat and the legion under Captain Combe of the 30th Regiment encamped in the open valley above Layou, the runaways continued to stalk the highways in the Roseau Valley and on the coastal stretches beyond Mahaut. Bala in the central part of the highlands and Sandy and Jacco in the lowlands of the West seemed to find innumerable ways to elude the military patrols set to contain them. Captain Marshall felt confident that he would soon eradicate the runaway slave camps in the area under his control.

He came to the estate one morning and sat with Georgette in the shade of the verandah. The rain had fallen the previous night and there was a cool freshness to the leaves of the trees and the grass in the open pasture before them. Looking out towards the horizon, they could see light clouds floating across the sky and creating pale patches on the cerulescent surface of the sea. They sat there all morning until lunch. Elise had kept to her room, never coming out even when Toma, with his usual cautious tread, brought lunch and spread the dishes and glasses out on a small table before them. Georgette had remained sitting sedately all morning. There was none of the boisterousness of past days. She listened attentively to his discourse, although most of his talk was about the dull social life in the town, the poor condition of the militia, and what he considered vain attempts to drill military discipline into the black soldiers that had been recently added to their ranks. The Council had recently decided to conscript slaves into the militia in the belief that they would betray the whereabouts of the runaways and use their knowledge of the woods to penetrate the defenses of their camps. In his view, those blacks were a pack of morons, good only for carrying the packs of the white soldiers on their sorties into the woods. Even so, they had to be watched since they were known to be a treacherous people.

Georgette listened to him all morning. There was an uncharacteristic pensiveness about her that he could not fathom. She laughed at his witticisms, but quickly relapsed into thoughtfulness. He flattered himself that she was deeply smitten with love and this had chastened her natural sprightliness. There was no doubt that she appeared to be consumed by some deep emotion. There was also a kind of hesitancy in her responses to him, especially when their conversation touched on Elise. She could not sit still, and shifted uneasily on her seat, her eyes cast down to the floor.

The afternoon sun had warmed the verandah and drove them to the shelter of the trees. At that time of day everything held still. The leaves appeared to droop and birds perched sleepily on the branches. Only the faint sound of voices in the far-away fields disturbed the afternoon's somnolence. Georgette and the Captain walked in the shade of the trees until they came to the bower of thick overhanging branches. They stood awkwardly and silently in the cool dark, until he spoke.

"Did you mean what you said the other day?" he asked her softly.

She nodded her head slowly and came quietly to him, gently resting her head on his chest. The rough braids on the lining at the front of his tunic lightly chafed her cheeks. He held her firmly to him, then raised her chin and kissed her softly on her lips. She did not demur, but held tightly to him as he lowered her to the ground. She whimpered sharply at first; then only the thrashing sound of their bodies on the dry leaves disturbed the silence. Afterwards she held him almost maternally to her bosom and stroked his damp hair.

After a long while he spoke. He was sitting against the rough bark of the tree and she sat leaning against his chest. She was still strangely quiet, head bowed, fingers twiddling with the dry twigs on the ground beside her.

"Something is bothering you."

"No. It is nothing."

"You have been quiet and thoughtful all morning."

"It is nothing, I tell you."

"Well, there must be something the matter."

"I can't speak of it."

"You might as well speak of it if it is bothering you so much."

"No. I can't speak of it," she said again.

She lapsed into another silence. Then she lifted her eyes to the dark branches above them.

"If only my father knew," she murmured absently.

"Knew what?" Captain Marshall asked sharply.

"I can't tell", she said, a look of dismay spreading over her face.

"It's about Elise, isn't it?"

She turned to him appealingly.

"Please," she pleaded, "don't make me tell."

He seized her by her shoulders and turned her to face him. His face hardened and his eyes bored into hers. She tried to avert her eyes, but he forced her to look at him.

"What of Elise?" he demanded. "You must tell!"

She dropped her head disconsolately.

"I saw her," she said almost inaudibly. "I saw them."

"Saw whom?" he asked gruffly.

"That slave. The one that ran away. Pharcel"

"With Elise?"

She nodded miserably.

"Impossible!" he almost shouted. "Not Elise. You must be mistaken."

She clutched desperately at his arm. Her words came out gushing as if a dam within her had been breached.

"I heard her that first night, and many nights after, wandering in the dark at the back of the house. I listened to the sound of their rapture in the trees and saw him standing naked in the night. I tell you, he was here. Many times. He comes with the night and she goes out to him. Here among the trees."

A dark cloud of fury clouded his face. He thrust her away from him and stood over her.

"It's a lie!" he shouted at her. "A wicked lie!"

Of a sudden, she leaned on her elbows on the ground and turned to face him, a mocking grin on her face.

"Your Elise!" she sneered. "Or is it his?"

He turned from her and hastened from the trees. Only the galloping of his horse as he rode to the encampment could quiet the thunder in his breast.

CHAPTER 6

Petit Jacques was a skilled woodsman and knew the forest and the innermost crevices of every valley and gorge among the surrounding mountains. He was a small man, tightly built of bone and sinew. Veins stood out prominently on his arms and legs which gave the impression of inexhaustible endurance. He moved through the dense bushes that grew in profusion in open swathes of variegated green between the darkly wooded hills, through the tangled vegetation that hung from the giant trees on the mountain slopes and over slippery ground and muddy swamps, with equal grace and sure-footedness. He was sharp-featured, with a chin that sloped almost to his thin neck. A morose companion who hardly spoke, except in a habitual whisper, he was a dependable guide through the most difficult terrain; but he was known to be shifty in his personal relations and wavering in his loyalty and attachments.

They had been warned of the legion stationed at Laudat and of the danger of running into patrols if they followed the shorter route through the lower hills of Grandbay and across the wider valleys above Roseau. Undaunted, Petit Jacques, with stealthy but certain steps, traversed the higher ground behind the eastern boundaries of Geneva in a seemingly unending series of sharp inclines and deep gorges choked with towering trees and mossy undergrowth, crossing numberless streams and rocky ravines.

Pharcel was accustomed to the woods above Dubique and Geneva, and he had learned to travel over long distances in silence and with the utmost caution. Here in the heart of the forest, he was profoundly moved by the awesome stillness around him. Giant gommier trees towered overhead, their thick branches forming a dark green canopy a hundred feet above them. Here and there, the light broke through the filtering leaves and streaked in bright slanting rays that lit up the dim and dank interior like the beams of light breaking through the high windows of a cathedral. There was a soothing silence among the trees, broken only by the screech of some unseen bird or the scuttling of some tiny creature in the soggy leaves and broken branches on the forest floor. In some places long ropes hung suspended from the branches way above their heads, so thickly disposed that they had to move them aside to make their way through. Tiny streams flowed at the bottom of gullies or in low fissures in rocky mounds, with water clean and clear like liquid crystal.

They had walked for hours without sight of a living creature when, out of the buttressed base of a giant chataignier, a figure, so desolate, gaunt and wild that Pharcel instinctively leapt several feet into the sparse undergrowth, rose before them. It was an old woman, naked and unkempt. Her hair lay in a tangled mess on her head, her eyes bulged out of deep sockets, and stumps of yellowed teeth gnashed savagely between foam-flecked lips. She let out tiny screeches and a string of gibberish while darting her claw-like fingers in menacing gestures intended to keep them at bay. Petit Jacques merely shooed her away and she crept bending low, her eyes never leaving them, into a burrow that she had made at the base of the tree. Petit Jacques explained that she was a runaway who had lost her mind and had been wandering the forest for years searching for her lost village somewhere in Africa. Many attempts had been made to take her from the bush into the camps nearby, but she always disappeared and returned to the forest.

After several hours walking through the deep fastness of the woods, they came upon the coarse, low vegetation surrounding the lake. They stood on a rise and below them was the lake, stretching out its several branches of grey, placid water for nearly a mile across. Above them, the sky arched between the mountains in unclouded blue. The sun was on its way down the valley that fell westward to the sea; and its waning light softened the greenery on the surrounding hills. A deep hush added to the serenity of the place as if nature itself had come to rest on the banks of the still, open expanse of water. They kept to the higher ground around the lake until they came to denser woods, moving eastwards until they encountered a trace that led to Bala's camp.

Bala's camp was a muddle of squalid huts and shanties scattered over a muddy clearing in the forest. Behind the clearing, the land rose in heavily forested slopes to serrated ridges overlooking the lakes. In front, it fell precipitously for nearly a quarter of a mile to a small stream and, beyond the stream, leveled off to a gentle descent along the crest of a lower ridge. The path that led from the camp veered left down the steep decline, and was cut into steps with strips of logs placed at each step as footholds. The stream below opened out across the path in a shallow basin before it tumbled down a declivity through dense bush and away into the woods. Straight ahead from the camp, the path dwindled to a thin, almost indiscernible trace into the forest.

Pharcel and Petit Jacques had been shown to Bala's hut, a large but shoddy structure set in the center of a muddy patch of bare earth. Cork, one of Bala's lieutenants, was standing at the door and grudgingly allowed them to enter. Bala was dressed in the grey trousers that he had worn during his visit to Coree Greg's camp, and a mud-stained white linen coat that barely covered his chest and hips, and was sweat-stained at the armpits. He was sitting on a carved wooden chair at a square, brown-stained table in the center of the room. Around him was a profusion of furniture of the kind found in estate houses—vanities that looked incongruous in the rough interior of the hut. Pharcel had crept in respectfully a little way behind Petit Jacques. He smiled expectantly, waiting for a word of recognition from the awesome warrior he had heard so much about, but Bala only raised his head and through narrowed eyes regarded them disdainfully.

"Now what does the old man want?" he asked gruffly.

Petit Jacques spoke in soft, halting tones and delivered Coree Greg's message.

Bala did not respond, but merely waved them away with a contemptuous gesture. He did not so much as enquire about their journey or their need of refreshment and rest after their arduous trek through the woods. Pharcel and Petit Jacques backed out of the hut, but in the brief moment of their exit, they both caught a cold, dark look of malevolence in Bala's half-shut eyes. Pharcel involuntarily shivered, wondering why it was he suddenly had this sense of danger. It was the kind of feeling that had come over him the first time he suddenly encountered a large boa in the woods.

As they stepped out onto the muddy ground outside, Cork glowered at Pharcel. There was a look of suspicion and dislike on his broad, mean face. Petit Jacques spoke to Pharcel in his soft whispery voice.

"Careful," he said. "Look to your back!"

Pharcel turned backwards reflexively; thinking to avert some immediate threat. Cork had disappeared within the hut and there was no one behind him, but he could not shake off the dark cloud of fear that had settled over him since he had that last look into Bala's soul. He was puzzled. He had not paid any attention to the vicious look on Cork's face, and he had not understood what Petit Jacques' warning words meant. He was disturbed by the cold, venomous glance that Bala had directed at him, though he could not understand its significance or any possible reason for it.

As they walked through the space between the houses, they could hear the sound of laughter coming from a jumble of huts towards the left. There were several men and women seated on stones and low stumps of trees within an elevated circle of dry earth. The laughter and the chatter stopped and hung suspended as the two men walked in, but resumed when they recognized Petit Jacques as if there had been no interruption. The men were dressed variously in cut-off trousers or the wide trousers of the estate overseers, with shirts of varying designs and colors. The women were outfitted in tight bodices and wide low skirts, stained and tattered from constant use. They were all young and mostly handsome.

Cicero was sitting amidst a bevy of girls of indeterminate ages. His eyes were darting all around the circle in his customary edginess; but as they came to rest on Pharcel, they seemed to darken for a moment, and then to shift quickly away as if fearful of making contact.

Pharcel stood nervously outside the circle listening to the laughter and gaiety coming from the group. There was much bantering and bawdy language in a lively exchange between the men and women. The carefree and jocular spirit among them contrasted with the staid and sedentary atmosphere in Coree Greg's camp. He yearned to be part of the youthful energy and untrammeled gaiety that pervaded this place. His mind refused to dwell on the squalor of the surroundings or the dark looks of enmity that he had encountered since coming here. He liked the free and easy relationship among the people. The women in particular seemed unrestrained in their behavior and free of inhibitions concerning their relationships with their male companions. One of them had been eyeing Pharcel speculatively since his arrival among them. She gave him a side-ways look, a saucy smile brightening her face.

"Is this stalwart cock going to stay with us?" she asked, brazenly appraising his youthful physique.

"Hey, Presente," Cicero remarked sternly. "There can be only one stalwart in this camp."

"Then Bala better watch out," she laughed.

Pharcel smiled, shifting uneasily on his feet.

"Where you coming from, boy?" Presente continued to gaze wantonly at him through long, fluttering eyelashes.

"Coree Greg's camp," he replied shortly.

"What are you doing among those old men?" Her smile widened just enough to show a pair of large, white upper teeth.

Pharcel could feel himself warming to the attractiveness of her look and the open invitation in her smile. Cicero regarded him intensely under lowering brows; but he said nothing.

"I came to see Alexis," he ventured quietly.

"What a young, handsome boy like you wanting to see Alexis for?" She gave him that mocking, teasing look, batting her eyelids and somehow constricting her lips in that cheeky, two-toothed smile.

The other women snickered and there was a low guffaw among the men. Cicero continued to scowl. He said something to Angelique, and her expression froze in a resentful frown. She turned away from him.

Victoire sat somewhat apart from the other women, holding her two year old son between her thighs. She must have been just past sixteen years of age, with eyes that seemed to be still searching for the rest of her childhood—clear and bright, but somewhat confused. She had a round head covered with short, brown curls lying close to her scalp. Everything about her face seemed to have been molded for roundness, from her curved forehead to her snub nose and her almost circular fleshy lips. Her face glowed with a glossy blackness that emphasized the orbicular curve of her high cheek bones. The little boy between her legs had the same rotundity about his face except that he had the ponderous brow that was such a prominent feature of Bala's countenance.

"Ah, Sussex," she said addressing Cicero, "why you so disagreeable? He's not about to take your place. Bala needs you to grease his pistol."

The others laughed volubly.

Victoire turned to Pharcel and she jerked her chin sharply upward, indicating a direction towards the eastern extremity of the clearing.

"You will find Alexis over there," she advised him crisply.

"But don't forget to come back later," Presente shouted after him as he turned to go.

He found Alexis sitting outside his shack, whittling at a long thin pole with a slim blade of knife. The knife had worn down to just a narrow strip of metal. Where the handle should have been, brown strands of the wet fiber of the balizier plant were wrapped tightly to give a firm comfortable hold. Alexis was obviously overjoyed to see him; but in his characteristic taciturn manner, only opened out his arms to embrace him. They sat on the log outside the shack until nightfall, retracing the events of the past months.

Alexis had left Dubique soon after the night of Pharcel's escape. He had loitered in the field at the end of a day's work and made his way in the dark through the forest until he came to a small Carib settlement just above Petite Savanne. There were only about twenty men and several women of varying ages. Most of the men lived in a carbet around which were a few separate ajoupas. The largest ajoupa stood somewhat apart from the others and was occupied by the chief and his family. The others housed the rest of the men and their wives.

He had simply walked in from the surrounding forest and gone to sleep in the carbet. When he awoke in the evening, the men gave him food from a large clay pot simmering on a fire just outside the carbet. For a whole week they took no notice of him except to feed him from their pot, until on the seventh or eight day they pointed to the North and signified that they were embarking on a journey. He had followed them down the steep side of a mountain to a rocky shore where their canoes were beached. The waves were coming in angry swells that rose and crashed thunderously on the rocks, and he wondered how they could possibly launch themselves through that dreadful turbulence. But they did.

By late evening they came to a cove on the shores of Delices. The swell was cascading even more furiously; and the Caribs waited just beyond where the waves crested until, at a signal, they rode upon a low swell that rushed swiftly to the shingled shore. They had then scrambled out of the boats and hurriedly dragged them over the stony beach. Alexis was left standing on the beach looking about him uncertainly. He entered a coconut grove and found a track through windswept, stunted bushes that brought him to Congoree's camp. He stayed there many days until one day he followed Congoree and a few of his men to Rosalie in a long day's march, and then to Mabouya's camp ensconced in a deep gorge below the long, high ridge that was Grand Fond. Mabouya was squat, bovine and middle-aged, but beneath his dull exterior was a temper so flammable that it would erupt at the slightest provocation. The few men and women living in a disorderly scattering of bamboo huts feared him and went about their business with a subdued dread that gave the camp an atmosphere of impending doom.

Many nights the distant sound of drums rolled down the steep mountain side into the somber quiet of the camp, and the men would whisper among themselves about the decadence and bawdiness of the life-style of their neighbors. Alexis had been drawn to the beckoning sound of revelry coming from the far away mountain above; and one bright day he walked the long, steep incline up the slippery slope to the track into Bala's camp, and never returned.

Pharcel sat with Alexis on a log outside a small, crudely built shack at the lower end of the camp. They had not seen each other since Pharcel escaped from the estate at Dubique. For months since then he had heard of Alexis' presence in Bala's camp and had planned to visit the little man who had first alerted him to the danger of Elise's too obvious and potentially fatal attraction. But he had also been eager to meet again the man he thought was the greatest among the runaway chiefs. He had been profoundly affected by Bala's dynamic personality and leadership during his visit to Coree Greg's camp and for many weeks he had harbored the thought of stealing away to be part of the exciting adventure that he imagined was a daily occurrence in Bala's camp.

Coree Greg had sent him with Petit Jacques to say to Bala that he agreed to a gathering of Chiefs to discuss mutual defense, but that he and his men would take no part in unprovoked aggression on the white planters. They were to pass on to Bala the information Joseph had sent from the house of Councilor Winston concerning the movement of the three legions of the militia. Pharcel had welcomed with exuberant excitement the opportunity to experience the thrill of being again in Bala's presence.

Pharcel told Alexis of his days in Coree Greg's camp and of Bala's visit there. He mentioned obliquely that he had on several occasions returned to Dubique, though he never mentioned Elise and the overwhelming passion that bound them together. Somehow Alexis sensed that there was much that was left unsaid.

"You should not go back." He shook his head sadly, knowing instinctively that his warning would be of no avail.

It was not long after dark that the dancing began. He and Alexis were still sitting outside on the log before a fire that was slowly dying, after eating from the black earthenware pot that Alexis had set on the ground between them some hours ago; and his youthful energy was subsiding into numbing somnolence when the chanting began. He recognized the song. He had heard it many times on the estate at Dubique, and he had been taught the basic steps of the dance. Behind the chorus of female voices, the drums rose and fell in alternating clangs and rumbles that defined the intricate and sinuous shuffles and capriole that would ultimately entirely possess the dancers in a kind of phrenetic dementia. He looked askance at Alexis who only shook his head from side to side.

"You can go," he said. "Enjoy yourself."

Pharcel rose to his feet and stumbled through the darkness back to the clearing where he had found the group. The place was lighted with flaming torches set in the ground around the elevated circle of earth and tied to nearby branches. There were many more persons gathered around the circle, the torches throwing fleckered shadows on their faces. He recognized Petit Jacques squatting at the edge of the circle, and close to him Cicero, his eyes for once fixed to the center of the clearing where the dancing was already in progress. Cork, almost unrecognizable in the dark, was leaning against a tree, alone and glancing sullenly at the shadowy figures around the clearing. Victoire and some of the other women stood in a group in the shadows. The drummer sat on a low upturned log with a drum made from a short length of a hollowed tree trunk, one end stretched over with a square of animal skin, held firmly between his knees; his eyes raised to the stars in a trance-like fixity while his hands thrashed and pummeled the resounding skin of the drum.

Presente was in the clearing with a male dancer whose leaps and shuffles and gyrations were increasing in a frenzy of motion as the throbbing cadence of the drums rose in intensity. She shuffled and gyrated before the male dancer, her eyes intent on his every movement. Each time he lagged in the lusty exhilaration of the dance, she would lift and flash the front of her skirt, exposing the dark jointure of her thighs, and he would leap in a frenzied resurgence of motion until he worked himself into a cataleptic fervor that seemed to take him beyond control. Then she turned to the drummer, flashing her skirt, and skipping and vertiginously whirling, her bare thighs glistening in the wavering light of the torches, until she collapsed onto him, her raised skirt finally falling over his drum. The silence of the drum broke the spell and the male dancer awoke from the depth of the ecstasy that had so completely possessed his spirit, braced his shoulders and, looking drained and dissipated, walked slowly from the circle. Presente grinned proudly and wiped the sweat from her brow.

Victoire detached herself from the group of women standing in the shadows and tripped over to the center of the circle. She beckoned to Cork who seemed to brighten suddenly, and he came proudly to her, strutting like a game cock, his arms stiff at his side. He skipped around her; head lowered in a sideways glance, and then came to a stand a few paces from the drummer. One man behind the drummer led the chant in a hoarse baritone, and the women responded with high quavering voices that kept the cadence of the music rising and falling in rhythmic undulations that seemed to stir every nerve in the dancers' bodies. Victoire took the lead in this dance while Cork leapt and twirled from his position beside the drummer. Every now and again he jerked his abdomen in lewd contortions forward and back as if to urge her dancing to ascending heights. His face beamed with ecstatic delight as he followed her movements around the circle.

Victoire moved her feet with lightening speed and a back and forth motion, dipping and rising, her arms gracefully flailing the air, her bosom heaving and subsiding as the drumming and the chanting took hold of her. Dropping and twirling with her knees spreading wide and coming together again in rapid quivering motions as if to clasp an elusive presence, the light of the flambeaus shone through the thin material of her skirt to reveal the firm outline of her thighs. She danced with her head thrown back, her eyes half shut and her dark pouting lips puckered as if she was wonderfully uplifted in the throes of an overwhelming freedom of spirit that broke through the shackles of reality and raised her to the acme of delight and ecstasy.

She flashed the front of her skirt upwards and down in complete abandonment as the dance seized control of her in every limb, briefly exposing the darkness of her belly and loins. Pharcel had never witnessed a dance so beautiful, so wild and so erotic. As the chant increased in vigor and the drumming quickened in tempo, her lissome body convulsed in a paroxysm of ecstatic release as she rose and fell on her flashing feet closer and closer to the stirring, delirious rhythm of the drum until, raising her skirt almost to her breast, totally entranced and help-less, she fell at last upon the drummer and silenced the reverberating beat of the drum.

She raised herself and stood there for a moment, head bowed to her chest, shoulders drooping; then she lifted her eyes to the sky and, as if freed from the bonds of some diabolic enchantment and filled with elation, she let forth an exultant laugh. She turned and looked about her, peering through the flickering light at the shadowy faces around the circle until her eyes came to rest on Pharcel. She beckoned to him to come within the circle. With uncertain steps, he walked into the bright light of the torches and stood languidly opposite her. Cork slunk out of the circle and into the darkening shadows. Bala was standing at the outer edge of the crowd and Cork went to join him. They spoke and after a while both turned abruptly away and disappeared into the night.

The chanting and the drumming began afresh, and Pharcel tried lamely to re-enact the sinuous movements of the dancers before him. His feet felt leaden and his movements clumsy as he went through the steps he had learned on the estate at Dubique. His awkwardness did not deter Victoire, however, and she went flit-ting and twirling and undulating as if she were alone in the center. At last, he got caught up in the voluptuousness of her dance and his feet moved of their own accord as the drums stirred him to a rhythm that was in time with her move-ments. But it was not as enlivening and titillating as the previous dance, and he was glad when it was over.

The dancing went on till near dawn. The flambeaus had burnt down to smoky glows, and the dancers appeared as mere twitching silhouettes in the center of the stage. The crowd thinned gradually and he found himself standing alone at one side of the circle. Then he felt urgent fingers clasp his arm and he turned sharply around to find Presente leaning towards him and resting against his shoulder. She looked up at him, the same seductive smile on her face.

He awoke in Presente's hut later that morning to find her bending over him. He saw the broad whiteness of her two upper front teeth between the fleshy con-tours of her lips.

"You must go," she said coolly. "Bala wants you dead."

A chill came over him and he hastened out of her place to find Alexis. He found him sitting in his shack, his head lowered between his shoulders.

"I must go," Pharcel said to him, a note of urgency strangling his voice.

Alexis nodded.

"Where is Petit Jacques?" Pharcel looked about him nervously.

Alexis jerked his head sideways.

"Gone already," he answered, fear puckering his brow.

"Then I must go."

Pharcel turned to the low gap that served as a door in the front wall of the shack.

"Wait!" Alexis stood and reached for a straw sack hanging from a peg on the wall, then he lifted his cutlass from a low shelf and, without another word, he walked out of the shack through the bushes at the back. Pharcel followed him.

They crept through the dense bush until they came at last to the track that led to the stream below.

"Where are we going?" Pharcel asked with a note of puzzlement in his voice.

"If you value your life, do not turn back," Alexis replied tensely.

They continued downhill and across the stream where the land straightened to a gentle slope along the edge of the long ridge all the way to Rosalie. They came to a juncture where the path diverged. Alexis turned to face the path that led across a broad river.

"I will go back to Congoree for a few days," he said. "For you, it is not safe even there."

He pointed to the other track.

"This will take you to the land of the Caribs," he said compassionately. "Follow this track across a river broader than this and across a wide flat valley. Continue up hill until you find them. You will be safe there for a time."

He turned and walked away.

Pharcel watched him as he waded across the river, the water up to his waist. Alexis never turned back and was soon swallowed by the thicket of bushes on the other bank.

For most of the day he traveled on the edges of windswept hills with the foaming sea roaring hundreds of feet below. The track took him up a long, steep hill that fell sharply on its other side to a beautiful cove where the sea shimmered in dancing billows that rolled continuously to a sandy shore. It was a narrow but open valley devoid of forest, filled with wild raspberry and guava trees. On its edges, sweet-smelling bay grew in profusion on the lower reaches of the surrounding hills, their waxed leaves glistening in the sun, before they gave way to the forest trees that darkened the hillside above them. A shallow stream gamboled its way through the valley until it opened out in a wide pool as it entered the sea.

It was the most beautiful spot that he had ever encountered, and he could not resist loitering on the bank of the stream, lying on the warm grass near the shore and gazing at the relentless waves as they rolled onto the sand.

His mind went back to the night from which now he was fleeing to save his life. He had had no intention of following Presente to her hut, but the lateness of the hour and her beguiling insistence had drawn him to follow wherever he could find immediate comfort. Neither was he bent on sharing the libidinous charms that Victoire had displayed in those scintillating minutes that she commanded the stage. He did not even think that his own indifferent performance had been worth noting by anyone. Yet here he was on the run from the one man he admired more than any other. He respected Coree Greg for his maturity, courage and wisdom, but he idolized Bala for his boldness and fearlessness. He could not be mistaken about those qualities that he had held in such high esteem. But surely, there must be awful flaws in Bala's character if he was prone to such unreasonable and unwarranted malevolence. He felt lost and betrayed more than he ever did when he was so unmercifully thrashed for a crime he did not commit. His feelings of resentment and hate for Jean and Brent had already worn thin, especially since the days of his desire for Elise. His mind was now in confusion and he could not define what his true feeling about Bala was. He sat there brooding for a long time before he rose again and began the long climb to the crest of another hill.

He came upon the broader river when the sun was already far over the sea. Looking down from the hilltop, the river seemed to curve in a wide arch from the thrusting base of three or four mountains through the wide valley towards the shore. It widened to a deep estuary where it joined the sea; and he could see the waves breaking far out and cascading in gentle wavelets that rolled onto the shore and a long way up the dark surface of the river. The valley below him opened out in a broad expanse of flat land that stretched out in the distance before it rose gently towards the base of the mountains behind it. The low sun slanted its rays over nearly a mile of cane fields that stretched almost to the edge of the sea, in the midst of which rose the stone bulk and up-thrusting chimney of a mill. Beyond the far side of the river, low hills ran into each other enclosing the valley right down to the sea. On their gentle slopes were open spaces of vegetable gardens interspersed with groves of fruit trees. On the side of the hill closest to the shore, slave huts huddled together; and a little way above them, in the middle of a wide grassy slope, was the country residence of the Lieutenant Governor, Captain Bruce.

Pharcel could hear voices coming from the fields below him, but as the sun sank below the crest of the hills, and shadows crept rapidly over the valley, the voices receded until the valley was deathly quiet. Only the smoke rising from the cluster of houses in the distance gave evidence that a hundred weary slaves were settling down for the night. Pharcel remained hidden in the bushes until he felt the deep, regular breath of the night. There was no moon, and only the flitting fireflies lightened the dark. He crept slowly down the thickly wooded hill to the bank of the river. There he turned right to where the river broadened in what he thought was a still, wide pool. He hesitated only for a moment, then walked to the edge of the water and dived in. He gasped with shock as his head emerged from the cold water and he struck vigorously out towards the other bank.

The water was heavy and the downward current threatened to sweep him to the sea. He could hear the hiss of the sea waves running over the surface of the river, splashing his face as he thrashed against the tugging current. He forgot all caution, pulling vigorously against the strong current, his arms and legs thrashing and thrusting noisily in the deceptively rapid flow of the water. For a moment, he felt his legs dragging; and the water closed over his head. With a frantic resurgence of energy he heaved himself to the surface and pulled himself towards the still far away bank, and did not stop until his sagging legs brushed against a boulder. Gratefully, he found a foothold, paused to regain his breath; then with a final heave, he waded through shallow water, pulled his way over the stony bed and collapsed helplessly on the grassy bank.

It was a long time before he could stand and look about him. The bank of the river stretched out in a sandy strip right down to the shore. He followed this until he came to the blacker sand of a wide beach that extended on both sides of the estuary to the foot of the low hills on either side. He crept along the beach, knowing he could not walk inland through the slave huts or the vegetable gardens or the fruit orchards without rousing attention. Even as he crawled along the shore, he could hear in the distance the growling and barking of dogs, so he walked below sloping walls of grainy rock where countless storms had gorged the land. Above the rough band of rock, rank vegetation, upswept by the sea wind, gave thick cover to the loose, sandy soil. He followed the line of the shore until he came abruptly to a small cove hollowed out of a section of the hill. There the sea came in endless surges that crashed on the base of the cliff. He turned back until he found a worn-out fissure in the grainy rock up which he was able to clamber to reach the thick, low cover of the brush. Crawling gingerly through them, he came at last upon a trail that wended its way westward through a sparse forest.

The sun was just popping out of the sea on the far horizon when he saw out of a gap in the trees, the broad sweep of a clearing on the side of a hill some way in the distance. He hastened in that direction, sensing that at this early time of dawn, there would be no one about to intercept his way into the village. He came upon it over a rise, perched on a slope, five hundred feet above the shore. The houses were scattered among a proliferation of brilliant flowers and sweet smelling herbs. They were tiny huts called *mwinas* made out of wattle and straw with sloping roofs thatched with the leaves of the roseau plant, and were propped on two sides with long poles to secure them against the force of the wind that blew constantly from the sea. In the center of the clearing on a flat strip carved out of the hillside was a much larger structure called a *tabwi*, similarly constructed, but with its roof sloping on both sides down to the ground.

Several women came out of the smaller huts and bustled about lighting fires and gathering herbs and other food for the day's breakfast. They were naked except for a short, narrow strip of colored cloth strung from their waists and dangling between their legs. The only other adornments were bracelets and chains made of colored beads or coral; though a few of them had rings of what looked like gold hanging from their nostrils. They were all of a rich bronze color with glossy black hair falling low on their backs and shoulders, and over their flat foreheads; and were of sturdy build with slanted eyes, short pert noses and slightly flaring nostrils. The men, he saw, as they emerged from the large central building or *tabwi*, were of similar complexion and build, and wore the same scanty covering over their private parts. They stood desultorily in the morning sun waiting to be fed. When the day's breakfast was served, they came bearing calabash dishes and helped themselves from the communal pot.

Pharcel stayed hidden in a clump of bushes until the men had settled down to breakfast. He was uncertain what to do, but he had been told about traditional Carib courtesy and hospitality, so he strode boldly forward to the *tabwi* and sat on a large rock not too far from the breakfast pot. No one paid any attention to him, but soon an old woman came and handed him a calabash dish with a mess of herbs and fish and a chunk of cassava bread. He ate silently while the men disposed themselves on the floor of the *tabwi* or in the shade of the stunted trees that grew beside some of the huts. As the morning progressed, the men either singly or in small groups disappeared variously towards the forest or down to the sea, while the women worked and chattered at the back of the huts where vegetable gardens and small patches of cotton were planted.

Pharcel sat on the rock until the heat of mid-morning drove him to the cool interior of the *tabwi*. It was a large, lofty building constructed of wooden poles and thatched with straw. Its design was simple but firm enough to withstand the strong wind that blew from the sea. Stout tree trunks supported a long ridge pole at the top from which long rafters descended on either side right down to the ground where they were firmly fixed in the soil. Across the rafters, thin lengths of wood were tied at intervals of about two feet from the top to a short distance from the ground; and over these, bundles of thatch were secured firmly to form a thick and impenetrable covering. Rows of hammocks were slung from the rafters and hung about four feet from the ground. Besides these, the *tabwi* was empty of any furnishing except for a few low stools and tables. The weather end was walled with wattle and straw where stacks of tools, weapons and fishing equipment, mainly harpoons and crudely made fish pots, were stored. Near the open end, three large stones formed a fireplace where food was cooked on rainy days.

He lay on the packed ground in the shade of the *tabwi* all day, not daring to climb onto one of the many hammocks disposed along the full length of the building. There was no one about except a few small children and a weathered crone who hobbled from hut to hut in search of something to do. Her bleary eyes roved curiously over Pharcel, but she said nothing to him. Towards evening, the women began to drift back to the little huts and then to the clearing in front of the *tabwi*. By and by the men returned and threw down heaps of birds, agoutis and crawfish which the women gathered for cleaning and cooking. Some of the men returned with only their fishing gear, and spoke gruffly to their women who quickly took up baskets and trooped down to the boats to collect the day's catch of fish.

Pharcel drifted out of the *tabwi* and again sat on the rock some distance away from the others. Later, the old woman who had served him breakfast, now accompanied by a stout young woman, came again with a calabash dish, brimming with crawfish, plantain and sweet potatoes and handed that to him. The stout woman had a merry look about her eyes and her lips seemed always curved in a half smile. She stood close to him as he ate and did not seem to mind the looks that the men directed at her.

As the light faded, giving way to sudden darkness, he stood and began to move towards the shelter of the *tabwi*. He was about to enter when the old woman emerged from between two of the smaller huts and beckoned to him. He turned hesitantly to her, but seeing her eager and urgent signal, he followed her to a small hut on the outer circle some distance away from the *tabwi*. The hut was as bare as the *tabwi* itself; but there was a wide mat stretched out on the hard packed floor. She lowered herself at the far side of the hut and indicated to him that he should sleep on the other side. In the dim light, he could make out another form stretched out close to the old woman. He measured the distance between them and feeling happily secure, he laid himself down and promptly fell into a deep, dreamless sleep. It was towards morning that he felt the warm wetness enveloping him and heard the short, breathless, stifled cries in the dark. His eyes opened to the stout woman writhing ecstatically over him. Instinctively, he made to rise; but suddenly overcome by a feeling of utter abandonment, he eased himself down again and remained still until her motions ceased and she collapsed weakly by his side. The old woman was sitting up gazing at them all this time, a happy gleam in her eyes. Pharcel turned away from her and drifted back into sleep. He did not stir until the heat of the sun woke him and he felt the hunger in his belly. There was a dish of fish and cassava close to him on the mat. He shook himself awake, ate and then walked out of the hut to sit in the shade beneath one of the low trees.

The men snickered and gave him leering looks when they returned and found him still sitting beneath the tree. Again the two women fed him and brought him a small gourd filled with a spirited brew made from fermented cassava juice. This seemed to have stirred an even greater amusement among the men who nodded to each other, gave short guffaws of merriment, and slapped each other's shoulder. Pharcel ignored them and when it was dark he followed the women to their hut and went to sleep on his side of the mat. In the depths of slumber he was dreamily conscious of many sensations, but he could not be sure which was dream and which reality, which was the buxom woman or which was the other. He awoke next morning to a fine day and strolled out of the hut totally at peace with the world.

Gradually, the men brought him into their circle and began to communicate with him by signs. Some of them knew a few words of the crude patois commonly spoken among slaves, and they began to speak with him in labored exchanges, using disjointed phrases that eventually became amplified by a curious mixture of Carib and patois expressions. In that way, he learned that the two women he cohabited with were widows whose men had perished at sea or had been killed during raiding excursions to the neighboring islands of Marie Gallante and Guadeloupe. Their names were Kumeni and Marika. He was also made to understand quite clearly that the seduction of a man's wife could be mitigated only by death, and that he should keep clear of the daughters and wives in the village; but he was welcome to the widows who were left for the entertainment of unattached men and visitors.

He stayed for nearly a month, and heard many tales of wars and adventures that took place up and down the many islands that stretched from the mouth of the mighty Orinoco in the South to the lands of the Incas in the North. They told of a fabulous treasure which their ancestors had salvaged from a wrecked ship after a storm, and hidden in a cave far distant from any habitation. No one was sure just where that might be. Only the old crone had a faint notion of its where-abouts, but her mind was now wandering and her speech incoherent. They had all but relegated the tale to the fantasies of history.

The women, too, told many stories; but when he mentioned the treasure hidden in a cave, they merely shook their heads as if to say it was all a fantastic legend. When he persisted, they grew impatient with him until one day they brought the old crone to him. The crone, bent and wrinkled and musty with age, blabbered as she gave a long inarticulate account while pointing eastwards. The younger woman, Kumeni, told him afterwards of an emerald river hidden in the forest a day's journey away where there were caves in which, it was said, the trea-sure had been stored; but she said it as if it were merely the ranting of a crazed old woman. Many days passed, and still every night Pharcel had them repeat the story of the great treasure hidden in the forest. He got so obsessed with it they thought that he, too, had lost his mind. They brought the crone to him again and again, more in jest than with any serious intent of enlightenment. Pharcel lis-tened to the blathering of the decrepit and wandering hag as if it was the most romantic of tales, but bit by bit his fevered mind pieced together directions and locations that moved in an ever widening circle further and further eastwards. He told himself that, if he had to, he would scour the forest until he came to the east-ern shore.

He spoke to Kumeni secretly one afternoon.
"We will find that treasure."
She nodded as if to dismiss an importunate child.
But when one day he picked up a pannier and a cutlass and signaled to her, she quietly followed him into the woods. The men of the village together with some of their women had gathered on the beach that morning and launched sev-eral canoes towards Marie Gallante. Only a few of the women, the children and a couple of older men were left behind. Pharcel and Kumeni slipped out of the vil-lage and were soon submerged in the dense vegetation of the forest.

All that day they trudged silently through the thickly wooded hills, up and down ridges that seemed always the same. As night was falling, they stood beneath a giant tree whose towering trunk distended in lateral growth forming hollows descending from eight feet above the ground. They slept that night in a dry hollow and awoke with the sound of morning. They continued eastward until, sometime past noon, they heard the sound of a fall of water behind them. Pharcel turned about and, not being sure of the direction from which the sound came, began to walk in wide circles back the way they had come.

At last they came upon the bend of a small stream running swiftly downwards. They followed this, breaking through dense bush and clambering over slippery rocks. The sound of the fall grew stronger and stronger, and by nightfall they came to the edge of the fall where the stream tumbled through an arched thicket of bushes to a rumble of sound far below them. The rocks around the edge were wet with moss and slime making descent from there too hazardous. The light had already faded, and they searched around the top of the fall until they found a cleared spot on the bank of the stream and laid themselves down to rest amid the needling buzz of a horde of mosquitoes.

They came awake to a torrent of rain pounding on their faces. It was a brief shower which drifted rapidly away towards the West leaving the skies a cerulean blue and cloudless. They skirted the edge of the fall, peering through thick bracken at a precipitous gorge below. It was slow progress walking along the edge through the prickly growth, but they came at last upon a sharp declivity down which they were able to scramble thirty feet to the bed of the stream. They could hear from where they stood the sound of the fall, but their view of it was obstructed by a mound of black rocks over which the stream cascaded in frothing splashes. On one side the wall of the gorge fell perpendicularly to the bed of rocks, but on the other there was a steep slope along which a narrow shelf undulated in the direction of the fall. Crossing the stream over the slippery rocks, they came to the other side and, clambering up the slope to the shelf, they inched their way cautiously towards the fall.

As they came over the top, their eyes became transfixed to a sight truly wonderful to behold. Below the edge of the fall was a solid wall of rock covered with a crisp, green tapestry of moss-like vegetation. As the water broke over the edge to a deep cobalt basin forty feet below, splashes of mist moistened the moss with tiny droplets of water which sparkled in the bright morning sun like a million emeralds stuck on the green tapestry that covered the wall. For a while they stood breathless at the marvelous scene before they pushed eagerly forward. The fall broke cleanly over the edge and fell onto a wide rock on the inner side of the basin. Ten feet from the base of the wall, a deep fissure, wet and dark and fringed with low fern, spread out on both sides of the falling water.

Hastily dropping the pannier and cutlass, Pharcel dived in and swam to the other side, avoiding the tight column of water that fell with such force and thunder from above. He hugged the dark, slippery rocks as he pulled himself onto a narrow ledge. Kumeni stood beside him. Together, they clutched at the wet slippery surface as they crawled upwards and over the lip of the cave. There they stood uncertainly in the dank, dark interior until their eyes adjusted to the blackness around them and they began to discern the irregular shape of the inner walls and floor. They both uttered sharp yelps of excitement as their sight fell on a peculiar pile in a far corner of the cave. Eagerly, they stumbled on the uneven floor until they stood over the pile. Even in the dim light they could make out the glint of gold and the sparkle of emeralds.

It was many days before they found themselves standing at the top of a sparsely wooded cone near the eastern shore. They had scrupulously avoided the obvious tracks through the forest that invariably led towards the camps of the runaways or to broader paths between estates. But there were many hunting trails that ran in all directions and they kept moving eastwards until one mid afternoon they heard the roar of the sea. Kumeni had an instinct for finding easy ground over which they trudged silently during the day, but when she came to this high mountain she could find no other way except up its mostly bald sides to the top. There they stood in the bright sunlight, and, looking southwards, they could see below them a sweep of thin forest stretching downwards to a distant shore. Somehow, Pharcel sensed that he was close to home. Kumeni with her keen eye spotted a clearing in the far distance on the crest of a lower hill and thought that it could only be a Carib village. They descended to the lower ground through the sparse forest in the direction of the village.

Pharcel had no intention of entering the village with his pannier full of the stolen treasure. He had carefully selected the sacks of coin and a bundle of chains and bracelets richly inlaid with emeralds. The profusion of plates and goblets and larger medallions and plaques he left where they were in a heap. The lighter objects he knew instinctively had greater currency, would be easier to conceal, and would be lighter to move at a moment's notice. He already knew where his hiding place should be. There were many nooks on the sheer sides of the cliffs above the shore just past Dubique where he thought his treasure would remain undisturbed and safe.

Though it was still early evening when they got to the foot of the hill above which was the village, he decided that they would remain there for the night. In the morning he would send Kumeni to the village while he continued round the base of the hill into the denser forest. By nightfall the next day, he hoped to be within sight of Dubique. Kumeni would be safe with her own people until his task was complete and he could return to find her.

CHAPTER 7

Captain Marshall had been several months encamped in the vicinity of Grandbay and still had not encountered the runaways. Not that he was actively in search of them, but he had his men on constant patrol of the main road and the estate paths extending from Grandbay and Geneva to the smaller estates and villages northwards along the coast. Occasionally, there were sorties to the east coastal plantations at Delices and La Plaine, although there were no signs or reports of any encroachments by the runaways in any of these places.

Captain Marshall was proud of his military discipline, and he thought that his reputation had so intimidated the runaway chiefs that they were forced to remain hidden in the deepest woods far from any contact with him. He could not know that, as far as Coree Greg was concerned, the old chief was content to be left alone in his camp where he could give shelter to any slave bold enough to make his escape from the white planters. Seasoned as he was in military campaigns against white colonists, Coree Greg understood that the time was not right for an all out war against white authority; not until the camps were united and properly armed.

Congoree, too, held out in the East, training his men and waiting for the day when all blacks on the island would rise in a united body and he and the other chiefs would be in command of a great army that would forever wipe out white domination on the island. He was not given to the profligate adventures typical of Bala and Sandy, who refused to accept that their constant depredations and scandalous atrocities were of no military value and only served to prejudice the moral cause of all runaway slaves.

After these several months of virtual inactivity, enlivened only by short furloughs in Roseau, Captain Marshall was getting bored. He spent his days drilling his men in endless parades and making tentative advances into the nearby bushes, guns primed and swords drawn and ready. After these fruitless exercises, he would ride to the village in search of any white companion who could spare the time from the humdrum activities of estate management to loiter in the shade of the only saloon there was.

The village was situated on a hill and consisted of a single dirt avenue which ran steeply down to the sea. Houses of various sizes and crude designs were scattered on both sides of the avenue among a profusion of breadfruit, avocado, mango and coconut trees. At the top of the avenue and broadside to it was a massive cross cut from a single stone, which had been carved and erected by a French planter many years ago, and stoutly defended by him against persistent attempts by the Carib Indians to remove what they considered both an architectural and spiritual abomination. At the bottom of the avenue, veering towards right, on a slight elevation above the shore, a stout grey stone building was erected, its conical steeple plainly denoting that it was the village church. Midway down that avenue stood a substantial two-storied building, more imposing than the rest, on the ground floor of which was the *Salon L'Aise*.

The *Salon L'Aise* was an open hall with an elaborate bar at one end and several plain tables and chairs randomly positioned around a billiard table. The saloon was owned by a freed mulatto whose enterprise brought to the shores of Grandbay both human and tradable cargo. He was indiscriminate in his dealings with human traffic, bringing in with equal circumspection white political escapees from the rigors of the French revolution and escaped slaves destined for the many runaway camps around the island. But his popularity with all sections of the community rested on the liberal stocks of fine brandies and rich wines which he sold at accommodating prices, unencumbered as they were from any customs excises or other government imposts.

The bar and the tables were tended by three or four mulatresses whose flimsy cotton garments enhanced the generosity of their buxom bodies. Here the small community of white overseers, engineers, carpenters and other tradesmen and estate factors gathered in the afternoons and evenings to regale themselves royally at prices that dishonored the prestige of the superb wines and brandies of which they partook so copiously; and to ogle the *cafe´au lait* damsels who attended them.

After many weeks of desultory association with the factors and overseers, the masons and the carpenters that he found loitering betimes in the saloon, Captain Marshall discovered a strange affinity in Brent, the white overseer on the Geneva Estate; not because his conversation was in any way more convivial than the others', but because of his inordinate capacity for holding an astonishing amount of liquor, and his rapacious appetite for anything sexual—an appetite that bordered on animalism if not outright brutality. Brent was a man of few words and unquestionable will. A mere incline of his rather bony head was enough to get the mulatresses scurrying to his side. Captain Marshall was impressed by the force of his personality and used him, albeit with utmost caution, to break through the habitual reserve of the inhabitants of the village, white, black and mulatto.

He had got to know the priest, too, a gaunt old Frenchman with a wry and often bawdy sense of humor. Sometimes he would saunter down the avenue to the small church and sit with the priest on the narrow verandah of his presbytery drinking a potent mixture of raw rum and lemon sweetened with molasses. They would sit there for hours watching the swell of the sea heave into curling billows that came rushing in and crashing down on the rocky shore; and speak of many things—the laudable objectives of the French Revolution and, more frequently, its excesses. The priest was not in any way defensive of the *doit de majeste'* or hereditary rights to property or privileges of class or station. His single social doctrine was one of charity to all men and women; beyond that he had no political interest in the shifting fortunes of the protagonists in the great upheaval that was taking place in his motherland.

Often, the simplicity of his character would emerge as he recounted with a mischievous gleam in his eye how he would induce some of the younger women slaves, totally naked under their organdy dresses, to climb the fruit trees in his orchard, while he stood underneath innocently catching the fruit as they dropped them down to him. He told those stories free of any salaciousness, being a worldly man and honest in the earthiness of his manners.

Captain Marshall had not been to Dubique for nearly a month. After Georgette's scandalous disclosure to him, he had stayed away for a time, not able to face Elise even though his mind refused to accept the probability that there could be some truth in what Georgette had said. He could not contemplate that there could in reality be the remotest chance that Elise should prefer the company of a slave, and a boy at that, to his; much less relate to the slave sexually. French though she was, he had to give her credit for at least a modicum of ordinary feminine decorum and Christian morals. White women, even white women of the lowest class, did not cohabit with slaves. Whatever lingering doubts there might still be in his mind, he had put that aside and returned one bright day to Dubique. But he could not get rid of the burning hatred he harbored deep down in his heart for the runaway slave. The mere thought of his name in association with Elise sent a violent rage coursing through him. Day after day that odious thought gnawed at his soul like irreversible corrosion on metal. He was like a man driven out of reason, obsessed by a single goal—to destroy the slave who so despicably challenged his manhood and his superiority.

Not that his visits to Dubique were in any way more rewarding than they had been in the past. Elise was as elusive as ever. She would sometimes appear in late morning with that dreamy, lost look on her face, walking sedately across the hall and sometimes drifting across the lawn to the tiny fall and the small pool in the hollow. Each time he had risen politely from the chair on the verandah where he always sat during his visits, but, except for a brief acknowledgement by a slight inclination of her head, or a fleeting stretch of her lips, it was as if he was invisible, a nonentity. He had tried staying over in the evenings when he would sit with Jean on the back porch drinking till the poor man drifted off to sleep. Still Elise would not even condescend to appear even briefly to see to their comfort, or to say a polite "good evening" before she disappeared into her bedroom for the night. It was always left to Georgette to refill their goblets after Toma left for his hut down in the slave quarters.

He continued his dalliance with Georgette whose youthful freshness and precocious forwardness excited his adventurous spirit. They had not spoken of Elise again since that day. It was as if whatever had been said was only of momentary importance, or mere ranting coming out of an intemperate fit of jealousy, or the natural antipathy of growing girls towards their mothers' romantic foibles. Except during the mid-morning hours when they sat on the porch, their time was spent away from the house in the seclusion of the bushes and trees that surrounded it. He passed many weeks in the company of the young girl, and he never ceased to be amazed at the inventiveness she showed in finding shady nooks or burrows in the most unlikely places. There they would lie in comfort and spend the warm mornings in each other's arms. He was content to indulge in the vast outpouring of her intemperate giving of herself, and he would have been quite happy to do all he could to assuage her obvious need for affection; but then, one morning, without preamble, she declared simply that she was pregnant.

He had not returned to Dubique from that day. There was a strange ambivalence in his attitude towards Georgette's pregnancy. He had found her young, capricious and seemingly virginal. At the same time he was often disturbed by what struck him as an odd mixture of innocence and feminine sagacity, of insouciance and instinctive sexuality, of puerility and worldliness and of vulnerability and predacity in the makeup of her character. He was not even sure if he had seduced her or if she had seduced him.

Normally, as an officer and a gentleman, he should have felt some sense of obligation for getting so young a child in trouble. But then she was French. What obligation should he have? If she was an English girl he would have been obliged to see her father and come to some understanding as to his intentions and as to her future. If he neglected to do so he would soon find himself cashiered out of the military. But this French family, especially remote as they were in the wilds of Dubique, was unlikely to raise complaints against him. Nor would their complaints have been seriously considered by the Commandant or even by the Council. So he simply stayed away while Georgette's pregnancy grew month after month.

Captain Marshall sat with Brent one early afternoon in the saloon. They were sipping a particularly mellow brandy and trying to find some common ground from which to sustain their usual desultory conversation. The interior of the hall was cool, dark, empty and quiet. Not even the clacking of billiard balls relieved the silence, for there were no players at this time of day. Captain Marshall looked across at Brent, an involuntary look of contempt distorting the usual sardonic smile on his lips. This man is a churl, he thought, a bounder of the lowest class. But he had his uses.

"Did you ever hear of a slave called Pharcel in these parts?" he asked.

"Did you say Pharcel?"

"Yes, Pharcel."

"Oh yes, I know him. Know him very well. I had to flog the skin off his back not long ago."

"You flogged him? Why?"

"Oh, Lyonnais called me to do the job. He knows that I wield the cat o' nine and the bull pistle like an artist. Wouldn't let me finish the job, though. He got soft in the heart and stopped me before I could break the brute's spirit. You have to break their spirit you know."

"But why was he flogged?"

"Something to do with their little girl." Brent bowed his head, thinking deeply for a while. "Something to do with her and him."

"Georgette?"

"Yes, that's her name. They found her touching him or something like that."

"Georgette?"

"Yes. They had to send her away for a time."

"That little tramp!"

"She is a wild one all right."

Captain Marshall felt the revulsion bubbling up his throat. His chest tightened and his face flushed with anger. He could hardly contain the fury raging within him. A slave? With Elise? And now with Georgette? For some reason he felt twice abused. The fact that Elise had so consistently repudiated his advances made these revelations even more heinous in his mind. His eyes darkened and his jaw tightened in angry lines. Brent looked at him curiously.

"Something the matter?" Brent asked with a mixture of concern and curiosity.

"No. No, it is nothing," Captain Marshall replied softly, recovering his composure.

He turned again to Brent, lowering his eyelashes to veil the anger that still darkened his eyes. His lips stretched to a thin, sour smile.

"Do you know where he is?"

"Where who is?"

"Pharcel."

"Oh, out in the woods, I guess. Like all the other runaways."

"Do you know where?" Captain Marshall asked with some asperity.

"How would I know? Must be in one of the camps. With Coree Greg up in those mountains yonder. Or with Bala over by the lakes."

"Can you find out?"

"What do you want with him?"

"I must see him; and it is urgent."

Brent's eyes dug deeply into the Captain's veiled look, hoping to get a gleam of emotion that would reveal his intent; but his face remained inscrutable.

"I will see what can be done," he said finally.

Brent sat brooding over his drink for a long time before he noticed that the saloon was quickly filling up. He knew just who he would call on for information about the slave camps. Old Joshua on the Stewart's estate was his man for the job, a wily old fellow who was piling up a fortune with the hope of buying his freedom before dying, who had lived most of his life a slave and did not intend to die one, and who sold the one commodity that he was free to trade to meet the price of his freedom—his intimate knowledge of estate slaves and of the runaways and their camps. There were already four men around the billiard table. Brent dismissed the matter from his mind and turned his attention to the game in progress. Captain Marshall regarded him for a while distastefully and, briefly excusing himself, moved away towards the bar.

Betty came out of the woods and skirted the low ridge above the village. The sun was poised just above the horizon in a blaze of scarlet and yellow. She knew that she had a few hours to wait before she should venture under cover of darkness to the upper reaches of Grandbay. So she sat in a thicket of bushes looking out to sea, watching for the green flash as the sun dropped below the horizon. When she was a child, the older women used to say it was a good omen if one was quick enough to catch the green flash, so she sat with her gaze fixed to the sun and waited. Suddenly, it was gone and nothing remained but a slowly darkening purple and grey. A chill set in immediately after, and she shivered as a cool damp rose from the ground at her feet where previously it had been warm. Her thoughts went back to the camp and Coree Greg's caution that she should not venture too far into the village as she was wont to do.

In the main part of the village from the stone cross down to the sea, the white tradesmen and freed blacks and mulattos lived in disordered segregation; the whites occupying the lower end of the village, closer to the church, but intermingling in the shops and bars that lined the avenue from top to middle. Beyond the cross where the land broke into a shallow ravine was a cluster of ramshackle huts where a community of poor, black laborers, independent in all but means, lived in miserable isolation. No one in the lower part of the village ventured in this section after dark because of the savagery of its existence. It was there that Betty found shelter when she visited the village, and it was there that she transacted her purchases, except when it was declared safe for her to wander further down the village.

As the gloom thickened around her and the sounds of night filled the bushes and the trees, her mind returned to the bitter exchange of words between her and Pharcel. He had accompanied her through the woods; and she had felt safe, inviolate and secure in his company until, emerging out of the deep cover of the woods, he had said to her that they should meet again at the crack of dawn. He would await her there, and she was not to leave without him.

"But," she protested. "Will you not return to the camp?"

"Not right away," he had replied distantly.

"It is that white woman, isn't it?"

There had been a note of resentment in her voice.

"I have to go by Dubique," he had responded testily. "To see someone there."

"Please don't go."

A deep and overwhelming sadness had come over her, and her chin had dropped on to her bosom.

"I won't be long," he had replied brusquely. "Just wait for me before sunrise."

"It is that woman. I know it."

"You know nothing."

"You are no different from the rest."

"From what rest?"

"Why pretend to be free if you are still chained to your mistress? Just be a house slave!"

"What do you know of freedom?" he had asked bitterly. "Is there freedom in those woods? Especially for you, cooped up with those old men and four derelict women. One day I will show you what real freedom is."

"You will show me nothing but a sad old grave if they do bother to bury you," she had flung at him as she turned away and walked through the bush.

"Wait for me later," he had shouted after her.

Those words resounded in her thoughts as she sat waiting for the night to settle. Soon a breathless calm came over the land as if the trees and the village below had gone to sleep. She rose from the cover of the bush and crept cautiously down to the village.

It was dark among the huts, but she knew the paths that twisted among them well. The huts were all asleep and the sounds of slumber came through their thin walls. Only the muffled growl of a few dogs marked her silent passage. She came to one of the huts and rattled its flimsy door. Immediately, there was a stirring within, and the door was unlatched to admit her. As she completed her exchange of commodities, the woman inside whispered to her that old Joshua wished to speak with her. She wondered what the old man wanted from her, but she pushed this question from her mind and continued among the huts.

Her transactions were swift and purposeful as she went from one hut to another, and her commerce was complete well before dawn. She was happy to begin the climb up the ridge where she would wait for Pharcel. It was still dark, but she knew that the first streaks of dawn light would soon break over the hills. She was almost to the top when she thought again of the old man's message.

She remembered Joshua as one of the great mysteries of her childhood. He was a lean man with thin, knotty legs and arms and a head that sat askance on a long neck as if he was always questioning the world's virtue. Even when she was a child, he had scabrous patches of hair on his elongated head and stubs of brown teeth attached to the blackest gums she had ever seen; and he was already well on his way to decrepitude. But his mystery was his unaccountable attractiveness to women of all ages. His one redeeming quality that she remembered was his irrepressible and infectious humor that seemed ever ready to spring from the gay lines shooting out from the corners of his eyes and from the permanent leer on his liver-colored lips. Part of his mystery was his ability to set himself apart from everyone else while maintaining his air of jovial sociability. Thus it was accepted as characteristic of him that he should build his hut on the very edge of the estate boundary away from the general community of slaves and at the same time maintain the closest intimacy with even the most private moments in each household. By subtle means he had abrogated unto himself the task of repairing tools for the estate from his hut away from the fields where the other slaves sweltered in the sun day after day. All these were part of the mystery that had surrounded him, a mystery that incited awe and respect in generation after generation of younger slaves.

Betty did not think that his summons had anything to do with his penchant for seduction, although, despite his advanced age, stories still abounded about his sexual prowess and seductive skills. Usually, news about the movements of the militia or activities in the capital would be relayed to her through her contacts in the village. It would have to be something of extreme importance for Joshua to want to communicate with her directly. She stood hesitating for a long time even as the darkness began to lighten.

Joshua sat in his hut waiting. He had already sent word to Brent to be in readiness to recapture the fugitive. Soon his task would be complete and he would be one Joe nearer to purchasing his own freedom. He entertained no qualms about what he was doing. It was a matter of survival in this mixed-up world of perpetual betrayal and distress, a world in which tribal loyalties were of no relevance and traditional tribal enmities, so proudly upheld for generations, were forcibly suffocated in this amorphous, confused and confusing mass of displaced humanity. All he was concerned about was that he, a Masai, alone and aloof, should survive. So he waited to sell another body in the way that he had been sold. He yearned for his freedom and he would have it soon.

His ears were attuned to the sounds of night, and he could hear every brush of branch on branch, the scurrying of creatures through dry fallen leaves and the soft fall of bare feet on the beaten path to his hut. He heard her footsteps approaching from the back of his hut and he waited in a suspension of time that seemed to last forever. He held his breath wondering what it was that arrested time and movement for so long. Then he heard it. The dogs. They were growling and snarling and howling and filling the night with alarm. The dogs were alarmed by an alien presence. She must have heard it too and understood. She must have sensed that it was a trap and there were white men about. Joshua threw open the door just in time to hear the sound of hurried footsteps on the track, back towards the bush.

"She is getting away," he shouted into the dark.

For a while he heard nothing but the rushing of feet in the shrub up the side of the hill. He followed thinking that he could never catch up with so young a girl in the dark up a steep incline. He wondered, too, about Brent. Did he get his message? The increasingly furious barking of the dogs gave him the answer.

Somewhere in those bushes the white men were lurking. Silently like hounds they were waiting or stalking their prey. He hastened up the hill intent only on following the sounds ahead. He thought he had lost the sound of her flight until he heard the whipping of branches coming from all directions way above him almost to the top of the hill. Then he heard her scream.

"Pharcel!" she hollered. "It's a trap. Run."

Joshua stopped in his tracks. The light was just beginning to filter through the dark over the top of the mountains to the East, defining the ridges in stark silhouette. He felt the chill of morning and the wetness of dew on his bare feet. He shivered. Above him, he heard the sound of bodies crashing through the bush and finally her snarl of fury as she tried to slip from their bodies piling on top of her.

They brought her down still struggling, past him down to the village.

The sun was high up in the sky as Joshua sat on a crude bench outside his hut chipping at a length of wood that he would make into an axe handle. It was already quite warm and beads of sweat were forming on the back of his hands and on his forearm. He had long since dismissed the capture of the girl from his mind. All he was concerned about was holding Brent to his promise to deliver one more Joe as payment for his service. The shadow of the man came over him before he sensed his presence. He turned quickly around and saw the half-naked man looking down on him.

"Morning, Elder," the man said quietly.

Joshua was startled and remained staring at the stranger for nearly a minute. He knew he was face to face with a runaway. Something desperate must be afoot when a runaway showed himself so far into an estate in broad daylight. This must be Pharcel, he thought. The young boy they said was Betty's protector. He peered closely at the face above him and, but for a slight pucker of a frown between the eyes, there was nothing unusual, except an unnerving serenity, about it. The man's eyes seemed to draw him into a fathomless pool, cold and dark. For the second time that morning, Joshua shivered.

"I am looking for Betty," the man spoke calmly. "They told me I could find her here."

Joshua steadied himself as he stood up, the laughing lines deepening at the corners of his eyes. He held his head at an angle appraising the man with a sideways glance.

"Oh, Betty!" he nodded his head agreeably. "Yes. She was here. A long while ago. I sent her to the village to collect tobacco, a fresh supply for Coree Greg."

"But where is she?"

"She should have been well away into the woods by now."

"But she hasn't returned."

Joshua hesitated. There could be another Joe for him if he could play this one well.

"I could go down to the village to enquire," he offered.

"Could you?" the man considered this for a moment, but remained silent.

Joshua regarded him speculatively.

"It won't take long," he demurred. "They would know what route she took."

"It is already so hot, Grandfather," the man said calmly. "Can I have some of your coconuts?"

Joshua looked at him dubiously, wondering at the suavity of his speech and the placidity of his expression. It was indeed warm; but if Pharcel was concerned at the disappearance of Betty to the extent that he would risk capture by appearing on the estate in broad daylight, why would he bother with coconuts at this time? The old man shrugged, the quizzical look deepening on his face.

"It's all right," he said. "Take as many as you want. If you can climb."

Pharcel reached the nearest tree with a few quick steps and clambered up to the crown of fronds at its top. With a swift slash of his cutlass, he sent a cluster of nuts crashing on the ground. He slid down the tree and brought the cluster to where the old man was still standing, sliced into the thick outer husk of one of the green nuts until he came to the soft shell underneath, scooped out a small aperture and, throwing his head backwards, brought it to his lips. The cool, sweet water gurgled down his throat. He belched as he straightened up.

"Want one, Grandfather?" he asked solicitously.

Joshua looked at him suspiciously. Pharcel was already bending to pick up another nut. He cut into it and handed it to the old man. Joshua held it uncertainly for a moment, then leaned his head backwards and brought the nut to his open mouth. Pharcel watched the old man as he swallowed, his Adam's apple rising and falling with every gurgle; bent away from him as if to pick up another nut; then with a quick but graceful pirouette, right arm unfurling in a wide arc with the cutlass firmly extended, he swiped across the old man's neck. Joshua's head and the coconut toppled at his feet. The rest of him stood quivering in spasms as the blood gushed in scarlet jets from his neck. At last the body fell, convulsed for a moment and finally lay still.

Pharcel picked up a slice of the green husk and wiped it across the blade of his cutlass. Then he strode into the brush and upwards to the hills.

"We have your girl", Brent whispered exultantly to Captain Marshall.

"What girl?"

Captain Marshall was preoccupied with the stern dispatch that he had received that morning, enquiring about his conduct of the campaign against the runaways and demanding decisive action. The Council, in the past, had been quite apathetic about the problem of the runaways, being satisfied that it had made sufficient budgetary arrangements to keep the militia engaged and that the main roads were now clear and the maroons safely confined to the woods. But recent dispatches from London had expressed concern at the number of estate owners and attorneys who had been driven to return hastily to England, abandoning their homes and lands; and raising questions about the efficacy of administration in the colonies.

Then, too, the rumblings of a social revolution were beginning to spread from Paris, over the continent of Europe and even among a scattering of intellectuals in Britain. It was feared that the new revolutionary fervor would inevitably spread to the colonies and find expression in subversive and treasonous action among the French residents in Dominica, acting in league with some of the runaway chiefs. It was imperative that the camps be destroyed and all vestiges of potential revolt completely eliminated.

The Council had, therefore, urged him to bring the campaign to a head and take full military action to apprehend the runaways or destroy them and their camps. He had his work cut out, but first he had to deal with Pharcel.

"What girl?" he repeated abstractedly.

"Betty," Brent replied impatiently. "The girl from Coree Greg's camp. The one they say is Pharcel's woman."

"Oh?" he remarked, suddenly coming to full attention. "Where is she?"

"Down in the village," Brent said, his voice filled with excitement.

"Well, take me to her."

"There is no hurry," Brent said smugly. "She won't be going anywhere."

They arrived at a low thick-walled building set behind a row of houses near the top of the avenue. It had once been used to store molasses, but had been abandoned when other storehouses had been built more conveniently closer to the shore. At one side, uneven steps led down to a basement, dark, cobwebbed and musty. Betty lay spread-eagled on the floor, her arms tied to rings set in the wall, her legs secured against the rough wooden legs of a work table. Even in the dim light of the basement, Captain Marshall could easily discern the ravaged body of the young woman. Her arms, discolored along their lengths where patches of purple and black showed evidence of prolonged and systematic torture, were twisted at a painful angle. Below her slightly flattened breasts, and around her rib cage down her loins and legs, similar markings and contusions occurred in irregular profusion. The girl stared out of half-shut, swollen eyes; and her lips were raw and puffed-up in a hideous grimace. She was all but naked. The white linen dress that once clothed her modesty was torn to shreds and stained with mud and faeces. She must have been raped over and over again, for there was what appeared to be dried semen between her open legs.

Captain Marshall almost retched at the sight. He turned angrily to Brent.

"What have you done to her?" He was livid with outrage and humiliation, not wanting to be associated with such an act of cruelty.

"I had to soften her up," Brent replied, turning a surly countenance on the Captain. "To make her talk. She must know about Pharcel."

"Make her talk?" Captain Marshall snarled at him. "You've all but killed her."

Suddenly, the look of shock and resignation faded from Betty's disfigured face, and her voice came out in a whisper.

"You the Captain?" she asked.

The sound barely reached Captain Marshall's ears, but he turned to her, a look of encouragement on his face.

"Yes," he said, "I am the Captain."

Her swollen lips stretched grotesquely and painfully, and her half-shut eyes lit up for a moment in triumph.

"He is better than you," she said provokingly. "He took your woman."

A wild scream escaped from the Captain, and his lips broke in a savage snarl as, drawing his sword, he made to run the woman through. Brent grabbed him around the waist and forcibly subdued him.

"Steady on!" Brent shouted in his ear. "We have more use of her."

"I have no further use of her," Marshall said sullenly. "When you are finished, bring her down to the shore. She must be sent to the Fort. The Council wants runaways, then here is the first."

He stormed out of the basement.

CHAPTER 8

Brent sat brooding at the bar of the saloon at eleven o'clock in the morning as he nursed a glass of brown, full-bodied rum, the kind he needed after the excesses of the night before. His eyes were blood-shot, and stubbles of graying beard covered the lower part of his face. He had been summoned here by Captain Marshall, told to leave his work minding slaves on the estate to come here for what purpose he did not know. He wanted no more to do with those militia officers who did not have the stomach for anything useful in these colonies, much less for fighting runaway slaves; who thought they were gentlemen and not fit to do the dirty work of disciplining slaves until their own interest was at stake. Now he knew why the Captain was so incensed against Pharcel. It was his woman who was no doubt raped by the slave, just as the same Pharcel had raped the woman's little girl. The namby pamby officer had rebuked him for softening the slave girl Betty and enjoying her while she was still usable, but was quite ready to run her through with his sword when she let out his humiliating secret.

Now the Captain had summoned him again, to help him revenge his honor, he supposed. Well, they both had a score to settle with this Pharcel. Look what he did to old Joshua: lopped off the old man's head, clean as he would a stalk of cane. The old man had been his most reliable source of information about what was going on among the slaves, and especially about the runaway camps. Now he was dead, and the vital link that he was could not easily be replaced. Brent recalled the gruesome sight of the old man's head, mouth gaping as if still in the act of drinking, lying beside the still half-full coconut. He hastily swallowed a huge gulp of the brown, bracing liquid. Pharcel must be destroyed, and how he would enjoy making him suffer before he would allow him to die!

Captain Marshall came and sat beside him.

"We have to find him," he whispered in a low, rasping voice.

"Who?" Brent looked into the glass of rich brown liquid as if searching for an answer.

"Who?" Captain Marshall turned to Brent with impatience. "Pharcel, of course."

"Where?"

"Wherever he is!"

"I thought it was your job to ferret out the runaways."

"We won't catch him in the woods."

"Then where?"

Captain Marshall seemed suddenly lost in a profound reverie. One of the waitresses placed a full glass at his elbow, but he continued deep in thought until Brent slapped his shoulder.

"Where?" Brent asked again.

"He will keep coming down to Dubique," the Captain said, shifting on his seat with embarrassment. "We should capture him there."

"When does he get there?" Brent swirled the rum in his glass ruminatively, watching the dark gold wetness running down the sides and settling again in the brown liquid mass at the bottom.

"That is for you to find out," Captain Marshall replied brusquely. "Go to the estate and speak with Georgette. She will know."

"But shouldn't you.......?" Brent paused not wanting to disclose what he had heard about the Captain's exploits among the bushes of Dubique.

"No, you should go. I have my reasons."

Captain Marshall picked up the glass at his elbow, swallowed its contents in one gulp, and grimaced as the potent liquid hit his gullet and coursed in spreading waves down his belly. He slipped from the stool and marched out of the saloon.

Elise was distraught. She had noticed the wan look about Georgette's face, the loss of appetite, and the sudden lethargy that had settled on her as if a burning fire within her had been put out. Two months had gone by and Georgette's listlessness grew to the extent that she spent most mornings in bed and the rest of the day lounging on the back verandah. Her usual rosy complexion had paled to a bloodless, pasty white, an unhealthy pallor that somehow deepened the lusterless vacuity in her eyes and the pale depression of her lips. Her body screamed of neglect as she abandoned all pretence of personal hygiene and would not even get out of her night clothes to complete the most rudimentary ablutions.

Elise had observed, too, that Captain Marshall had not been to the estate for more than a month. Georgette had always attended to her personal appearance with meticulous care whenever she thought the Captain would visit. But now she appeared to have lost whatever zest had possessed her to make herself presentable, as if she no longer cared.

Elise was happy for the respite in not having to hide away from the Captain week after week. His frequent visits and especially his hang-dog look had left in her feelings of guilt at the turbulent and complex emotions that had so drastically changed her feelings about herself. The Captain's presence was a constant reminder of the day when she had so recklessly surrendered what she had always thought was her unassailable virtue. No doubt the Captain thought that the brief and aborted episode between them was the cause of her withdrawal. He had no way of penetrating the dark secret that lurked deep down in the innermost core of her spirit. Even in her personal consciousness, that secret lay buried in the light of day to emerge with pulsating urgency only under cover of night. She was as virginal in her appearance and her emotions during the day as she had always been. Only the dark of night opened out the bursting bud of her sensuality and the dark and irrepressible desire for the body of the slave, Pharcel.

She could not share her concern about Georgette's decline into neglect with her husband. For months now Jean had been preoccupied with the affairs of the estate, which he never discussed with her; but she knew that his letters of credit in Martinique were being dishonored, and she was also aware that the factors in the capital and the mill owner at Geneva were discriminating against the French planters, and that Jean was having considerable difficulty getting fair treatment for the sale of his produce. Jean was not of the inner set of Dominican society and, being French, was treated always as an outsider.

She thought that she could have made a difference if only they socialized more, even among the few white planters in their neighborhood; but Jean had virtually become a recluse, laboring together with his slaves all day and drowning his failures in the numbing vapor of raw factory rum night after night. Even the occasional presence of Captain Marshall failed to stir in him any awareness of his social obligations, except to proffer the comradeship of a few drinks on the porch in the dark.

So she bore the burden of her daughter's fall alone, knowing from the sudden swell of her breasts and the barely observable thickening of her waist that she might be with child. She had not noticed from the weekly washings the usual signs of her monthly flow, and that added to her anxiety. Elise raised the matter with Bessie one morning. The old cook went ashen with sudden fright as she blubbered that she had not washed Georgette's linen for two months and that this could be a sign of pregnancy. She could brew a concoction that would remove the problem if that became necessary. Elise patted her shoulder affection-ately and walked away to find Georgette.

It was already late morning, and Georgette was still asleep. Elise entered the dark recess of the room closely shuttered even in the rising heat of mid-morning. Georgette stirred but did not get up. Her hair lay in tangled coils about her head, and Elise could smell the acrid odor of her unwashed body and the rancid breath from her mouth and nostrils. She wanted to open out the shutters to bring in the morning air, but she steeled herself and sat beside her daughter, not wanting to startle her or raise the recalcitrance of her spirit.

"Are you awake?" she whispered tentatively.

"What do you want?"

Georgette's response jolted her to the sensitiveness of her intentions. She hesitated, choosing her words carefully.

"I want us to talk," she said calmly.

"What about?" Georgette raised herself on one elbow.

"About you." Elise leaned forward, her hand hovering over her daughter's hair as if in the act of patting the disordered coils. "I am concerned about you."

"About me? Why should you be?"

"I am your mother."

"Why should you be concerned? What's wrong with me?"

"You are pregnant aren't you?" Elise blurted out the words, not being able to contain her anxiety any longer.

Georgette remained silent. Defiantly, she turned her head away, her gaze lost in the dark interior of the room.

"It's that Captain, isn't it?" Elise leaned closer to her daughter, wanting to hold her face to her bosom.

Georgette kept her face turned away from her mother.

"Oh, Georgette!" Elise cried, reaching forward to embrace her.

Georgette tightened her lips. Her eyes puckered, on the verge of tears. She wanted to lay her head on her mother's bosom. She yearned to be folded in her protective arms the way she used to be when she was a baby. She wanted her mother to hold her and to make all that was wrong with her go away. Instead, she stiffened and a cold expression replaced the vulnerable look on her face.

"It would not have happened if you'd wanted him. Instead of that slave!" She spat the words out at Elise like a snake striking out at an unwary victim.

The words smashed Elise painfully in the center of her stomach. She gaped, horrified at the meaning of her daughter's accusation. Elise reeled in utter confusion, overwhelmed by a sensation of falling eternally downwards into a bottomless abyss. The shock and the confusion on her face revealed her vulnerability. Georgette regarded her with contempt.

"What are you saying?" Elise said weakly.

"You didn't think it was a secret, did you?" Georgette sneered. "They all know. The Captain and Brent. They'll capture him soon enough. You'll see."

"Oh, Georgette!" The cry came painfully deep from within Elise's bosom. She fell upon her daughter, clasping her close to her breast. They lay there in each other's arms, their heaving bosoms racked with bitter sobs. Tears flowed down their cheeks and mingled as they held closely to each other.

"I am sorry, mommy," Georgette pleaded. "I am so sorry. I told the Captain and he sent Brent to speak with me. They will be waiting for him tonight. I am so sorry."

A pang of fear constricted Elise's breast, but she held on to her daughter, stroking her tangled hair and kissing her wet and grimy cheeks.

"It will be all right," she said plaintively. "It will be all right."

Coree Greg was furious that anyone of his camp should have been so easily taken. For many years he had successfully defended his camp against any incursions by the militia. He had purposely not drawn attention to himself, living quietly in the deep forest and avoiding any acts that would call for retaliation on the part of the government or the militia. Only once had Young's detachment of soldiers, in a sudden flush of legionary zeal, attempted to penetrate the defenses of his camp. He had dealt with them quickly and decisively and they had not even returned to recover the bodies of their dead. Since then they had left him and his followers alone. Betty's capture disturbed him immensely. It was an act of treachery, he knew. But the reason for this had to go beyond the mere capture of a runaway slave girl. Betty knew her way around the nearby estates and she was well liked and trusted. There had to be some greater reason why anyone would betray her. It had to be part of a grand design to invade his camp again and destroy him and his followers.

He turned to Pharcel, his worried eyes searching for an answer.

"How did this happen?"

Pharcel recounted most of what he knew; how they had gone separate ways the evening before to meet again in the dawn of the next day; he had sat and waited in the dim light of approaching day until the sun began to appear over the hills, and still she had not returned; then he had crept down to the slave huts at the top of the village and learned of Joshua's message to her, and of the hideous sounds of pain and agony that came from the abandoned warehouse afterwards in the early hours of morning. Then he told of his visit to Joshua's place and of his swift dispatch of the old man's life when his lies had blackened the look in his eyes.

Coree Greg nodded, satisfied at the summary punishment meted out to the old traitor. He had known of old Joshua for a long time, but he had never had any trouble from him until now. Joshua had always lived a life of cunning, using subterfuge to appease both black and white; but his acts of betrayal had been minor until now. Well, he had paid a fitting price. Pharcel had dealt with him appropriately. In true African fashion.

"But why did you separate?" Coree Greg searched his face closely. "Where did you go?"

"I went to visit some of my friends at Dubique," Pharcel replied, stirring uneasily where he sat beside the old chief.

Coree Greg noted his discomfort and knew he lied. There was much else to be said that the boy would not say. His eyes roved over Pharcel's face and sturdy frame, now bowed down in distress and sorrow. Despite his suspicion, he felt moved by the sadness that fell like a grey mantle over the boy's usually bright countenance. He had observed Pharcel for a long time since the day he had crept into his camp escorted by Jacko and Hall. The boy was no doubt intelligent and courageous, but there was something inscrutable about him, an impenetrable mask that made it impossible to look far into his soul. It was not so much deceit as an unconscious withholding of himself. A deep-seated fear of opening up to others. Now Coree Greg wondered what dreadful secret the boy carried that had led to Betty's capture and possible death.

"What will become of Betty?" Pharcel turned to his old chief, a note of despair hanging heavy on his voice.

"They will flog her, sell her and transport her." Coree Greg looked down at his feet. "We will soon find out."

He sat quietly for a while thinking, then he turned again to Pharcel.

"You had best not go back there," he cautioned. "At least not for a time."

Pharcel stood as the old man gave him a dismissive nod. He turned and walked away into the gathering dusk. Already he could feel the desolation settling on his shoulders as he approached his empty hut under the towering trees. He thought of Betty, beaten and bound like a beast, her fragile spirit broken by the degradation of her torture and rape at the hands of the men she had so fervently despised. The women in the huts in the dark depression at the top of the village had described to him the piercing screams and pitiful wailing that had gone on for so many hours before she was taken out again and sent to the shore for transportation to Roseau. Some of them had even seen her bruised limbs and lacerated face as her limp body was being dragged through the avenue down to the boats.

He sat in the dark in his hut, her broken image haunting his thoughts, and wondered what might have been if he had returned to her earlier and had gone in search of her when she did not appear at their appointed time. He felt heaviness in his heart as his mind returned to the blissful hours he had spent with Elise while Betty was being tortured and violated. He blamed himself for not being there to prevent her falling in Brent's trap and for not being there to save her when she did. Even the thought of his revenge on Joshua could not assuage the guilt that weighed down his soul.

Marie Claire came to his hut with a bowl of ground provisions and stewed agouti. He saw the stout columns of her legs and smelt the musk of her body before he raised his eyes to the robust firmness of her belly and breasts. She held a smoking torch in one hand and the full bowl in the other. Her broad face looked down on him with a half smile as if wanting to cheer him up and at the same time to commiserate with his woefulness. She offered the bowl to him, but he shook his head. He found the mere thought of eating revolting to his stomach. Marie Claire set the bowl down on the ground and sat beside him, stroking the thick brown hair on his head. His chest was tight with misery and regret, and he retched as the full force of dismay welled in him. Marie Claire continued to stroke him as his body shook with the sadness of his loss and the frustrating helplessness that he felt as he sat there in the creeping dark. After a while, she left.

Pharcel sat alone in his sadness, thinking of the night before and the words that he and Betty had exchanged before they had separated. He recalled her reproachful tone as she rebuked him for his faithlessness and his weakness in not resisting the attraction of the woman who had enslaved him since he was a child. He had tried to deny what she had perceived so clearly, that though he was physically free, emotionally he was totally enslaved. He knew in his heart that however strong and earnest his affection for Betty, he could not break the bonds that kept him chained to Elise and her fatal attraction.

Marie Claire returned out of the pitch-black night, her torch throwing shimmering shadows on the walls as she entered the small room where he still sat. This time she brought another bowl with fresh scented oil which he was sure must be snake oil. She set the bowl on the ground beside him and proceeded to draw his pants down over his feet. She cupped her hand, drew some of the oil onto his chest and abdomen, and began to mould his muscles as a baker would mould his dough before setting it to rise. Front and back she pinched and pummeled until he felt the knots in his neck, chest, legs and arms loosen and unravel. She turned him over on his back, and squatted over his loins, the thick coarse bush of her lower abdomen rubbing his belly as she leaned over and continued her firm but soothing massage. He remained limp even as he felt the wetness from her sex dripping onto him. Her rough hands gentled as she pressed lightly on his face, neck and shoulders until a deep drowsiness overcame him. He slept. When he awoke in the brightening morning light, she was still lying beside him.

He felt refreshed and wonderfully calm as if his body and his spirit had been freed of a million bonds and the weight of a mountain of rocks. He turned to look at the woman sleeping beside him, her massive blackness rounded into seductive curves and mounds from her heaving breasts to the jointure of her loins. He tore his gaze from her and rose to his feet. Drawing his pants over his nakedness, he crept quietly out the door.

For many nights he wrestled with his despair and his guilt. Each night Marie Claire came and ministered to him, but she no longer slept at his side. He accepted her care with subdued gratitude, a shy smile brightening his lips, his eyes smoldering with a warm devotion that remained unspoken even after many days. During the day, his thoughts were filled with Betty and her winsome prettiness, but at night his dreams went riot with visions of Elise and the warm nights among the trees, the scent and feel and stirring sounds that gave them the dimensions of reality; then the gentle sound of Betty's voice would intervene as if to lure him away from the enchantment that so completely possessed him.

Many nights lying in the dark and thinking, he could not understand why it was that he had found love so exciting and yet so unsatisfying among the women of his race, even with Betty, while Elise never failed to bring him to such fathomless joy and inexhaustible pleasure. She seemed always to open out more and more to him the closer they came together, as if the cavern of her love could eternally soften and expand into an embrace that was so alive and so limitless in its possibilities. At those times the urge would seize him to see her one more time; but as each new day dawned he would settle back into his misery until night came again and Marie Claire returned to put him to sleep.

It was almost a week after Betty's capture that he stole away long after the day began and drifted in the direction of Dubique. His dreams the night before had been so intensely arousing that no phantom or disembodied voice could tear him from the rosy effulgence that had so palpably enveloped him. When he woke up the next morning he was obsessed with the single desire to live once again the overwhelming passion of his dreams. And so he drifted further and further out of the forest as if drawn to an irresistible fate. He was like one bewitched, moving thoughtlessly and without will to a certain danger that he could no more avoid than the fly avoid the spider in his wide-spun web.

It was already dark when he found the path that led through the cane fields down to the house. The path was wide enough to admit the narrow, mule-drawn wagons that conveyed the stems of cane down to the shore and to the mill at Geneva. The fields were full, approaching harvest time, and the cane fronds arched on both sides of the path. His footfalls were deadened by the soft earth of the cart wheel tracks, but occasionally dry fronds crackled under his feet. He felt the usual surge of excitement as he got closer to the fringe of trees that grew at the back and sides of the house, knowing that Elise would be waiting in the dark. His thoughts were filled with her and her total surrender to the intensity of their passion every time they met, as if always reaching out to new heights of fulfillment. His breath came quickly as he approached closer and closer to the house. In the dark, he did not see the shadowy bulk stretched across the path until he stumbled over it. Instinctively, he rolled towards the side and plunged into the thickness of the cane field. He heard a sharp almost inaudible hiss and a subdued whisper of his name. He remained still, peering through the thick clumps of cane. The shadowy bulk was standing and he could discern the short, rotund form of a woman.

"It's me, Bessie," the form whispered.

He came cautiously out and stood at the edge of the path.

"You must go back," Bessie said urgently. "They are waiting for you."

He leaned over her and brought his lips close to her ear.

"Where are they?" he asked. There was a slight tremor in his voice but his eyes were steady in the dark.

Bessie pointed at the stand of trees directly at the back of the house. Pharcel nodded and grinned, his teeth flashing in the dark, his eyes gleaming with mischief.

"How many?" His voice had taken on a sudden harshness.

She held up one hand, fingers outstretched, close to his eyes.

"You must go!" she whispered desperately. "Elise sent me to warn you."

He nodded again and pushed her gently into the clumps of cane. He heard a brief swishing sound as she brushed through the dense growth and then the silence of the night settled over the field. Pharcel stood in the dark and took a deep breath of the cool night air before he turned and walked up the path the way he had come. Near the top of the hill, the fields of cane gave way to a fringe of low bush that bordered the forest. Pharcel plunged into the bush to the left creeping silently in a half-circle until he came to the opposite side of the house. There was another stand of trees on this side near the low brush that bordered the clearing. He clambered into branches, thick with dark green foliage that hung low to the ground. Pharcel climbed to the middle and sat in the fork of a thick branch, his back against the trunk. Through the foliage, he could see the back of the house and the trees where the white men were.

He saw when Elise came out, the faint glow of her white dress a ghostly blur in the dark. She walked as if for a stroll in the night air, took a couple turns about the narrow strip of yard, and disappeared again into the house. He remained where he was, listening to the night, his eyes fixed on the trees on the opposite side. He heard the rustling of leaves as the men shifted about among the branches, and he listened to their mutterings as the night crept on. It was past midnight when he heard the sound of bodies noisily dropping to the ground and saw three men emerge from the shadows into the clearing. They disappeared around the corner of the house and their subdued voices faded down the hill past the meadow towards the shore.

The waiting seemed interminable, but he remained motionless against the trunk of the tree, his eyes penetrating the dark. Just as the darkness lifted and the first grey light began to filter over the brim of the hills, two figures crawled stiff-jointed from below the low branches of the trees on the other side. They were the Captain and Brent. Both came out to the clearing and stood hesitantly in a brief and animated conversation, then Brent turned and walked dejectedly across the lawn and down the track towards the shore. The Captain stood pensively, alone, as if reluctant to discontinue his fruitless vigil.

Pharcel slid down the tree and slithered through the low brush towards the ravine north of the clearing where the house stood. At the higher elevation the sides were steep; but, holding on to the slender trees that grew down its slope, he slung himself down to the bed of the stream and hastened down it past the slave huts, still asleep in the first wink of dawn, until he came to the road beside the shore. There was no one in sight. The three men had long since gone back to the village, and Brent was still trudging down the path from the house. There was a pile of rocks beside the road a few paces from the bank of the stream where chunks from the overhanging cliff had fallen. He hid behind the rocks and waited.

After several minutes, he heard the sloshing of a horse's hooves across the stream and, peering around the rocks, saw Brent riding towards where he was hid. Brent seemed lost in thought. He held the reins loosely in one hand, the other hand hung listlessly down his side. As the horse came abreast, Pharcel leapt from the cover of the rocks and swung his cutlass in a wide arc. The horse reared suddenly in fright as the sharp blade sliced into its shoulder. Brent leaped to the

ground, and in a twirling motion turned to face Pharcel, at the same time drawing the knife that hung from his waist. They circled each other, neither of them
noticing the horse that was madly bolting away down the road towards Geneva.

Brent stalked his adversary, his athletic legs planted firmly with every step, his
neck outthrust, thickening with tension, holding his knife point outward in the
palm of his hand. Pharcel bent loosely forward, stepping aside, keeping his distance, his cutlass dangling from limp fingers. Brent suddenly leapt sideways and
Pharcel tensed in readiness, leaning to his left, his fingers closing firmly over the
handle of his cutlass. But it was a feint, and he was slightly unbalanced when
Brent quickly changed direction and rushed head forward into his abdomen. The
impact sent the air gushing out of his lungs and drove him backwards. Brent was
an experienced fighter, and seeing his advantage closed in on Pharcel, his knife
poised for striking as Pharcel desperately tried to regain his breath; but the
younger man swung nimbly away and they again faced each other, moving in
tense circles.

The sun poured its heat on the deathly struggle beside the stream. Brent's garments were already soaked, and rivulets of sweat ran down his face and neck.
Beads of water stood out all over Pharcel's glistening upper body where the oil
formed a protective layer over his skin. Their eyes were fixed on each other in a
cold, deadly glare, each taking in the slightest signal of the other's intent. No
words were spoken and the silence between them was unbroken except for the
sound of their deep breathing and shuffling feet. Again Brent feinted and
plunged forward driving his shoulder into Pharcel's solar plexus and knocking
him flat on his back. The shock of the blow momentarily disabled Pharcel and
caused the cutlass to slip out of his hand, leaving him unarmed. Brent leapt over
him, knife descending in a swift plunge. Pharcel reflexively rolled away from him,
but not quickly enough. He let out a cry of rage as the knife dug into his shoulder. Brent raised his hand for another stab, but Pharcel with surprising agility,
caught him at the back of his neck, reared upwards, and butted him painfully,
shattering his jaw. The knife flew out of Brent's hand and blood spurted out of
his mouth and nostrils.

They grappled each other, rolling in the dirt and down the bank of the stream
into its swift, cascading flow. Brent wrapped his long, muscular arms around
Pharcel, trying to crush his back; but the snake oil spread over Pharcel's skin
made his body as slippery as an eel's, and Brent was unable to hold his advantage.
They both leapt to their feet at the same instant, but Brent, acting swiftly, swung
Pharcel's body around and locked his arms around the runaway slave's neck in a
deadly grip that had him choking and sputtering. Pharcel began to weaken and

his chest burned as his breathing became more and more labored. A whirling and roaring began in his head and his arms flailed helplessly at his sides. Brent strained to hold him down, and had him slumping lower and lower in the stream. For a moment, it looked as if the fight had gone completely out of Pharcel, but, suddenly, with an agonized roar, he heaved upwards and sent Brent sprawling onto the rocks in the middle of the stream. He was on Brent in an instant, one knee pressed into the small of his back. Quickly, he wrapped one arm around Brent's neck and jerked his body upward. There was the crack of bone splintering and Brent collapsed helplessly; his arms and legs giving only feeble movements as he tried to raise himself out of the stream; his mouth opening as if to scream, though no sound came. The water gurgled and splashed around his body as it flowed merrily to the shore only a few yards away downstream.

Close by above the further bank, the clopping of a horse's hooves broke the silence. Pharcel stood over the man who had flogged him so severely, and who had so viciously abused and raped the woman who had been so good to him and for whom he had such a warm affection. With a last look of contempt, he kicked the lifeless body further into the stream.

He looked up to see Captain Marshall reining his horse only a few yards away. The look on the Captain's face was one of shock and horror as he reached frantically for his pistol, but before his nervous fingers could release the weapon from his waist, Pharcel had already sprinted up the nearer bank of the stream and disappeared into the bushes.

The captain would never forget the impudent, mocking grin that had so unnerved him as he fidgeted with the catch on his weapon. He realized then that he had come face to face with a mortal enemy.

CHAPTER 9

Paulinaire was being watched. Although he was free to move about, he knew that every step he made was being followed. The authorities had declared him a seditious person, but could not find sufficient evidence to apprehend him and have him either in jail or deported. He was a free mulatto of French origin who had fled Martinique because, despite his education and independent means, the *code noire* debarred him from attaining a social status of significant respectability; he was not allowed to appear in public dressed like a gentleman. He was careful to conceal the more credible reason that he had been at the forefront of the revolutionary agitation that had seized the poor whites, mulattos and freed blacks in all the French colonies; and that white society in Martinique had marked him for summary extermination.

Here in Dominica he was well known, even among the upper class, as a man of gracious affability and social refinement. Though he was not fully accepted in "polite" society, he found ready welcome among the whites and colored in the more popular bars and saloons. And he was allowed to dress as he pleased. Besides, many of the leading merchants and other businessmen had found it profitable to cultivate his friendship because he was their principal link to back-door trafficking in smuggled goods. It was an open secret that Paulinaire supplied most of the fine wines and brandies that graced the shelves of the most successful commercial establishments in Roseau.

What was a closed secret was that he also smuggled guns and ammunition which he somehow was able to conceal at various spots around the island. He was also able to keep hidden the large store of revolutionary tracts and other subversive literature which he arranged to be circulated among the few literate free blacks and mulattos in the town and even as far away as the northern district. But the authorities had been informed of his private meetings with blacks and mulattos under cover of elaborate and interminable balls and dances that were arranged in the larger towns and villages. There Paulinaire was used to gathering around him in private rooms the more intelligent and articulate, and expounding on the writings of Abbé Raynal and others who had embraced the cause of blacks, especially the enslaved.

At the beginning, the French Revolution had very little to do with the colonies, being essentially confined to the interests of the landed gentry in France and their rebellion against the irrational power and privileges of the nobles and clerics. Louis XIV's inept fiscal management supporting expensive wars against foreign governments, and the avaricious and grossly extravagant demands of the nobles and clerics, had drawn France into huge debt that could be supported only by oppressive taxes and other imposts on the already overburdened peasants and small landowners. The growing disaffection of this group coincided with the flaring discontent of the masses impoverished by rising prices and increasing shortages of basic foods and consumer goods. The fall of the Bastille and the storming of the Tuileries gave rise to the emergence of the Third Estate, the declaration of the *Rights of Man and Citizen* and the revolutionary call for liberty, equality and fraternity. Gradually, the literary outpourings of the greatest minds in the influential circle of French and English intellectuals—*Voltaire, Montesquieu, Diderot, Rousseau, Locke* and others—filtered through to the underprivileged whites, mulattos and blacks of the West Indian colonies, sparking high expectations that the conscience of Europe was at last awakened to the plight of the downtrodden and oppressed.

In this grand effluxion of philosophical thought and rational social analysis, no one understood the limits of liberty, equality and fraternity as it applied to the specific issues of gender, religion and race. The question of slavery in this new social and political environment was even more complicated in the light of its critical importance for the survival of the French economy, dependent as it was on the profitable commerce from the colonies. Thus the moral values so grandly declared in the *Rights of Man and Citizens* became subjugated to pragmatic concerns about economic survival in France and other colonial powers, including England, and especially in the colonies. Even the increasingly strident voice of the *Society of the Friends of Blacks* in Paris could not penetrate the mercenary wall of resistance as more and more white planters in the French colonies agitated for representation in their National Assembly to protect their commercial interests.

Naively, the free blacks and mulattos in the colonies had adopted the revolutionary cockade (red, white and blue ribbons) as their banner for the struggle for liberty and equality, thinking that they could free themselves from their social condition in the same way that the white masses had liberated themselves from the shackles of feudalism and autocracy by executing their king and nobles. All that had to be done was that the slaves kill their white masters, free themselves and take possession of the estates which had been made profitable with their sweat and blood. The bloody insurrection in San Domingo resonated among the blacks and mulattos everywhere among the colonies as they waited for the signal to rise and join the march to freedom.

In this electrified atmosphere, the voice of Paulinaire, informed as it was by the advocacy of Abbé Raynal and others of his philosophical inclination, was a clarion call to action among the mulattos and free blacks. Their hope was that the spread of revolutionary fervor in nearby Guadeloupe and Martinique would give them the support they needed to overthrow their English colonial oppressors and to take control. But events in Guadeloupe and Martinique had shown that the whites in those colonies had no intention of relinquishing their colonial interests which were ineluctably tied to the continuance of slavery and the maintenance of the *Code Noire*.

Paulinaire quickly understood that the few mulattos and free blacks on the island could not take any meaningful action to improve their social and economic condition. The example of San Domingo in conjoining the interests of the mulattos, the free blacks and the slaves was the only means of achieving their revolutionary objectives. Therefore, an alliance with the runaway slave leaders was essential to any attempt at social upheaval.

These matters he discussed with the core groups of mulattos and free blacks that he met at the many soirees, balls and dances that he attended in several towns and villages. Not all the mulattos and blacks were in favor of joining with the slaves and, especially, the runaways, who they regarded as uncouth and brutal savages. But Paulinaire argued the pragmatism of using the strength of the masses wherever it could be found. They agreed finally to send out missives to the runaway slave leaders to mobilize their support and bring them together in one grand army that would annihilate all vestiges of white domination as was done in San Domingo.

Among the whites of the island, very little sympathy existed for the plight of the mulattos, the freed blacks, the slaves and least of all the runaways. But there had recently come to the island a young curate of the English Church, a scholarly man of impeccable virtue and high principles, educated at the prestigious Oxford University, whose social conscience had been stirred by what he had witnessed and the accounts he had heard of the terrible conditions under which slaves lived, and the brutal treatment that was meted out to them for the least cause or offence.

Paulinaire had met the curate accidentally one afternoon while taking the air in the open parade ground near the Fort, and both men had found common ground while discussing the issue of slavery and its degrading effect on society. It was clear that the curate had a low opinion of the moral and intellectual capacity of the white population, and their preoccupation with maintaining their status quo. He thought the curate could be a useful ally in any future struggle for liberation of the society from white prejudice and abuse, especially with regard to the educated mulattos.

Thus Paulinaire moved on the margins of colonial society, admired for his suavity and daring business acumen, but detested for his obsessive desire for acceptance among the rich and privileged. Reports of his activities among the blacks and mulattos and of his frequent sojourns in the countryside soon came to the attention of officials who, already jealous of his increasing wealth and frustrated by the illusiveness of his disreputable traffic in smuggled goods, looked to any cause that would bring him down to justice and disgrace.

Their suspicions increased as murmurings of revolt against English domination began to be heard among the French population especially in the riotous town of Colihaut and the nearby villages. To add to the sense of danger, subversive tracts had been found circulating among slaves in the western villages and Grandbay who, though mostly illiterate, held on with superstitious awe to the grimy pamphlets that promised freedom and equality for all men. Inevitably, a finger of suspicion was pointed at the mysterious, colored Frenchman whose gregarious activities around the island could not easily be explained. Paulinaire was marked for destruction.

The encounter with Pharcel was one of those portentous happenings that changed the course of events on the island. Since his narrow escape from capture on the Dubique estate, Pharcel had refrained from visiting Elise; but he continued to be drawn to the vicinity of the estate, spending nights in the woods close by. He had also taken to visiting the small Carib settlement where he had left Kumeni several weeks earlier after he had hidden the cache of gold coin and jewels that he had taken from the hidden treasure of the Caribs. Kumeni had received him with characteristic passivity and he had wandered in and out of the settlement for several days, receiving only restrained acknowledgement from the rest of the community.

It was during these wanderings that he met Jacques who confided to him that a secret gathering of blacks and mulattos was to take place deep in the forest above Geneva the following night, and that Paulinaire, the French mulatto revolutionary, was to speak of recent developments in France, and especially of the magnificent victory of the blacks in Haiti. He urged Pharcel to attend, as he thought this could be the initial rallying point for all true revolutionaries in the march to freedom.

At first Pharcel received him with instinctive skepticism, knowing how easy it was for betrayals to be arranged and executed. His recent experience had also shown him that self-interest too often overcame the noblest sentiments in people of whatever class or race; but he knew a lot about Jacques who, though not aligned to any group, had faithfully assisted so many slaves to escape and find refuge among the runaway camps. Jacques was a trusted emissary among the blacks, free and enslaved, and could walk into any of the camps from Delices to Grandbay without fear or suspicion.

Pharcel's misgivings soon gave way to curiosity about the man whose reputation for intelligence and cunning was spoken of with respect if not veneration everywhere among blacks and mulattos. He stayed with Jacques all day and through the night, never leaving his side even when he ventured among the slave huts on Geneva in the dead of night. He listened to the excited whisperings among the slaves as if they thought that their freedom was nigh and Paulinaire was the long-awaited deliverer who would lead them to liberty and return them to their homeland.

Pharcel's feelings towards Paulinaire were at best ambivalent. He had lived in Coree Greg's shadow, and had learned to respect the old man's sagacity and bravery. As for Bala, though he distrusted him, he could not help but admire the staunchness of his leadership and his boldness in facing up to the white planters and the militia. But this man of words, a city dweller, unseasoned in bush fighting and unused to the discomfort and privation of life in the woods, what had he to offer them? Nonetheless, he spent the next day impatient for the night to come.

The place was in a clearing nearly a mile into the bush. The land dipped into a shallow bowl with thick clumps of bamboo leaning in an unbroken ring around its edge. The thin and narrow leaves of the plants formed a dry, smooth cushion over the bare ground. The land fell away on two sides of the bowl, looking towards the estates below; but rose to thick forest at the back and the other side. The spot seemed secure enough if guards were posted on the lower sides. Nevertheless, Pharcel remained standing on the outer edge of the circle, the dense, dark woods a few paces at his back.

It was a warm night. A half moon was already high up in the sky, its wan light filling the bowl within the circle of bamboo. Only the groaning of the stems rubbing against each other disturbed the silence as the dark shadows of men and a few women emerged from the surrounding bushes and descended to the inner sides of the depression. They sat with hardly a murmur, slaves and free blacks together, waiting.

Paulinaire entered the clearing surrounded by a few free blacks and mulattos from the village. He stood tall and erect, walking with delicate steps down the lower side of the clearing, his shoes slipping on the dry, smooth leaves. Hands reached out to steady him until he found firm footing at the bottom of the depression. He stood uncertainly looking at the shadowy faces around him until someone placed a fallen log at the higher end of the circular hollow. Without invitation, Paulinaire stepped gingerly forward, whisked a handkerchief from his coat pocket, spread it on the dry log and carefully sat. The night listened as he began in a mellifluous voice to weave a pattern of words and expressions that formed magical thoughts in French and patois and that instantly held his audience in thrall.

He was over six feet tall, slender and nattily dressed in the fashion of the times. Even in the wildness of his surroundings, he maintained the elegance of his person as if he were comfortably ensconced in the most luxurious boudoir in the city. His features were slightly elongated with a high forehead, arched eyebrows, long, thin nose that flared noticeably at the nostrils, tight, lean upper lips that stretched incongruously over the fleshy protuberance of its lower companion, and large ears extending outward as if to intercept the slightest whisper. His eyes peered narrowly from deep sockets, their light shadowed by thick, overhanging eyebrows. Crisp, wooly, black hair covered the top of his head down to the nape of his neck and contrasted oddly with the ruddiness of his complexion. Even under the narrowest inspection, he could have been mistaken for a white man.

After many years of living on the island, Paulinaire had not lost the Gaulish habit of using his hands generously during conversation and, as he spoke, his long, delicate fingers seemed to weave his words into a fascinating pattern that gave added eloquence to his speech. At first, Pharcel paid little attention to the flurry of words that rose in mordent harmony from the hollow over which he stood. He leaned tensely forward looking past the ring of dark faces, nervously scanning the darkness beyond for any sign of unexpected intrusion. But as Paulinaire continued to speak into the night, snatches of his well articulated thoughts on the equality of all men and their inborn right to liberty captured his attention and drew him closer into the circle; and soon he was sitting gape-mouthed, drawing in the captivating intonations of the mulatto who was almost a white man.

Paulinaire told them in simple terms of the struggle of the masses of the people of France who had been as downtrodden as they themselves were, and how they had seized the reins of power in their hands and now controlled their own destiny. He spoke of the great intellectuals of France and England whose writings had sown the seeds of the massive changes that had overthrown privilege and oppression in Europe. In particular, he praised the progressive thinking of Rousseau who had upheld the formidable principle that "the person of the meanest citizen is as sacred and inviolable as that of the first magistrate", and who always insisted on complete equality between men. It did not occur to the slaves that these principles might not apply to them who were not regarded as citizens anywhere. But the noble thoughts of Rousseau and so many others fired their imagination, and opened out in their minds possibilities of liberation and independence that they had previously held to be unattainable. All they had to do, Paulinaire said to them, was seize the time when they could eradicate white oppression forever.

Through the night they listened as he lauded the work of Abbé Raynal who pursued his sacred mission to relieve the terrible condition of the slaves, against severe opposition from the delegates of the French National Assembly and in particular the delegates from the colonies, charged as they were with advocacy for the interest of the white planters. Even here, the new curate of the Anglican Church, a man of learning and human sympathy, was taking up the cause of the enslaved and was using his considerable influence to advocate to the Council a new code of conduct towards the enslaved.

He derided the vulgarity and lack of learning of the planters and their degraded factors who spent their days in constant inebriation, and whose animalistic tendencies drew them down to the lowest moral standard to which any human can descend. He declared to them that though white society despised the slaves and others of African descent, they detested themselves even more.

He ended by extolling the brave and noble struggle which Toussaint, Desaline and the thousands of the heroes of San Domingo had upheld with such spectacular distinction and which had brought them complete freedom to determine their own destiny. He exhorted his audience to take up the banner of freedom, the same banner that had so inspired Toussaint and Desaline; and to seize the hour of their liberation. At the end there was complete silence, but within each breast there swelled a growing and irrepressible emotion, a rousing surge of confidence and valor as if in that instant they were already charged to rush towards the lines of battle and face their hated enemy. The spell was broken as Paulinaire slowly rose to his feet and walked across the clearing the way he had entered.

Pharcel roused himself from the trance-like absorption in which he had been held all night, and seeing Paulinaire's retreating figure surrounded by the mass of the people, he dashed around the rim of the hollow to intercept him. They faced each other at the outer edge where the land began its decline to the upper reaches of Geneva.

The half moon was hovering half way over the sea and its faint light filtered through the saplings that grew on this side of the clearing. Soon the dawn light would first darken the woods before breaking over the top of the hills and spreading in brightening shades onto the hillsides and into the valleys.

Paulinaire took in the tight muscular frame and bold expression of the young man standing before him. Jacques sidled up to them, elbowing his way through the crowd until he stood at Paulinaire's elbow, and whispered something to him. Paulinaire turned sharply and looked again at Pharcel with a new and lively interest. He had heard of him and his deadly exploits at Dubique and Geneva. Though he abhorred bloodshed, he knew that in the kind of struggle that would inevitably ensue, bloodshed was unavoidable. They would have need for soldiers to do the bloody work. He took Pharcel by the shoulder and walked with him all the way to the boundaries of Geneva.

Pharcel sat with Coree Greg and several of the other men of the camp the following evening. The sun was already dipping below the tops of the bushes at the far end of the ravine and the community of huts stood in deep shadow. The men had gathered around Coree Greg where he sat against the side of his hut smoking. Claire was squatting on the bare earth inside the hut listening to what she knew to be important news. Her son, Joseph, sat with her quietly studying the intent look on his mother's face as she took in the stilted account that Pharcel gave of his encounter with Paulinaire. After a while she stood and leaned across the door jamb and looked directly at Coree Greg who turned towards her and, catching the dark frown on her face, knew that she was not pleased at what Pharcel had spoken. He shrugged and said nothing, allowing the bubbling enthusiasm in the young man's voice to simmer to more rational discourse. Claire withdrew herself and sat in the darkening interior of the hut in silent consternation.

Pharcel told them with obvious pride of his private conversation with Paulinaire after the gathering had broken up and they had walked together down to the boundaries of Geneva. He beamed at them as he described the intimacy that had been established between himself and the learned mulatto and the confidences they had exchanged in that brief moment before the sun dissolved the lingering remnants of the night. Coree Greg's frown deepened as Pharcel imparted with near condescension that Paulinaire held the old chief in high esteem, respected his sagacity and valor and would like to meet him and through him, the other camp leaders as soon as possible. He also revealed that a group of insurgents, mostly colored, would be entering Grandbay from Martinique within a short time and that they would be willing to make money and guns available to support a revolt.

The other men spoke quietly at first and then with rising heat as they analyzed the implications of this new development in their struggle for freedom and independence, each point of view receiving a brief nod of acknowledgement from Coree Greg. Mention of the money that could be made available and of the weapons in which they were so badly lacking excited the interest of many of them, but Coree Greg continued to sit in unruffled serenity, quietly smoking his pipe.

Tom, too, remained still, glancing furtively at the inscrutable frown that clouded his old companion's face. He said nothing as the arguments continued to rage around him.

Abruptly, Coree Greg rose from his seat, his old frame exuding wordless authority. He took the pipe from his mouth and for a moment his brow contracted as if in profound contemplation. Then he raised his eyes to the eager faces around him and almost spat his words.

"I have never known a mulatto who was not treacherous and a coward!"

He turned and walked sedately into his hut. It was already dark inside. Claire regarded him worshipfully. She smiled in silent reassurance.

Later that evening, Pharcel sat in his hut thinking. He still felt the shock of Coree Greg's dismissal, and the deathly silence that had followed his departure from their meeting. He thought he had conveyed quite clearly and forcibly the essence of the discourse he had heard that night in the bushes and the importance to them of the forces that were gathering outside their camps. Clearly, Paulinaire was a man of vast knowledge and immense resources, a man who could give invaluable support to the struggle in which they were all engaged. Paulinaire was no warrior; but he knew the inside of the white man's mind. He moved among them, knew their secrets and could be a useful ally in strategizing the war that was to come. Furthermore, his account of the splendid victory in San Domingo had shown how important it was for the blacks and colored to band together to overcome the formidable military and economic strength of the white government.

Pharcel sat in the dark feeling alone, more so than he had ever felt. He thought of Betty and her quiet companionship. He missed her terribly. Word had filtered into the camp that she had been tried and, because of the terrible condition in which she had been found, had been dealt with leniently. The judge had simply ordered that she be auctioned and deported to one of the French islands. Joseph, the councilor's man-servant in Roseau, had sent word that she had been bought by a French planter and sent to Martinique. He vowed to himself that one day soon he would find the means to secure her release.

Alone in the dark, his thoughts drifted to Dubique and the captivating white woman who had so completely possessed his spirit. Her essence, the raw fragrance of her body and the warm, yielding softness of her flesh, seemed to pervade the darkness around him. He spent the night in erotic dreams and lurid phantasy, and when he finally awoke late in the bright morning he felt utterly drained and listless.

It was many days before he bestirred himself to move beyond the circle of huts. It had been raining and the spatter of rain and the dripping of leaves onto the thatch roofs of the hut added to his melancholy. When the sun came out his spirit rose and he was filled with an inexplicable feeling of expectancy. He could not remain cooped up in the dreary confines of the camp one more day. He drifted off among the trees further and further away. Without any sense of direction he followed unconsciously the faint trace that ran to the borders of Geneva. From there a brief diversion would lead him to Dubique; but he hesitated, knowing the risk to himself and to Elise.

His mind wandered to the night in the bush when Paulinaire had stirred his spirit with promises of equality and freedom. Those words meant more to him than the wise words of caution with which Coree Greg had dismissed his high expectations; more to him than the treasure he had hidden in the secure fissures of the cliffs below Dubique. He had to find Paulinaire, but first he had to find Jacques.

He wandered all day among the trees and the bushes, and when night came he took the track down to Geneva. He came upon Jacques loitering on the edge of the estate. In the half light, they both scampered into the bushes, but after a moment Jacques spoke.

"It is me, Jacques."

Pharcel came slowly out and they faced each other grinning happily.

"It is too early," Jacques said softly. "They will not gather till much later."

"Too early for what?" Pharcel was confused. He had meant to ask Jacques how he could arrange to meet with Paulinaire again.

"The meeting." Jacques looked at him querulously. "The meeting tonight. Didn't you know?"

"Whose meeting?" Pharcel asked.

"Paulinaire has gathered a few men from Martinique who sneaked in through Bagatelle last night," Jacques explained patiently. "They will meet in the abandoned warehouse across the river."

Pharcel immediately recalled his conversation with Paulinaire. The man had mentioned a group of insurgents who would bring support to the grand revolt of slaves and mulattos together. He had not forgotten, but he had not expected matters to progress so quickly. This was clear indication that Paulinaire was a man of decisive action and, more importantly, a man of his word. He became quite excited about meeting Paulinaire again and being part of a great and well organized movement to overthrow white rule in the shortest possible time.

"It is still very early," Jacques said. "We can bide here until it is safer to cross the fields."

They sat on a grassy mound beside the track. The moon was already poised over the hills, its soft beams giving a magical glow to the bushes around them and to the extensive fields below. Jacques unwound a small bundle and brought out a round of cassava bread and a slab of smoked pork. He tore into both and handed a share to Pharcel. They sat and munched quietly, listening to the whispering night.

"What did the old man think of Paulinaire?" Jacques asked suddenly.

Pharcel hesitated, not wanting to prejudice his relationship with Paulinaire by conveying too starkly Coree Greg's negative and dismissive reaction. After a while he raised his head and spoke simply and earnestly.

"He does not trust him," he said.

Jacques nodded.

"You should listen to him," he cautioned. "He is a wise old man."

Pharcel regarded him, a look of bewilderment furrowing his brow.

"What do you mean?" he asked suspiciously. "You are with Paulinaire, are you not?"

"I am with him all right," Jacques assured him.

"But why, if you do not believe in him?" Pharcel's perplexity strained his voice.

"We have to see what's in it for us." Jacques leaned towards him and rested his hand on his shoulder. "We may have common cause, but not common interests."

Pharcel remained silent, pondering this anomaly.

They remained there a long time. The moon was already midway through the skies, throwing a silvery sheen over the landscape around them when they rose. They trudged silently down the track listening to every sound, alert to every movement in the bushes through which they passed.

At last they came to the barn-like structure and walked cautiously around it to the single entrance facing the river. Two men emerged from the shadows on either side of the building and recognizing Jacques, they melted again in the dark of the surrounding bushes. There was a subdued murmur coming from inside and they knew that the men had already gathered. A faint light seeped below the door. Jacques gave three rapid knocks and a sudden hush fell within. The door creaked softly and through the thin gap a pale brown, lean face peered at them apprehensively. Jacques stepped forward and put his face forward in the narrow streak of light.

"It is Jacques," he whispered.

The door opened wide enough to admit them. A company of faces turned towards them, ranging in color from pink to sallow brown, to ebony and even to oriental yellow, no doubt the product of mating of a colored male and a Carib female. The features, too, varied from near white to decidedly African. Paulinaire, beaming, stepped from the shadows at the back of the group. He extended one arm and wrapped it around Pharcel's shoulder; and then turned to the gathered faces.

"This is our man, Pharcel," he declared grandiloquently. "He is our man, young, brave and handsome."

He proceeded to introduce some of the men around him—Jean Louis, Jean Baptiste, Michael and Paul, all light-skinned mulattos of diverse shades and facial contours. Cocque was the wizened, brown-skinned man at the door. There were also a number of elaborately accoutered men furtively clinging together and speaking in hushed tones in demonstrably elegant French. Pharcel noticed quickly that in this gathering there were no other slaves present and that, besides Cocque and Jacques, he was the only one of decidedly African origin. Even Cocque appeared different as he carried himself with a certain sophistication of manner that held him apart from Jacques and him. He began to feel that he had walked in on an alien convention. But Paulinaire continued to hold him in a close embrace as he led him to the centre of the gathering.

One of the men had been reading from a French Gazette titled *L'Ami de la Liberté. L'Enemi de la License.* He resumed reading, pausing intermittently to discuss the resounding phrases of revolutionary denunciation. Pharcel could not follow the rapid flow of French words, and Paulinaire, sensing his dilemma, patiently translated a few of the more virulent condemnations of white supremacy in the affairs of Martinique and Guadeloupe. There was brief mention of the persistence of slavery in the English colonies and the imperative of extending the noble principles of the revolution to those benighted and crassly uncultured English colonists. Nowhere was the concept of equality for all ever mentioned.

Towards midnight the door was thrown open and a troupe of women entered bearing loaded baskets on their heads. They were preceded by a stiff-jointed old slave dressed in white linen tunic and worn grey pantaloons. The women walked with their bodies erect, balancing the baskets on their heads, their hands swinging loosely at their sides. The act of balancing the loads on their heads without the aid of hands gave each of them a proud and dignified look with neck up-stretched, breasts uplifted and hips swinging. They wore long plain dresses loosely belted at the waist, and intricately tied turbans on their heads. As they came close to the group inside, they set their burdens on the floor and proceeded to remove tureens of soup and platters of meat and provisions which they set on a high table on one side of the room. Some others drew bottles of wine, crystal glasses, plates, dishes and silver cutlery which they laid carefully on the table before retreating to the middle of the room.

Immediately, the men scrambled to the table, drawing an assortment of rough benches with them. The old slave walked ceremoniously forward and stood beside the table, surveying the layout critically. At a brief signal from him, the women came forward again and, leaning over the assembled shoulders, began to ladle out soup into waiting bowls.

Pharcel found himself sitting on a low bench at one end of the table. Jacques came and sat beside him. Cocque sat in near isolation a few places from them, while the rest crowded together in intimate companionship. Pharcel, having been a house slave, was familiar with eating implements, but had never had occasion to use them. Neither had Jacques. So after fiddling awkwardly with his spoon for a while, he impatiently set this aside and drew the soup directly into his mouth from the bowl, slurping happily as the delicious mix flowed down his gullet. The others, disgust showing on their pale faces, paused, gaped at him, bowed their heads in shocked humiliation and dipped delicately into their bowls. Jacques defiantly followed Pharcel and emptied his bowl in a few mighty gulps. Paulinaire smiled at them indulgently. He avoided the strained look on the faces of his companions.

The old slave again gave a discreet signal, and the women came forward to remove the now empty bowls. He then proceeded to open one wine bottle after another, carefully pouring into the glasses measured portions that fell almost exactly the same distance from the brim of each glass. The wine seemed to have released a sense of rakishness among the men at the upper end of the table for, as the women came forward and bent over their shoulders to serve the meats, exploring hands sneaked under the low hems of their dresses and playfully rose to their upper thighs, mauling and pinching in gay abandon. Some of the women giggled shyly at the intrusion, but most sullenly moved away as quickly as they could, splashing meat and gravy carelessly on the plates. The old slave stood impassively as stiff as the wooden posts that supported the roof.

Pharcel was furious. He could not understand how anyone who professed to the high principles of equality, fraternity and liberty could so openly affront the dignity of any female, especially the women of his own race. He did not then understand the gradations of color that set mulattos apart from the rest of the black community. He strongly resented the liberties that were being taken with the persons of those helpless women.

One woman in particular, a young nubile slave with a rich ebony color and plump, firm, curvaceous body, seemed to be in dire distress. Jean Louis had casually lifted her dress and was stroking her loins absent—mindedly while carrying on a ribald conversation with the rest of his group in the center of the table. The girl lowered her head and her dark cheeks flushed with shame and anger. Pharcel could see her fidgeting to dislodge the intrusive fingers from her thighs, but she could not shake off Jean Louis who kept on oblivious to her discomfort and resentment. Boldly, Pharcel clattered his plate on the table and signaled to her that she should attend him immediately. She looked apprehensive at first, then quickly disengaged herself from the lecherous mulatto and rushed over to Pharcel's side. There was an ominous hush around the table. Jean Louis turned an angry, disbelieving frown at Pharcel. He raised himself from his seat, his fists balled in fury.

Paulinaire deftly rapped his knife on the table and stood. He smiled benignly at the gathered faces and spoke in his usual well modulated voice.

"This is an important epoch in the history of our countries. Whether we are French or English we are all bonded in a common cause to overthrow the shackles of colonialism and the insufferable indignity of white domination. The great minds of the Enlightenment have paved the way with philosophical thought that freed the mind of Europe from the absurdities of god-given privileges and the inborn superiority of the aristocracy. From Diderot to Danton, from Rousseau to Marat, we have witnessed the destruction of class and a leveling of society, with privilege based only on merit and the elevating condition of intellectual achievement. But we have to be careful not to follow the misguided politics of the Jacobins and their preoccupation with government by the masses. Nothing will be more disastrous than to entrust the sacred duty of governance to the hands of the unwashed and the unlearned. We hold in trust the future of our generation and we must be careful not to endanger that future by wanton disregard for the realities of our society.

"We are here because we have to work together, and we recognize that each of us will have his appointed task according to his ability to carry it out. Those of us who are privileged to be in advance of our black and colored society must lead. But we must not forget our sacred duty to nurture the interests of our less fortunate brethren. They need our wisdom even as we now need their strength.

"The time for philosophical thought and disputation has passed. The century of the Enlightenment has given us a surfeit of moral and social analysis. It is now a time for action. The storming of the Tuileries and the recent revolt in San Domingo have shown that it is not words that win a revolution but war. So we must band together and fight. Those of us who are gathered here, the slaves on the white man's estates and our brothers in the hills.

"This is the hour of our redemption when we must show ourselves as men. Right this minute guns and ammunition are being offloaded on a coast nearby to be given to the great army of our brothers. There will be clothes and supplies in abundance as befits the preparation for war. But it is not only force that will lead our army to ultimate victory, but the sagacity of our leaders who know and understand the heart of our enemy. We who are gathered here must lead and we must be careful to prepare our vast army to die for a noble cause—the freedom of blacks and the emergence of a new and more worthy class of governors."

Paulinaire raised his half-filled glass to his lips and sat down amidst a thunderous rapping of glasses.

Pharcel sat dumbfounded. He could not be sure whether he had been insulted or warmly embraced into a common and honorable cause. He sat pensive while the conversation resumed around the table and the clattering of cutlery announced the termination of the banquet. Soon the men were milling around the door, preparing to slip into the night. He and Jacques slunk quietly out. As he stepped out of the door, Paulinaire clapped him on the shoulder and spoke hurriedly in his ear.

"You must not forget to pass the word to the camps. We will soon need them."

Pharcel nodded absently, walked hurriedly out of the light and vanished into the dark bushes.

CHAPTER 10

It was not long after the Geneva meeting that Jacques came into the camp one bright morning bearing a message from Paulinaire. Coree Greg received him with courtesy and listened attentively as he delivered his missive in formal tones as if reciting an official proclamation. In brief, Paulinaire wanted to meet the chiefs of the runaway camps to discuss with them plans for a grand revolt island-wide. He wished to assure them that there was ample support forthcoming from sympathetic groups in Martinique and Guadeloupe who had already sent large quantities of arms, ammunition and other needed supplies which were now ready for distribution. Already, his network all over the island had infiltrated the estates, and slaves everywhere were sufficiently roused to join a tri-partite revolutionary army. All he needed presently was to meet with them to agree on a strategy to execute a summary overthrow of the white planters and their pernicious system of oppression.

Coree Greg sat through all this, his whole body slumped in somnolent repose. At the end, he raised himself to an erect position and nonchalantly turned to Jacques.

"Who will lead this mighty army?" he asked cynically.

"Paulinaire", Jacques replied.

Coree Greg nodded.

"You will see the other chiefs?" he asked.

"I am on my way to see Bala," Jacques assured him.

"Then give him my respect and say I will be willing to meet to discuss all this among ourselves."

Coree Greg rose and returned to the cool interior of his hut.

Pharcel and Jacques spoke late into the night. They discussed the last meeting in the isolated warehouse on the bank of the Geneva River and the vague and vacillating relationship between the free blacks and mulattos and slaves that Paulinaire had described. Jacques recalled the obnoxious attitude of the arrogant mulattos towards the women slaves and the nearly explosive incident between Pharcel and Jean Louis which Paulinaire had so subtly diffused by his diplomatic intervention.

"There is this in his favor," Jacques said admiringly. "If he has any class preju-dice he hides it well. He makes everyone feel included and important."

"But his tongue is like the penis of a pig," Pharcel replied with a broad grin. "It is twisted and moves in all directions."

"He is a clever man, no doubt," Jacques admitted. "He tries to appease every-one. How else will he bring slaves and freedmen together to fight on the same side? He knows that we need each other. They have the guns, we have the men."

"The old man does not believe we need guns," Pharcel said ruefully. "He thinks we can fight the militia with cutlasses and spears. He still imagines we are African warriors."

He remained silent for a while, lost in thought.

"I wish I could get one," he said wistfully.

"Get what?" Jacques asked.

"A gun," Pharcel explained.

"I could get you one," Jacques responded quickly.

Pharcel glanced at him searchingly; but he saw only a bland look on his face. The torch that had been lit earlier in the night began to disintegrate. They snuffed the light out, and stretched out on the floor. Soon they were fast asleep.

Bala's response to Coree Greg was swift and decisive. He had sent out invita-tions to Sandy, Mabouya, Congoree and Jacco. They would meet the following Saturday in Congoree's camp on the east coast which, for the moment, was the safest place, since it was a considerable distance from the nearest militia posting. Coree Greg proceeded to make arrangements immediately for travel. He chose to follow the eastern coast to Delices to avoid any patrols in the vicinity of the lakes, and decided that Petit Jacques, Hall and Pharcel should accompany him, leaving Tom and the others to take care of the camp.

Congoree's camp lay in a flat stretch of wooded land that extended from the bank of a broad river on one side to the sea on the other. Behind, a tall, precipi-tous mountain provided a formidable defense. It stood like a gigantic cone, its sheer sides lightly wooded. A hardly perceptible trace spiraled down it from its southern approach. It was down this track that Coree Greg and his men had come, slipping and sliding in the loose soil, and holding on to the slender stems of the meager trees that populated the slopes. On one side the mountain dropped perpendicularly to a narrow bank of huge, black rocks on which cascading waves crashed in thunderous collision. On the landward side, a series of serrated, thickly forested hills stretched out in the distance, lost in a covering of cloud that seemed always to hover over the center of the island.

Where the flat land ended on the shore, huge waves rushed from the heaving ocean beyond to break in roaring splashes on the stony beach. They rose and fell with such fury that this part of the coast was practically unapproachable by boat. The Caribs had found a landing further down the shore beyond the other bank of the river, but entering on that side required boating skills which only they possessed. The only easy approach to the camp was from across the river whose open sides made visible any incursion by hostile visitors. These natural defenses made the camp as safe as could be.

It was a sprawling area with several small huts hidden among stands of cassava and coconut trees. To one side closer to the shore, Congoree had cleared a wide portion of land on which he had hastily built additional huts to accommodate his guests and a spacious, open-sided structure where they could gather for meals and for discussions.

Towards evening of Friday the delegates began to drift in. Coree Greg coming from the South was the first to arrive; and Congoree received him graciously, assigning to him and his contingent one of the new huts. Mabouya came in soon after from across the river accompanied by two of his men. They immediately selected one of the huts closest to the shore and disappeared within it. It was nearly dark when they heard the sound of raucous laughter and a great bellowing cry from the other side of the river.

Bala strutted into the camp with his usual commanding presence. He was closely followed by Cicero, his gun-bearer, holding an old rifle across his chest, its rusted barrel resting in the crook of his left hand. Cicero stayed close to Bala's elbow as if always waiting to hand him his weapon. They were followed by seven more men ebullient with fun and laughter, looking about them as if in total possession. Cork, looking sullen and embittered as usual, was among them. Congoree came out and embraced Bala warmly. He escorted Bala to his assigned hut, but the young chief shook his head sullenly and demanded private quarters separate from his men.

Bala left his men in the common hut and followed Congoree to another close to his own which was occupied by his valet. The boy understood and left hastily. He hardly ever slept in the hut anyway, being always on call to warm Congoree's bed. Tonight, Congoree would not have to summon him. He had nowhere else to go and he would take his customary place at his chief's side. Bala ensconced himself comfortably in the boy's hut and waited for the companion whom he was certain Congoree would send in to him later that night.

It was late when Sandy and Jacco trudged into the camp. They had the longest journey of all coming all the way from the west coast and they were exhausted.

There were only six of them, and they were brought directly to the long open shed where dinner was about to be served. A clamor of greetings came from the assembled guests, which they briefly acknowledged as they dropped gratefully to the dry earth floor and received the first libations of the night.

A number of torches threw a flickering light on the faces around the floor of the shed. Rough planks overlaid with balizier leaves extended from end to end, on which gourds of bush rum and calabash dishes of cool water were placed at intervals. Congoree sat at one end with the other chiefs on both sides of him. His valet, a young, slender, delicately built youth called Romain, stood at his back, solicitously seeing to his wants. Before long, a troupe of women entered the shed and, leaning over the shoulders of the men seated around, emptied platters of roasted pork, smoked agouti and cooked cassava, yam and bananas onto the balizier leaves. Congoree extended his hand and picked up a lean leg of smoked agouti. At this signal the gathering reached out for the savory morsels nearest to them. The women came and sat among the men. In this lightened atmosphere, ribald phrases and risqué stories whirled around the shed, and the laughter and merriment pervading the gathering belied the gravity of the cause that had brought them together.

As if in spontaneous and logical response to the delightful repast that had been provided for them, the men and women moved to the open ground in front of the huts where a drummer already sat, a barrel drum clasped firmly between his thighs. Soon the stirring undulations of the drum beat drew dancing couples to the center and, when the chanting began in earnest, they quickly lost themselves in the mesmeric rhythm of the dance.

Bala withdrew early to his private quarters and, not too long after, the unmistakable sound of his exertions filled the little hut and sometimes intruded in the intermittent silence between the throbbing and resounding music outside. It went on for most of the night. Congoree in his hut next door listened to the sound of Bala's unrelenting and turbulent engagement with mounting excitement. He pulled the delicate form of his little valet closer to him and stroked him tenderly.

The morning broke in brilliant colors over the horizon. The early sun sparkled on the dew-drenched leaves, and the vibrant sounds of birds twittering and cattle lowing mixed with the gentle murmur of the river on one side and the roaring waves of the sea on the other.

Pharcel was up early, and he came out of the hut where Coree Greg and the others of his camp still slept. He stood in the warming air outside, absorbing the brisk energy of the rising sun, and thought he should walk down to the river to refresh himself in one of its clear, deep pools. As he strode across the clearing, he saw Bala standing almost naked at the door of his hut.

Bala was wearing a loin cloth only, and the muscles of his abdomen, arms and legs rippled and glistened in the sunlight. He caught sight of Pharcel and seemed to scowl darkly for a moment, but his face suddenly brightened and he waved invitingly.

"Hey! I know you," he called across the yard. "You are that boy in Coree Greg's camp."

Pharcel was astounded. He had made up his mind to stay out of Bala's way after the cold reception in his camp and the threat from which he had to make such a hasty escape many months ago. He stood hesitantly for a moment wanting to distance himself from the danger that he thought he was in, but Bala was already walking towards him, a friendly smile on his face.

"I have heard of your doings," he said. "You are no longer a boy now; not after those brave executions you carried out."

He came right up to Pharcel and clapped him on the shoulder.

"You are the man I need." He looked at Pharcel appraisingly. "You are wasted among those old men. Come and see me soon. Presente will be glad to see you."

Pharcel nodded, still at a loss for words.

Not far away, Cork listened to the unexpected warmth between his chief and Pharcel. His face darkened and turned even more acerbic when he saw Bala's friendly, almost brotherly gesture towards Pharcel. A consuming jealousy took possession of him. He did not want anyone, not even Cicero, to come between him and his chief. He recalled how Bala had wanted to do away with Pharcel because he had resented his lack of success in seducing the pretty young woman in Coree Greg's camp away from the younger man. Cork had not been able to catch up with Pharcel up to this time, and Bala had dealt with him severely for this failure. And now he would have to watch closely that Pharcel did not supplant him in Bala's favor.

All through the morning Pharcel pondered the sudden turn in Bala's attitude towards him. He had not given much thought to the reprisals he had carried out against Joshua and Brent, but somehow those two natural acts of retaliation seemed to have elevated him in Bala's esteem and apparently had also earned the respect of Paulinaire. He was standing on the bank of the river staring into the dark, glassy surface of a pool when he was startled by movement at his back. He spun around ready to defend himself or to dash to the nearest cover. It was Jacques emerging from the fringe of bushes that lined the bank. He grinned broadly as he handed a polished rifle, its dark barrel gleaming in the sun.

"It is from Paulinaire," he announced grandly. "He sends his compliments and bids you to remember."

Pharcel's eyes widened with excitement as he saw the almost new weapon in Jacques outstretched hand. He reached out eagerly for it, but withdrew his hand abruptly, hesitating. He looked quizzically at Jacques.

"He asked me to remember what?" he asked suspiciously.

"Oh, what he said at the meeting," Jacques reminded him, "that we all must work together."

"Oh, that?" Pharcel grinned. "Our meeting today will decide that."

He reached out again and took hold of the gun. He held it out at arm's length for a while, turning it around in the brightening light and admiring the sleek lines from stock to muzzle. Then cradling the weapon closely to his breast, he turned to Jacques.

"When did you come?" he asked.

"This morning," Jacques replied. "I traveled all night through the lake road. It was tricky evading the patrols up there, the black militiamen especially."

"The meeting will commence soon," Pharcel informed him. "We don't have much time."

They stripped. Pharcel laid the gun carefully on his trousers. Shivering slightly with anticipation of the coolness that the dark, placid water promised, they dived in and thrashed about for a while until their bodies adjusted to the invigorating cold. The sky above them was a clear blue with thin veils of cloud drifting from the hills, but dissipating as they came closer to where the sun was rising. They splashed about the water for a long time before they heard the sound of many voices approaching. They quickly scrambled out, hastily dressed and moved away back towards the camp.

Pharcel was diffident about carrying a gun around the camp. He was particularly concerned about Coree Greg's reaction if he saw him with the weapon; so he did not enter the clearing with Jacques, but, swinging away towards the shore, he searched for a secure place where he could leave it until it was safe to bring it out. He found a piece of the dry fibrous membrane that fell from the upper trunk of a coconut tree and, wrapping the gun, he hid it in the hollow of a fallen tree not far from the last row of huts.

The meeting began with desultory accounts of what they knew of the disposition and strength of the militia in the various districts. Coree Greg expressed concern about the recent government decision to conscript slaves in the colony's militia.

"We will be fighting against our own people," he lamented.

"Anyone that wears the uniform of the white man is not our people!" Bala reposted. "He becomes our enemy."

Nonetheless, it was generally acknowledged that the conscription of blacks in the militia could present difficulties for the camps and that special care had to be taken so that the camps would not be infiltrated by black soldiers purporting to be runaways.

It was when the discussion turned on the proposition from Paulinaire that all blacks and mulattos come together in a common cause to drive the white inhabitants out of the island that the meeting really came to life. Congoree briefly introduced the subject, saying that they had all received emissaries from Paulinaire putting forward his views on how the camps and free blacks and mulattos could work together to mobilize their forces in a quick frontal attack on the white population. Paulinaire had offered guns, ammunition and supplies in aid of the campaign, some of which had already arrived and was stored in safe places in the South. There was no doubt that the camps were poorly armed, and arms and supplies would strengthen their forces to fend off the encroaching encampments of the militia which had made it unsafe for them to traverse their usual routes across the island.

Sandy, standing tall and lean, his long neck exposing his Adam's apple which bobbed up and down as he spoke, was harsh in his comments about consorting with mulattos in any cause. He had hawk-like features which gave him a predatory look, especially as his hooded eyes appeared always half-shut. He leaned forward as he gave an account of a meeting with Paulinaire, his guttural voice adding to the severity of his sarcasm and contempt as he described the character of the mulatto and his egotistic aspirations. They had met at a secret rendezvous in the heights of the Layou valley many weeks ago. Paulinaire had spoken a lot of rubbish about the role of intellectuals in precipitating the revolution in France and the indispensable contribution of the educated blacks and mulattos in freeing Haiti from white rule. In his view Paulinaire spoke with the tongue of a serpent, championing fraternity and equality on the one hand, but on the other hand speaking with words that set him and his mulatto companions apart from the mass of the black people.

"I do not trust any man who adopts the dress and the mannerisms of the white man so faithfully. He wants to be one of them," he ended.

Coree Greg sat silently and listened intently as first Mabouya and then Jacco expressed their suspicion about the motives of the mulatto group. Their cause and the cause of the enslaved could not be the same. Nonetheless they had mutual interest in overthrowing the whites and if Paulinaire and his supporters in Martinique could provide supplies and weapons then they should take advantage of their offer; but in no way would they subject their ranks to control by men who had no knowledge of war and especially of war in the forests. Working with them should not mean subjecting the camps to their control. The runaways were already the dominant group. Together with the slaves in a general uprising, they could defeat the meager legions that were too soft even to venture beyond the safe boundaries of the estates. They should look at what was happening in Haiti. Whatever part the mulattos might have played in the revolt there, Desaline had firmly taken control, and the country was in the hands of the masses.

After that there was a lull in the discussion. Neither Coree Greg nor Bala showed any inclination to speak. Congoree, wanting to keep the discussion alive, suggested that Jacques, being one of Paulinaire's emissaries, should give an appraisal of the resources that the French activists had already brought into the island and his own impressions of Paulinaire's intentions.

There was a long pause before Jacques began to speak. In halting and labored phrases he told of the meetings in Grandbay and the number of French mulattos that had sneaked in to the island to meet with Paulinaire's group. He knew of a cache of weapons and supplies that was hidden somewhere near the southern coast, but he had never found out how much there was or the places where the caches were hidden. Paulinaire was an extraordinary and mysterious man who appeared to keep to his word though his motives were unclear and it was difficult to gauge the depth of his sincerity. Maybe Pharcel, who had also been present at the meeting, would give his own opinion.

At the mention of Pharcel, Coree Greg frowned and looked sharply and searchingly at him. Pharcel tried to evade the old man's accusing eyes, and allowed his gaze to drift around the gathering; but he was disconcerted at the circle of eager faces waiting expectantly for what he had to say. He bowed his head in anguish and stuttered a few random phrases before he finally took hold of himself.

"He wants our help and he embraces us," he said lamely. "But some of his men disrespect the women slaves. He wants to lead, but he does not say what place there is in it for us. They talk only of themselves as the new government."

Pharcel subsided into an awkward silence. He was relieved when Bala thundered an oath that had the entire gathering suddenly galvanized.

Bala leaned forward, his firm, square jaw jutting out in furious challenge. A cold but piercing light flashed from beneath his lowering brow, and one corner of his lips curled into a one-sided sneer.

"What are we doing here," he bellowed, "talking about union with mulattos? Since when have blacks anything in common with the bastards of the white men? Have we forgotten our own history, or the misery and torture that we have been through at the hands of the white men and their yellow-colored overseers and house slaves? Since when do those yellow bastards have anything in common with us? Haven't they spent all their wretched lives trying to be white men? They have failed because all their ranting about equality and fraternity has not brought them anywhere. The white man will not share equality and fraternity with any colored, no matter how pale-skinned he thinks he is. He will not even share equality with those of his own race who are less privileged than he is. That is reality.

"For many years we have carried out our own struggle. We have harried the white men on their estates and driven many of them away. We have done all this, working as separate units. Each chief has secured his territory, and we are on the verge of victory. If we band together now, then we will hasten the end of our struggle. We want arms? They are there for the taking. We will raid the estates. We will snatch them from our enemies. And if necessary we will plunder the caches of the mulattos. But we will have no union of any kind with them.

"Now is the time to show our strength. We are assembled here in a body. Let us show our worth by acting in concert. Let us begin by destroying Rosalie Estate and sending a clear message to the white man and to those presumptuous mulattos.

"We have spoken enough words. Let us now do something meaningful together."

There was stunned silence when Bala sat upright again and smiled benignly on the assembly. Before any applause could begin, Coree Greg spoke in a low, level voice.

"My younger brother and I speak with one voice," he said. "We do not want anything to do with mulattos. I have seen too many betrayals in my life, and it would be foolish to lay myself open to more."

He paused and looked around at the ardent faces hanging on his every word. Bala turned a quizzical look at him, wondering what new cunning was in the old man's mind. Coree Greg lifted his face, lined with a life time of weariness, as if studying the thick thatch that formed the roof over his head.

"But let us not be hasty in our decisions," he continued evenly. "We have lived quietly in the woods, and our camps have been a haven for all those who have succeeded in gaining their freedom. Our numbers are growing, but we are not yet strong. I feel in my bones that the time will come when the mass of all blacks will rise in spontaneous revolt. That time is not yet come. Let us be patient and send the message out to all our enslaved brethren that they can gird themselves for the hour of their deliverance. Now is not the time for impetuous sallies against the strength of the white men. Even the mulattos recognize the need to build our strength in unity, though I do not accept that they have any place in our final destiny."

He looked around again at the expectant faces.

"We are all brave men," he said, "and brave men do not have to act rashly."

"But only cowards ignore the tide of opportunity," Bala roared. "Do we have to wait for mulattos to stir us to action? We are here together. Let us plan an immediate assault that will herald the start of our campaign!"

His words were greeted with tumultuous acclamation, though there were murmurs of dissent coming from some of the older men. Bala beamed at the eager faces around him.

"Then it is settled," he said triumphantly.

"Yes, it is settled," Coree Greg replied with sullen resignation. "But my men and I will have no part in this madness."

"I am sorry to hear that, old man," Bala sneered. Then he turned expansively to the rest of the gathering. "We have time to plan and prepare. Let us send word to the camps near by for as many men as can be available to gather near the Rosalie River four nights from now."

The meeting came to an end suddenly. There was still some time before lunch could be served.

Pharcel was in a quandary. He had personally met and spoken with Paulinaire and had been won over by his vast knowledge and the high principles he appeared to espouse. He did not altogether trust the group of mulattos, but Paulinaire had shown himself to be considerate, tactful and a man of his word. Even though his motive in wanting to collaborate with the chiefs were not completely altruistic, he appeared sincere in his efforts to mobilize the strongest force to carry out a general revolt against the white population. He had reached out to them with promises of support and resources which the slaves and the runaways could not ever hope to assemble themselves. And now the meeting had roundly rejected him and his offer. And he, Pharcel, had been too tongue-tied to stand as an advocate for the man who had confided in him and who had demonstrated his sincerity by sending him his own personal musket.

To add to his confusion, Coree Greg had turned a cold shoulder at him after the meeting. Pharcel had not told him of his last meeting with Paulinaire because he had been reluctant to bring up any matter regarding the mulatto after the curt dismissal he had received that first time. Jacques' untimely revelation of their involvement with Paulinaire had taken him off-guard and had plainly angered Coree Greg. After the meeting the old man had gone to his hut attended only by Hall. Pharcel came in soon after and found them gathering their belongings in preparation for departure.

"You seem to have many secrets," Coree Greg said to him with suppressed anger. "On whose side are you?"

"I should have told you," Pharcel had muttered.

"It is too late."

Coree Greg turned away. He collected his few articles, and stood still for a few moments, his eyes downcast, his narrow shoulders slumped as if a great weight had descended on him. Turning to Hall he laid his hand on his shoulder.

"We will leave immediately after lunch," he decided. "That should get us home before nightfall."

Then he spoke over his shoulder to Pharcel.

"You may stay if you wish," he said darkly, "but I warn you not to follow this rashness."

Pharcel stayed in the hut long after Coree Greg had left it. His mind was in turmoil as it swung around the rationality of Coree Greg's caution, the boldness of Bala's call for present action, and Paulinaire's ideas about programmed unity among all colored people and an organized campaign against the white government. He trusted the wisdom of Coree Greg, and he wanted to follow him; but he found the stirring challenge put forward by Bala irresistible. Also, in the face of this valiant call to action, the philosophical ramblings of Paulinaire about equality and fraternity appeared superfluous and irrelevant. If they could snatch victory now, what did it matter about changing men's minds on the issues of equality and fraternity? Those issues would no longer arise since the black man would be free and equal and belonging to the same black brotherhood.

He was still groping in the confusion of his thoughts when Petit Jacques entered the hut. He looked at Pharcel with surprise and some disquiet as his restless eyes darted to every corner of the hut.

"You're still here?" Pharcel asked.

"I thought you'd be gone," Petit Jacques replied evasively.

"I wanted to stay," Pharcel said earnestly. "This is too important to miss."

"They have started preparations," Petit Jacques informed him. "The chiefs are gathered in the shed."

The meeting went on till sunset. It had been like a war council. The chiefs sat in a tight circle with only Cicero, Jacques and Romain in attendance. Romain stood doggedly behind Congoree, his eyes steadfastly observing every movement that his chief made and responding to them at the slightest signal. The other men sat outside wherever they could find shade within the clearing, waiting for their chiefs to summon them. Pharcel sat among them.

Dinner was served immediately after the meeting ended, the chiefs being served where they sat at the meeting place, and the men out in the open. The drums began to beat just after dinner. The chiefs came out of the shed and sat on logs in the middle of the clearing while their followers lounged wherever they could find dry stones or patches of grass close by.

It was already late when Rosay, slim, black and handsome, whirled in the center and began a dance which, in raw eroticism, exceeded all those that had gone before. As she began a slow skipping around the circle, the deep ebony of her skin shone in the light of the torches and the whites of her eyes and the brilliant flashes of her pearly, closely set and regular teeth contrasted with the glossy blackness of her face. Her lips were sensuously full and liver-colored and seemed to pout and part invitingly as she twirled around the circle of men. She wore a knee-length, loose-fitting dress which ballooned out and rose higher and higher up her thighs as she twirled and thrashed and swayed her body in rippling convolutions around the small circle.

Sandy joined her in the middle. He was a graceful dancer, and his long legs and arms easily picked up the rhythm of her dance. As the drums rose in tempo their legs shuffled and their tense bodies quivered and writhed in uninhibited rapture that had the audience spell-bound and breathless. It was as if Rosay had been transported to a world of pure sensual desire as she threw her head backwards, her face reaching up to the stars, breasts jutting out like an offering, bare thighs flashing darkly beneath her raised skirt. She appeared lost in the violence of her passion until at last, naked up to the shaded juncture of her thighs, she collapsed helplessly on the drummer. Sandy reached out to hold her and led her, breathing heavily, beads of sweat running down her face, to the select group where the chiefs sat.

Bala grabbed her hand and drew her to his side.

CHAPTER 11

Coree Greg's mind was disturbed. He could not understand why he had been unable to sway the meeting away from the rash decision it had come to. He thought he had put the case clearly and convincingly that the camps should first consolidate their resources and prepare for a grand assault before attempting any major aggression against the white planters. But the reaction against Paulinaire's invitation to join forces with the mulatto group had been so strong that it had stirred the current of contempt and hate that was never too far below the surface, to that surging wave of determination that had driven them on their present course. He understood that for most of them, especially Bala and Sandy, it was a matter of pride that they should not appear to be powerless to manage their own affairs; and most of all, that they should not be upstaged by a bunch of pretentious mulattos. It came to him suddenly that he was no longer in cinch with the rest, and that his authority as an elder and an esteemed warrior was not as respected as it was in the past. A gloom of weariness that was only partly physical descended on him as he labored up the twisting path to the summit of the precipitous mountain. In the cloud of despair that suddenly settled over him, he felt the heaviness of age and the futility of a vision that had diminished in its definition and purpose.

Even in his own camp he seemed to have suddenly become irrelevant and a burdensome anachronism. For many years they had gathered around him, the few men and women who had drifted to the sanctuary of the small community that he had established in the forest. Unlike the other chiefs, he had not set out to build a combative encampment, a base from which to wage war on the white planters. He wanted only to establish a viable community of independent blacks, secure in the woods and undisturbed by unnecessary conflict with the outside world. He had welcomed many into his camp, but over the years he had seen most of them drift away to the more convivial and riotous living that the other camps provided. Those who had remained had entrusted themselves entirely to his care and protection, and he had not failed them. For the most part their loyalty was unquestionable, and there had never been any cause for concern until the

125

viper of doubt and suspicion had raised its menacing head at the culmination of the morning's meeting.

The revelation that Pharcel had been plotting with Paulinaire and his group of mulattos was particularly galling, and he had been embarrassed beyond words that a member of his camp should be in league with forces outside his control and without his knowledge. He had known from the beginning that he had to be circumspect about his dealings with Pharcel. The boy was brave and undoubtedly intelligent, but he was from Guinea stock and his nation was known to be unpredictable and perfidious. Coree Greg did not believe that Pharcel had acted out of deliberate disloyalty. He had no reason to doubt his sincerity and honesty; but he had observed the restlessness in his eyes; and he had known that he could not for long suppress the unexpressed yearning that showed in the younger man's look, a yearning that would only be satisfied by adventure and action. Thus he was not surprised when Pharcel lingered after the end of the meeting before coming to him, nor was he in any way jolted by the eagerness with which he accepted the suggestion that he could remain behind for the rest of the meeting.

He hoped that Pharcel would heed his warning and not rush into any impetuous action that would be sure to lead to strong and punitive retaliation by the white authorities. But he doubted that the vibrant spirit of his youthful protégé, already charged with revolutionary fervor and illusions of equality and fraternity within easy reach could resist the grandiloquent sentiments and lofty visions of war and conquest that he was certain surrounded the later discourses of Bala and his warlike companions.

He had instructed Petit Jacques to stay behind to observe the preparations that were being made, and he also cautioned him about joining any dangerous raids on the estates. He had expected some degree of concern or disappointment on the part of Petit Jacques at his decision to leave him behind, but the little man's bland and shifty-eyed response made Coree Greg wonder if he, too, had been impassioned by Bala's call for immediate war. Petit Jacques was an excellent woodsman and a brave fighter, though he was never sure of his dependability, loyalty and steadfastness of purpose.

As he came to the crest of the hill, the full brilliance of the sun lit up the landscape before him in its fullest splendor. On all sides the land dropped precipitously. The plateau where he stood was no larger than a plot surrounding a normal-sized hut. Southwards, the land angled steeply for about two hundred yards, and then leveled in a broad sweep of forest that curved outwards until it was lifted by the far away mountains. Behind him, several hundred feet below, the plain of low trees upswept by the ocean breeze stretched to the shore on one side and to the rising hills on the other. Down the center of the plain the broad river in frolicsome turns and tumbles made its way to the sea. Looking seaward, the deep undulating blue of the ocean broke into foam-flecked waves that rolled in incessantly from the far distance where the smoke-grey outline of Martinique hovered on the horizon.

A strong breeze blew at the top, and Coree Greg and Hall paused for a few minutes in the sparse shade of a stunted tree. Streams of sweat ran down their chest and back into the soaked waist of their trousers. It was still a long way to sunset, though the sun was already poised not too high up over the top of the mountains beyond. They would have time to get to familiar terrain well before darkness set in. They began the steep down-hill climb scrambling from tree to tree until they came to flatter ground. From there the track opened out in a well-used path that would take them to the boundary of Bagatelle. It would be an easy walk until they had to make a diversion through the woods to camp.

Though the path had leveled out to a gentle gradient they were still high up above the sea. The inner side of the path was lined with a row of sparse trees emerging out of a field of guinea grass; and only a few feet beyond, the dark forest crouched as if waiting to repossess the cleared terrain. On the other side the land dropped precipitously to the sea two hundred feet below. Thick, tangled brush overhung the edge so that the sharp fall was hidden from view.

Coree Greg had returned to his thoughts. Just ahead of him Hall trudged forward, his compact, muscular body swinging easily, his cutlass held loosely in the crook of one arm. It was at the time of day when nature seemed to pause for breath. Except the muffled pounding of the surf a long way below, only the intermittent melody of the mountain whistler broke the silence. The air was still. No birds flittered in the trees, and no breath of wind disturbed the drooping leaves.

As they came around a wide bend, a brief crackle broke the silence. Hall stopped instantly, his body tense and alert. Coree Greg looked about quickly, listening for the slightest sound of movement in the thick cover of grass beside them. They had already straightened up and eased the tension from their bodies when they heard the explosion. Coree Greg threw himself sideways through the thick tangle of brush. He felt himself hurtling a long way down, and he thought for a moment that he would crash onto the rocky base of the precipice and into the pounding surf. His body jolted in pain as he slammed into the angle of a large tree clinging precariously to the stony cliff. He remained still, his fingers grasping the loose shale around the base of the tree. He could hear loud voices and two more explosions coming through the overhanging bush several feet above him. Below him the surf thundered on the rocks incessantly.

A long silence ensued, followed by a string of expletives and violent exchanges. Then the silence returned. He stayed motionless for several minutes before easing himself gently upright, his back against the cliff, his feet anchored securely on the base of the tree. He flexed his arms and his legs, but except for a dull pain on his hip he felt no sign of injury. Looking cautiously around, he saw that the face of the cliff extended on both sides and was almost bare of vegetation except for a few scraggly plants that hung insecurely in loose soil. Below him he could see past an overhang of rock the heaving swell of the sea; and above, rough tangled brush hanging over the edge of the path. Lean, scantily leaved trees clung to the rocky face at intervals. Only a few large trees, widely spaced, held tenaciously to the craggy surface. He turned his face to the cliff, feeling the base of the tree on which he stood, firm and secure. Reaching upward, he grasped one of the smaller trees directly above him, testing its strength. Loose stones and sand splattered on his face, but the tree was securely rooted in tight fissures in the grainy rock. For a long while he studied the pattern of growth of the small trees, tracing a course up to the margin of coarse brush above. He had to make the attempt. If he slipped, he knew that he would not be saved again by the same large tree. It could be certain death in the crashing waves below.

He tested his weight carefully against the strength of the sapling; then heaved himself slowly, his bare toes digging into the crumbling surface. Painfully he crawled upwards, from one tenuous stem to another, dislodging showers of loose soil and stones which fell soundlessly to the depths below him. Near the top, as he grabbed on to another stem, a large slab of shale loosened from its root and slammed into his shoulder. The sudden pain caused him to loosen his hold, but he quickly grasped for an exposed root, took hold of it and drew himself up. Pausing weakly, he gasped for breath.

He was not too far from the top. Two more trees upwards and he would be able to reach the more sturdy brush at the edge of the path. He stayed perched on the narrow angle of the tree against the barely sloping side of the precipice, listening intently for any sound. It was deathly quiet except for the now distant sound of the surge. He reached out again at the height above him and, holding on to the nearest tree, he strained against it, his feet trying to gain purchase in the loose soil. Then he heard it, a low groan coming from above on his left. He clung to the slender tree listening fearfully.

He found Hall suspended on the strong but pliant branches of the brush a few feet below the path. Drops of blood trickled from his side. The brush formed a thick cover, and was rooted firmly in the crumbly soil. Coree Greg crawled through the tangled branches until he lay flat against the side of the cliff close to

Hall's shoulder, his body supported by the strong stems. Wordlessly, he extended his hand and pressed his fingers into Hall's arm. Hall turned an agonized face to him, but he remained silent. They stayed where they were until nightfall. Certain that their assailants would no longer be there, they began a slow climb to the edge. Although the land above them sloped gradually upwards, offering a more secure footing for their climb, the thick enmeshed branches made it difficult to crawl through, and Hall was having difficulty pulling through the thick meshes. Carefully Coree Greg turned him over and, placing his arm under the shoulder of his good side, he dragged him through the low branches until they came to the top.

Hall's injury was severe but not fatal, but the anxiety to get out of the precarious edge had stirred him to move on his own strength. They lay in the thick brush watching the path as the light faded. There were no sounds or movements except for the birds settling in the trees nearby and ground creatures scuttling to their nests or burrows.

"Can you make it into those woods?" Coree Greg asked, looking critically at Hall's face and indicating the thick cover of forest in the background across the path.

Hall grimaced at the pain in his side, but he nodded bravely.

"Then let's make a dash for it," he urged.

They slithered out of the brush and paused briefly to glance up and down the path before bolting across and into the field of guinea grass. There they crouched low as they ran through the field until they came to the dark cover of the forest. Only the swishing of the long blades of grass marked their passage. There was hardly any undergrowth beneath the trees, and they were able to move quickly until they came to a hollow through which a shallow stream dipped and turned before it disappeared over a fall. Above the stream a giant chataignier spread its thickly-leaved branches over a wide patch of ground. The base of the tree extended to slab-like distensions that began at a height taller than an average man and descended diagonally to run horizontally two or more feet above ground for several yards. The hollows formed at the base of the tree provided shelter for roaming animals, and were a favorite nest for boa constrictors and other reptiles. Coree Greg inspected them quickly. They were dry, empty and safe. He helped Hall to sit in one of them; then leaned him over on his good side while he inspected the wound.

The bullet had chipped a lower rib below Hall's right shoulder. The wound was painful and was still dripping blood, but it would not be fatal unless the blood flow was not stemmed or the abrasion became infected. Coree Greg dug into the black soil near the edge of the stream and moved away the topsoil until he came to yellow clay below. Scooping out a handful, he molded it to a plastic softness and flattened it to form a plaster which he spread over the wound. He searched and found nearby the broad leaf of a balizier tree and removing the central rib to make the leaf more pliant, he wrapped it around Hall's abdomen, securely covering the plaster and the entire area of the wound. He kept the plaster and its covering in place with lengths of vine tied firmly above and below them.

"That will keep it clean until we get to camp," he said comfortingly.

He sat in a hollow next to Hall. They were both silent for several minutes as if the recent crisis had left them disoriented and they were still trying to find their bearings. The full horror of what he had just been through came back to Coree Greg. He relived briefly the moment when he had held precariously to the edge of the precipice with the turbulent sea crashing on the rocks and the bare sides of the cliff a hundred feet below him, and the agonizing climb from sapling to sapling until he came to the relative security of the brush. After a while he turned to Hall.

"Did you see those men?" he asked him.

"I made out only one," Hall replied somberly, "a slave from the Langston estate not too far from here."

"I thought the white man who shot looked like Dixon, the white overseer on the Pendleton estate; but I can't be sure," Coree Greg said.

"There were only two white men," Hall returned.

"The French planters would not bother us in this way, so they must be English," Coree Greg surmised.

"There was not time enough to recognize anyone of them with certainty," Hall replied cautiously. "All I thought about at the time was to get away."

"We are lucky," Coree Greg nodded his head wonderingly. "They must think we plunged all the way over the precipice."

Hall shifted uncomfortably as the clay began to tighten around his wound. Coree Greg looked at him solicitously.

"I had better fetch some water."

He moved down to the stream, broke off the wide leaf of a wild tuber that grew on its banks, and formed it into a scoop which he dipped into the stream. He brought it to Hall and held it to his lips as he drank. Then he drained the rest of the cool water down his throat. As the chill hit his stomach, he suddenly remembered that they had not eaten since mid day. They would both be hungry and there was nothing to eat. Had it not been for this unprovoked assault they would have made camp and they would now be resting on a full stomach. He felt a growing anger at their situation. Here they were hiding in the forest without food. They had been almost killed. The irony of the situation struck him forcibly. Bala and the others were out there planning war while he had been the only one advocating moderation. He was a man of peace, wanting only to be free and to be let alone in the privacy of his existence. Yet here he was hiding like a hunted beast. To be set upon like this by two white men and their slaves was an affront not easily appeased. After all, he was a warrior of the Kingdom of the Kongo and he could not let this humiliation go unavenged. He had to do something if only to preserve the dignity and honor of his camp. With these dark thoughts he fell into a fitful sleep. Beside him Hall turned restlessly as his wound festered.

In the morning Hall burned with fever. He was weak and dispirited; and the crude plaster had dried to a rigid form that chafed the already painful and sensitive wound. He sat up with difficulty, groaning with the pain and discomfort. Coree Greg removed the dressing to uncover the inflamed and suppurating laceration. The bleeding had stopped, but the wound was already getting discolored and was oozing an unhealthy fluid. He had to get Hall back to camp in the shortest possible time. That would be difficult since they could not continue along the path where they had been attacked. The only safe way was through the woods and across the difficult terrain of steep hills and precipitous gorges. He wondered if Hall could survive such an ordeal, but it was the only way to get safely back. Though Coree Greg was familiar with the area, he did not know his way through the forest as well as Petit Jacques did, and for a moment he regretted having left the little man behind. He braced himself for the strenuous journey ahead.

All day they plodded up and down the steep sides of hills that seemed to twist and turn in a maze-like pattern. It was as if some humongous centripetal force had squeezed the land on all sides, leaving broken ridges and sunken gorges choked with dense, green vegetation. The floor of the forest was alive with the sound of scuttling creatures, and the overspreading branches above fluttered with the swift and almost indiscernible flittering of a multitude of birds. On all sides the pungent smell of toxic herbs and decaying vegetation assailed their nostrils.

Hall staggered along stoically, pausing at every stream to drink its cool, clear water, trying to subdue the fever that burned at his wounded side. At last they came to a ridge which looked familiar. Looking through a gap in the thick foliage, Coree Greg thought he recognized a clearing on a high hill in the far distance. It was still a long way off, and the light had already faded among the trees. They found a dry spot beneath an outcropping of rock on the bank of a ravine, and settled there for the night.

The lulling sound of the shallow stream that flowed through the ravine soon put them to sleep, but later, the sound of Hall's groans and delirious cries broke the silence of the night. Coree Greg lay beside him feeling the heat of his body and the sweat that ran profusely down his neck and chest. There was nothing he could do except to keep chafing his companion's shivering arms and legs. It was a long night, and sleep came fitfully until the morning broke. Coree Greg supported Hall as best he could, plunging recklessly down the ravine, crawling under huge, fallen tree trunks, and climbing over distended roots that occasionally formed low barriers across their path. They came out of the woods to the clearing near midday and Coree Greg saw that they were on a grassy plateau above the valley where his camp was located. He would have to descend a hill, and a short distance from there the outer end of the narrow ravine led to the camp.

Hall was almost limp in his arms when he dragged him through the ravine. As they staggered into the camp, Claire raised her eyebrows questioningly; but she quickly understood the look of exhaustion and distress on her husband's face. She examined Hall's wound clinically and nodded knowingly to Coree Greg. She called out to Genevieve and Marie-Claire to come in and assist her. Together they placed Hall on the wide mat stretched at one side of Coree Greg's hut, and set about boiling water and gathering medicinal herbs and roots. The three women ministered to Hall for a long time while Coree Greg and a few of the men who had gathered after they had heard of their chief's return, looked on helplessly. It was many hours before Coree Greg could eat and stretch himself out on the bare ground beside Hall. He slept the night secure in his hut, his wife holding him closely to her breast.

Hall's fever had abated and he was sound asleep. The rest of the camp—men, women and children—gathered outside Coree Greg's hut as he sat on his customary bench and spoke to them about the meeting in Congoree's camp and the decision that the other chiefs had arrived at concerning the message from Paulinaire. They were annoyed when he related the debate on whether or not the time had come for immediate and independent action by the camps. They trusted Coree Greg's judgment, and were fully in support of the position he had taken. As for Pharcel, they had known that he could not be trusted, and many wondered if he should be allowed to return to camp. But all pacific thoughts were thrown aside as Coree Greg told with mounting anger about the ambush that had been laid to capture Hall and him. There was a general outcry for revenge, and both men and women expressed vociferously their determination to avenge the injury that had been done to Hall. Coree Greg nodded in satisfaction.

"We will have our revenge," he said solemnly. "Prepare yourselves for tomorrow night."

It was a solemn group that crept through the forest, moving like shadows in
the dark of the night. They had left Marie-Claire to attend to Hall and the children. The rest of them, men and women, armed with machetes, clubs, axes and
unlighted torches, moved with silent purpose through the woods and down to
the narrow coastal strip where the lands of Pendleton and Langston adjoined.
They walked through the gloom of the night and headed to the low depression
where a decaying estate house and a miserable cluster of slave huts that comprised
the Pendleton establishment lay hidden from view. A deep-voiced hound barked
in the night which prompted them to rush the remaining distance to the house.
In swift, decisive order, they lit their torches, and set fire to the four corners of the
house. The hound was leaping frantically from one end of the yard to the other,
barking ferociously, but too confused to attack any of the intruders. They
retreated to the shadows of a row of trees that bordered the yard, and watched the
flames creep up the sides of the building and then leap to the dry, shingled roof.
The house was already engulfed when Dixon appeared at the door, his gun pointing uncertainly at the darkness beyond. Seeing the danger, he leapt back into the
house and soon emerged again dragging his bewildered and screaming wife out of
the house.

The whole operation had been conducted quickly and soundlessly. Only the
barking of the hound gave any indication that hostile forces were about. Soon,
the confused faces of a dozen slaves came out of the huts, staring blankly at the
roaring conflagration that used to be Dixon's residence. They made no move to
put out the fire, but stood in miserable consternation as they watched Dixon and
his wife helpless in the face of the disaster that had so suddenly visited them.
None of them saw the obscure and shifting forms at the periphery of the yard disappear into the night.

Over the top of the depression and in a closed-in dell lay the Langston estate.
The main house sat in an open meadow, its front verandah looking out to the
sea. Perched on the slope above it, crude huts nestled under the shade of breadfruit and mango trees. A small stream ran at the base of the slope, through the
open field and down to the shore. The small community was already alive with
commotion. A few slaves ran about excitedly from their huts to the house, while
others huddled at the edge of the meadow, waiting for some indication of what
new danger lurked in the night.

Langston stood restlessly on the step down from the verandah, looking
towards the top of the mound above him where a mushrooming cloud of smoke

was rising to the sky. He held a gun closely to his chest as he looked anxiously about. Two slaves, armed with cutlasses, stood beside him. The silence hung suspended over the dell as if all creatures had paused breathless, waiting for the unknown.

Langston began an uneasy pacing up and down the yard. His two attendants looked wild-eyed and fearful at every shifting shade among the trees around them. The tension was almost palpable in its intensity and the deep quiet stirred a disturbing restiveness among the frightened group huddling near the bottom of the slope. Then a light flared as the thatch of one hut suddenly burst into flames. First one and then another, until the slope was ablaze with fire. Many of the slaves rushed towards the burning huts, carried away by an instinctive urge to protect their scant possessions; but most of them rushed in fear to the opposite side of the dell where close stands of coffee and cocoa trees gave them cover. Langston stood his ground shooting blindly at every movement real or imagined.

The blow came out of the dark. A rock as big as a fist struck Langston with such force that he flipped over onto his back and lay senseless on the ground below the verandah. His two attendants looked wildly around the burning slope, then dropping their cutlasses they fled into the nearby fields. Coree Greg came out of the trees and walked leisurely towards the house. His followers set their torches to the four corners and stood back as the flames rose into a roaring blaze. One of the men pulled Langston's inert body away from the heat and the flames, and left him in the middle of the meadow. He walked away with Langston's gun. As silently as they had come, the group of men and women vanished into the night.

It was not till morning that they discovered that Genevieve had not returned. In the elation of their triumphant march back to camp they had not noticed her absence. Two days later, word reached the camp that she had been captured on the road leading from Bagatelle. Somewhere in the dash into the woods she had lagged behind and, fearful of being lost, had returned to the road and ambled along the coast searching for familiar territory. She was apprehended by a gang leader who had been rushing in the direction of the clouds of smoke. At first she had not thought she was in any danger, seeing he was a slave, until she saw the whip rolled up at his waist. In panic she plunged into a nearby bush, but he quickly leapt on her and had her subdued.

Captain Marshall received his second captive with mixed feelings. Here he was, with an entire regiment under his control, with responsibility to clear the woods of a band of mostly unarmed runaways, and all he had done was receive two captured women, one so badly mauled that he had been hesitant in sending her to the authorities in the capital; and now the other, helpless and unarmed except for an unlighted torch. He was even more reluctant to send this overwhelming proof of his vigilance and martial skills to his already dissatisfied and cynical superiors at Fort Young. Nonetheless, he could not keep her in his barracks, so he made arrangements to dispatch her with a small escort to the town where the Council and the Court could deal with her suitably.

Coree Greg was dismayed at the disappearance of Genevieve. As he sat with his men going over the events of the previous night, his mind drifted to the night many years ago when a strange, bruised and forlorn woman had staggered into his camp, her thin garments torn and ripped in several places and revealing the ravishing attractiveness of her young and curvaceous body. He had taken immediately to her, and went out of his way to look after her comfort. That had been a difficult time with Claire. With time, however, they had found implicit acceptance of the triangular relationship. Claire ignored whatever infatuation that might have driven him to the young woman's hut as long as he took his place beside her at nightfall. Now for many years they had lived serenely without the disturbing passions of the past.

He listened to his men gloating over the deeds of the night. They were full of satisfaction that they had redeemed the honor of their camp. Coree Greg shared their glory and exaltation, though the loss of Genevieve continued to lower his spirit. It was not until Hall came out in the sunshine, still wan and unsteady on his feet, but standing erect and proud, that his spirit rose within him.

"We've done it, Hall," he said exultantly. "We have taken our own back!"

He had no way of knowing that coincident with his mild act of retaliation, a major and brutal act of revenge was being perpetrated on the other side of the mountains that loomed so heavily above them, an act of vengeance that would shake the very foundations of white colonial society and that would set the stage for half century of bitter and violent confrontation between the white planters and the runaway camps. It would be a bitter and unequal struggle that would result in many deaths and that would eventually lead to the creation of dark and mystifying legends surrounding the principal actors.

CHAPTER 12

It was a bright, cloudless and cool morning and there was that special solemnity that always descended on the town on Sundays. Streams of people dressed in their fineries walked solemnly to the churches that stood stolidly above the town. The little Anglican Church was already filled, and more people, even those of the Catholic Church, were filling the belfry searching with anxious eyes for a space in the pews where they could be squeezed in. Rev. Peters would be preaching again. He had delivered a sermon to a half-filled church the Sunday before that had disturbed the entire town. Those who had not been there came today to hear for themselves the radically provocative views of the little scholar from the elitist society of Oxford University.

The congregation spilled over the lawn at the front and one side of the church. On the other side, among the few gravestones that were scattered in the small burial ground, a crowd of black faces crowded the windows, unable to find a place in the belfry as they usually did, and looking in as best they could. Slaves and black freedmen were standing together.

The crowd inside sat restlessly through the introductory part of the service. Although the morning was cool outside, the unusual press of people generated a heat inside that brought out beads of sweat on the ruddy faces of the men, and moistened the carefully powdered and rouged faces of the women who sought relief in the frantic movement of their fans. At last, Rev. Peters mounted the pulpit to deliver his homily. His eyes gleamed with holy satisfaction as they scanned the crowd of faces stretching out on all sides and rising to the chancery. There was a hush of expectation as he raised his eyes to the vaulted ceiling as if seeking inspiration from the heavens. Then lowering his head, a beam of welcome lighting his aristocratic countenance, his arms extended theatrically, he began his sermon.

He thanked his congregation for coming out in such large numbers. It seemed evident that the divine wisdom that had guided him to speak a message of truth last Sunday must have touched their hearts and awakened in them an awareness of the natural humanity which was given to all men at the hour of their birth. He wished to explore further the theme of his last sermon—the responsibility of masters towards their servants and slaves. He surveyed what he thought were the eager faces around him, missing completely the dark scowls which had appeared on the faces of most of the men.

With masterly elocution, he exhorted his flock to be just and fair to their servants even as they would expect the divine master to be fair and just to themselves.

"Masters," he intoned, "give unto your servants that which is just and equal knowing that ye also have a master in Heaven."

He paused to allow the profundity of his declaration to sink in the minds of his audience. He was a dapper little man with the refined features of a scholar. As he spoke he moved beside the lectern to lean over the edge of the pulpit. He looked remarkably elegant in his new and elaborate gown, and faced his audience with supreme confidence as should be expected of an esteemed Fellow of Queens College, Oxford. With his habitual scholarly eloquence, he continued his sermon, the inflexion of his voice rising and falling in harmony with his impassioned words.

He spoke at length about the relationship between masters and their servants, putting forward the ideal of a principle that gave privileged and superior persons the unalterable responsibility to look after the well-being of those less privileged and economically and intellectually less endowed than themselves, especially their unfortunate servants; and binding them to a charter of social justice that left no room for human exploitation in any form whatsoever.

"The relation which subsists between masters and servants originates in a principle so intimately blended with the welfare and indeed so essential to the very existence of civil society that it requires little depth of reasoning or research to trace it to its source; it is sufficient, therefore, for me to observe upon this head that as long as some members of every political community shall continue to excel others in strength, in skill, in application, in economy or in judgment, and as long as it shall be permitted to the individuals thus excelling to transmit the fruits of their honest and meritorious exertions to the lineal or collateral descendants, so long must it unavoidably happen that one portion of mankind will abound with the comforts and what we want to term the superfluities of life while another (and that comparatively greater part) will possess scarcely any other property than such as they are in the habit of acquiring by their daily labors.

"The basis, then, for the connection between master and servants being thus evidently established by nature or (what is virtually the same) by the judgment of laws of civil society, it remains only for me to enforce some of the most important duties which natural and revealed religion has annexed to the respective stations."

By this time the congregation had become quite fidgety, due in part to the rising heat which came from the press of bodies which filled the church, but also partly because the circumlocutory discourse had already gone past their rudimentary understanding, and they were hearing words that in some elusive way sounded critical of them. Colonial plantation society of the time was never renowned for its intellectual sophistication, and the elegance of language used by this scholarly rector was more than they had been accustomed to, and more than they could feel comfortable with. They began to glance questioningly at each other as he continued to speak.

Then his discourse hit directly on the condition of slaves and the treatment accorded to them by their masters. While he did not go as far as condemning the practice of slavery itself, there was no doubt in anyone's mind that he deplored the condition in which slaves were held, and held the slave owners to account for not treating their slaves fairly and humanely as should be expected of every Christian person.

"One of the first and indispensable duties required of every colonial proprietor or manager of slaves is to adopt the most judicious and equitable regulations for the purpose of providing them with the means of comfortable subsistence.

"I do not hesitate to express an entire conviction that a state of servitude (both voluntary and involuntary) would have been positively forbidden by the Supreme Lawgiver had not that state been in its own nature alike conducive to the happiness of the employed and the employer."

A low murmur began at the back of the church among the mostly journeymen and artisans, standing there. Rev. Peters, not understanding the nature of the disturbance, raised his arm for silence and continued in firm and commanding tone.

"It is evidently the design of Providence that the laboring part of every community should derive from their exertions advantages in a great measure proportionate to the services which they perform, and because, secondly, the laborers in the present instance depend exclusively for the satisfaction of their wants on the care and kindness of their masters."

Among the slaves at the windows, an excited whispering began as some of the literate and more intelligent freedmen gave in more simple terms the meaning of the earnest rector's dissertation. Many of them gaped in wonderment at the small figure of the man who had so bravely come to them preaching a message of hope. They continued to gaze open-mouthed as the rector heartily came to the hiatus of his homily.

"I hesitate not to declare from the full conviction of my soul that in the eventual hour when I shall stand before the tribunal of my Heavenly Judge to answer for every deed which I have done I would infinitely rather appear before him as the murderer of my own brother than as the quondam master of a gang of slaves some of whom the dictates of my inhuman avarice had year after year condemned to an untimely grave."

At this point the murmuring had spread to the entire congregation. Those at the back began a loud clamor; and cries of "Bloody Republican!" were thrown irreverently down the nave of the church. A few men rushed to the group of slaves, now confused and frightened, and drove them from the windows and out into the street. It began to dawn on the unfortunate rector that somehow the logic of his sermon was lost to his congregation and that he had succeeded only in rousing the ire of those that he had so ardently hoped to convince by his rational arguments. Nonetheless, he continued doggedly though with less enthusiasm and confidence.

"Unless, therefore, we can bring with us to the Lord's Table a temper of mind inclining us to the practice of universal charity we are evidently unmeet to be partakers of this holy supper."

If Rev. Peters had hoped that he could calm his audience with the threat of excommunication, however temporary, he had made a gross miscalculation. Rows of men and women stood and turned their backs on him, jostling each other to get out of the building as quickly as possible. The rector paused uncertainly, looking at the diminishing crowd with dismay. He faltered for a few moments, and looked appealingly at the remaining faces that were regarding him now with a mixture of pity and reproach. He faced the crowd with ruthless determination as he continued his sermon.

"But on what grounds do men pretend to establish a distinction so unfavorable to the slave? Are we to draw this conclusion from the peculiar formation of his body or his mind? I must needs confess for my own part that I find nothing either in the pages of the Gospel or in the history of Human Nature which in the least warrants such an inference.

"To make, therefore, the dependent and helpless state of negroes a pretense for deducting from their comforts or for endangering their health is at once to violate one of the most plain and peremptory commands of natural religion and to manifest a disposition diametrically opposite to the spirit of the Gospel."

Perhaps if the entire congregation had remained to listen to the conclusion of the rector's homily, the consequences of his daring and unusually scholarly and critical diatribe would not have been so severe. Even among those who stayed and suffered to the end, his message seemed to have left only a stunned and coldly embarrassed condition of mind. At the end of the service most of them slunk through the side door, avoiding any word or contact with him. He understood then that, contrary to his noble and high-minded intentions, he had managed to fall irredeemably to the lowest depth of public detestation and that, in this small and backward society, his erudite and well-intentioned homily would certainly earn for him a disreputable record of socialist agitation.

Sadly, he walked alone and thoughtfully across the now empty lawn to his small cottage beside the church.

A number of the men who were present at the church, not for worship but to hear first hand the revolutionary uttering of the new rector, had gathered in the small cottage on the main street after the service. It was a motley crowd of councilors and officials, traders and factors as well as military personnel. They were all unanimous in their condemnation of the new rector's indiscretion for choosing for public dissertation such a sensitive subject as the rights of servants and slaves at a time when rumors of revolt were rampant in all parts of the country. What made it worse, in their view, was that it was all said in the hearing of a number of slaves and other blacks who needed just so much encouragement to think that they were entitled to a better condition of life and it was their right to seize it if it was not being offered to them.

It was the general view that the matter should be taken up in Council, and that steps should be taken immediately to relieve Rev. Peters of his duties and return him to the liberal halls of Oxford University where his indiscretions could be better directed to the enlightenment of his privileged class. The colonies were not a suitable place for republican intellectuals who, notwithstanding their erudition, could not understand the complexities of plantation economies or the peculiar vulnerabilities of a slave society. Even though he was a man of the cloth, Rev. Peters was a misguided upstart, more interested in showing off his learning than in keeping the society stable, as his primary duty as rector required him to do. He should no longer be tolerated; and all decent men and women should shun his presence.

The discussion had become quite heated when news of the fires at Bagatelle reached the gathering. It was reported that two estates had been burnt to the ground, and the estate owners had been assaulted by a gang of runaway slaves. It was said that the attack was in retribution for an attempt which had been made to ambush one of the runaway chiefs on his way back from the east coast where, it was alleged, the camp leaders had been meeting to plan an insurrection. Before the rage of those who were present could subside, word came in of unspeakable atrocities that had occurred at Rosalie that same night. A number of persons had been butchered and two estates burnt to the ground. The group of men on the portico had gone silent with horror and fear.

The news of the fires at Bagatelle paled in significance as details of the destruction of Rosalie Estate came in. Rumors abounded about the extent of the killings; and the numbers of the dead and mutilated mounted higher and higher as the hours passed. Speculation was rife about who the perpetrators could be, and no one was sure whether it was an internal revolt of the estate slaves or the work of the runaways. By evening, though no eye-witnesses had yet come forward, accounts of the enormity of the disaster had reached gargantuan proportions. There were reports that all the white men on the estates had been brutally murdered, and white women, including girls at very tender ages, had been first raped and then mercilessly slaughtered. The brutes had escaped into the woods leaving the thriving and well-developed plantation a pile of burnt-out rubble.

It was a somber and apprehensive group that sat on the little porch that Sunday evening pondering the awful calamity that had so suddenly come upon them. Joseph, the slave butler, flitted in and out of the drawing room, bearing glasses of punch and other light refreshment, moving like a shadow among the white men so deeply immersed in their own fears and forebodings.

"These are troublesome and dangerous times," Somerville remarked broodingly.

"Well, we have to be better prepared," Grove said. "There are signs of revolt coming from everywhere."

"It is not only the runaways that we have to look out for," Winston joined in. "There is much agitation among the slaves and mulattos, stirred by Paulinaire and his associates."

"Do not overlook the French republicans," Stewart cautioned, "they are everywhere around the island. They have been coming in droves through the hidden coves of Grandbay and Anse du Mai. With all these rumors of French preparations for war against England, we have to keep a close watch on the activities of our French inhabitants."

"I think the situation is sufficiently grave for there to be an emergency meeting of Council tomorrow," Winston concluded. "I will ask the Governor to convene it."

"But what could be the purpose of such a meeting?" McPherson asked. "Didn't the Council vote a large sum for dealing with the runaways? What we need now is some action."

Captain Marshall, sitting at the far end of the portico, shifted uncomfortably in his chair.

"What is the militia doing?" McPherson persisted, "besides fattening their men from an overabundance of rations and excessive idleness."

"Well, here is Captain Marshall," Grove turned to the Captain. "Maybe he can tell us."

"Oh, Captain Marshall has brought in two females," Winston said with heavy sarcasm. "One of them was near dead."

There was a slight tittering among the group which brought a deep blush to the Captain's face. He fidgeted with embarrassment.

"Well, Captain, why don't you tell us?" Grove said.

"We have managed to contain them," Captain Marshall stuttered. "They have not been out of their camps for weeks."

"Contain them?" McPherson jeered. "I thought you were sent to exterminate them!"

An uneasy silence followed McPherson's outburst. The men straightened up in their seats as if waiting for a signal to rise. Dusk was already falling and it would soon be dark and time to depart, each man to his separate quarters. Just as Somerville reached out behind him for his hat and cane, a great commotion arose somewhere in the back of the town towards the river. There was a loud clamor coming closer and closer until, around the corner of an intersecting street, an excited, vociferous crowd of men and women, white, black and mulatto, appeared. A short, white man in baggy trousers and close-fitting jacket led the jostling crowd, his grizzled face flushed with excitement and, evidently, a fair day's consumption of liquor.

"They've caught him!" he was shouting above the noise. "They have Cicero!"

At the edges of the crowd several blacks were peering curiously at a central figure. As the procession approached, the men on the portico could discern a short, compact man securely bound with his arms tied to a pole slung over his shoulders, his ankles hobbled with short lengths of rope. The figure walked upright, eyes nervously shifting from side to side, lips set in grim determination. He wore cut-off trousers, stained with mud and soot, and a worn-out vest that was too tight at the armpits. His unkempt hair stood out in tufts, and wisps of beard surrounded his lips, and grew randomly on his jaw and chin.

Cicero appeared to be unaware of the commotion around him, although his eyes continually darted from one side to the other as if seeking a way of escape. Next to him on one side the sharp, thin features of Petit Jacques glanced furtively at the crowd as he stumbled painfully on the graveled street. A large man, black as ebony, strode triumphantly behind them. He stood well above the crowd, and his massive shoulders and bulky limbs swung ponderously as he walked. His large head was oddly shaped, like an angular block of stone, with overhanging brow and strong, wide jaw that somehow diminished his other features so that his lips and nose looked disproportionate to the rest of his face. Five or six other blacks trotted briskly at his heels. As they came abreast of the portico, somebody shouted to the men inside.

"We have the Rosalie killers!"

"They look a miserable lot," Winston said sardonically. "Surely that is hardly an army to wreak such havoc against a whole plantation."

"At least we have two men and not two women," McPherson jibed with a loud guffaw.

As the procession turned in the direction of the Fort, Captain Marshall left hastily and followed them.

"Well, there goes our salvation!" Grove remarked with irony.

The other men laughed nervously. The events of the day had kept them engaged in cogitations of the most profound gravity, and they understood that, as the leading men in the community, it rested on them to find immediate solutions to the crisis that now threatened the entire colony. The Council would have some serious work to do on the following day.

Paulinaire was furious. After all his intense planning and careful preparation, the wretched runaways had gone on a rampage of violence that was bound to put the white government on the alert. He had worked out an intricate strategy to use the various forces on the island to work together in a well-coordinated campaign that would take the authorities off-guard and bring down the colonial government. Rev. Peters' homilies should have been the spark that ignited the bonfire of discontent that had been building up for so long, but the over-zealous scholar had gone too far and had precipitated the anger and suspicion of the entire white community. And now he was to leave on the next ship to England. The Council had been unanimous in its decision that the fiery rector should not be given another opportunity to stir dissention and spread his seditious socialist doctrine anywhere in the colony.

Paulinaire was convinced then that moral suasion would never be a viable option for righting the social ills that continued to blight the future of the island. There was no question that force would be necessary. The mulattos everywhere on the island had been effectively mobilized, and were waiting for the signal for a general uprising when they could take control and lead the masses of the black population to massacre all whites and occupy their plantations. His plans had brought in colored dissidents from Martinique, who had already supplied guns,

ammunition and supplies to wage a quick and decisive war against the white militia. The black corps of militiamen had been infiltrated, and many of them were
already prepared to join the revolt and support the leadership of the mulattos. In
addition, he had been in touch with French inhabitants at Grandbay and Colihaut, who had pledged support for a grand uprising if that could coincide with an
invasion by the French navy which was already in active preparation for a war
with the British.

He had spent a lot of time designing the strategy for what he understood to be
a very complex operation, one which undoubtedly required careful and intelligent coordination. He saw himself as the commander-in-chief responsible for the
sequencing of events and for pulling the pieces together in a military maneuver
no less brilliant than that so successfully carried out by Toussaint L'Ouverture,
the black general, and Pinchinat, the mulatto politician, in San Domingo. But
unlike the situation in San Domingo, he did not intend to share power with any
black man, slave or free. It was his destiny to command the revolution and to
establish a new republic that would be governed by men of color who were
endowed with the intellect and social refinement necessary to undertake this kind
of responsibility. He needed the runaways and he needed the slaves just as the
Paris revolution needed the mass of the people. However, he would not go the
way of the Jacobins. He had no intention of putting political power in the hands
of untutored blacks.

But now his brilliantly conceived plans were in danger of being pulled apart
because of the stupidity of those hot-headed runaway chiefs whose lack of vision
had put the revolution at risk. The Council had listened to a deputation from the
east coast that had painted a grim picture of the lack of security in that area.
White men, women and even children had been brutally murdered, and a substantial part of the wealth of the country destroyed while the militia sat ineffectu-
ally in the safe confines of their encampments.

The white planters on the neighboring estates had reluctantly come to the
conclusion that they could not rely on the assistance of an administration that
was so inept that they could not take simple and firm action to eradicate a few
miserable slave camps, mostly without weapons and under-supplied with food
and other basic necessities. The white planters had decided to form their own vig-
ilante group, and take pre-emptive action to prevent further atrocities and
destruction on the plantations on the eastern coast.

The Council's response to the deputation was to summon Commandant
Young, and to order him to provide men and weapons to aid the planters in the
eastern district to destroy the runaway slave camps in that area. From now on the

militia was to wage an all-out war against the runaways wherever they could be found on the island. Any black or colored man, woman or child found living or wandering in the woods should be apprehended and brought to justice. Resistance was to be met with as much force as required, even summary execution.

Paulinaire heard this decree with mounting apprehension. In such a state of martial law his activities would have to be curtailed. He would have to conduct his affairs with the utmost circumspection. On the other hand, the spotlight was now on the runaway slave camps, and it was unlikely that much attention would be paid to him and his excursions around the island since he did not pose an immediate threat of aggression against the white planters. Through his network of connections in the villages and towns, he could continue his work with the mulattos and among the growing number of militant slaves on the estates. He had been badly let down by the runaway chiefs who had rejected his overtures for joint action and opted for the kind of brutal and senseless action that was bound to lead to their defeat.

He had followed the trial of the captured runaway, Cicero, which had been nothing but a travesty of British justice. Judge Brayshay had summoned the court and within an hour had condemned the man to die on the gibbet. The white deputation that had the day before stood before the Council with their irate demands for retribution against the runaway slave camps had given evidence of what they had seen of the burnt-out plantations and the charred remains of the white planters and their families. They retold what had been said to them by the frightened slaves on the plantation at Rosalie, but no first-hand evidence was presented to the court except that of Petit Jacques who, it was clear, was intent on saving his own skin and protecting his own chief. Even Augustine, their captor, could only vouch that he had found them in the early morning of the day after the disaster hastening up the path leading from the plantation house, and that he and a few men with him had subdued them and brought them into town. They were clearly runaway slaves and he had brought them in. He was entitled to a reward.

It was Petit Jacques and his word alone which gave any substantial weight to the charges against Cicero. They had looked a pitiful pair standing in the dock of the tiny courtroom amidst a sea of white, angry, threatening faces, with only a few mulattos standing at the door on one side. Half-naked and cowering with fright, they sat in the dock like caged animals while the scale of justice tipped menacingly against them. There was nothing heroic in their helpless resignation as summary condemnation glared out of every eye in the courtroom. When he was called upon, Petit Jacques spoke tremulously, exonerating first his chief,

Coree Greg, who had no part in the attack on the plantation, and second, himself, who had been left only as an observer to take note of the happenings and
report back to Coree Greg. He made it plain that Coree Greg had been against
any unprovoked attacks against white planters, and had advised restraint in their
actions against the white population; but Sandy, Bala and Hall had incited the
gathering to carry out that raid on the plantation.

As for Cicero, he was Bala's gun bearer; and was part of the planning group
which had met in Congoree's camp four days before the attack was carried out.
He, Petit Jacques, was not present during the killings on the plantation, but he
had heard Bala command Cicero afterwards to return to the plantation and set
fire to the houses and factory. He had stayed behind to distance himself from the
riotous group that was madly intoxicated with the violence of the night. He had
intended to find his way to his own camp as soon as it was daylight, but he had
come upon the group of black men who had obviously mistaken him for one of
the perpetrators of the night's disaster. He was in their custody when they apprehended Cicero while he was running up the path leading from the plantation
houses.

Paulinaire listened with cynical anticipation as the court delivered sentence.
Cicero was to be brought to the outskirts of the town, there to be gibbeted alive.
Petit Jacques must remain in custody to be later auctioned and transported out of
the island. Augustine was to receive 33 Joes for his service to the colony. The
crowd of mostly white persons was jubilant as it squeezed out of the narrow
courtroom and spilled onto the streets.

At the end, Paulinaire had to admit that Cicero had died a heroic death. As he
faced the stark frame of the gibbet, he seemed to straighten his compact figure so
that he appeared taller than he actually was. For a moment he was no longer the
half-naked runaway slave, grimy and unkempt, but a valiant soldier standing in
the presence of his enemy, waiting for an honorable execution. Erect and com-
posed, his eyes no longer darting from side to side as if in fear, but steadfast and
looking to the distant hills, he remained silent to the last as the provost marshal
read his doom. Then he mounted the block and received the rope around his
neck with dignified calm.

Paulinaire remained in the shade of a large flamboyant tree long after the noisy
and exuberant crowd had dispersed. In respectful silence he regarded the now
limp body of the slave whose soul had now fled to eternal freedom. He pondered
the last moments in the life of this simple man who had faced death with such
calm and fortitude, and he wondered if his own end would be so serene and dignified. He did not doubt that the multitude in the hills were men of valor. But

such bravery was like the wind in the open sea, of no object unless it could be harnessed to some specific purpose. If only they could be disciplined to act together following a well conceived campaign, then the chances of success would be indubitably greater. Only Coree Greg had shown the wisdom to understand that emotive and impulsive decisions were not the way to lasting conquest. But the old chief had the toughness and cunning of an aged opossum, and was unlikely to fall for the subtlety of his kind of diplomacy. Coree Greg was simple and pragmatic. He had made it abundantly clear that his single and overriding objective was survival in the freedom of the woods. He was entirely devoid of any political ambitions.

Paulinaire recalled his conversations with Pharcel. The bright, sharp, personable youth, though lacking in sophistication, had shown an avid desire to be exposed to the refinements of civilized living. He had shown himself to be brave, intelligent and decisive; and able to mix quite well with those who were his superiors in intellect and class. It may very well be that Pharcel was his answer to the problem of gaining the cooperation and support of the masses. In any event the runaway camps were doomed. It was only a matter of time before they would be overrun and destroyed. He had to find Pharcel and warn him before it was too late.

The hand tapping on his sleeve startled him out of his reverie. He turned to find Jacques looking up at him, a worried frown on his face. He pointed at the inert body of Cicero hanging from the wooden frame and shook his head sadly.

"Where did you spring from?" Paulinaire asked, looking wildly around to see if there were still observers left on the field.

Jacques pointed to the side of a low hill overlooking the open space where the gibbet stood.

"I saw it all," he answered, "from that tree over there."

He pointed to a large tree standing above smaller growths towards one side of the hill.

"They would not listen to me when I tried to speak," he said wretchedly. "They even refused to hearken to Pharcel."

"Where is Pharcel?" Paulinaire asked.

"I left him at Delices," Jacques replied. "He was excited about that gun."

"You must find him," Paulinaire said anxiously. "He is in great danger."

Jacques nodded. It would be dangerous walking the woods in that area. Pharcel must be still caught up in the wild celebrations which he was certain would have followed the successful raids on that rich plantation. But he would find a way to reach him.

Paulinaire watched him scuttle through the bushes at the perimeter of the field until he was lost to view. Then he walked slowly the long mile into town.

CHAPTER 13

The band of men and women had been jubilant as they crowded into the inner side of the circle of huts. Most of them had followed Bala into his camp, carrying loads of food, liquor and an assortment of household articles, which they had secured after the raid on the plantation. Several guns and a quantity of ammunition had been seized, and these were piled in a corner of Bala's hut.

Sandy and Jacco and their few followers had joined the group. They had traveled a great distance from the west coast and the central part of the island, and they were pleased to accept Bala's invitation to spend a few days in his camp and to join the celebration of their brilliant victory over the white planters.

Mabouya came; but after one night of riotous revelry, he had quietly returned to his camp in the hidden valley below, taking his followers with him, except Rosay who stayed because Bala would not suffer her to be taken away from him.

Congoree had returned directly to his camp after the raid; but he had left Romain, his cherished valet, to follow Bala and the rest. He thought it would be good for the boy to be among other mature men since he was growing out of adolescence and fast losing the delicacy of youth. He had to let him go to grow into the toughness of manhood.

The celebration went on for many days. They felt secure in the forest, having blocked the entrance to the lakes with fallen trees. They were certain that the militia would not breach the barricades that they had set up. Each night the flambeaus were lit; the drums beat deliriously, and the sonorous chanting filled the night with enchantment that possessed every soul in the camp. Women vied with each other to display the most stimulating and seductive movements, enacting hymeneal rites in the sensual design of the dances. But the men found nothing so arousing as to watch Victoire and Rosay, in undisguised sensuality, whirling, writhing and joggling their bodies in delirious abandon in the flickering light of the torches. Pharcel sat on the outside of the circle, fascinated and aroused, as the torrid music took possession of the dancers and brought them to unimaginable heights of ecstasy. Beyond the circle, out in the gloom, the sound of coupling filled the night, and added to the surreal quality the experience.

Pharcel had found an unexpectedly warm welcome in Bala's presence. The days following the grand meeting in Congoree's camp had been filled with preparations for the raid on the Rosalie plantation; but Bala had gone out of his way to meet with him, and to lead him among the other chiefs, as if he was his newfound protégé. Bala became even more comradely when he found out that Pharcel carried his own gun. During the raid, he had urged Pharcel to stay by his side. Bala carried a small sack slung from his neck which he said contained the spirit of his ancestors that would always protect him from harm; if Pharcel stuck with him, he would suffer no injury, and he could not be killed.

Pharcel was standing close to him when Bala had ordered Cicero to return to the plantation and set fire to the buildings. At that time Bala had taken him by the shoulder, and urged him along, calling him his brave young warrior. When Cicero did not appear by morning, and word reached the camp that he had been taken, Bala simply shrugged and signaled to Pharcel that he should attend him in his hut. No specific instructions had been given, but Pharcel understood that he was now to be Bala's new gun-bearer. That same morning Presente came boldly to him, and led him to her small hut. Bala watched them go, a mean and calculating look in his sunken eyes.

The days went by in undisturbed tranquility as the body of men lounged around the camp, and the women went about their tasks of preparing meals and fetching water. The dancing went on night after night; and Pharcel sometimes sat in the shadows, enjoying the sight of the lissome bodies of the women gyrating in the dim light of smoking torches. But most nights Bala demanded his attendance as he sat with Sandy and Jacco till the early hours of morning discussing plans for an island-wide insurrection.

Pharcel hardly took in the disjointed flow of ideas that came from the three men sitting around a crude table. Clearly, neither Bala nor his associates understood the complexities of planning coordinated action. Their assessment of the degree of organization among the plantation slaves and of their willingness to respond to a sudden call to fight for their freedom was entirely wrong. They did not understand that the state of readiness of the slaves for spontaneous revolt was still extremely low. Paulinaire understood this, and so did Coree Greg.

He allowed his mind to drift to Presente and her half-concealed smile. He was charmed by the way she puckered her lips when she smiled to reveal only her upper two front teeth, and the way her long eye lashes fluttered when she looked at him as if beckoning him to possess him instantly. Despite her provocative ways, she was strangely timid in the ways of love. He remembered their first night together on his previous visit to the camp when she had lured him to her hut to spend the night. He remembered when he had entered her that first time, how he had felt the sudden backward curving of her abdomen as if she wanted to withdraw herself, and as he began to thrust deeper into her she had writhed and squirmed around the floor, seemingly in pain or some other frightful agony. Head bent backwards until she rested on the crown of her head, eyes starting intensely as if in fear, she had let out sharp, gasping cries that rose higher and higher until the little room quivered with the sound of her throes. He had tried to pull away from her thinking he was causing her physical distress; but each time she had desperately grabbed onto him and pressed him down to her even as her body uncontrollably pulled away from him. It was still the same with her; but now, her tumultuous response stimulated his desire, and her frantic and tempestuous convulsions drove him to a frenzy of lust that seemed unquenchable. Still, after every night's encounter, emptiness took over his soul, and the image of Elise so far away would possess his thoughts, and his mind would be filled with her and the musky odor and warm, yielding softness of her flesh.

Despite these many distractions, Pharcel was uneasy. He had witnessed the assault on the plantation and had been left drained of any moral justification for what he had seen that dreadful night.

It was a courageous band that had crossed the river from Congoree's camp and charged into the pitch-black forest—men and women charged with righteous anger at the inhuman conditions in which they had been forced to live. With flaming torches, they had rushed through the woods for many miles until they came to the valley where the plantation spread out in the arms of encircling hills. At a signal from Bala, the lights had been extinguished, and the men had crept through the bushes until they came to a path that led through fields of sugar cane. An eerie call as of an owl hooting came from someone in the group, which was answered from two directions. The calls continued until the separate groups of men and women converged near an intersection, one arm of which led to the plantation buildings.

The night was dark, with not even a sliver of moon to lighten the gloom. Banks of cloud obscured the faint glimmer coming from the far-distant stars. Only the flickering, ghostly lights of a multitude of fireflies hovered over the path and among the dense fields on both sides.

The band of men and women crouched together and then began to move down the path towards the cluster of buildings. As they approached, two dogs began a low growling. Bala signaled for a halt, and dispatched two of the men to move quickly ahead. They crept along the shelter of low hedges that led to and circled the main building. The furious barking of the dogs turned to an angry growl, followed by sharp yelps and then silence. A light shone from a window in the upper story of the main building. With a single wave of his arm, Bala plunged into the darkness. The mass of his followers, their weapons flashing in the surrounding darkness, roared in the night as they rushed forward and circled the plantation houses. What followed was an exercise in insanity.

Men and women tore into doors and windows and ripped them apart. Pharcel was jostled and pushed through the main door of the mansion. He stood aghast as his companions, in maniacal rage, broke into the rooms and cupboards, smashing and tearing as they went along. A lean white man, still in his night shirt, came down the stairs, brandishing a shotgun. Before he could fire into the crowd, a machete buzzed through the air and buried itself in his neck. The man toppled over the banister and fell lifeless on the floor. The crowd howled in satisfaction.

Pharcel elbowed his way out of the crowd and into the yard at the back of the building. Three more houses were under attack. He saw the body of another white man spread-eagled on the ground. As he looked, dark shadows fled from the other houses and faded into the adjacent fields.

He was standing there in the dark, stunned by the unbridled furor that had possessed the men and women who had so calmly walked with him, when he heard a painful screaming coming from the upper floor. With uncertain steps, he reentered the mansion and made his way quickly through the kitchen and into the dining room. Sandy, Mabouya, Congoree and Jacco were sitting at a large, round table, loaded with loaves of bread and slabs of cheese as well as several jars of jams and preserves; and were being served from flagons of wine. Around them men and women milled amidst piles of clothing and sundry articles. Pharcel picked his way cautiously until he came to the stairs leading to the upper floor. The screams were louder there, and they seemed to come from a room near the top of the staircase. He crept upwards until he came to the landing. The door to the room was ajar and he stepped hastily forward as the sound of a woman in agonized distress struck his ear. What he saw held him transfixed for several minutes.

A middle-aged white woman was stretched out on a wide, canopied bed. A little girl no more that seven years old, unconscious and bleeding profusely from a deep wound on one side of her head, lay on the floor. The woman's body was contorted in agony, neck and head arched as far back as they could go, eyes popping in naked terror. Her gown was thrown all the way over her bosom leaving the lower part of her body uncovered and open. Bala stood between her spread-out thighs.

Pharcel stood there fascinated, unable to move for what seemed an interminable time before Bala, sensing his presence, disengaged himself and turned around. Unabashed, he grinned at Pharcel triumphantly, and turned again to the woman.

Pharcel felt his stomach heave, but nothing came up. He whirled around, ran down the stairs, and out into the courtyard at the front of the building. He stood there alone, shivering in the dark. He had never seen such evil as the look in Bala's eyes at the moment of his shameful triumph. Growing up in a slave camp, he had many times come upon men and women coupling in the fields or in their tiny shacks; but he had never associated the act with such unrestrained violence. Somehow he felt sullied by the experience. He wanted to run away. He had carried his gun securely in his arms all this time, but now he wondered to what object he was armed to kill. He was still outside when the others came and marched past him, carrying armfuls of plunder. Pharcel followed blindly.

By the time they reached the lower heights of the hills leading up to Grand Fond, the mansion was on fire. Tongues of flame leapt from several points behind the main building, and the edges of the surrounding fields began to blaze as the wind carried flurries of sparks beyond the periphery of the courtyard and the open spaces behind the buildings. Bala turned to look, a bland expression on his face. He had not told Cicero about the woman whom he had left inert and devastated with her child in the room upstairs.

As he sat alone in the shade of a tree near Presente's hut, Pharcel's mind dwelt on the senseless violence and inhuman brutality that he had witnessed, and he thought of how different that was from the high principles behind the orderly revolution that Paulinaire had espoused. True, some of Paulinaire's associates had shown blatant disrespect for the black slaves that had attended them on that memorable night when they had dined on the bank of the Geneva River; but Paulinaire had clearly discountenanced their actions. Even so, that kind of disrespect was a far cry from the cruelty to which he had been unwittingly a party. He continued to be disturbed in the many days that followed, and he dreaded the hours when Bala would call on him to be in attendance at his hut.

One afternoon, he sat with Alexis on the bench beside his hut, and spoke with him for a long time about the conflict that was raging within him. Alexis listened to him with his usual restraint until Pharcel turned to him questioningly. Still, he remained silent for several moments before he began slowly to speak.

"Sometimes," he said, "men are made by the acts done to them."

He relapsed into silence for a few more moments.

"Have you seen Bala's back uncovered?" he asked.

"No," Pharcel replied. "He is never without a shirt or vest."

"The white man's clothes on his back covers a multitude of the white man's sins," Alexis said ponderously. "If you saw him naked you would see the mark of the white man's barbarism. His flesh was torn apart from his neck to his thighs. He is always careful to conceal those scars of shame."

"But most of us carry those scars," Pharcel protested. "In most cases that is what brought us together here."

Alexis bowed his head in thought. He had spoken quite a bit and he was never one for too many words.

After a while he spoke again.

"You should not be too quick to condemn a man for his warped nature," he said softly. "Some of us are more sensitive and vulnerable than others. Those who are born to privilege feel humiliation more acutely than they who are the lowly."

"How do you mean?" Pharcel became curious about the significance of Alexis' words.

"Bala was the son of a chief," Alexis looked directly into Pharcel's eyes as if to emphasize the importance of what he had to say. "He saw his father killed, his mother raped and mutilated, and his little sister violated in the worst possible way. The Portuguese did it, but he draws no distinction between them and other white people."

Pharcel looked at him aghast, unable to find words to express his feelings. He felt a chill in the pit of his stomach as if he was in the presence of something evil.

"God created Bala with princely qualities," Alexis continued somberly. "But it was the Portuguese that recreated him into what he is now."

It was many days after that Pharcel accompanied Presente to the stream nearly a mile away down the steep track from the camp. It was unusual for the men of the camp to be helping in women's chores; but he wanted to be away from the camp, away from constant attendance on Bala and his companion chiefs, even for an hour. So he followed Presente down the track to the shallow basin where the gourds were filled and clothes and utensils were washed. It was only mid-morning, the time of day when most people were still lying abed after the carousing of the night before. No one else was at the stream, so they removed their clothing, and waded into the clear, shallow water. Pharcel laid his gun carefully on a flat stone on the edge of the stream.

It was a clear, sunny day; beams of sunlight came through the branches of the overhanging trees, and sparkled on the surface of the water. The air around them was quite warm; the water was invitingly cool, so they sat on the gravelly bed of the stream and let the water flow over their shoulders. From where they sat, they could see the track running on a low gradient for almost half a mile, and then rising sharply to the brow of the hill before turning towards the camp. The land on both sides of the track dropped steeply down to deep, thickly forested gorges right up to the sharp incline, and then broadened on either side in an almost precipitous climb. Across the stream and on the lower side, the track continued gradually downwards in more open terrain through forest trees that were less dense than those that choked the higher gorges. The stream gushed down a narrow channel on the ridge of a low hill formed laterally across the deep gorge on the left; and ran across the track where it opened out in a wide basin before dropping suddenly several feet on the right of the track down a fall, the top of which was concealed by a heavy growth of wild fern. Through the clear surface of the stream, they could see crawfish scuttling on the gravel bed and yellow crabs crawling below the overhang of large stones, their claws opened wide in ostentatious defense.

They lolled comfortably in the refreshing flow, washing away the labors of the night. Neither of them had any thought of intimacy as they sat side by side, although Presente could not resist mischievously titillating him in the slow depth of the stream. He himself was always captivated by the uncommonly fleshy contours of her body, and he could hardly take his eyes away whenever she stood naked before him. He stared fascinated at the graceful curvatures of her form, its rich ebony-black shades so well defined, and he wondered why it was that he had found her so exciting and yet so unsatisfying.

They were lost in this quiet abstraction when they heard subdued voices some distance below them. Pharcel leapt to his feet and peered around some bushes at the lower end of the track across the stream. There were a large number of men trotting up the track. At first glance, he could see that most of them were white, and some wore uniforms of the militia. There were a few black men, also in uniform trailing the group. He immediately saw the danger they were in; there was not much time in which to make their escape; so he looked desperately up the channel where the stream flowed downwards, and then turned to the lower end where it disappeared over the fall. In panic, he seized his gun, and called urgently to Presente.

"Run!" he cried frantically. "Run, Presente!"

Pharcel leapt over the fall through the thick cover of fern. He felt himself hurtling down, his back scraping against the slimy face of the drop before he plunged feet first in a deep pool at its base. He waded through the water, and climbed onto a ledge behind the fall. Above him the cover of fern hung like a crest over the edge. He pressed himself against the perpendicular wall, and waited.

He heard them scrambling in the bushes above him, muttering among them-selves. They had obviously seen the clothes on the bank of the stream, and were looking about for the persons who wore them. He could hear them swearing and beating about the bush for a long time, until he heard an exultant shout; and then the loud wailing of a woman in distress. They had found Presente hiding behind a rock under a large tree some distance up the channel where the stream flowed from above. The loud wailing had abruptly stopped, and there was silence for a long moment, followed by the sound of thrashing and by harsh swearing in the bushes above his head. By and by, the swish of many feet moved up the track. He remained motionless behind the fall for a long time until the sharp reports of gunfire came from the hills above.

The stream continued below the fall down a narrow channel between huge boulders, slippery and covered with lichen. He squeezed himself between the boulders, and followed the stream downhill. Dense bush overhung the narrow flow as it twisted its way through a dark fissure scooped out in the volcanic rock by rain torrents that fell for months in every year. He was not sure where he was headed; but he knew that, somewhere in that dark and forbidding wilderness, Mabouya's camp was securely hidden on the lower side of one of those thickly wooded gorges.

The assault on Bala's camp had been planned over the past two weeks. The Council had given orders that the planters, their overseers and engineers should be given adequate support by the militia; and Commandant Young had himself led a detachment to join the white vigilantes. Young and his men had traversed the island through the central district to Castle Bruce and thence to Rosalie where they rendezvoused with the men from the nearby plantations. They had seen first-hand the destruction on the Rosalie estate, and this had fired the men to a boiling passion for revenge.

Reports had reached the planters of the unending celebration in Bala's camp following the Rosalie massacre. They had sent a few trusted slaves to keep surveil-lance over the daily routine of the camp, and were shocked and encouraged by the intelligence that security watches had been virtually suspended during the nightly celebrations and the early part of the morning. They were also pleased to learn that Sandy and Jacco were still enjoying Bala's hospitality, and were deter-mined to move against them as early as possible with sufficient force to eradicate the lot.

Young had sent stern orders to Captain Urquhart to clear the barricades across the track to the lakes, and join them at the appointed time. They were to wait on the upper flank above the camp until they had been contacted by Young's detachment which would occupy the lower flank. Urquhart's men had spent the night in the woods above the camp, and they had heard the sound of revelry until the early hours of morning. A few of the black soldiers had removed their tunics, and crept to the edge of the clearing where, from the high branches of balata trees, they had watched the dancers in the circle of light.

Urquhart waited impatiently all morning for the signal from his commandant. It was a bright day, and the sun penetrated the thick canopy of leaves to heat the damp ground on which they stood. A warm, uncomfortable vapor surrounded them which, added to the needling of the hosts of mosquitoes, caused the men to complain irritably and to move restlessly among the trees. The sight of the camp just a short distance below them, and the seeming absence of vigilance which, even at that distance they could easily discern, provoked such an aggressive response from them that the Captain had much difficulty in restraining them from dashing from cover and getting the attack over with in the shortest possible time.

It was while they waited that they heard the sudden, eerie wailing coming from below the camp. It was a woman's voice, and the sound was quickly hushed; but it seemed to have awakened some activity in the camp. Men rushed out of their huts, looked about suspiciously and, seeing nothing to occasion alarm, drifted back indoors. A few moments later, Urquhart heard a disorderly rush of feet as Young's men took up their position on the lower flank. There was hardly much time to receive any signal from the Commandant. More of the runaways had emerged from the huts, looking questioningly at each other and scanning the woods that surrounded the camp. Most of them were already armed, a few with guns, and most with cutlasses, axes and even clubs. As soon as Urquhart saw the flash of uniform approaching, he didn't wait to receive the command, but moved his men closer to the periphery of the clearing around the camp.

The signal came as a single pistol shot. A thunder of feet followed as a hundred men rushed madly towards the camp. The men on the lower flank had difficulty negotiating the steep slope below the camp, and were several minutes late in moving up to a position where they could engage the runaways that were now forming in a defensive phalanx around Bala and Sandy. Jacco had been taken completely by surprise; but he had swiftly assessed the situation, slipped through the gap in the lower flank with a number of women and children, and taken to the woods.

Bala was unprepared for an attack on that scale. He had not expected so quick a response from the militia, and he had not had time to dress or even arm himself properly. His men were already out in numbers in the clearing, and he quickly pulled them together in a tactical retreat to the edge of the woods behind the camp where they could fire into the oncoming soldiers under cover of the bushes and trees.

The fight went on for hours without any obvious advantage to either side. But towards late afternoon some of Urquhart's soldiers broke through the woods on the upper side in an attempt to outflank Bala and his men. Sensing danger, Bala quickly gave the command for further retreat deeper in the forest. He stood among them, fighting hand to hand against the unending tide of uniforms that filled the trees, until one of the soldiers who had clambered to the branches of a nearby tree spotted him among the men, and shot him before he could gain the cover of the deeper woods.

Bala staggered with the shock of the impact. He felt a burning in his thigh, but undeterred he drove his men to cover. The fighting became furious among the trees as the runaways led the soldiers into bushy depressions only to leap and hack at them while they were still unsteady on their feet and unprotected. Where thick undergrowth covered the ground, guns were useless, and bayonets and machetes flashed in the gloom. Men staggered with wounds and patches of blood covered the ground.

Sandy, surrounded by a few of his men fought furiously, using the butt of his musket to jab and swing at any flash of uniform that came within his vision. He was still unscathed; but when he saw Bala stumbling and bleeding from his thigh, he quickly ran to his side, and drew him away from the center of the struggle. He soon realized that the number of the enemy was overwhelming and that the men could not hold out for very long.

It was still some time before nightfall, and he doubted that they could hold the enemy at bay for so long. He took Bala by the shoulder and drew him away towards a jagged outcrop of rock that he had spotted some distance to the left. Bala lurched through the trees, his wounded leg painful and stiffening with the loss of blood. Sandy helped him along until they came suddenly upon the face of a low cliff. Only a few feet away, the outcrop of rock hung over a deep precipice. There was nowhere else to go. Below the overhanging rock, chunks of the cliff had been scooped out by constant falls of the loamy soil forming a shelf that was partly hidden from view.

The sound of the fray drew closer and closer even as its fury decreased. Then suddenly there was dead silence. They remained standing over the precipice for what seemed a long time. It was already late evening and night was beginning to fall under the trees. Bala was obviously in distress. His lips were compressed in a painful grimace, and he groaned involuntarily as intermittent pangs lanced down his leg. Sandy searched around the area, and gathered some lengths of vine and twigs which he formed in a crude tourniquet above the wound. He also collected an assortment of leaves from nearby plants which he crushed and packed into the small opening where the bullet had entered the flesh, hoping it would prevent infection.

There was an air of stealth about the place, and they could not understand why until some distance away points of light began to appear stretching from one side of the woods to the other, like a wide net that seemed to be drawing closer and closer. At the same time looking up into the trees above them, they observed the night sky had turned a bright scarlet, and they realized their camp was on fire. The line of flambeaus came closer, drawing inexorably towards the two men crouching on the precipice. Sandy began to pace back and forth looking frantically for a way out. He stopped suddenly at the top of the cliff and peered below. It was a sheer drop to a narrow shelf that jutted out a few feet just below and sloped upwards at the further end. Desperately, he dragged Bala to the edge, lowered him onto the shelf, and then followed. The two men crouched precariously on the ledge, the inner side of which opened inwards just enough to provide a slim overhang that sheltered them from overhead view. There they stayed for what seemed an eternity listening to the sound of approaching footfalls.

A few soldiers, spotting the cliff, rushed eagerly towards it; but finding only what looked like a dead end, swore vilely in frustration. The two men below could hear them trampling the earth as they searched the sides of the cliff for any signs of a passage through which the fugitives could have escaped. At last, after much muttering and swearing, the footsteps receded and the woods settled down for the night.

A pale moon rose over the trees, and hung suspended over the precipice, offering a dim light to the two men occupying the confined space on the ledge. They were cramped and cold, and Bala's injured leg had to be stretched awkwardly so that it extended partially over the edge. To remain where they were would have meant certain death because they could not have controlled their movements much longer, cramped as they were in the confines of the shelf. Sandy whispered to Bala that they had to try to regain the safety of the upper ground. He led the way, crawling slowly up the sloping end. Bala followed, dragging his wounded leg, and using his hands to clutch at the sharp points and fissures in the rock. They came to the top at last, and, holding on to the craggy face of the overhang, they regained level ground. They stayed there panting and heaving for several minutes, not so much from exertion, but from the tension of hanging on to what seemed to them the edge of doom. It was already past midnight, and the night was still.

They left the cliff before dawn broke, and followed a gradual rise until the contour of the land rose to a high plateau covered with thick bush and a scattering of scraggly trees. They knew that they had come to the lake region, and they decided to turn inwards to the higher hills where they would find a small lake hidden away in a bowl almost completely encircled by a rim of mountains some distance upwards from the more expansive fresh water lake. It was still early morning when they came upon a tiny stream that ran through a small pasture surrounded by dense bush. The land had begun to slope upwards more steeply, and Bala was showing signs of exhaustion as he dragged his lame leg painfully behind. Despite the cool of the morning, beads of sweat dropped from his forehead and rolled down his face and neck onto his back, chest and abdomen. The two men were glad to sit beside the stream for a few moments' rest. They felt secure that the search for them would not extend so high in the mountains. Both men had held on to their muskets, and they carefully loaded them and laid them on the grass close to where they sat.

There was a quiet peace about the place, not like the oppressive silence of the deep forest. Birds chirped in the bushes, and myriad butterflies hovered over the low, bright green growth that covered both banks of the stream. Beyond the small patch of grass, the bushes rose in a broad sweep to the upper reaches of the mountain, intercepted only by the edge of another sparsely forested hill that jutted into it. The sky above was clear, with only a few thin patches of cloud which drifted rapidly across. The sun was already warming the earth, but the hills and the covering vegetation gave the appearance as if they were newly washed. There was a reassuring serenity about the surrounding hills and the open land at their feet. The little stream gurgled, its crystal clear water sparkling in the early sunlight.

Sandy sat beside Bala and, sensing his discomfort, turned to examine his injured leg. He released the tourniquet, and examined the wound closely. The flesh around the bullet hole had darkened to a shade deeper than the surrounding ebony skin, an unhealthy pallor that showed signs of infection; and the leg from thigh to ankle was swollen to a feverish gloss. They both knew that Bala could not go on without proper treatment.

Scooping some water in his cupped hands, Sandy tried to wash away the herbal treatment that he had applied the evening before. Then he searched the low banks of the stream for clean deposits of unmixed clay. He found a vein behind a large rock, and dug out a handful which he spread over the wound, forming an airtight plaster. It would be some time before the plastic consistency of the clay would harden, and Bala's movements would not be unduly constrained until much later in the day. They were both so absorbed in this painful operation that they failed to observe the sudden flutter of birds' wings and the flurry of butterflies some distance away in the direction from which they had just come.

They continued to climb through thickening forest, and suddenly they came upon a wide expanse of water. The lake was circular in shape, surrounded by a rim of rusty grey pebbles; and its still water reflected the cloudless blue of the sky in the late afternoon sun. The forest encroached right up to the rim of stones, and threw dark, shifting shadows on the near side of the lake, giving the water an appearance of cold, unfathomable depth. The two men skirted the edge until they came to an opening in the trees.

A faint trace led them upwards to a grassy slope from which they could see the massive bulk of Morne Trois Pitons in the distance. Sandy had been pressing towards the western coast where he would be back in familiar territory and able to rejoin his camp in safety; but Bala's painful progress made the journey more tiresome and slow than it could have been. The trace that they had found made it easier to traverse the forest, and they continued to follow it in a northward direction, getting closer and closer to the other side of the great central peak.

Darkness overtook them not too far from the base of the mountain, and they looked about for the nearest shelter where they could rest for the night. The trace they were on curled inwards towards the foot of the mountain, and brought them to an escarpment formed by a fall on the side of a low ridge extending from it. The crumbling soil, almost blue white in appearance, had formed a cave in the side of the escarpment. They dragged themselves in and fell into unconsciousness immediately.

Despite Bala's torment from the festering wound, he slept soundly; but he was awake long before the first light of dawn. As the darkness began to fade, he shook Sandy and called urgently to him. Sandy rolled over, looked about him in confusion, and then rubbed the sleep from his tired eyes. He helped Bala up, and supported him out of the cave.

All at once they were surrounded by a dozen or more black and colored men, naked to the waist, and wearing the grey trousers of the militia. For several moments the two fugitives just gaped at them, startled, but even more mystified by the suddenness of their appearance. The soldiers stood about, their muskets held carelessly in their hands, gazing at the two men emerging from the mouth of the cave. There was a look almost of commiseration on their faces. Bala relaxed, and a wide grin began to form on his face, thinking that they might possibly be deserters in sympathy with his cause; but a sharp command from behind the circle of black faces jerked them to instant attention.

"Seize them, men!" the voice bellowed.

That voice of authority sizzled through Bala's consciousness, and, despite the pain and stiffness, galvanized him to action. He shook himself free of Sandy's supporting arm, his musket clutched by the muzzle in one hand. Glaring fiercely and holding the musket outwards like a club, he dared the soldiers to approach nearer. Sandy stood beside him; but, sensing the uselessness of resistance, he dropped his gun in an act of surrender. The soldiers hesitated, gazing in fascination at the cornered and wounded fugitive still so defiant and dangerous.

"Seize them!" the voice echoed against the walls of the cave.

At the sound of this urgent command the soldiers, in a concerted rush, fell upon the two men. In a trice, they had them subdued and bound hand and feet.

Bala struggled against his bonds, and never stopped his railing at the black soldiers until they reached the encampment in the center of the island.

It took a week to complete the mopping up of the woods. Presente had been kept in close custody by the soldiers in Young's detachment. All week the men of both regiments combed the forests, aided by a few slaves from the eastern estates. They found Rosay wandering in the coarse bushes on the banks of the lake. Victoire with Bala's two-and-a-half year old son slept in the woods several nights, but was finally apprehended not far from where Bala had made his last stand. Romain, Congoree's prized valet, was intercepted in the heights above Rosalie, trying to find his way back to camp. Few men died; and many were wounded. Most of them were scattered in the woods. Bala's camp was totally destroyed.

The place where the men and women had danced so vigorously and with such intense pleasure and joy was now left to the empty night. The drums which had throbbed so vigorously the night before were now silenced.

CHAPTER 14

Pharcel blamed himself bitterly. He had not intended to abandon Presente when they were both surprised by the approach of the militia only a short distance from where they were, naked and unguarded, in the stream. When he had called on her to run, he had expected that she would follow him, although he did not know what he was leaping into. She must have known that the fall on the other side of the track was deep and dangerous, and she had chosen the lesser of the two hazards by slipping up the stream, hoping to find a secure place in which to hide. He had been devastated when he realized that the soldiers had found her and were holding her captive, but there was nothing he could do against such a large number of armed men. Neither was he able to find a way back to the camp ahead of the detachment to warn them of the danger which was approaching. In frustration, he had scrambled down the rocky ravine for nearly two miles; and then he saw wisps of smoke rising from a depression between two hills. He had clambered up the steep side of the ravine, and made his way through thick bush until he had gained the forested ridge where Mabouya and his men were encamped.

Late in the evening of the same day Jacco limped into camp, leading a number of the women and children, who had managed to slip through the cordon of Young's men advancing on the lower flank. Jacco was slightly injured when he slid down an incline and landed on a jagged stump which tore into his heel. Mabouya welcomed them, though he was very much concerned that they could have inadvertently led the militia to his hiding place. He immediately proceeded to station men on the surrounding ridges and at various points along the trace that was regularly used to enter his camp. After two weeks they had felt secure again. The tension eased and life returned to normalcy.

One man who had been able to escape and find his way to Mabouya's camp the following morning reported that the battle with the soldiers had been furious and prolonged. Despite the odds against them, the men in Bala's camp had fought valiantly, and had held their own, fighting under cover of the bushes and dense wood, until Bala was shot in the leg and Sandy had to drag him to safety. Even then the men continued to fight, drawing the soldiers into the bushes and attacking them with machetes and any weapon that they had had time to seize. Though none of the soldiers had been killed, many had been wounded and several of the officers had to be carried out of the bush with serious injuries. Pharcel's heart fell when he heard that Alexis had been taken. The little man had been the last to surrender. He and Jupiter had been fighting back to back when Jupiter was shot in the chest, his lifeless body falling heavily onto Alexis as he prepared to leap to another assault. Disheartened, Alexis had thrown down his machete and offered to be shot; but, instead, the soldiers had surrounded and captured him.

News of Bala's capture did not reach the camp for several days. A cloud of dismay had descended on the community of men and women when they heard that Bala and Sandy had been found by a detachment of black soldiers and taken into custody. The camp was put on alert as they expected that the militia, buoyed up by their success, would no doubt be planning to eradicate all the runaway camps that they could find, especially as they had the help of black soldiers who were more fitted to forest warfare. But no attack came.

The camp settled down to its peaceful and dreary existence. There was none of the gaiety and excitement that had enlivened Bala's camp. The days were filled with purposeful activities, and the nights were devoid of enchantment. Rosay had not returned, and the few lusterless women in the camp offered little entertainment after dark as they fell in with the daily drill of work and sleep. After the second week, both Jacco and Pharcel decided to brave the insecurity of the woods and return to their respective camps.

Pharcel had decided to follow the longer route along the coast since it had been reported that the militia was still combing the area around the lakes where they had picked up several of the fugitive men and women, including Bala's wife, Victoire, and their son, as well as Angelique, Agatha and Juba.

The return to Coree Greg's camp had not been without danger. Self-appointed vigilantes, both white and black, were scouring the woods hoping to earn the mounting rewards offered for any runaway slaves captured. He came across bands of slaves set to prowl the estate tracks at night in an attempt to intercept any strange black man found traversing the area, but he had quickly found shelter in the bushes along the tracks and watched them go by. Afterwards, he kept to the forested hillsides as much as possible all the way to Congoree's camp. There he learnt that Jacques had come looking for him and had decided to return to Grandbay after he had found out that Pharcel was still in Bala's camp.

The route along the eastern coast took him again to the small Carib village where Kumeni had remained after she had stolen away with him and helped him to find the lost treasure. He found her lodging in a *tabwi* with another old woman who appeared to have adopted her, and who, at first, resented Pharcel's intrusion in their constricted space. However, Kumeni seemed to have prevailed on her to suffer his presence, and. he was allowed to spend several days in the village where he endured the phlegmatic acceptance of the men and the curious, questioning gaze of the other women. Though Kumeni's reception had been somewhat indifferent, she never failed each night to come to his side; and it was soon evident that the old woman took vicarious pleasure in Kumeni's breathless and ecstatic nights with the black, robust stranger in the close intimacy of her hut.

He learnt that the militia had come prowling around the village after the fires at Bagatelle; but the Caribs had driven them away, regarding their uniforms with suspicion and antagonism. As an independent and tribal people, they would not tolerate any other authority but their own in territories which they occupied. Pharcel knew that the woods were no longer safe, although the militia had not yet penetrated the fastness where Coree Greg's camp was hid. He spent a few idle days among the Caribs, sharing their common pot of maize, crabs and fish. A few of the younger men had at first followed him with awe as he drifted around the village with his musket cradled in the crook of one arm though when he offered to show them how to load the weapon they would have nothing to do with it. They continued to admire it at a distance until he went away.

Many times as he sat in the shade for hours, silent in his own thoughts, as the Caribs themselves were accustomed to do, his mind wandered to the exhilarating nights in Presente's hut when he had been stirred to such heights of unquenchable desire by her tremulous response to his virility. But his mind always returned to Elise and the voluptuous nights of a passion that was both exhilarating and satisfying. He had not seen Elise for many months, and the thought of her brought out in him an overwhelming hunger that could be assuaged only by the feel and the smell of her extraordinary and delightful feminine charms. He could not endure much more time without seeing her.

Times were different, he knew. The white population was in panic. The recent attacks had brought to the fore the enormity of the threat against the survival of the planters and all other persons who were not black or colored. In this atmosphere of insecurity and turmoil, most planters had placed harsher strictures on their slaves, and the estates were being fortified against any insurgency by the runaways or against insurrection among the slaves themselves. He would have to observe extreme caution if he were to venture anywhere near Dubique.

As he gathered his belongings the following day, Kumeni regarded him with characteristic apathy; but when he left the tabwi her eyes followed him all the way until he was lost to her in the gloomy shade of the trees. He kept away from the less dense fringes of the forest, slipping and sliding up and down steep gorges, through muddy patches of ground and over rotting fallen trunks of trees until he came to the dark, brooding mountain over Geneva. He could go on from there to Coree Greg's camp, or turn to the ridge that would bring him to the heights of Dubique. Undecided, he sat on the bole of a tree that had fallen across a faint trace that he knew only the hunters of his camp frequented. He sat with his musket across his knees listening to the silence. His ears were so attuned to the sound of the forest that he could hear the scuttling of the padded feet of an agouti among the rotting leaves on the wet ground, or the sudden muted flutter of wings as a hawk or a parrot drifted down on to a branch overhead. Now and then the faint twitter of the tiny robin or the long, sad monotone of the mountain whistler came to him from the distance.

He wondered why it was that such peace and tranquility could be found in the woods while the rest of the world was embroiled in such turbulence. Was this why Coree Greg preferred to enjoy seclusion in the wilds than to fight for freedom among a people who themselves could never be free? Was this freedom ever to be found among the classes of people that constituted colonial society, a people that were forever striving for dominance over each other?

He thought of Paulinaire, rich and a freed man who yet was not free, a man who, unshackled by the bonds of ownership, was willing to join with slaves to secure another kind of freedom that seemed as elusive as gold at the foot of the rainbow. Was this freedom then merely the right to choose the manner and quality of his individual servitude? But his mind recalled the grandiloquent sentiments that Paulinaire had brought to them in the clearing in the woods that wonderful night when he and the other men and women had been given dreams of equality, fraternity and liberty. In the broader context of humankind, the relevance of these noble principles still seemed plausible. At least Paulinaire had implanted in his soul a dream which, however distant, still seemed attainable and kept him from the barrenness of despair.

In contrast, Bala's dream had been one of destruction, and his principal weapon was hate. His was a philosophy of doom without the shining light of fulfillment at the end. Pharcel felt deep sorrow that a life of such bravery and fortitude should now be condemned to futility. He was resolved that somehow he would have to find a way to inextricably weave the context of Bala's struggle and the valor and loyalty of those who had surrounded him, into the tapestry of history so that the blood which had been shed in the valley of the lakes should not have fallen on infertile ground. He would accommodate himself to Coree Greg's strategy of passive resistance for the present; but that would only be a transient pause in a journey that would lead him to a destiny that was still vague and undefined, but which he was certain would bring him to the centre of the struggle for liberation from the enslavement of his race. But first, he would have to find Paulinaire.

The sun was already descending over the sea when he began the climb to the ridge that would take him to the upper reaches of Dubique Estate. When he came to the edge of the forest he climbed into the thick foliage of a rosewood tree and sat in the crook of a thick branch until nightfall. He had hoped that he would find Jacques somewhere in the outer fringes of the forest, but he had not appeared. No doubt, Jacques had retreated further into the woods to avoid confrontation with the militia or the many zealous and reward-crazed vigilantes who were forever on the lookout for runaway slaves.

Pharcel lingered in the bushes on the boundaries of the estate, unable to make up his mind about what he should do. He wanted to make contact with Paulinaire, but he knew that he had to find Jacques to do so. On the other hand, lured by his desire to hold the woman of his nightly fantasies one more time, he felt a desperate need to see Elise. He wandered aimlessly for some time in the dark, and then, without conscious volition, began the descent to the cane fields.

A half moon was hanging over the sea, casting an eerie light on its waters. In the cane fields an uneasy somberness cast a pall over the surrounding land, and trees stood like ghostly silhouettes against the grim, grey landscape. Pharcel crept along the path, all senses tuned to the sounds and movements of the night. At his approach, small creatures scurried noisily in the cane trash; an owl hooted in one of the trees close by; a dog bayed chillingly down by the ravine on the opposite side of the estate house. As he neared the perimeter of the clusters of trees that bounded the house on three sides, he veered left towards the ravine, then crept through the bushes until he was a few feet from the clearing; he crouched there more still than the branches that surrounded him.

His mind conjured images of Elise languorously moving about somewhere in the house, her thin cotton chemise clinging to her voluptuous form. Her presence seemed to possess him more and more in closer intimacy—the clean scent of her hair, the warm, fresh smell of her half-exposed breasts and the musky odor of her charms. His desire stirred as he thought of the last time he had held her to him and of the quickening sound of her soft cries and sighs as their bodies locked together in intimate embrace. He was so lost in his imaginings that he almost missed the flash of white around the far corner of the house. His breath came quickly. Panting with excitement and uncontrollable desire, he darted from the cover of the bushes and, crouching low in the dark, rushed towards the further side of the house.

He rose up in the dark on the other side, arms extended, bending forward with eagerness. The figure in white stopped as if sensing an unexpected presence and turned sharply to him. He stayed rooted to the spot even as the full bloated belly of the woman jutted out towards him. He saw her face, sullen, strong-jawed and disdainful. Her eyes seemed to cloud in uncertainty for a brief moment, and then they suddenly flared into recognition. Georgette glared at him with unimaginable malevolence as she began screaming into the night, an unending, terrifying screech that tore through the branches of the trees and lifted to the hills far away.

Pharcel stood transfixed, unable to react to the shock of the unexpected encounter. He heard the pounding of boots on the front verandah, but still he remained rooted where he stood. A loud explosion shattered the state of traumatic immobility which held him fast and he turned and bounded into the nearby bushes. He heard Jean shouting to Toma, and a second explosion ripped through the bushes close to him. He ran headlong towards the stream, virtually somersaulting over the side of the ravine, and did not stop until he had gained the cover of the trees at the top of the ridge. He was breathing heavily and his limbs quivered with fright.

A storm of emotions ran through Pharcel's body, and his heart pounded in pulsing surges in his bosom. He could not tell whether it was from the danger which he had so narrowly escaped or from the sudden exposure to the hate and contempt that he had seen on Georgette's face.

He had felt secure in his daring encroachment in the vicinity of the estate house, knowing that Elise would come out some time in the night looking out for him in the privacy of the dark. The house had always been asleep after Jean retired from his nightly bouts of drinking, except for Elise who had never failed to appear even for a brief moment, hoping that he would be somewhere among the trees waiting for her to come out to him. Now he sensed a new alertness as if the place had suddenly been fortified against some expected incursion. Even Jean seemed to have awakened from his drunken somnolence. And what was Toma doing there so late in the night instead of being safely asleep in his hut in the slave quarters? He could not know how much had happened since his last visit, and he wondered whether Elise's nocturnal trysts had somehow been revealed to her husband.

Totally confounded by these questions and the storm of emotions that raged within him, he paced about restlessly under the trees, feeling like an animal caged and abandoned. He had come down to see Elise and he had been hounded out of her presence by hostility which he had never expected to find. The hunger for her was still boiling in his loins and his heart burned for even a moment's brief reunion with the object of his desire. He had not seen her for so many months, and the thought of her had filled his heart with a yearning that had stayed with him through the weeks of his tumultuous adventures. He had come so close to seeing her, but now she was beyond his reach. Frustrated and downcast, he sought for a place to rest for the night.

He remembered the hollow in the bamboo grove where he had first met Paulinaire. It would be dry and secure, and the cushion of soft, smooth leaves would make a good resting place. He found it without much difficulty and lay down on the sloping sides of the hollow. The night was cool and dark. The moon had dropped further to the horizon; a spattering of stars hung high in the sky over the circle formed by the overhanging tops of the bamboo trees, but their light barely penetrated the gloom of the night.

His mind raced over the events of the past weeks, the meeting with Paulinaire, the convocation with the chiefs, the massacre at Rosalie, and the recent retaliatory attack on Bala's camp. He wondered what would be the outcome of all this. He recalled Bala's sudden change of affection and the attention he had paid to him among all the other chiefs and their followers. He had felt privileged and singled-out among the army of men that always surrounded Bala. Even Sandy and Congoree had taken time to be attentive to him. But the glory of his association with such heroic figures had somehow faded after the repulsive acts and emotions that he had witnessed during the attack at Rosalie, and he felt lost and alone and disillusioned.

He fell asleep at last just before dawn, and dreamed of birds whistling in the trees. He awoke when the sun was already up over the hills. There was whistling in the trees, but not of birds. He looked up to see movement behind the bamboo clumps, and sat up, and felt about quickly for his musket. It was Jacques grinning at him through the swaying stems of bamboo. Pharcel returned a welcoming grin, and Jacques came down into the hollow, regarding him with some amusement.

"Chasing white wives again?" Jacques asked mockingly.

Pharcel looked at him with an insouciant smile, not acknowledging the taunt.

"What could you have against our black girls?" Jacques challenged him again to respond.

"Nothing at all," Pharcel replied.

"Then why do you so recklessly risk your neck to go after that white woman?" Jacques persisted.

Pharcel was nonplussed; and hung his head, thinking of a way to avoid responding.

"And a married one at that?" Jacques prompted him.

"She loves me," Pharcel said defiantly.

"Love? You think white people have love?"

"Why not?"

"You think white people can love black people?"

"But why not?"

"Black people have love. White people, they do not even have heart."

"Then we are not the same?"

"No, and never!"

"Then we are not equal?"

"Never."

"I thought you believed in Paulinaire?" Pharcel said. "What was all that about liberty, equality and fraternity?"

"That is something different," Jacques said, scowling defensively. "Nothing at all to do with white people's love."

Then he turned impatiently to Pharcel.

"We don't have time for this kind of talk. Paulinaire wants to see you."

"When?" Pharcel asked.

"I will let you know," Jacques replied. "I will arrange a meeting."

Pharcel nodded.

"And keep away from the white woman," Jacques grinned at him amiably. "Next time Toma's buckshot will rip your behind."

As he reached over the top of the hollow, he turned again towards Pharcel, looking gravely down at him.

"Tell the old man to prepare," he said. "The militia is on the march. They plan to visit him one of these days."

"Where are you heading?" Pharcel asked. He was anxious to make contact with Paulinaire as soon as possible.

Jacques hesitated for only a moment.

"I am going to the execution," he replied gravely.

"What execution?" Pharcel asked again, a look of confusion on his face.

"Bala and Sandy," Jacques explained tersely.

"Bala and Sandy?" Pharcel was momentarily dumfounded. He had not given thought to the fate that awaited the two captured chiefs.

"Yes," Jacques said solemnly, "they are to die on the gibbet tomorrow."

"Good God! I did not know. I must come." Pharcel decided without hesitation.

"It is risky," Jacques cautioned. "Your presence is too remarkable for you to hide as easily as I can. Nobody notices me. That is why I can move freely without drawing attention to myself."

"I will be there," Pharcel insisted.

Jacques nodded and strode towards the thick wood a short distance from where they stood. He turned northward, away from the trace that Pharcel had traveled by.

Coree Greg's camp was crowded. Several of the men and women who had escaped the attack on Bala's camp had been wandering for days, torn and hungry, in the woods. Some of them had been captured by the militia as they came through the open and more accessible scrub surrounding the larger fresh water lake; but many had kept to the cover of the thick forest, down steep gorges, and over countless ridges until they came to the narrow valley where Coree Greg's camp lay hidden and secure.

Coree Greg received them with characteristic graciousness, and set about a methodical disposition of places in the few huts that were available, including his own. Claire assisted him with the sensitive task of finding places for the women and children so that personal frictions and tensions could be avoided as much as possible. Even so, on the first night, two of the men confronted each other for right of precedence into Marie Claire's hut, but Claire quickly reassigned a houseful of women and children there. Marie Claire was evidently resentful of the change, and the situation was finally resolved when she generously moved to the open shelter of the spreading branches of a tree not far from her hut where the men, in recognition of their mutual and instant need for collaboration, busied themselves with setting up a rude, temporary shelter for the night. The fulsomeness of Marie Claire's appetite and capacity for giving soon filled the night and each man quickly discovered that he alone was inadequate to master the exceeding generosity and excessive lubricity of her offering. Harmony prevailed in the camp after that.

Until Pharcel returned.

It was still bright morning when he entered the camp. Finding his shack occupied, he ambled over to Coree Greg's hut to let him know that he had returned. He stood hesitantly, taking in the many new faces milling around, before he called to Coree Greg. A few new huts had been erected, and men and women were bringing in poles and bundles of thatch to construct others. Claire came out and squinted at him, her bony face showing displeasure. She re-entered the hut without a word; and soon, Coree Greg came out, and stood at the door. He peered at Pharcel with a dour look, saying nothing.

"I am back," Pharcel said.

Coree Greg continued to gaze at him sourly, as if he had not spoken. Pharcel shifted uncomfortably.

"I see my hut has been taken," he ventured, reaching out for some response.

Coree Greg nodded.

"Should I build myself another?" he asked.

Coree Greg continued to look at him, a blank expression on his face.

Pharcel shifted uneasily, wondering why it was that he suddenly felt a stranger to this camp.

"You no longer belong here," Coree Greg said at last. He turned to go.

"What have I done?" Pharcel's voice was heavy with distress.

Coree Greg stopped. Then, turning his head slightly, he spat the words over his shoulders.

"We do not consort with traitors."

Despite the shock of the words so scornfully leveled at him, Pharcel's response was controlled.

"I have betrayed no one!" he replied evenly.

Coree Greg did not reply. Stiff-backed, he walked slowly into his hut.

Pharcel could not understand what went wrong. Clearly, there must be some misunderstanding, but he did not have the faintest notion of what that could be. He sat under a tree for the rest of the morning wondering what he should do. His shack was fully occupied by a few of the men who had recently drifted in; he could build another, but Coree Greg's attitude towards him had been one of scorn and dismissal. He could go back to the Caribs who were never warm in their reception, but who, at least, tolerated his presence. At lunch, Marie Claire brought him a bowl of cassava and river crabs, however, she would not stop to talk, and quickly turned her back on him as he was about to thank her.

Despite his hunger, having been without a meal since he left Kumeni in the Carib village, he ate slowly and with little appetite. His musket lay at his feet. No one took any notice of him, and everyone went about his business as if he didn't exist. A cloud of depression settled on his shoulders, followed by seething anger at the injustice of his own people rejecting him so cruelly and with no apparent cause. He sat there for a long time, his brown handsome face darkening with mounting fury. He looked up after a while and, recognizing one of the men from Bala's camp, he addressed him directly.

"What did I do?" he asked, desperation choking his voice.

The man stopped in his stride and glanced at him. He was about to turn away again, but, seeing the look of anguish and frustration in Pharcel's eyes, he turned and faced him squarely.

"You ran away," he said with a vicious sneer.

"I did not run away!" Pharcel protested.

"You are a coward!" another man shouted at him.

Pharcel leapt to his feet. Anger convulsed his body. He sprang at the man and seized him by the throat and shook him fiercely.

"I am not a coward!" He kept shouting the words again and again as his fingers tightened around the man's gullet.

Several of the men rushed forward and tried to dislodge Pharcel's deadly grip from the man's throat. They fell to the ground and rolled in a seething mass as they seized him by the arms, neck and waist. Outrage and resentment gave Pharcel strength as he thrashed about and threw the men off him. But they subdued him at last and held him to the ground. He looked up to find Coree Greg staring down at him with a fleeting brightness in his eyes, a brief smile of admiration on his lips. But Coree Greg's eyes clouded again and the sternness returned to his countenance.

"You will have to leave," Coree Greg said coldly.

"Is that the wisdom of Africa that you always boasted about," Pharcel retorted, still lying flat and breathless on the ground, "that a man should be condemned before being heard?"

Coree Greg looked startled. Then a faint smile warmed the frostiness of his words.

"You will be heard," he assented shortly.

He walked away back to his hut.

The sun was already withdrawing its warmth from the clearing in the forest, and its light flashed onto the top of the trees, when the men and women gathered in the open space in front of Coree Greg's hut. The old chief sat in his usual place on the small rustic bench. Today he wore the rusty red sash over his shoulder and he held a staff with elaborate carvings down its length. A bright colored cap with a strange, tribal design, was perched on his head. His wife, Marie, came and sat at his feet, her infant son held close between her thighs.

The atmosphere was as formal as it could get. The blood tingled in Pharcel's veins as if he had been spiritually drawn into some primordial ritual that had been carried through the generations of his ancestors out of Africa and into this alien forest. He looked around at the glowering faces and at Coree Greg sitting in authoritative dignity on the crude bench, and the symbolism of what was about to happen struck him forcibly. No matter what the outcome of all this was, he would remember this day when he had been part of the genuine culture of a land he had only heard about, its sense of democracy, fairness and justice, and the best demonstration of fraternity and equality that he felt certain he would ever experience.

Coree Greg, in a deep, level tone of voice, explained the purpose of the gathering and the established practice and procedures for conducting an enquiry of this kind. It was not yet a trial, and no words of condemnation should be uttered until everyone was heard. Then he began his own testimony, telling of the account that Pharcel himself had given of his initial meeting with Paulinaire and how he, Coree Greg, had forbidden any further communication with the mulattos. He spoke with evident bitterness of Pharcel's declaration at the recent and disastrous meeting of chiefs, that the mulattos had instructed him to convey an invitation to the camps to join with them in a collaborative uprising against the planters and the rest of the white community, which showed two things—that Pharcel had disregarded the communal decision of his camp and that he had become an emissary of the mulattos and so could not be trusted. Furthermore, there had been rumors that Pharcel was consorting with the wife of a white planter, thus putting the camp to enormous and unnecessary danger.

The men tittered at the mention of Pharcel's inter-racial liaison, unconsciously admiring and even envying his boldness. The women scowled and muttered, their body language conveying feelings of betrayal. Pharcel stood uncomfortably in their midst, unhappy that Elise had been brought into the discussion. Somehow he had never associated Elise with his camp or with the world of runaway slaves. Theirs had been a world apart, a magical world which had nothing to do with the reality of his personal existence.

Coree Greg's voice jolted him back to the proceedings. He called on anyone present to come forward with his or her complaint. One by one several of the men who had been in Bala's camp on the day of the raid stood, and gave testimony to Pharcel's perfidy. The gist of their complaint was that he had not appeared to fight with the other men on the day in question. Instead, he had left the camp early in the day. They thought he must have gone to lead the militia up to the approaches to the camp. Why else would he have left the camp when all the other men were still in bed? One woman came forward, and said that she had seen him leave with Presente with whom he had been bedding since the day he came into Bala's camp, and she thought he must have delivered her to the militia since Presente had been taken by them even before the fighting began.

The scowls deepened and the muttering became louder.

There was a long pause when the testimonies were over. Coree Greg's eyes roved over the circle of faces, but no one else came forward. He nodded silently to Pharcel. Night had fallen and the faces had faded in obscurity as the darkness settled over the camp. Someone came with a bundle of lighted torches which he planted at intervals on the inside of the circle. The flames flickered and threw dancing shadows on the eager faces of the men and women sitting around.

Pharcel began to speak, slowly and hesitantly at first.

"I have been a steadfast and dedicated member of this camp," he said. "My loyalty and devotion to our chief, Coree Greg, has been unwavering and will always be so."

He paused and looked around at the shadowy faces as if to appeal to their understanding and sympathy. They were his judges and he had to make them understand.

"I am innocent of the suspicions and charges brought against me," he continued, "though the circumstances of my life might have led me to strange paths and even stranger associates. If I am to be judged, then let it be on the basis of truth and reason, and not on mere prejudice and spurious speculation."

As he spoke, his voice became stronger, and he seemed to stand taller with a presence that became more and more commanding. His words grew more impassioned as his heart swelled and the hidden secrets of his life came spilling out in wave upon wave of intense emotions. He spoke of his childhood among men and women who seemed forever displaced and searching for the return of a lost identity, and of the shadowy existence that he himself had led in the household of the white planter who had had complete ascendancy over him. He related the injustice that had been done to him when he was so severely flogged for unwittingly witnessing, and being subjected to, the wanton and reckless behavior of the planter's daughter; and of his fears after his own person had been violated by the planter's wife.

Stumbling for words, he tried to describe the passion that had been ignited in his heart, drawn him inexorably and dangerously back to the white woman, and had almost been the occasion of his death. Then he told of his encounter with Paulinaire on that fateful night when the mulatto had awakened in him a new sense of himself, when he began to understand that he had run away not just out of fear of punishment or of the hatred and contempt of the white persons who had claimed him body and soul, but because of something grander: the revelation that he was seeking to establish his right as a human person to equality and liberty.

He repeated as best as he could what Paulinaire had said about the universal struggle for liberty, equality and fraternity even among the poor and down-trodden whites in their foreign lands; and spoke of the magnificent successes that the fraternity of blacks and mulattos had achieved in San Domingo, and especially of the pre-eminence of Toussaint L'Ouverture and his army of blacks.

At this point in his testimony, despite the unsteady light, Pharcel could discern a softening of Coree Greg's countenance as if he had found some empathy with the higher principles which had so drawn Pharcel to the preaching of the mulatto. But the old man lapsed again into abstraction as Pharcel continued.

Carefully and with long pauses, he related the circumstances that had led him to the grand banquet of the mulattos on the bank of the Geneva River; but he was quick to disclose his disillusionment at the treatment which had been accorded the women slaves that were in attendance, and the doubts which had assailed him when he listened to Paulinaire's statement regarding the inevitable ascendancy of the colored intelligentsia, and the subordinate role that he had offhandedly assigned to the black community in the new society that was to come. His disillusionment and uncertainty were the main reasons why he had not bothered to convey Paulinaire's invitation directly to Coree Greg. Indeed, he had had no intentions of doing so at all until Jacques had called on him to corroborate what he had said to the chiefs.

In simple terms and without visible emotion, he dismissed the charges made against him regarding Presente's capture and his failure to join in the defense of the camp. His account of his own narrow escape from capture, and the arduous trek in full nudity down to Mabouya's camp, seemed to have mollified the other members of Coree Greg's camp; but the visitors grumbled vociferously and remained skeptical. At the end, a dark curtain seemed to have descended on Coree Greg's face. He looked impassively at the assemblage and extended his arms palm upwards, inviting judgment. An angry murmur rose among the men, and the women turned to each other in agitated whispers; but no one came forward. At last, Coree Greg struck his staff firmly on the ground and all eyes turned to him. A sudden hush fell on the circle as the old man prepared to speak.

"Nothing that we have heard completely absolves the accused," he began.

His words sent shivers down Pharcel's body. He felt as one caught up in a bad dream. This couldn't be true. It was not the end. There was something more, something important to be said. Then it came to him in a flash: the last thing that Jacques had said to him.

"The dangers that surround us are too great," Coree Greg continued, "and the risks too high for us to harbor among us anyone who is not entirely beyond suspicion."

"Wait!" Pharcel shouted. "There is something more."

There was a loud muttering among the assembly. Many of them gestured with clenched fists in his direction, as if to shut out any further argument.

"The militia is coming!" he shouted in desperation. "The camp will be under attack!"

There was a moment's stunned silence followed by shouts of incredulity.

"No more lies!" they shouted at him. "No more betrayals!"

Coree Greg raised his staff high over his head. The assembly fell into an abrupt silence. Only the faint sound of a light breeze in the trees disturbed the night. Coree Greg slowly lowered his staff.

"What are you saying?"

Coree Greg's fiery eyes flashed a dire warning. He turned a wary look on Pharcel, searching his eyes for any sign of duplicity. The news had obviously unsettled him, and he was searching for a way to draw out the truth from Pharcel.

"The militia is planning an attack on this camp," Pharcel said, emboldened by Coree Greg's concern.

"How do you know this?" Coree Greg asked suspiciously.

There was more murmuring and the men glanced at Pharcel accusingly.

"Jacques told me this morning. He asked me to warn you that they will be coming soon," Pharcel replied calmly.

The men and women all knew Jacques. He had helped most of them to find their way to camps as far away as the east coast. At the mention of his name they looked uncertainly at each other, then leaned forward and waited for Coree Greg's response. The silence dragged on for a long time. Claire turned and looked at her husband expectantly.

"When did you meet with Jacques?" Coree Greg asked, deep concern adding to the heaviness in his voice.

"We met three days ago," Pharcel replied. "He was on his way to the execution."

"What execution?" Coree Greg asked in alarm.

The circle of faces leaned forward anxiously. All ears were fixed intently on Pharcel's words.

"Bala and Sandy," he said, turning to the circle of faces now gaping awfully at him.

A low moan rose from the crowd. A high pitched keening came from the women huddled close to the nearest huts. Coree Greg's chin fell upon his bosom.

"They died valiantly," Pharcel said simply. "It was truly the bravest thing I ever saw."

Coree Greg stared at him in wonder.

"You were there?" he asked.

"I went with Jacques," he replied proudly, a slight elation heightening his voice.

The murmuring among the group increased and they stared at him with something close to admiration. Coree Greg stood, and spoke quietly, as if to the stillness of the night.

"It is late," he said. "We will discuss all this tomorrow."

CHAPTER 15

The little town was in a fever of excitement. From sunrise, town-criers had been to every corner with a proclamation that the two notorious runaway chiefs, Bala and Sandy, had been found guilty of sedition, incitement and murder, and had been sentenced to be hung on the gibbet on the open grounds at Woodbridge Bay. The public was invited to witness the executions. Come one, come all!

Captain Urquhart sat on the portico reading the *Colonist* of 4th June, 1786, and the *Journal or Weekly Intelligencer* of the same week. The two journals gave full praise to the planters on the east coast, without whose initiative the raid on Bala's camp would not have been carried out and so successfully executed. While the support given by the two companies of the militia was gratefully acknowledged, it was as if they had played a minor role in the rigorous battle that had taken place in the difficult interior of the forest surrounding the camp. No mention was made of the black militiamen from Urquhart's company that had tracked the two fugitive chiefs and cornered them in the cave below Morne Diablotin.

As for the battle itself, the papers had made it appear that the white planters and the militia had easily routed the runaways, who were described as a pack of cowardly, undisciplined savages, unschooled in warfare and without the courage to withstand an organized attack. Captain Urquhart knew that fighting had been fierce in the woods and, despite the element of surprise which favored the militia, the runaways had quickly marshaled their forces, and made a tactical retreat into the cover of the forest. By doing so they had made it difficult for the militiamen, using their advantage of superior numbers and better arms, to surround and capture them. Indeed the militia had been forced to resort to close order fighting with swords and bayonets against the machetes and clubs of the runaways.

He was full of admiration for the way Bala and Sandy had rallied their men to withdraw into the woods where they would be less vulnerable than in the open clearing around the camp. The result might not have been so decisive had not Bala been wounded so early. Even so, the runaways had continued to fight in rear-guard action to protect their chiefs and give them time to make their escape.

Contrary to the reports in the two journals that there had been wholesale slaughter and capture of the majority of the runaways, he knew that most of the men had simply vanished after their chiefs had gone safely into hiding and when it was clear that there was no point in prolonging the battle. A few had been injured during the fight, some of whom had been taken prisoner. He also knew that most of the women and nearly all of the children had been led safely away as soon as the attack began.

His men had carried out the mopping up exercise in the scrubs and bushes around the lakes which had brought in Bala's wife and son, as well as a number of other fugitives trying to make their way to the nearest camp. It was his men who had brought Bala and Sandy in, but no mention had been made of this crucial fact. Instead, both journals continued to bewail the inaction of the militia in whom the planters and other worthy citizens had entrusted their safety and properties, and on whom such a large part of the colony's funds was being expended. They were being urged to take heart from the bold initiative of the worthy planters who had girded themselves to defend their lives and their economic interest, and to set about completing the task that had so splendidly been started for them.

Captain Urquhart was disgusted at the disparagement of the conduct of Bala and Sandy during the harrowing days of their trial. The truth was that both men had bravely endured nearly four days of brutal harassment, and had stood heroically firm against a judicial authority that was blatantly abused by the court officials. Bala in particular had shown his mettle as a warrior and leader. His wound had not been attended to, and his thigh and legs down to his toes had swelled and turned to a gangrenous blackness. But despite the intense agony which assailed him, he stood tall and proud, disdaining to answer to the court on the many charges made against him.

Sandy had maintained a quiet dignity throughout the proceedings and spoke, not in answer to any questions put to him or to any accusations made against him, but with passion and eloquence against the inhumanity of white colonialist society and the injustice meted out to all slaves on the island. He claimed that freedom was his by right and that he did not have to depend on any man, white or black, to grant it to him. He had retaken his freedom, and he would make no apologies for that.

Instead, the journals had painted a picture of abject cowardliness and unrepentant barbarism in the two men, qualities that could not be considered heroic in the eyes of the superior race of white men and women that constituted the citizenship of the colony. They made much of the savagery of the attacks on the Rosalie plantation, which they said had amply demonstrated the beastly nature of the perpetrators of the crimes committed there; and they boasted of the refinements of British justice which they said were too precious to be wasted on creatures that could hardly be considered human.

Captain Urquhart threw the journals away from him. As a soldier, he had often encountered fear, and he knew what true bravery was when he saw it. He could not stand by and see genuine courage as displayed by the two men so outrageously disparaged. What was even more galling was the pettiness of the rabble that had filled the courtroom. Devoid of any sensibilities, they had jeered and railed at the two prisoners, hurling insults at them as they stood already condemned even before their trial had begun. He wondered how many of those vociferous men in the courtroom would have dared to stand against the two in open combat anywhere, here or in the forest. He could not help but feel ashamed at the crassness of those in this narrow colonial backwater who claimed superiority among other men and women because of the color of their skin, although for the most part they themselves were illiterate and uncultured in the ways of civilized society. It seemed to him that there was far more nobility in the two men standing bound and nearly naked in the docks than could be found among those who were intent on belittling them.

He had been educated at Cambridge before joining the West India Regiment. There he had been embroiled in heated arguments about slavery and the true nature of the African black. To him the issues had been conducive to lively and interesting discourse, and he had enjoyed the intellectual exchanges, especially as he had never been called upon to take any definitive position. He had joined the regiment filled with romantic notions of defending the empire and the King; but now he had come to the degrading realization that he was instead drawn into the unpleasant and indefensible task of giving support to a decadent and vulgar society of white men and their coarse, graceless women in their abhorrent, inhuman treatment of a helpless, displaced, oppressed and dispossessed people.

A large number of blacks had been assigned to his company, and he had reluctantly accepted them at first; but he had seen first hand how responsive they were to training and discipline, and he had grown to admire their intelligence, loyalty and courage under the most difficult conditions. Few of the white soldiers in the ranks, even though they gave themselves airs about their superiority over all black and colored men, had shown similar dedication, discipline and sense of duty. For one thing, the black soldiers' unfailing care for personal cleanliness set them apart from their white counterparts who were often unkempt in appearance and unclean in their personal habits.

Captain Urquhart drew himself out of his reverie. He was still alone on the portico. No doubt his host, Winston, was still with the Governor and the rest of the Council making final arrangements for the execution. This was no ordinary event. The last execution of the runaway slave, Cicero, was not of such importance even though it had created a great stir among the population. These two chiefs, who had aroused so much fear and panic in the countryside, had now been taken and condemned. The Council wanted to ensure that their execution was seen as a warning to all slaves and especially runaways everywhere that it would meet any insurgency or insurrection with the full severity of its will. It was to be a demonstration of the determination of the Council to eradicate the chiefs and all runaways, and to keep all slaves in rightful subjection.

Word had been sent all along the west coast and to the southern part of the island that the planters there should gather as many of their slaves as could be spared from estate work to witness the execution of judgment on the two men who had dared to use violence against their white masters, and who had violated the virtue of the white woman and her innocent daughter on the plantation. The gibbeting of the two notorious chiefs was to be a signal lesson to all runaways still in the woods that a similar fate awaited them if they did not quickly surrender and return to their masters; and to all slaves everywhere that they should not rob their masters of what was rightfully theirs through any misguided notions about their right to liberty.

In response to this call, gangs of slaves were herded across the river to the open savannah where the gibbeting was to take place, and a steady procession of gaily dressed men and women of many shades and gradations of color filled the narrow road that led northward out of the town.

Captain Marshall had been summoned from his post at Grandbay to help strengthen security at the Fort, as it was feared that an attempt would have been made by the other chiefs still at large to rescue the two condemned men; but there had been no signs of any infiltration of the black population in the town or of any incursions anywhere near the boundaries of the district. His own company had been in a state of readiness for nearly a week awaiting the command to move against Coree Greg's camp in the mountains over Geneva. It was a mission that he was looking forward to with eagerness since he was sure that he would find the slave, Pharcel, hiding there.

Since Brent's death at the hands of the slave, he had zealously patrolled the lighter woods in the hills above Dubique; and he had set watches in the fields around the estate house, but Pharcel had not shown his face for many months. Finally, he had sent word to Jean about his suspicions, urging him to keep watch day and night, and to shoot on sight if Pharcel were ever to return to the estate. He was looking forward to the opportunity to get rid of the pernicious slave once and for all, the memory of whose taunting eyes had haunted him for so many months.

Captain Marshall, resplendent in his dress uniform, walked smartly across the street and up the flight of steps to join Captain Urquhart on the portico. He gleamed all over with spit and polish, and his thin moustache, turned up with a special twist at the corners of his mouth, emphasized the sardonic look that always appeared on his face. He looked about him uncertainly, searching the dim interior of the sitting room.

"Nobody here?" he asked.

"I am," Urquhart replied teasingly.

"Of course," Marshall exclaimed, "you are nobody!"

"Oh, come on," Urquhart chuckled with a pleasant smile.

"So where are the others?" Marshall asked again seriously.

"Winston is still with the Governor," Urquhart ventured. "Everybody else seems to be heading down to the gibbeting."

Joseph came in quietly bearing a small tray with two glasses. He looked particularly downcast, and barely murmured a greeting. Marshall looked questioningly at him.

"What ails him?" Marshall asked, tipping his head towards the departing slave.

"Looks rather gloomy today, don't you think?" Urquhart remarked.

"I don't trust those black bastards," Marshall said viciously.

"Oh, Joseph is all right," Urquhart assured him. "A bit under the weather, I suppose?"

"Don't be so sure," Marshall replied portentously. "There seems to be a widespread conspiracy going on. You never know who to trust."

"I think you exaggerate," Urquhart protested. "It can't be so bad."

"I tell you. These slaves are devious," Marshall insisted.

"These are brave men out there," Urquhart said. "You cannot help but admire their courage."

"Courage?" Marshall smarted. "Killing women and children? You call that courage?"

"Well, you should have seen them fighting," Urquhart said wonderingly. "I have never seen men face death so fearlessly. And what about the trial? Did you see either of them even flinch at any time during the long days of prosecution?"

"I will show them 'courage' when I meet with them in the woods,"

"Don't be too complacent. There is a lot of fight in them. Even in old Coree Greg."

"I have one mission to perform in Coree Greg's camp and that is to destroy that slave, Pharcel."

"Why are you so obsessed with him? After all, he is only a minor figure."

"You will know one of these days. He is more dangerous than you think."

"Well, don't let this mission become an obsession, lest it consumes your good judgment."

Marshall snorted disdainfully.

"We might as well go down to the execution," Urquhart said, changing the subject. "It will soon be time."

Joseph watched them go. A dark frown furrowed his brow. He knew he had to act quickly. He cleared away the empty glasses and hastily left the house as soon as the two officers disappeared around the corner.

It was a bright day. Thin wisps of cloud floated under the clear, blue sky. The mountains surrounding the town stood out in clear outline against the sky. A gentle breeze blew from the sea, ruffling the dark, green leaves of the many trees that spread over small clearings and sometimes over roof tops. The streets were alive with a bustling throng heading towards the river. A few white men rode horses, and two carriages nudged cautiously through the crowd. Several white women with parasols over their heads walked daintily in the center of the road, trailed by young slave attendants with picnic baskets on their heads. Most of the white women wore white or plain colored garments embroidered with lace or with crocheted blouses, while their slaves were clothed in the uniform drab grey or coarse blue cloth stitched in tubular, formless fashion that nonetheless could not hide the vibrant sensuousness of their bodies. Several mulatto women swung gaily by dressed in colorful, sweeping, multi-layered dresses and gaily-colored head-ties. The men looked almost effaced in their simple linen suits and straw hats. Most of the male slaves wore trousers cut off at the knees with short vests, though many of them preferred to go bare-back.

The road veered right at the last row of houses towards a ford in the river. A crowd had gathered on the sandy bank as the horses and carriages edged into the stream, and plodded across the stony bed. Several men hoisted some of the women on their backs and waded to the other bank. The women slaves, their baskets perched precariously on their heads, hoisted their skirts far up their thighs, and stumbled over the rocks across the swift current of the stream. Bawdy cries and calls came from the men standing on both banks as the women slaves struggled to reach the further side. It was a jolly, carnival atmosphere so much at odds with the macabre scene that was to be enacted on the savannah at Woodbridge Bay.

A narrow, rutted road continued from the further bank through a patch of roseau plants, its cane-like fronds and light, fluffy blossoms waving in the breeze; and beyond that was a row of seedy houses occupied by some of the poorer French refugees from Guadeloupe and Martinique. Past the row of houses, the road opened onto open grassland which was interspersed with tamarind and flamboyant trees. Further towards the North, a small stream flowed through a thick copse of dark wood that stretched to a narrow valley into the adjoining hills. The level, open ground was already filled with horses, carriages and a multitude of persons milling about in general disorder. Hawkers called out their various offerings of fresh coconuts, cane juice, roasted corn and nuts, fried fish and cassava bread. A stand had been set up under a spreading flamboyant tree where a group of white and colored men stood drinking from gourds and goblets.

It was a pleasant morning. The warm sun was cooled by a refreshing breeze which came wafting from the sea. The faces of the people were alive with excitement and a curious elation, the kind one unaccountably feels at times like this when death and suffering was in the air. Only the small groups of estate slaves bound together and huddled under the trees towards the back of the field showed sullenness and despair. All others were in high spirits as if to celebrate the grim ceremony that was about to be conducted.

The sound of military drums came from the distance; and soon, emerging from the row of houses, the two Captains, Marshall and Urquhart, appeared, erect on their prancing horses, leading a procession. Following them, between two lines of militiamen, the condemned runaway chiefs stumbled forward. In the vanguard were the Provost Marshall and three other men dressed in the tawdry robes of court officials. They sat on plodding horses, their sallow faces tight with judicial authority.

As the procession came closer, a feeling of awe ran through the crowd as it beheld the two men, clothed in the raiment of savagery, being led by ropes tied to their waists. They wore thin, white trousers cut off at the knees and were bareback. Their arms were bound across their chests, and a long pole had been forced in the crook of their arms and across their backs, forcing them to bend forward slightly. Their ankles were shackled with short lengths of rope, so that they were only able to shuffle forward with short steps.

Bala walked with a painful limp; but, despite his obvious agony, he held his head steadfastly forward and his shoulders hunched. His jaw was firmly set, and his eyes burned with unshakeable passion. Sandy walked beside him; but because of the pole that held them together, he was made to stoop to compensate for his taller stature; nonetheless, the boldness of his countenance remained undiminished by the forced indignity of his posture; and his eyes flashed defiantly as he scanned the gawping multitude. As they came through the crowd, a way opened out before them. Many of the white and mulatto women gasped and held their hands to their mouths with feigned and exaggerated horror as the two men passed near them. Others stared in silent dread at the matted hair, grimy bodies and fierce mien of the two men as they would at the wild mane and predatory eyes of a caged lion. The field slaves hung their heads, and moaned softly as they saw the two chiefs, bound and helpless, approaching the instrument of death.

As the procession passed on its way towards the gibbet, the crowd began to jostle forward. A loud murmuring arose from among those closest to the condemned men, and loud abusive epithets came from those hanging back under the trees. Some persons had rushed forward with upraised fists, gesturing aggressively until they came to the front line; but they came to an abrupt halt, fearful of the defiant posture of the prisoners even though they were securely bound. The militia formed themselves into a half circle in front of the gibbet, keeping the crowd at a safe distance from the condemned men.

Out of the crowd near the half circle of militiamen, a woman and her young child were prodded into the open space a few paces in front of the gibbet. Victoire appeared disconsolate, and wrapped her son protectively in her arms, his face buried in her robust thighs. Her garments were torn in several places, and she seemed to want to fold into herself to hide her partial nakedness. On seeing her, Bala made as if to take a step forward, but the restraining pole that kept him fast to Sandy held him back. He shook his head in frustration like an infuriated bull securely roped; and the great mass of his tangled hair lifted and fell over his ears and the back of his head. Bravely, he pulled himself together again, and directed a proud and warm glance to the woman who had borne his child.

At that moment he looked almost regal as he rose to his full height, and with awful fearlessness cast his eyes affectionately on his son. Victoire responded visibly to the warmth and inspiring courage that she had seen in Bala's eyes, and she, too, stood erect, and a wonderful look of composure seemed to settle on her youthful countenance. Bala's valiant spirit seemed to have touched his son also, for at that moment he turned from his mother's thighs and looked directly into his father's eyes, unafraid and filled with admiration.

A drum rattled and the murmurs and jeers of the rollicking crowd subsided quickly as the Provost Marshall stepped forward, and, in a high, commanding voice, read the warrants of execution. He enumerated the several crimes which had been attributed to Bala and Sandy, and in tremulous tones read the sentence of death. Then two of the militiamen strode smartly to the prisoners and released them from the pole that kept them together. Bala and Sandy strode directly beneath the gibbet and the nooses that hung loosely over their heads. One of the officials came forward and placed the nooses around their necks.

A solemn hush fell over the small field. Even the wind seemed to have paused in its gentle ruffling, and the leaves hung limply from the branches of the trees. It seemed that the earth had stopped its breathing, and all life hung suspended waiting for some imminent doom. A dark cloud crept over the mountains to the East, but no one noticed it even though its shadow spread like a pall over the inner part of the field where the slaves huddled in fear.

Suddenly, Bala's voice boomed across the open space.

"I have never been a slave," he shouted, "because in my heart I was always free. Free to do with my life whatever my will told me that I should do. Free to take my freedom in whatever way that I could. Free to punish those that sought to enslave me. And now free to die as nobly as I shall."

A loud murmuring began among the crowd; and the men under the flamboyant tree, already besotted with rum, shouted angrily, hurling insults at the already doomed men.

"Hang the niggers!" they yelled, "hang the villains!"

"I do not ask for anything," Bala raised his voice in defiance, "except that you bury my juju with my body, that I should take the spirit of my homeland with me wherever I go."

The men under the tree jeered.

"You may do what you will," Bala shouted defiantly, "but my spirit will not die! As long as my son lives, vengeance will be mine! My spirit will not rest until this day is avenged, and the day is coming when the agony of all those like me who have suffered under white oppression will be wiped clean with the blood of our oppressors!"

Sandy, who had all this while maintained a dignified silence, lifted his eyes to the skies, raised his manacled hands high above his head and shook them in triumphant solidarity.

The field slaves under the trees at the back of the field were visibly moved by Bala's invincible defiance. They all stood erect and proud, and raised their shackled arms over their heads. A few among them cheered and ululated. Among them a figure of a man, tall, brown and handsome, moved unobtrusively, unnoticed by the throng of men and women intent on Bala's last words. Captain Marshall, sitting stiffly on his horse, turned irritably to the sound of cheering, and saw the stalwart figure flitting silently through the line of field slaves. He could not mistake that brown face with the halo of brown, matted hair. Unconsciously, he jerked the reins, and the horse reared, flailing its front legs in panic. He spurred the horse, and it bolted the short distance to the trees. He pulled up among the slaves and saw, to his dismay, the brown figure heading for the thick copse that engulfed the stream. A cry of alarm went up from the crowd, totally unaware of the reason for the Captain's precipitate action. Many of them dashed towards the stream, curious to know the cause of the disturbance. There was nothing there. The copse and the hills beyond were silent. A bit crestfallen, Captain Marshall returned to the open space before the gibbet.

"What was all that about?" Captain Urquhart enquired, leaning forward with a puzzled frown on his face.

"The runaway slave, Pharcel," Captain Marshall replied. "I am sure it was him."

Captain Urquhart smiled enigmatically.

"Don't you think this obsession is gone too far?" he said.

"I know it was him," Captain Marshall insisted.

Captain Urquhart sniffed meaningfully and turned away from him.

Bala's voice thundered over the commotion that had stirred the crowd.

"There will be rivers of blood!" he shouted. "My son will avenge me!"

The Provost Marshall gave the signal and the noose tightened around his throat strangling the words that continued to pour from his mouth. They did not break their necks as was the custom in most executions; but they kept them hanging while the noose tightened slowly, choking the air from their lungs. The two bodies hung there gasping, limbs quivering in agony, while the crowd danced, and jeered, and sat in boisterous groups, passing refreshing drinks and sundry delicacies from group to group.

The dark cloud which had approached gradually over the field suddenly exploded in a torrent of rain. It poured in drenching splatters as if a huge dam in the sky had suddenly been breached. A collective wail of dismay rose from the crowd, and the men and women rose, and scattered among the trees seeking shelter. The cloud seemed to darken, and the rain poured down as if there would be no end.

"The river!" somebody shouted above the noise of the rain and the cries of distress that came from the women.

"The river!" passed from mouth to mouth.

They all understood the significance of these words. The river would soon be in flood, and would then be impassable. They had seen it many times when the heavens opened and poured torrents of water onto the hills, and the valleys flowed with streams of earth and debris, swelling the rivers to overflow with a rush of brown water like a solid wall speeding towards the sea. There was a mad dash to the road that led back into town. Soon, the field was almost empty.

Only the two Captains and their company of militiamen remained to witness the last miserable twitches from the dripping bodies hanging from the gibbet.

"You cannot help but admire them," Captain Urquhart muttered thoughtfully.

Captain Marshall looked at him aghast, wondering what could be ailing his friend.

"Soon," he said darkly, "there will be nothing to admire."

A low thunder rumbled in the distance.

CHAPTER 16

Coree Greg had spent a sleepless night. All through the night he had tossed about restlessly in the dark, struggling to empty his mind of the conflicting emotions which assailed him at every turn; but the oblivion which he so desperately sought continued to evade him. He had listened carefully to Pharcel's defense and though he had reservations about his constancy, he could not doubt the earnestness and abundance of courage with which he had spoken.

Pharcel had revealed the heart of a lion when he had been driven to defend his honor against the two men who had branded him a coward. It was difficult to associate such courage with the craven acts of desertion and betrayal which the men of Bala's camp had laid to his charge. Nor could he reconcile the sincerity which Pharcel had always shown in his dealings with everyone in the camp with the treachery that was the basis of the accusations against him. On the other hand, Pharcel had maintained communication with Paulinaire and his mulatto associates against Coree Greg's wishes, and he was in frequent contact with the wife of the white planter at Dubique for whatever shady reasons.

Coree Greg could not accept the incidence of any attraction, physical or emotional, between a black person and a white person as natural and socially acceptable. In his world, the two races were separate and apart; and there could be no room for cohabitation between them. There had to be some sinister purpose in this kind of intimacy, a plot of some kind. It was well known that the Captain of the detachment at Grandbay was used to regular visits at Dubique. It was also evident that the French were in constant conspiracy to overthrow English dominion over the colony, and to take control by force of arms, if possible with the help of the mulattos and blacks. It was quite possible that Pharcel was being used either to attempt to infiltrate the defenses of the runaway camps or to inveigle support for the seditious cause of the French, just as the mulattos were clearly also trying to do.

Coree Greg had become suspicious when Pharcel had returned to the camp carrying a musket, a weapon which was generally beyond the reach of black men, even the chiefs; and had come bearing news of the death of Sandy and Bala so soon after the event. Most disturbing of all, Pharcel had shown that he had access to intelligence concerning the movements of the militia, albeit that the source of this intelligence had been Jacques who was well known to and trusted by the several camps around the island. It was all too mysterious.

Claire had tried to soothe him with tender caresses during the sleepless night, her bony fingers fluttering lightly over his chest and belly and lingering gently at his loins. But response to her ministration was suppressed by the mental agony which had beset him. She coddled him and whispered softly in his ear.

"He is dangerous," she said, "He will never be loyal to you."

"He is young, but I think he is earnest," Coree Greg replied thoughtfully.

"He is of Guinea blood," Claire reminded him, her eyes hardening with distrust, "brave, but never dependable."

Coree Greg had been bitterly disappointed when the report had reached him that Petit Jacques, a member of his camp, had given testimony in the white man's court of justice that had condemned Cicero, Bala's gun bearer. Although he had always despised Bala's brutal way of dealing with the white planters and even some of his own followers, he could not condone any act of cowardice and betrayal as Petit Jacques had committed against one of his own race. He himself had felt let down and shamed that anyone from his camp should be so craven as to prefer dishonor than death. And so he was doubly cautious about the uncertainties surrounding Pharcel's conduct and the mysteries that seemed to cloak so much of his young life. He could not have his camp associated with any more of the disrepute and infamy which had hung over the place since Cicero's trial and execution.

"There is something in him which I find remarkable," Coree Greg said wistfully, "something rare. Few of the men among us have anything like it. He has vision, though it is still so clouded. If I can help him clear it he could make a good warrior and leader."

"You give him too much credit," Claire cautioned. "You can only lose by it."

His mind turned to the shattering news concerning an imminent attack on his camp. He had expected that, after the debacle at Rosalie, the militia would be on the march. With the destruction of Bala's camp and the capture of the two chiefs, he knew that it would be only a matter of time before similar attacks were made on the other camps; and he had kept a close eye on the detachment at Grandbay until he was satisfied that they kept to a strategy of containment rather than outright aggression. But now it was clear that the success of the militia at Bala's camp had spurred them on to a more daring strategy of pre-emptive assault. Still, he was confident that the natural defenses of the terrain leading into his camp would make it difficult for them to carry out the kind of surprise attack that had taken Bala and his men unprepared and without adequate defense.

He was aware that the character of the militia had changed since the last attack on his camp more than ten years past. Now they were better equipped, and the conscription of blacks to their ranks would certainly bring in a new element to the battle strategy that they would employ. Blacks were familiar with bush warfare, and the difficult approaches which had so daunted the white soldiers would not be much of a challenge to them.

The first stirring of the new day woke him and he opened his eyes to the faint light of early morning seeping beneath his door. Claire held him closely, purring softly in a late sleep. He gently disengaged her arms, stole silently out of the hut, sat on the bench outside and listened to the rustling of the forest creatures waking up. The camp was deathly still. Only the low snores from the nearest huts came to his ears.

He heard soft footfalls on the damp earth approaching, and raised his head quickly to see Pharcel walking across the clearing. Coree Greg thought that he must have slept under the trees because there were twigs standing out of his hair and his movements were stiff as if he had lain on a hard, uneven surface. His eyes were bleary, and his youthful brow was creased with worry. He came and stood nervously before Coree Greg.

"I did not do all those things," he muttered.

Coree Greg bowed his head for what seemed a long time. Then he looked fixedly at the young man standing before him.

"I believe you," he said softly, "but you are walking a risky road. You have to be more careful."

He shifted sideways on his seat, and gestured for Pharcel to sit beside him. Quietly, they conversed in the stillness of the morning while the birds shook themselves awake and began their melodious chirping. Coree Greg wanted to know the details of Bala's and Sandy's execution, and Pharcel told him of Bala's defiant words and Sandy's courageous stance up to the hour of their death. His face brightened when Pharcel told of the field slaves that had been shackled together under the trees and who, inspired by Bala's bold and courageous words and Sandy's serene confrontation, had cheered the heroism of both men; but it clouded again when he heard of Bala's last request that his juju be buried with him, because he knew that such a sacred wish would not be understood by ignorant white men or, even if understood, would be ruthlessly disregarded.

He could not elicit much from Pharcel about the impending attack by the militia since Jacques had not communicated any details. Coree Greg gently prodded Pharcel concerning his liaison with Elise; and Pharcel spoke quietly, but with suppressed feeling, about the strong bond that had kept him and the white woman seeking each other over so many months, and that he thought was beyond mere sexual infatuation. Coree Greg shook his head sadly, but said nothing more.

As they crept out of their huts, the men and women of the camp were astonished to see the old chief and the young man who the night before had stood before them in disgrace, sitting in the warming sun and conversing genially. They could hardly contain their curiosity as they went about their morning's chores. Claire with a fierce, defensive look in her eyes, came out and stood by her husband. Pharcel, sensing her disapproval, rose from the bench and walked away towards the cover of the trees.

Before the sun had reached its meridian, a visitor arrived in the camp. He was a field slave from a nearby estate near Geneva, and he had slipped away from his labors tending cattle to bring an important message. He went straight to Coree Greg's hut, and remained there for a short time. He did not delay in the camp, and returned posthaste the way he had come.

Coree Greg sat in brooding silence as the men and women assembled in front of his hut in the late evening. A heavy burden seemed to have settled on his lean shoulders, and a cloud of anxiety darkened his drawn countenance. Claire stood at the door of the hut looking at him solicitously. She came and sat quietly at his feet. Tom stood over his shoulder, somewhat perturbed at the disquiet which he sensed troubled his old companion and chief. The other men and women sat in gloomy silence, wondering at the sombrous mood that appeared to have settled on the camp. They cast furtive glances at Coree Greg, pensive and unmoving on the bench, and at Pharcel, somewhat downcast and nervous, sitting at his right, a bit removed from their circle.

At last, Coree Greg raised his eyes to the assembly. He spoke in measured tones, almost without emotion, as he addressed his followers.

"We have dreadful news," he began. "Pharcel was right. The militia is about to attack."

The men shifted uneasily where they sat and the women whispered among themselves fearfully.

"Who says this?" Cork stood in the background, squat, strongly-built and mean featured. He had been a leading figure in Bala's camp, and considered himself the natural successor to Bala's leadership. "How do we know this is true?"

"Pharcel told us so last night," Coree Greg retorted.

"We still cannot trust him," Cork strode importantly to the center of the circle. "He should not be among us."

"We had a visitor this morning," Coree Greg said evenly. "He carried a message from an important source in Roseau. The message confirms what Pharcel said."

"We do not want him here," Cork said vehemently. "We will not fight with cowards or traitors."

Turning to the other men he asked, "Who wants to have to defend his back while he faces the enemy?"

Several of the men murmured their agreement; but most of them remained silent, waiting for Coree Greg to respond to this challenge. Pharcel turned to look at Cork cautiously, remembering the animosity that he had shown to him during his days in Bala's camp. He recalled that Cork had appeared to be resentful of the closeness which seemed to have developed between Bala and him during the grand assembly at Congoree's camp and in the days following the attack on the Rosalie plantation, but he could not understand the cause of the vicious enmity which Cork was now leveling against him. He bowed his head thinking of the sudden change in the men and women among whom he had lived so harmoniously over the past two years. Even Marie Claire averted her eyes whenever she came across him.

Coree Greg's reprimand cut through his thoughts.

"This is not the time for recrimination," he said, an edge of annoyance sharpening his voice. "Our camp is in danger, and we must consolidate our strength. We have a common enemy to do battle with. Let us not fight among ourselves, put aside dissention, and work together to defend this camp."

He paused, watching Cork glowering in the fading light.

"In times of war there can be only one authority and a single body." He stood to his full height, his staff held firmly at his side. "There will be no more talk of betrayal. It is time for preparation and watchfulness. We do not want to share Bala's fate or Sandy's misfortune."

Cork stood somewhat abashed, but still defiant. The other men shifted about uncomfortably. They knew where they stood with Coree Greg who had led them to a life of safety and relative ease in the woods. Most of them had little regard for Cork who was known to be treacherous, brutal and arrogant while he walked in the shadow of Bala's supremacy. They knew that underneath this arrogance was a man who was not dependable in any way or capable to lead them in times of crisis.

"We are still few in number, and so we will need all the help we can get," Coree Greg continued. "Our friends are far away and it is too late to call them to our defense. But there are others who will help us. I propose to call on our neighbors, the Caribs, to guard our northern flank while we strengthen our defenses around the ravine and on the exposed southern side. Tomorrow we will have a council of war. In the meantime, I will dispatch a message to the Caribs over the hills beyond to come to our aid. Pharcel will go since he is well known to them."

He turned and walked stiffly into his hut.

Cork stared unbelievingly at the old chief, his eyes darkening with fury at the personal insult which he felt in the old man's arbitrary dismissal of his accusations against Pharcel. He turned and looked around at the other men, thinking that they shared his outrage; but the men and women were already moving quietly and complacently to their huts. They left him standing there still full of thunder, but without a bolt of lightening to give force to his anger.

Claire too had remained disconcerted at Coree Greg's decision. Over the past years she had seen the fire in him dying out slowly. He was old, and the strength of his leadership had dwindled to a benign but feeble authority that could be sustained only because of the deep love and loyalty of the aging men who had remained with him. It was as if the sap in him had dried, and all that was left was the brittle remains of his once powerful and glorious manhood. She had been with him through the many years of struggle to protect the men and women who had gathered around him and to find the one spot in the vast and forbidding maze of twisted valleys and precipitous hills and mountains where they could be safe to enjoy the rudimentary life of freedom which they had yearned for and found at last; and she had grown to love him with a deep and abiding love that had not diminished even as the years enfeebled him physically more and more. She could not abide to see him dwindle to a nonentity as she knew he would if he were to give way to younger men.

Tom had been his faithful companion for many years, but there was no threat from him since they were both aging venerably together. But Pharcel in the prime of youth, adventurous and resourceful, bold and personable, was definitely a challenge. She had seen the subtle change in Coree Greg as he became more and more indulgent of the younger man's foibles, qualities which he would have snuffed out ruthlessly in the past.

She was deeply upset at the turn of events at the meeting. It was the first time that Coree Greg had deliberately disregarded her opinion. He appeared to have softened up towards the younger man, and to have given in to what could only be a sentimental weakness as if he, Coree Greg, had suddenly discovered something in Pharcel which he wished he could find in himself.

As Cork turned to go, his face still taut with anger and humiliation, she beckoned quietly to him.

"You must not let this happen," she whispered tensely as he came up to her. "We are all in danger, now more than ever. He must be removed."

Cork nodded eagerly. He understood perfectly what it was she wished him to do.

"You must meet him on his way back," she said with quiet determination. "He must not return to this camp."

"He will not," Cork replied confidently. This time, he thought, there would be no mistake. He had failed to carry out Bala's command that first time because somebody had intervened and warned Pharcel. This time there would be no warning and no escape. He would make sure that this was so.

Claire smiled grimly. She did not trust Cork either, but he was not as great a danger as Pharcel was. Cork had adopted a lot of the brutality that was characteristic of Bala, but he did not command respect since his vision went no further than his present needs and emotions. Impetuous and given to malicious intent, he would never inspire confidence or loyalty in those around him. Bala had used him as an instrument for evil and that is what he would always be. He was a man to be watched, but not to be feared. His boldness and vigor could never be a match for Coree Greg's sagacity and courage.

It was already dark when she reentered her hut. She went straight to Coree Greg and folded him protectively in her arms.

The Caribs had come to enjoy the evenness of their lives after centuries of constant fighting. They had arrived from the southern mainland centuries before, and displaced the more sedentary and peaceful Arawaks whose women they had taken as their wives. Now the white men had driven them further and further from the coast and taken most of the lands in the gentler valleys and open hillsides. For more than two centuries they had kept the island as their own, but constant fighting and the pestilence of the white man's disease had reduced them to a pitiful community.

They no longer fought to defend their island. As long as they were left to carry on their daily existence in their villages and there were no further encroachments on their territory by the avaricious white men whose appetite for new lands seemed insatiable, they had no cause for war. They had long since abandoned their reputation as a warlike people, and they no longer made daring raids to steal the wives and daughters of the planters from islands as far away as Antigua and St. Kitts. They had also withdrawn from getting involved in any alliance in the unceasing struggle between the English and French for possession of the lands of the Caribbean islands because they had been duped so many times by representatives of both nations.

Now they lived peaceful lives fishing the seas and rivers and hunting the forests. They provided sanctuary to runaway slaves only because of their natural graciousness in giving hospitality to any visitor and because of their own passion for personal liberty. They had been known throughout history to embrace death rather than allow themselves to be kept in bondage, and so they would not hesitate to give succor to those who rebelled against captivity. On the other hand, they had no regard for the growing legion of slaves whose docility in bondage they had come to despise.

They were few in number now; and they kept to themselves, having little to do with the growing hordes of black men and women and their white oppressors that seemed to hem them in closer and closer to the more remote parts of the island. Only a tiny settlement remained in the southern end, miles apart from the more numerous communities further north.

Pharcel had brought Coree Greg's appeal for help before the elders as they sat in a circle in the middle of the *tabwi*. They had listened to him patiently while he described the desperate situation that had forced his chief to seek their aid, and then they had risen as if in concert and walked away wordlessly, leaving him sitting there dumfounded and mystified. He could not understand their silence and the fact that they had so quietly turned away from him. He pleaded with Kumeni to explain the strange behavior of the old men, but she merely shook her head, looked at him dourly, and set about feeding him fish and cassava bread.

No one spoke with him the next day. All morning he had waited, and tried to engage one or the other of the elders in private conversation; but their expressions had remained distant, and their tongues silent. Even the younger men who had been so fascinated with his musket on previous visits kept away from him. He left while the sun was still high in the sky.

He was still brooding over his failure to get a response from the Caribs when he came to the juncture where the track split into separate traces, one leading down to the ridge overlooking Dubique and Geneva, and the other fading out into the woods in the direction of his camp. It was a pleasant spot, and he had sat there some time ago listening to the sweet sound of the birds and the whispering of the branches as the faint wind from the sea fluttered the leaves.

The trees grew tall. Their spreading branches formed a thick canopy through which sunlight descended in bright beams to the ground. Only a sparse under-growth of thin trees, their skeletal branches almost devoid of leaves, broke the wide open spaces between the giant trunks which rose like unbroken columns forty feet upwards. The ground was thick with leaves slowly rotting, forming a springy carpet pleasant to walk on. The air beneath the trees was clean scented with the freshness of dried leaves mixed with the oozing sap of the vast crusted tree trunks. There was none of that acrid dankness that hung heavy in the air among the choked-up woods of the gorges.

Pharcel sat on a dried tree trunk that had fallen across the path. It was still held a few feet above ground by its rotting branches, providing a comfortable perch from which to observe the almost still life and cathedral silence of the for-est. His mind went back to his meeting with the Caribs and the cold abstraction with which they had listened to his plea for help. He was accustomed to their indifference to those visitors that came in and out of their settlements. He had experienced it many times, but he had always understood that beneath this indif-ference was genuine courtesy and generosity. They were certainly not an emo-tional people, except when roused to anger. Then they could be extremely vengeful and dangerous. Still, their impassivity mystified him; and he could not understand how, in the face of such a crisis in their neighborhood, they had shown no interest in what he had to say. They had all cast their eyes to the ground as he spoke, then looked at him with blank expressions as they rose together to walk out of the *tabwi*. They had left him with no response, tacit or otherwise, that he could take back to Coree Greg.

He recalled the night with Kumeni and he felt his loins stirring as he thought of her subdued cries as the agony of pleasure seized her. Their previous encoun-ters had always seemed tentative as if she sought temporary relief from some oppressive loneliness. It was almost an act of self-gratification, with him being the passive partner. But when she came to him in the dark that night, she lay beside him for a long time as if holding out herself as an offering. He had turned to her, intrigued by her unusual docility, and felt the smooth firmness of her skin and the flowing sleekness of her hair. She had parted her legs eagerly, and her soft cries rose in the night as she opened out to him. Kumeni had stayed by his side the whole night, and did not move from his embrace until the morning broke.

Pharcel was lost in his memories, blissfully unaware of the world around him. His mind wandered back to the time of his trial when the men and women of the camp had turned against him. His heart grew heavy as he thought about Presente and the joyful moments they had spent together. He remembered her lying naked and care free in the stream, and the panic that had seized her when he had urged her to run. Now she was languishing in goal waiting to be transported to another island. He felt saddened that he had been unable to save her. Anger seethed within him as he recalled the accusations made against him. How could they ever think that he would betray the woman who had given him so much joy? As for being branded a coward, his deeds spoke strongly on his behalf. Even Bala had had to acknowledge his worth as a young warrior.

A dark shadow flitted past the large tree trunks, circling the clearing where he sat. The clearing was deathly quiet. The sound of birds chirping was strangely muted. The air seemed to hang still. The canopy of leaves overhead ceased its airy fluttering. The sunbeams steadied, fixed in irregular patches on the ground. A few feet away, a small boa slithered through the dry leaves. Pharcel watched it go, its silent passage leaving him strangely disturbed.

His mind returned to the night of the assembly and the way he had been vilified even by those who had known him and lived with him for so many months. How had this come about when he had not done anything to deserve their distrust? He regretted not having confided more in Coree Greg. He had not intended to deceive him by withholding information from him. He had merely tried to avoid confrontation with the old man. Coree Greg understood, and had it not been for his wisdom and understanding, Pharcel would already have been an outcast, wandering the forest without friends and without a home. Now he had to contend with Cork whose animosity appeared irrational, but, nonetheless, extremely dangerous. Like the boa, if Cork got a hold of an enemy, he would crush him to death. He would have to keep a close eye on him and destroy him quickly if that became necessary.

The shadow moved at his back and slid behind the wide trunk of a balata tree. A slight breeze ruffled the branches overhead. The sun had slanted westward, and the sunbeams flittered in bright circles on the dry leaves. The clearing seemed to have come alive with a new vigor as the sea wind stirred the trees. There was a flapping of wings as numerous birds rose to the current of air and flew around in close circles as if to cool their sun-drenched feathers. Somewhere far away, a wild boar crashed through a ravine, its raucous grunts fading away in the distance.

Claire's unwonted frostiness was what disturbed him most. He had seen the venom in her eyes when Coree Greg had dismissed the charges against him and entrusted him with the important mission to win support from the Caribs. He had always respected her, and considered her the mother of the camp. She was stern, but caring towards men, women and children alike, healing their wounds, relieving their pains and sorrows. He had thought at first that she was especially mindful of his youth as she appeared to take particular care to see that he was properly housed and adequately provided for; but now he sensed that Coree Greg's recent indulgence of his youthfulness could be the cause of her sudden resentment. More and more he regretted having done anything to disturb the simple harmony of the small community of which he had been so happy to be a part.

Pharcel pulled himself upright, his ears alert, his eyes darting from side to side. He thought he heard a soft crackling in the dry leaves that covered the ground, and he shifted in his seat, and turned around so that he could drop from the tree trunk onto the ground. Out of the corner of his eye he saw the blur of a figure crashing through the meager undergrowth towards him. He was still unbalanced as the figure came upon him, arms raised for a strike. Pharcel saw the bright blade of a machete flashing briefly in a beam of sunlight as it came down to him. He toppled backward and lay sprawled as the machete sliced through the dry branches of the fallen tree trunk where he had been sitting. Cork stood over him, his face suffused with hate and anger, his machete a deadly menace poised for a second strike. Pharcel lay helpless on his back. Panic seized him as he saw the gleaming weapon descending on him. He shielded his face with his hands, waiting for the fatal blow. Instead, he heard a gasp of surprise followed by an agonized roar. Looking through his fingers he saw the startled eyes, the gaping mouth and upraised arm fixedly arrested in mid-strike. Blood seeped from Cork's mouth. His knees trembled as his body fell slowly forward. Pharcel rolled away as Cork's body crashed onto the ground. A knife was buried deep at his lower back.

He looked up, still stunned by the sudden attack and his miraculous escape. Jacques stood a few feet away, his head at an angle, a broad grin brightening his face.

"I saw him lurking around since morning," Jacques explained. "He was so impatient and so full of anger. I knew he would be up to no good."

Pharcel remained speechless. Cork's lifeless body lay crumpled on the ground beside him. He looked around him in consternation, unbelieving that he had come so close to death.

"Come on!" Jacques urged. "He is dead. He can do no more harm."

Pharcel's heart still thundered and his chest felt constricted. He took a deep breath and felt the tension easing out of him as he exhaled.

"He would have killed me," Pharcel uttered the words breathlessly.

"Yes he would," Jacques laughed, "for whatever reason."

"What brought you here?" Pharcel asked curiously.

"Paulinaire sent me to find you," Jacques looked at him reproachfully. "You have still not come to see him."

"I have trouble in the camp," Pharcel said. "They think I am a traitor for consorting with the mulattos."

"Was this what that was all about?" Jacques inclined his head towards the dead body lying between them.

"Possibly," Pharcel replied. "Quite possibly."

"Paulinaire is disappointed in Coree Greg and the other chiefs," Jacques spoke with a note of disapproval in his voice. "He thinks as things stand the camps will be destroyed one by one."

"They will not listen to this kind of reasoning," Pharcel said sadly. "You were at the grand assembly. You know what happened."

"Yes," Jacques assured him, "I know."

"I got into enough trouble trying to persuade Coree Greg," Pharcel said disconsolately.

"You should leave," Jacques said firmly. "The situation is dangerous. We have word that the militia will attack soon. They are awaiting reinforcements from the detachment stationed at Laudat."

"Where will I go? Nowhere is safe now." Pharcel hung his head, his shoulders slumping dispiritedly.

"Paulinaire wants you to join him," Jacques stepped forward and gripped him by his shoulders. "He is amassing men and guns. The revolt will be soon."

"I cannot leave at this point," Pharcel muttered uncertainly.

"But it is useless," Jacques protested. "You will be killed out there."

Pharcel remained silent for several seconds. He thought of the suspicion and hate which he had recently encountered in the camp. He remembered the venom which had appeared in Claire's eyes when she had seen him in intimate converse with Coree Greg. His heart was filled with resentment and bitterness at the way he had been treated. The sight of Cork's body, still menacing even in death, reminded him of the hostility which he would have to face on his return to the camp. But then he thought of Coree Greg, dignified and strong, without whose intervention he would have been an outcast among his own people. The old man had treated him with respect, and had shown him a fatherly understanding which he knew he would not find in any other man. He lifted his head and his eyes gleamed with a burning fire.

"I will not leave," he said finally.

Jacques nodded his head, a faint smile of admiration in his eyes.

They both turned about and walked away in opposite directions.

CHAPTER 17

Since his return to camp, Pharcel had busied himself building a new hut. He went out alone into the forest to gather lengths of wood, ropes and vine which he dragged into the camp. He was soon joined by Marie Claire who brought with her a new girl, one of the fugitives from Bala's camp. Together, they brought loads of twigs and balizier leaves for covering which they placed in a pile near an open spot close to the stream that flowed through the ravine. Soon they were joined by several men. Marie Claire's irrepressible cheerfulness kept them working until dark. By that time the hut was almost complete except for a section of wall at the front. He did not protest when Marie Claire spread a bundle of dry leaves on the bare earth and invited the new girl to lie down. Exhausted, they slept soundly till late morning.

The girl was only seventeen years old. Not much younger than he was. She stood in stark contrast to Marie Claire's bulky frame. Thin and erect of posture, she glided along with a natural grace and dignity that seemed out of place in the crude ambience of the camp. She was of a light copper complexion, with frizzled brown hair, bleached by the sun; her skin stretched tautly over a thin angular face, with a nub for a nose that was perched provocatively over small, plump lips; her eyes were long and slanted, almost concealed by drooping lids, and were over-arched by thin, glossy eyebrows; and her pointed chin accentuated the angular cast of her face. The rest of her body stood in graceful proportion, with long, thin, almost arching neck, narrow shoulders, flat abdomen, long, sleek legs and breasts hardly bigger than small oranges. The only startling part of her anatomy was her abnormally plump buttocks which stood out like two full-sized bread-fruits from her slim waist. She moved about shyly and spoke in soft mellifluous tones.

Her name was Marie Rose. At first Pharcel was nervous about her presence, but, as she set about efficiently making the new hut livable, he began to admire her sense of organization and her abundant energy. He quickly saw that she possessed a robustness of body that belied her slim and delicate build. By the second day, she and Marie Claire had cleared the narrow strip of land along the stream and planted an array of vegetables and herbs. The three of them settled down to a comfortable living in the hut that they had built, sharing the straw mat stretched out on the bare earth at night, but respecting each other's privacy as far as possible.

Coree Greg had received Pharcel's account of his meeting with the Carib elders with characteristic patience. He had never had much to do with them as neighbors, but he respected their fortitude as a nation, and had a great admiration for their sense of personal independence and collective valor. He had not expected much assistance from them because he knew that they were a people who maintained neutrality among all nations and kept aloof from black men who they generally considered inferior. But they were known to be generous in their living, and always received with patient hospitality fugitives, especially escaped slaves, and other non-threatening visitors.

As soon as Pharcel told Coree Greg of Jacques' report that the militia was awaiting reinforcements and would soon be on the move, he set about strengthening the defenses at the southern end, what he had long considered the only negotiable approach to the camp. With the heavily forested mountains at his back and precipitous hillsides on either side, he thought the invaders would be forced to attempt to rush through the narrow defile formed by the perpendicular sides of the deep ravine that led directly into the camp. He therefore spent most of his time setting up defenses at various points along the ravine, putting up barriers and concealed pits and trenches where his men could attack the enemy from hidden places. This strategy had worked many years ago when the camp had been attacked for the first time. The defenses had proved to be impregnable, and the militia had suffered heavy losses before it was forced to retreat. Since then no other attack had been attempted.

The camp had been busy with preparations for war. A brief council had been held the day after Pharcel's return, at which Coree Greg had outlined the defense strategy that he proposed to adopt, as well as the various responsibilities to be assigned to the men. The women were to remain in the camp and take care of the children and the camp's provisions, although a few of the more hardy and mature volunteered to fight along with the men. A stocktaking of the weapons revealed how poorly armed the camp was: only two muskets and a few rusty swords and poniards, several machetes, a few axes, pitchforks and axe handles. These would have to be supplemented by crudely made wooden spears and clubs. As the council was breaking up, Pharcel asked diffidently about the plan for retreat. There were loud snickers; and the men looked at each other meaningfully, but Coree Greg nodded thankfully towards Pharcel.

"A wise leader knows when to retreat," he said. "It is not cowardly to do so if his position becomes indefensible. He should never risk the lives of his warriors uselessly. Pharcel is right. We must have an escape plan."

"Then let him do that," a voice in the back muttered irritably. "He is quite used to escaping."

There was a roar of laughter at this remark. Coree Greg's features remained stern. His voice rose above the merriment, cutting it short.

"It is an important task," he said seriously, "maybe the most important of all. I agree Pharcel should take care of it."

The council ended in stunned silence. The men and women drifted quietly away to their assigned duties.

Cork's disappearance had not been noticed until several days had passed. Men were accustomed to spend days away from the camp either on hunting expeditions or visiting friends in nearby camps; and even on nightly visits to neighboring estates. When he had not returned after several days there was speculation that he had left the camp because he had been so riled by Coree Greg's refusal to support him in his cause against Pharcel. Most of them were accustomed to his arrogance and high handedness. They had often suffered from it under Bala's leadership, and it was well known that Cork had been one of Bala's protégés. They soon dismissed his absence as a voluntary act of protest against Coree Greg.

Claire, however, was not so sanguine. She had not expected Pharcel to return, and when he did, she was startled out of her wits and slunk quickly back into her hut, a fearsome look in her eyes. At first she would not come near him as if she feared that he carried the spirit of his ancestors around him to protect him against all evil. There was no sign that he carried his juju on his person; but she was certain that he was possessed of a powerful magic, one as strong as the charm that had protected her husband all his years. How else could he have escaped Cork? She had remained silent and aloof for a few days; but one evening, as he came out of the bushes at the upper end of the camp, she sidled up to him and looked at him searchingly for several moments.

"Did you see Cork?" she asked darkly.

"No," he replied calmly, "he must have gone to hell."

Her dark skin had paled for a brief moment, but she quickly regained her composure. They stood looking deeply into each other's eyes as if measuring the strength of each other's will. Then she nodded, a look of grudging respect filling her eyes. She kept lurking about wherever he was day after day after that, until one day she joined him and some others in preparing the escape route out of the camp. From that time she was always attentive to whatever he said and whatever he wished.

Pharcel led a few of the men and most of the women past the circle of huts towards the rising ground that lifted sharply to the encircling hills. First he cut a swathe through the tall grass and bushes past the clearing, leading to a thickly wooded and precipitous gorge on the left. The cleared path continued a considerable distance to the entrance to the gorge where it ended. Beyond was the dark, sodden, narrow and steeply rising floor of the gorge choked with mossy boulders and rotting tree trunks.

The men wondered why he led them to such an impenetrable pass, and they muttered critically among themselves as he led them back to camp at the end of the day; but they began to understand the next morning when he began systematically partially cutting the stems of the low bushes and bending them backwards, clearing a path that led in a different direction a long way uphill towards the right until they reached the edge of the forest. On the way back along the cleared path they carefully bent the bushes back to their natural position so that they appeared undisturbed to any casual observer. The men marveled at the ingenuity of Pharcel's retreat strategy and spoke proudly about it all week.

For days afterwards, alone, he scouted the hills above the camp, traveling further and further into the woods each day until he was sure he had found his bearings. He carefully mapped out in his mind the lower ridges beyond the hill following an eastward route. He knew how deceptive these ridges could be; but he quickly surmised that if he kept at his back the tallest peak that loomed over the hollow where the camp was hidden, he would be traveling eastwards towards the small Carib settlement not too far from the coast. He had always been welcome in their midst, and he was confident that those who escaped the battle would find refuge there. From there he would locate a secure place to rebuild their camp.

As soon as preparations for the defenses and for an escape route were ready, men were posted at strategic points along the approaches to the camp to keep a constant watch on movements of persons in the vicinity of the camp and along the trace commonly used by visitors right up to the edge of the forest. Days passed uneventfully, and the watches had nothing to report except for a few half-naked blacks that they took to be slaves on the run. The blacks had waved briefly as they continued on their way to the upper slopes above the camp deep into the forest.

The men on watch had paid no attention to this especially as word had reached the camp that the slaves in the southern region were becoming more and more restive and were planning mass escape from the plantations. But on the second week the numbers on the move increased, and the men began to wonder why none of them sought refuge in Coree Greg's camp. They quickly sent word to Coree Greg about the strange and increasing traffic passing through the hills above them.

Meanwhile Pharcel had been keeping watch on the movements of the militia in their encampment on the Geneva flats. For the first few days he noticed nothing unusual. Certainly he did not observe the stream of half-naked, raggedly attired black soldiers making their way up the northern ridges into the woods. He saw the constant daily drill and the ordinary movements of soldiers among a colony of white canvas tents. It was a week later that his attention was awakened to the blare of trumpets and the beating of drums as the parade ground filled with orderly rows of men in full dress uniform.

At first he thought that this was the signal for the march into the interior of the woods; but as he peeked through the branches of the trees way up on the hillside above, he saw columns of men arriving from the northern track that joined Grandbay to the capital. Soon the encampment came alive with increased activity as new tents were erected and more men milled about among them. He learnt later that Captain Urquhart and his men had arrived to augment the forces under Captain Marshall.

Through Jacques, he had quickly made contact with one of the stable boys in the military camp. Every day, soon after nightfall, he crept down to the upper reaches of the Geneva River and waited for the boy to appear in the dark. There was not much to learn at first. Marshall had been impatient to begin the attack, but he was forced to wait for the arrival of Urquhart and his men. There were about fifty white soldiers and twenty blacks, but many of the blacks had disappeared over the past few days. The boy was not sure that they had deserted. He had seen some of them throw off their tunics and slip quietly through the bushes taking muskets and long knives with them. Pharcel listened intently as the boy informed him of unusual movements in the encampment. Captain Marshall had been spending a great deal of his time at Dubique for several weeks past. But now that he was fully engrossed in preparations for the coming expedition into the interior, he had not left the camp for many days.

The mention of Dubique brought his mind back to Elise. He had not seen her for months. Though his mind had been preoccupied with many things of late, and Marie Claire and Marie Rose were exuberant in their attention to his nightly comfort, he still felt that unquenchable thirst for a drink from the well that had kept his young heart so filled with enchantment. The thought of Elise's abundant womanhood, so accommodatingly warm, wet and vibrant, stirred him to an irrepressible hunger. He had to find her again. He had to visit Dubique one more time. If Captain Marshall was so engaged in his martial duties, then there could be little danger of his being intercepted there. Besides, if Georgette had given birth so recently, she would still be confined to her maternity bed as was the custom among white women. It was one of the absurdities of the racial divide that black women, being hardy animals, were fit to work immediately after childbirth; whereas their white counterparts, being considered frail and tender, had to be confined for at least three months after the birth of their children.

That same night Pharcel crawled along the track through the cane fields and hid in the thick foliage of one of the trees near the house. Elise had not come out, and he remained there all night. Through gaps in the foliage, he saw the slaves trudging up the track. It was later in the day than usual, and, as he watched them go by, he thought he sensed a new truculence among them. The driver continuously flicked his whip at them which they ignored as if the threat meant nothing in their present state of desperation. At Dubique, the whip had seldom been used as an instrument of motivation. The frequency of its use now suggested that conditions had deteriorated badly since his last visit. Jean followed an hour later, sitting listlessly on his horse. He looked dispirited and wan, his face a sickly, yellow color. There was still no sign of Elise.

She did not appear until late morning. He saw her step down from the front verandah dressed in a loose, white gown, her bleached hair in disorderly curls about her head. Barefoot, she walked pensively across the lawn and down the hollow to the tiny waterfall. He had not seen her face clearly, but there was a look of dejection in her slow, bowed walk, as if she carried an unbearable burden on her shoulders. Robust of frame though she was, she looked frail and vulnerable in the bright morning sun. He sighed as he watched her disappear into the hollow.

Pharcel remained where he was, uncertain what to do next; she was only a few leaps away; but it was open ground, mostly covered with prickly raspberry bush; he would have to crawl through the bush several feet to the edge of the stream. Waiting seemed interminable, and he could not control the restlessness in his limbs as he shifted about anxiously, wanting only to make a dash for the hollow where she had disappeared. After what seemed hours of suspense, he slid down the tree and lay low to the ground.

The house was only a few yards away across the clearing, and he caught a glimpse of Toma's grey head as he peered briefly through the kitchen window. Pharcel remained fixed until he was sure that there was no one to observe his movements. Then he crept slowly out of the dark shade of the trees into the sunlight further away from the house. Crabwise he crawled towards the hollow, keeping low to the ground until only a few feet separated him from the bushes. Bessie came out of the kitchen door carrying a pail of slop which she splashed onto the garden of herbs and flowers at the edge of the clearing. She turned, and looked squarely in his direction. He paused, petrified, his chocolate brown body gleaming in the bright sunlight. As soon as she turned away he rolled over and plunged into the prickly mass.

The thin, wiry stems of the raspberry bush clawed at him as he crawled through them. His back, arms and legs burned as the tiny thorns raked his flesh; but he did not stop until he came to the lip of the hollow. The raspberry bush hung over the edge, forming a protective screen around the small basin below the fall. Gently, he parted the bush and saw her in the full splendor of her nakedness standing uncertainly below the fall of water, her hand stretched out as if reluctant to touch the glistening flow. Sunlight filled the hollow with bright warmth and flashed on the crystal surface of the stream.

Her back was turned to him; and when he dropped beside her, only the soft splash of water told of his presence. She turned, and gave a stifled scream as she saw his matted, shining brown hair and glowing nakedness. He quickly muffled her cry with his hand over her face, and held her as she struggled weakly against him. He felt her relax in his embrace, and he released her gently. She looked frantically about, her face pale, her eyes wild with fear.

"You must not stay!" Her voice was tight with distress, and her eyes were distraught as they searched the surrounding bush. "You must go at once. He will kill you!"

He smiled at her and put a finger against her lips.

"Yes, I will," he whispered in her ear, "soon enough."

He drew her to him under the cool splash of the fall and let his hands wash over her back and legs. She quivered at his touch and at the sensuous flow of the water over her limbs. As he raised her to him and entered her she whimpered softly. But soon her arms folded around his neck and she engulfed him fully as her abdomen came against his. Soft cries escaped her parted lips, and she groaned as he pressed her closer and closer to him. For a long time they remained lost in the rapture of the moment, feeling only the wondrous warmth and firmness of their union, and the swirling tide that brought them higher and higher to the peak of ecstasy. Afterwards, she collapsed at his feet, weak and quivering and blissfully confused. He stooped to her, holding her to him and whispering words of tenderness in her ear. She pushed him away from her, gently and reluctantly.

"You must go now," she said sternly. "It is not safe."

He stood over her, his soft eyes dancing with devotion and triumph.

"Go!" she pleaded. "You must find a place to hide. The militia will be coming for you soon. I heard it from the Captain."

"I will be all right," he said firmly, "and I will return."

She nodded, her eyes a desperate plea for his safety. He turned to go, and her arms stretched out to him as if to hold his presence still. He hesitated only for a moment before he leapt upwards to the edge of the hollow and scrambled through the prickly bush. He left her there, curled into herself, desolation filling her staring eyes.

Pharcel came down to the Geneva River when it was night, and saw two figures lurking in the dark. He remained concealed by the bushes that covered the steep hillside that gave onto the grassy bank, thinking that he had been betrayed and that a trap had been set for him. Despite his caution, Jacques must have heard his approach down the hill because he called out softly to him.

"It is me, Pharcel. Paulinaire is with me."

He came slowly out of the bush. His body was still in a state of euphoria after the steamy morning in the hollow below the fall. He sauntered over to the two men whom he now recognized in the grey light of the night. Paulinaire looked as debonair in the bush as he had been in the bright light of the dining hall several months ago. Beside him, Jacques looked squat, shabby and subservient.

"Where is the boy?" Pharcel asked with concern.

"There are restrictions in the encampment," Jacques informed him. "The whole place is under guard. No one is allowed out of the perimeter of the tents."

Pharcel looked at him questioningly.

"The boy sent word," Jacques reassured him. "It will be tomorrow. There are orders to harness the horses well before daylight, and the men have been issued full weaponry overnight."

"Then I must return to camp immediately," Pharcel said hurriedly. "Coree Greg is already on the alert, but I must let him know they are coming in the morning."

Paulinaire stepped forward.

"Why do you want to waste your precious life and a glorious future?" he asked reasonably. "It is a lost battle, and you and all the rest will be killed uselessly."

"The men are armed and ready," Pharcel replied boldly.

"Armed with what," Paulinaire asked tartly, "pitchforks and machetes? This is not agricultural work," he said impatiently. "This is war."

"The men have been prepared to fight," Pharcel responded, a note of annoyance in his voice. "They are brave and strong."

"War," Paulinaire said, drawing himself up to his full height, "is not about brute strength or about bravery. War is about common sense and about effective strategy and leadership. How can a few men with only agricultural tools, led by an old man stand against a militia armed with muskets, swords and even small cannon. You will be massacred!"

"Those agricultural tools and the man you call old repulsed an attack ten years ago," Pharcel replied weakly. He was not convinced about his own arguments, but he had no choice but to hold on to his loyalty to his chief.

"That was ten years ago," Paulinaire said patiently. "Coree Greg is now an older man, and things are different. We fight not only white men but black soldiers as well. They know the woods as well as you do."

"He is right," Jacques said firmly. "Save yourself for the bigger battle."

"I can't," Pharcel turned to him ruefully, "I must return to Coree Greg."

"I offered help and friendship. I offered weapons and the benefit of my experience, and they refused," Paulinaire lamented. "Now one by one they will be slaughtered like sheep."

"Coree Greg knows this is not the time for war," Pharcel said regretfully, "but he has no choice. And I must stand by him."

"You are foolish," Paulinaire said witheringly. Then he looked sternly at Pharcel. "But you are brave and loyal."

"We are ready for them," Pharcel said confidently.

"Save yourself, then," Paulinaire urged, embracing him warmly. "Come to me when this is over."

Pharcel nodded silently. He backed away quickly and was soon lost in the bushes.

The battle was short, swift and brutal. The dawn had barely begun to lift the blanket of night when the troops were lined up on the parade ground on Geneva Estate and marched silently over the hill and into the forest. A small detachment of black militiamen led the way through the woods carrying a few small cannon, each placed on a wooden pallet fixed on horizontal poles. The larger detachment of white militiamen marched behind, bearing swords and muskets. As the sun broke through the trees, its brilliant rays shone on the bright scarlet uniforms and oiled weapons of the troops as if to flash a warning that danger was approaching. But the signal had long since reached Coree Greg's camp that the militia was on the move.

Coree Greg's men stayed on the steep sides of the ravine, waiting for the troops to scramble over the barricades; but they did not. What happened was both unexpected and out of the ordinary. The black detachment marched right up to the ravine with their heavy burdens, placed the small cannon a short distance from the entrance, and retreated. A dozen or so white soldiers marched briskly forward, loaded the cannon, and proceeded to demolish the barricades. So loud and devastating was the onslaught that many of the men hidden in the bushes on the sides of the ravine broke cover and fled towards the camp. In the confusion that arose, the militiamen broke through the defile, and began a headlong charge towards the camp.

Coree Greg leapt into the ravine and his men followed. In the narrow confines of the ravine there was little room for musket fire and the militia was soon forced into hand to hand combat. There brute strength prevailed, and the militia were being driven slowly back to the entrance of the defile. Pharcel had found a bush-covered outcropping near the inner end of the ravine, and, under cover of the bushes, he was able to use his musket to deadly effect. He saw many white soldiers crash to the ground either wounded or dead.

Over on the left flank, he observed a wonderful sight. The hillside above the ravine was covered with gleaming brown bodies, and a rain of arrows fell through the trees on to the militiamen. The Caribs had joined the fight. For a while it looked as if all was over for the invaders; but still they stood their ground, advancing a bit, then retreating a short distance. Pharcel wondered at the foolhardiness of the commanders and the reckless bravery of the troops.

Suddenly, on the right flank, the forest thundered, and a mass of black shadows plunged through the bushes and down the side of the ravine. Black, half clothed bodies surged around Coree Greg's small army, and Pharcel quickly realized that these were not friendly auxiliaries but part of the militia. The hill on the left flank became deathly quiet; and when Pharcel searched the hillside, it was empty. The Caribs had disappeared. Either they had sensed that the tide of war had turned against Coree Greg or they had become confused seeing black men turn against black men.

Pharcel turned to find Coree Greg's wife, Claire standing beside him, her face drawn with dismay and anger.

"You should join the women and children," he told her hurriedly. "I will soon come to take you away."

"You go," she replied defiantly. "My place is with my husband."

With that she leapt from the outcropping straight into the fray below.

Pharcel looked with alarm at the small circle of his companions surrounded on all sides, battling furiously for their lives. Claire's wiry form stood beside Coree Greg, swaying with the surge and press of men in all directions, her machete flashing in the bright sun. Coree Greg stood firm, his staff clutched defensively before him, his right arm swinging a knobbed club, seasoned with the blood of many battles. In the melee below it was not easy to distinguish between Coree Greg's men and the black militiamen; and Pharcel could never be certain who it was that plunged the knife into Coree Greg's chest; but suddenly he was on the ground, stricken by the mortal blow. Tom stooped to draw him up and he, too, fell, cut down by the saber of one of the officers. Claire's wail of desolation rent the fury of the fight as she beheld Coree Greg's body in its last throes, blood streaming from his chest, back and mouth. The battle came to an abrupt end and a fearful silence fell on the ravine.

Pharcel hastened from his perch and down into the camp. He did not pause for anything, but headed straight for a covert where the women and children crouched in the shade waiting for him to lead them out. Many of the men who had panicked at the first cannonade he found hiding in the bushes on the inner side of the camp. He herded them quickly out of their hiding places, and led them together with the women and children to the rising ground on the right.

He had to restrain the men whose precipitous haste to escape from the terror of the militia threatened to disrupt their carefully laid plans. At one point, he had to turn his musket on the terrified group and swear he would shoot the first man who trampled the vegetation carelessly. Soon they calmed down and began slowly to lift the partially cut branches of the low bushes and let them fall again naturally as they passed through. Pharcel brought up the rear, ensuring every branch was carefully replaced. They heard the triumphant roar of the militia as they poured out of the ravine into the camp, and could see their scarlet tunics blazing in the bright morning light. He led the group slowly and cautiously all the way up the hill and into the forest, leaving no trace of their passage. They did not stop until they had gained the top of the eastern hill overlooking the camp.

Their camp, now a mass of billowing smoke and rising flames, lay below them. The women huddled together under the tall trees; and the men, panic-stricken, glanced anxiously into the forest gloom, wanting to be far away from the place of disaster. The children gaped at the wondrous sight of the mushrooming cloud of smoke brightened by a million sparks coming from the valley where they had lived so peacefully. Over towards the opposite hill, scarlet figures slipped and tumbled along the swathe which they had cut through the grass and bushes up to the impenetrable gorge. They knew then that they were safe, but not for long. They would have to make time before the deception was discovered.

The men and women looked anxiously to Pharcel. He felt overwhelmed and uncertain; and wondered how he could manage to bring that bunch of cowering men, shivering women and sniffling children to safety over those daunting hills and narrow valleys, pristine ground that had scarcely been trodden on except by the wild creatures of the forest.

Pharcel braced his broad shoulders, turned eastwards and led them onwards.

CHAPTER 18

Rain fell incessantly day after day. It drenched the sodden trees whose branches drooped listlessly, weighed down by the crystalline drops which clung tenaciously to them. Streams of water trickled down the trunks of the trees or splattered from the branches on to the soggy ground. Sudden gusts of wind shook the branches, raising showers of diamond drops which glistened in streaks of light as they fell. Water seeped through the wet leaves on the ground, and formed tiny rivulets that rolled and grew and cascaded downwards to the closed-in valley below. The small stream that flowed through the valley gurgled happily as tiny tributaries flowed into it from all directions. It swelled and spread over its grassy banks, sweeping the earth clean of the detritus of many months.

It began the day after their escape from the burning camp. They had stumbled through the tangled forest over steep hills and narrow valleys, always keeping the high mountain at their backs. The men surrounded the women and children, and pushed them mercilessly onward, fearing pursuit by the black militia. All day they fought their way through the dark woods, their footfalls deadened by the rotting leaves which padded the wet earth. They crossed deep gorges spanned by rotting tree trunks, and clambered over mossy boulders which clogged dry ravines.

In this part of the forest, rank vegetation grew in utter profusion underneath the trees, filling the air with pungent fumes. Insects buzzed around them, and clouds of tiny flies rose from the damp decay on the floor of the constricted gorges. By night fall, they had come to the open side of a hill, and they could see the fires of the small Carib village some distance away along the curvature of the hill. Pharcel left them there and disappeared into the night.

He returned by sunrise next day accompanied by a number of the villagers, Kumeni among them. They bore quantities of food and drink in baskets and gourds which they placed carefully on the ground like an offering. The Caribs then stood away silently while the fugitives fed themselves. The day had opened with a sultry stillness that seemed to drain the energy from all living things. The trees did not wave their branches as there was no wind, and the birds stayed still among the deadened leaves, waiting for a resurgence of life among them. It took some time before Pharcel could rouse his dispirited group to lead them further into the hills.

The Caribs led the way through twisted gorges and over disorderly ridges, always further and further into the maze of hills and valleys. The tall mountain stood like a beacon, rising sharply among the hills; and it seemed that they had circled it because it was no longer behind their back, and its face had changed to a rugged steepness that was different from the smooth gradient at the side from which they had come. At last they descended into a deep valley that was surrounded on all sides by precipitous hills. It looked like a huge bowl scooped out of a large plateau and filled with a variety of plants. It must have been an old habitation because there were remnants of an old garden covered by vines and creepers. A small stream ran through it, and disappeared through a narrow gorge. Along its banks, coarse vegetation covered the ground; but here and there open patches showed the remains of fireplaces and the rotting pillars of old structures.

As silently as they had come, the Caribs turned back into the forest, and were soon over the crest of the hill by which they had descended. Kumeni had lingered for a brief moment, but she, too, left quietly and followed her people. The valley was silent. It was as if they had never been there.

Pharcel and his men set about clearing a bit of ground raised above the stream. They collected the slender trunks of several saplings which they planted in the ground. Over these they built a sloping frame to support a covering, and the women used branches and twigs interwoven with the broad leaves of the balizier to form a roof. The sky had darkened over them adding to the gloom of the valley. The heat clung to them like a sickly vapor, and sweat poured down their bodies as they busied themselves in their collective tasks.

They were still hastily building the temporary shelter when the rains came. It poured out of the sky in a drenching torrent that had them scampering beneath the half-finished shelter where they stood close together in a vain attempt to avoid the drops splashing into the open sides. All day it poured until at last, the men, braving its cold, wet drenching, stripped naked and hurriedly piled the last twigs and leaves on the unfinished part of the roof. They returned shivering into the shelter. The work was hastily done; and the further end of the roof was dripping, but there was more room to find dry spots on which to lie.

The rain continued incessantly for many days. The little stream which had gurgled merrily as tiny rivulets flowed into it now grumbled and frothed angrily as the hillsides poured cascades of water loaded with the debris of many years of degeneration into its narrow bosom. It rose and roared and brimmed over its banks, sweeping through the rough vegetation as it sought to escape the crush of water that flowed in all directions. The water spread over the floor of the small valley, and was soon seeping beneath the shelter that the men had built.

That first day they had eaten the remains of the food that the Caribs had brought, but when that was finished the men had again to venture into the wet. They searched and found wild yams which they dug out of the soaking ground and roasted over a fire that they built in the middle of the shelter. They ate and slept as the rain drummed on the roof over their heads. They ate and slept as the earth filled with water, until the excess flowed out of its pores and spread all over the valley floor. The branches of the trees drooped and snapped under the press of the unceasing flow. The roof of the shelter sagged as pools formed in weak places, and dribbles of water flowed through crevices between the layers of leaves onto the ground.

On the fifth day it stopped suddenly. The sun came out brightly, casting a wide smile on the new-washed hills and warming the wet valley. The stream moaned reproachfully as its waters ebbed lower and lower, leaving the scrubbed earth around clean and clear. The earth breathed cleanly, and the trees shook themselves free of the weighty wetness that had them drooping for so many days. It was as if the earth had gone through a prolonged ablution that had washed it free of all pollution and decay. The air was vibrant and clear, and the light sparkled on the bright green of the hillsides. The men, women and children came out of the damp shelter, and looked about them in wonderment. They, too, felt clean and newly washed.

As soon as the rain had stopped and the sun had come out confidently to warm the shivering earth, Pharcel began to look critically at his surroundings. The deluge had revealed to him the danger of setting up camp in the low ground of the small valley. There was risk of serious flooding; and in spite of the thick forest cover on the hillsides, landslips could occur under extremely wet conditions. Furthermore, the camp would be too vulnerable to attack, encircled as it was by the surrounding hills. He recalled that not even the well defended ravine had been able to save Coree Greg's camp as long as the attack could come from the high ground above it. That same day Pharcel began to explore the hill on the side of the bowl opposite the track by which they had entered it.

Leaving his men to grub for whatever roots they could find, he approached the steep slope, and forced his way purposefully through thick undergrowth until he came to higher ground. There the forest floor was almost free of secondary vegetation, and he could see through the trees a gap in what had first appeared a continuous ridge. He headed towards it, and suddenly, through the trees and close to the gap he saw a broad expanse of pasture lying flat along the edge of the ridge. It ended in a sheer drop falling cleanly down to the valley below. From the pasture he could look clearly at the circle of hills around the bowl.

He made his way to the gap. It was but a narrow defile, thinly wooded. As he came out the other side, a bright light burst upon him and shimmered over a wide expanse of forest falling gracefully down a long way towards the coast. Further away he could see the silvery flash of what he thought was the ocean. He felt secure in this spot. He returned through the gap, and wandered about the pasture until he found a fissure in the ground where a spring gushed from the side of the hill and fell away down towards the valley. He marked the spot where his hut would be, retraced his steps and began the steep decline to the floor of the valley.

Pharcel led his men to the higher ground the next day. Sweltering in the bright sun, they began to build a new habitation where they would be secure for many years to come. It was not a great distance to the bottom of the bowl; and the men and women, having already assessed the rich potential of the deep loamy soil down there, had quickly decided to return to rehabilitate the fruit trees and plant new stands of cassava and new gardens of herbs and vegetables; but they were happy they would not have to remain in the oppressive closeness and steamy heat of the valley.

Up on the higher ground, although more exposed to the sun, the air was always cool, and a constant wind gushed through the gap and wafted on all sides of the pasture. In the morning there was often the faint smell of sulphur, and Pharcel knew they could not be far away from the dreaded lake that boiled. It was a grand vista looking around at the surrounding hills. On a bright day the towering form of the ever present mountain stood clear in the far distance, a thin veil of cloud settling on its crown. It was the kind of refuge that made the small colony of men, women and children feel protected and invincible; and they soon settled to their daily lives as if they had always been there.

Pharcel built his hut against the side of the cliff close to the spring, and one for Marie Claire and Marie Rose beside it. The two women looked after his needs while he spent his time organizing the life of the camp, leading the men and women in their daily labors, and joining them in their occasional nightly celebrations.

Then they came. At first it was a trickle, and then it was a flood. In the beginning they came one by one down into the deep valley, and then up onto the sunny plateau. They came, brimming over with the excitement of their freedom, telling tales of a coming insurrection and war. The slaves in the South were in agitation, whipped up to the pitch of rebellion by the mulatto call for revolt.

Paulinaire had been active in the South, sending his agents among the slaves on the estates, promising arms and money if they would join with him and his group in a general revolt that would unseat the white government. Since he had failed to marshal the support of the runaway chiefs, he had decided to mobilize support directly among the slaves. Filled with the desire for freedom from the strenuous labor to which they were driven daily, from the constant threat of punishment and even torture, and from the personal indignity to which they were constantly exposed, they listened eagerly to the words of Paulinaire's agents; and their minds longingly embraced the vision of a state free of the white man's domination. But in the end, they escaped, not to Paulinaire's dream of liberty, equality and fraternity, but to the reality of the independence of their own people in the mountains. The daily flow increased, and more and more men, women and children came wearily up the steep hill and into the camp.

The small camp grew into a sizable community as word got around that the young Pharcel had founded a bastion of freedom where no white man could find him. Many came from the other camps, journeying from the other side of the high mountain, and from the eastern shore. Soon word came from Mabouya and Congoree, urging him to hold the camps together; but nothing was heard from Sandy's camp, or from Jacco who seemed to have gone in hiding. Pharcel returned courteous greetings and assurances that his people were at one with all others of their race. Now was the time to build on the foundation that had been laid, and his people were fervently engaged in securing themselves and their future. In times of peace there should be preparations for war. His people would strengthen themselves and wait for the day of their deliverance.

It was not long before Paulinaire paid a visit to Pharcel's camp. He had been quick to discern that his agents had succeeded only in driving the slaves to escape the plantations, and that they had not joined his ranks. They were all heading to Pharcel's camp. He walked into the camp one evening, barely able to lift his legs. His grey suit was stained with the green sap of trees, and his shoes were muddy with the black soil of the valley. Jacques came in with him, as breezy as usual. They sat in Pharcel's hut for a long time before Paulinaire could regain his composure. With his wrinkled, stained and mud-splashed clothing, he looked less debonair than he normally was; but he soon pulled himself together and his commanding presence filled the spacious hut.

"It was as I said it would be," he told Pharcel. "Coree Greg alone could not withstand the force of the militia. Now he is dead, I hope common sense will prevail."

"He fought bravely," Pharcel said somberly. "We should honor his name."

"This is not about personal glory," Paulinaire replied, "it is about war. When the war is over, there will be time to honor the brave."

"It is over," Pharcel responded emphatically. "Here we live in liberty and peace."

"But for how long?" Paulinaire asked patiently. "You are still the white man's property. White people, and especially white colonists, are obsessed with the idea of property. They will never leave you alone."

They spoke all night and Paulinaire's natural eloquence deftly worked the tapestry of the grand vision that he had of a world controlled entirely by blacks and men of color, a world elevated to the rule of justice and the principles of liberty for all, equality among all men, and fraternity among the brethren of black and colored men. He, Paulinaire, had the means to support the realization of this noble dream. He had the money and the weapons. He had the intellect and the experience. And he had the full support of the mulatto community and even some from the more enlightened white men in the town. He would provide the weapons, and he would coordinate the union between the black and colored communities. All Pharcel had to do was to bring the blacks together and they would be invincible.

Paulinaire was impressed with the growing numbers in Pharcel's camp. All the next day he observed the comings and goings of the men and women. There was no rigid discipline as in a military camp; everyone went about his business independently; but there was a sense of togetherness which promised easy mobilization and consolidation whenever danger threatened. Pharcel's leadership was not intrusive; he appeared to be one among many; but the other men and women never failed to turn to him whenever difficulties arose or disputes had to be settled. He ruled merely by the pre-eminence of his own person.

Paulinaire told Pharcel of the state of affairs in the colony. The white population was in a state of unease with news of an imminent war between England and France. The French inhabitants on the west coast and down in Grandbay were planning an upheaval to coincide with the date of the French invasion. They refused to countenance any direct collaboration between the blacks and mulattos and themselves, but they encouraged any action that would improve their chances of overthrowing the English and driving them from the island.

Paulinaire's position was to appear to be sympathetic to the French, and encourage them in their plans for insurrection as a means of diverting the attention of the militia away from him and his group. When the French rose up in arms, that would be the signal for the combined force of the blacks and the mulattos to take the South and march on the capital. With the militia engaging the

French on the west coast, there would be little resistance to the combined strength of the blacks and mulattos down in the South. Pharcel marveled at Paulinaire's duplicity, but he said nothing. Meanwhile, Paulinaire promised to furnish Pharcel's camp with a large quantity of arms and ammunition. He knew two black soldiers who could be induced to desert from the militia and join Pharcel's camp. They would be useful for training the men in the use of arms.

Paulinaire kept his word. Within two weeks a huge cache of arms and ammunition awaited them at an appointed place in the forest. Pharcel had the place thoroughly reconnoitered before he would allow his men to approach the cache. The men struggled through the difficult terrain with the heavy boxes, and, by the end of the day, they had carried most of them all the way up the steep hill and into Pharcel's hut.

Jacques returned two days later with the renegade soldiers. Pharcel was uneasy with their presence in the camp, remembering what had befallen Coree Greg and his brave warriors, and the part that the black soldiers had played in breaking through Coree Greg's defenses. He had them watched closely for several days before he admitted them into his hut to open the stack of boxes and commence their work.

Before long, Marie Claire's enormous appetite drew one of the soldiers to her welcoming arms. Night after night the sound of their delight in each other floated out of the hut into the quiet of the dark. On those nights Marie Rose left them alone, and laid her mat beside Pharcel's in his hut next door.

The man was only of medium height, but big-boned and muscular. He held himself erect, and spoke with a commanding voice wherever he was, even in moments of casual conversation. It was soon apparent that the authority in his voice was a cloak for his lack of intelligence. He could teach the men to shoot, but little else. They called him Napoleon and he thought himself as great as the Emperor himself.

His companion, Samba, was a man of modest countenance, equally skilled in the use of arms; but he also had an inventiveness of mind that gained the admiration of the men and set them to orderly preparations for the defense of the camp in the event of an attack. He spoke little, but he had about him that quiet charisma that drew the men to his company whenever he sat in the wide circle in front of the huts. They came to him and listened to his stories of life in the militia among the white officers and soldiers.

He told them that when there was not any military work to be done, the black soldiers were treated no better than the slaves on the plantations, being required to do the most arduous and repugnant tasks; but that when they were on the march, they were treated almost as equals. He asserted that no black soldier could feel comfortable fighting people of his own race; but, having been steeped in military discipline for so long, they had no choice but to obey commands. Still, there were many who would readily desert if the opportunity came for a successful rebellion. He was proud to be among the men of Pharcel's camp in this atmosphere of freedom and independence. He felt he was already one of them.

Months had passed, and the men and women had transformed the closed-in valley into a luscious profusion of herbs, vegetables, fruits and root crops. On the higher ground pigeons and doves abounded among the trees, and provided excellent, quick targets for the men to practice their shooting skills. Wooden traps were laid for small game, including the lean-bodied deer that roamed in occasional open grasslands on the windward side of the hills; and pits were dug to entrap wild boar that sometimes ravaged the rich harvest of roots and vegetables in the garden below.

Napoleon strutted about the camp as he would on a parade ground, sometimes bellowing orders which no one paid attention to. It was as if he had appointed himself commander of the forces and he had forgotten to declare this to anyone. In his blubbering sentimentality during his nights in Marie Claire's arms, he often boasted of his military prowess; and claimed that he was the only one who could credibly lead the men of the camp in any struggle, either of defense or of aggression. He considered Pharcel a raw, untutored youth, who did not have the experience, the intelligence or the courage, to lead such a body of men in battle. Contented as she was with Napoleon's diligence in assuaging her nocturnal and muliebrile desires, Marie Claire nonetheless felt obliged to warn Pharcel of his incipient ambitions.

She did, and Pharcel acted swiftly. He banished Napoleon to a smaller hut at the extremity of the camp on the other side of the gap in the hill, and instructed him to attend to his duties as a shooting instructor and not to leave the camp on pain of death. Pharcel had him watched at all times. It became clear that the men regarded Napoleon as a buffoon, a man who fancied himself as a leader but who had no following.

For some time, Napoleon moped about the camp in sullen anger. Unlike Samba, who had fully integrated himself in the life of the camp, doing his fair share of labor in the gardens down in the valley, Napoleon shirked any kind of work that was not strictly military. He marched about the camp all day, carrying a musket; and intruded himself among any group of men or women to voice his complaints about Pharcel and his incompetence as a leader. His audience dwindled day by day until, after a time, he sat alone in the shade, watching resentfully as the camp went about its daily routine.

Then one day he vanished. The men came to Pharcel and said that he could not be found. He had left in the night taking his musket and a quantity of ammunition with him. When he had not reappeared after the second day, Pharcel summoned Samba to him.

"He is not to be trusted," Samba said.

"Why not? Paulinaire sent him," Pharcel reasoned.

"Oh, he sucks up to anyone," Samba replied, "even the white officers when it suits his purpose. We were never very close. I hardly knew him."

"Do you think Paulinaire could have been mistaken?" Pharcel asked doubtfully.

Samba hesitated for just a moment.

"I do not think Paulinaire is very discerning in such matters," Samba said thoughtfully. "He can be impressionable, and Napoleon impressed him with his vociferousness."

"Is he a threat to us?" Pharcel asked him anxiously.

"He is a bit bombastic, and his bark is often sharper than his bite," Samba said light-heartedly; "but he is also a slimy bastard. I would not put anything past him."

"You think there will be trouble?" Pharcel looked searchingly into Samba's eyes.

"It does not hurt to be prepared," Samba replied, his eyes steady on Pharcel.

"Then let's do it," Pharcel said decisively.

The small party crept cautiously along the almost indiscernible trace. Only the faint signs of the press of bare feet on the dead leaves that covered the ground and the occasional bent branch of the thin bushes that grew under the towering trees indicated that human traffic had passed that way. There were two white officers and four black soldiers; and they were well armed, the officers with swords and pistols, and the others with muskets and long knives. They crawled slowly towards the lip of the bowl, their ears alert to every sound. The sound of laughter and brief snatches of song coming from the men and women laboring in the valley below rose to them. The two officers moved boldly forward and peered curiously through the bushes over the edge. The others hung back uncertainly.

They had been sent on a reconnaissance when word had reached the encampment that Pharcel had set up camp deep in the interior, that his numbers were increasing day by day, and that he had been well supplied with arms. One of the muskets taken from the camp showed that it was of French manufacture, and the authorities were quick to link Pharcel's mobilization of so many runaways with the seditious activities of Paulinaire and his group of rebellious mulattos and French revolutionaries.

Dispatches had immediately been exchanged with London about the growing tensions in the colony and the new threat of a large body of renegade blacks securely hidden in the most difficult part of the island, and who were undoubtedly in league with Paulinaire, the educated mulatto who had now become the arch enemy of the colonial government. London demanded that Pharcel be taken by any means possible. They wanted an end to the runaway problem. As for Paulinaire, they were to entrap him in any act of sedition, and summarily dispose of him and his misguided followers.

It also became known that Pharcel frequented that area around Geneva and Dubique. Captain Marshall would not have let out the nature and significance of Pharcel's activities at Dubique, notwithstanding the extreme resentment and hate which he bore against the young African. Pride would not allow him to admit to any association between the upstart black and the woman he had so desperately desired, and he subtly insinuated the intelligence that Pharcel was known to visit friends on the estate at the ebb of the moon. The entire militia had been put on alert. In addition, the authorities had notices posted in all parts of the island offering a huge reward for the capture dead or alive of Pharcel, the fugitive slave and leader of a band of runaways.

The two officers and the small party of black soldiers, guided by Napoleon, had been sent to locate the entrance to the camp; and to observe the layout of the surrounding territory. Encouraged by his success with the destruction of Coree Greg's camp, Captain Marshall was confident that he could penetrate the defenses of Pharcel's, and destroy him and his followers once and for all. He entertained no doubts about this. The young slave, with no knowledge of or experience with military strategy, could not match his superior skills as a soldier and accomplished leader of his men. All that was necessary was for them to locate the camp; and he would soon have it burnt to the ground, and all the runaways returned to their rightful masters. And that would be the end of it. Except that he had a special fate awaiting Pharcel. He would make him pay.

As the two officers moved silently forward, their eyes closely scanning the ridges that surrounded the deep hollow below them, the men muttered among themselves. They had done their jobs and located the camp, and they saw no reason to loiter in such a dangerous place. They kept well back as the two officers edged further and further over the precipitous decline. When the bushes around them suddenly came alive with the dark forms of a dozen or more runaways, the soldiers broke away, and vanished down the trace by which they had come, leaving the two officers helpless and in panic as the runaways surrounded and hustled them down the trace into the valley, up the other side and into the camp.

The officers were kept standing in the shade of a low tree that spread its branches over the side of the clearing close to Pharcel's hut. After a while, Pharcel came out to meet them. He signaled to his men to strip them of their swords and pistols, and then he turned and smiled winningly at them.

"Welcome to our camp," he said politely. "I do not know what brought you here, so far away from your own encampment; but you are most welcome."

The two officers turned to each other, and then together nodded in acknowledgement.

"You must be hungry and thirsty after such a long march," Pharcel continued solicitously, "and it is close to dinner time. I hope you will accept our humble hospitality."

Pharcel called, and Marie Claire came out, gathering her wide skirt about her stout legs. He spoke with her quietly, and she inclined her head sideways, an arch expression on her broad face. She looked at the two officers appraisingly, and smiled sweetly at them before turning back. They watched her formidable haunches vibrate with every step as she made her way back to her hut.

"Marie Claire will take care of you," Pharcel reassured them. "We will talk later."

He left them still standing in the shade surrounded by their captors. As he entered his hut, he signaled to one of his men to join him inside.

"Were they alone?" Pharcel asked.

"No, there were others; but they fled before we could get to them."

"Did you see them?"

"We did not. They were like black shadows in the forest. I am sure they were black soldiers."

"Was Napoleon among them?"

"We could not be sure. There was no time. The others turned their backs and ran so quickly."

Pharcel nodded.

News of the capture of the two officers would certainly reach their encampment by nightfall. This would no doubt precipitate action to rescue them immediately. He knew he had to be careful not to detain the officers longer than was necessary. The camp was secure; and it was well armed, but he was not ready to engage in hostilities. When he fought, it would have to be on his own offensive.

It was no good being drawn to defensive action, especially when there was no purpose in it. He took his companion by the shoulder.

"Pass the word that the officers are to be treated kindly, but they must be watched at all times."

The man inclined his head quizzically. He nodded, and left.

When Pharcel rejoined the officers they had eaten; and had been refreshed by the cool, clear water of the nearby spring. He sat with them in the shade, and spoke openly to them about life in the camp. As the men and women returned from the day's labor in the fields, he spoke of the industry of his people and how well they had adapted to the productive and orderly life of the camp, producing all their needs and not venturing into any properties outside their own. His people planted and harvested. They snared and hunted in the vicinity of the camp. They kept within the confines of their own territory and did not steal, nor appropriate, nor destroy anyone's property. They lived in peace. All they asked for was to be left alone.

As night fell and the light gradually faded, he escorted the officers to a small hut opposite his own on the inner edge of the clearing. A few of the men dispersed unobtrusively around the hut. The officers remained indoors, knowing that they would be closely watched.

Pharcel summoned Samba to his hut. They sat late into the night discussing the importance of the event which had occurred that day. It was clear that the officers had been part of a reconnaissance party sent to test the defenses of the camp. The men had reported that there had been others, black men like themselves, but in the uniform of the militia. They appeared familiar with the woods because they had quickly disappeared in the forest, leaving little trace of their passage. The men had not pursued them far, being more concerned to secure the white officers. Samba felt certain that the party had been guided to the camp by the treacherous Napoleon.

The capture of the two officers would bring consternation to the military encampment at Geneva, and would most certainly rouse the anger of the colonial authorities. No doubt Captain Marshall would soon be pressured to march his men into the forest to attempt a rescue. Samba was confident that the defenses of the camp were sufficiently formidable to repel any attack, especially if it were to come from across the deep valley. It was unlikely that anyone would attempt to approach from the more exposed and virtually unexplored and heavily forested slope on the other side of the gap.

When Samba left his hut well past midnight, Pharcel stayed awake. For hours afterwards his mind shifted about exploring all possibilities and examining every option. He understood the danger they were in if they were to detain or execute the officers. He also understood the risk of releasing them after having revealed to them the situation of the camp and the only possible approaches to it. He reasoned with himself as to which was the greater danger. When he fell asleep at last, he had still not come to any decision.

He awoke when the camp was already alive with activity. Many had gathered around the hut where the officers were, curious about the prisoners and what their fate would be. Many of them, remembering the route that had occurred in Bala's camp, and the recent massacre in Coree Greg's, were impatient about the delay in deciding what should be done with the two intruders. If this was a continuation of war they should have been executed instantly. Pharcel should not hesitate when he had the upper hand. They were surprised and disconcerted when he summoned the two men to have breakfast in his hut.

Marie Rose brought in roast mountain doves, boiled corn, wild raspberries and a gourd of the fresh sparkling water. The three men dined silently, the officers frequently glancing at each other, uneasy about the solemnity of the meal and the uncertainty of their situation. When the meal was finished, Pharcel led them outside, and, surrounded by a number of his men, he strolled around the circle of huts until they came to the track that led down into the valley.

They descended at a leisurely walk, pausing now and then to glimpse the gangs of men and women diligently tilling the ground on the valley floor, or clearing the weed and other noxious plants from the cultivated gardens. At the bottom of the valley they moved among the workers scattered over the several vegetable patches. They sat with them at lunch, and shared in the provisions that the women had cooked. The shadows had already crept over the valley when Pharcel led them back to the camp.

The next morning, Pharcel again summoned them to breakfast. They sat as before munching silently on the simple fare, and when they were finished, Pharcel led them outside. He signaled to the men hovering near the hut where the officers had slept. They came and stood expectantly before him.

"You may go now," Pharcel calmly announced to the officers. "My men will take you safely to where you can find your way back to your detachment."

The officers turned eagerly to each other, then stood uncertainly, a look of suspicion and fear darkening their faces.

"Oh, I will keep your weapons as a memento of the wonderful time we had together". Pharcel chuckled with amusement.

The officers still stood, hesitant to follow the troop of men that Pharcel had assigned to escort them.

"You may go now," Pharcel urged them. "No harm will be done to you."

The officers moved slowly forward, turning nervously to look over their shoulders. They continued to turn and look backwards until they descended the track that led them to the valley.

Pharcel watched them go.

CHAPTER 19

It was late afternoon and the *Salon L'Aise* was packed to overflowing. There had been a general unease in the Grandbay community over the past weeks. News abounded about the state of affairs between England and France. There was the continuous threat of war between the two countries; and the French inhabitants, especially in the South and in the west coastal villages of St. Joseph and Colihaut, were in constant readiness to support the French cause in the event of an invasion by the French fleet. To add to the uneasiness that pervaded the southern villages, the agents of Victor Hughes, a rabid revolutionary from Guadeloupe, were all over the territory, instigating the slaves to revolt. Chief among those agents was Louis Paulinaire, the well educated but virulently disaffected mulatto, who had recently left his comfortable living in the capital and moved among the estates, stirring the slaves to rebellion.

Many of those agents had infiltrated southern society, posing as wealthy émigrés from Martinique. Most of them were mulattos, and so large was their number that they overwhelmed all attempts to keep them from the restricted sanctuary that the *Salon L'Aise* had formerly so jealously guarded as the preserve of the white planters and their factors and more respectable journeymen. They had even invaded the one place where Captain Marshall could be sure to find quiet, intelligent and witty conversation. On many occasions when he had sought the company of the priest in his modest presbytery near the shore, he had found the place teeming with the loquacious Frenchmen who seemed forever stirred to vigorous expositions or disquisitions about the social upheavals that had taken place in their mother country.

To add to the anxiety of the planters and other white residents, the slaves on the estates had become unusually restive. Many of them had recently taken to the woods, swelling the ranks of the army of runaways that was building up in the forests. Most of them had found refuge in Pharcel's camp, and it was feared that the young chief was preparing for an all out assault on the estates.

It was rumored that large quantities of arms had been left in stacks hidden in the woods where the runaways had collected them and conveyed them to their far distant camps. From all accounts the situation was becoming uncontrollable, and the militia was being urged to take a more aggressive stance in their campaign to drive the runaways out of the woods and back to their rightful owners.

That day the saloon was filled with their unceasing garrulousness; and the two friends, Marshall and Urquhart, retreated to a back room where they could converse in relative quietude. A plump, peach-colored mulatto girl came in to serve them. Her face was round and full with eyes that glittered out of narrow slits between puffy eyelids, and fleshy lips the color of ripe papaya. Her breasts rose proudly from a generous bosom. Below them her abdomen rolled in voluptuous curves down to her ample thighs. She beamed coquettishly at Captain Urquhart, but stiffened instantly as Captain Marshall, frowning, and regarding her with scorn, barked a sharp order.

"Bring me rum. The best."

Captain Urquhart smiled at her warmly, his eyes softening as he took in her pretty face and curvaceous figure. He kept her standing at his elbow for a long while, pretending to deliberate over his order. At last he turned to her grinning mischievously.

"You know what I want," he said teasingly.

"No, I don't," she replied coyly.

"That fine wine you served me yesterday."

"There is no more. They," she indicated the noisy crowd in the open saloon, "gobbled it all last night."

"Then bring me the old cognac. The one you keep hidden."

She giggled impishly, and cast an inviting look at Urquhart as she hurried away, her proud, rounded bottom quivering enticingly. His eyes followed her to the door, and he smiled inwardly remembering.

He had gone with one of the black soldiers to a clearing near the Geneva River one night, where there was to be a festivity of some kind. It was unusual for any white person to be allowed among the slaves when they had their special feasts, and at first he had felt most unwelcome as he stood against a tree, and watched the swelling crowd moving uncertainly about and giving him suspicious glances. But as the evening went along and the men and women drank again and again from the gourds of raw liquor that were being passed around, they had gradually settled down, and he found himself warmly accepted by many of them. They brought him food which he ate from the broad leaves of the dasheen plant, and he had smiled winsomely at the women who served him. As the heady liquor lightened the mood of the crowd, drummers had come out and set up their drums to the side where he stood. Instantly the crowd parted and drifted towards the edges of the clearing.

They started tentatively at first. A few men and women came out and shuffled vigorously about, the whites of their feet flashing rapidly as they leapt and cavorted over the bare ground. As the night progressed, the dancing had become more and more seductive, tantalizing and lewd until they were nothing less than a parody of some savage sexual rite. Suzanne had been one of the late dancers; and he had found himself transported to a world beyond anything that he had hitherto experienced as he followed her rhythmic motions. In the end, she had collapsed helplessly on the ground, fully spent, but blissfully happy. He had applauded her loudly, to the amusement of the crowd. Afterward, she had come and stood beside him.

The noise from the open saloon was muffled. Through the wooden partition, the clattering voices of the Frenchmen and the squeals of the mulatto serving girls as they fluttered among the crowd, dodging its many darting hands and clawing fingers, reached them. They waited in silence, listening to the hubbub on the other side until the mulatto girl returned with a bottle of rum, dark as old oak, a flagon of rich roseate wine and two crystal glasses.

"There was one bottle of that wine left," she said with a glittering smile. "It was tucked away at the back of the cupboard. I have secured it for you."

Captain Urquhart nodded, and smiled at her appreciatively. She gave him a provocative glance as she left the room.

They raised their drinks.

"To the confusion of all blacks," Captain Marshall proposed.

"Ah!" exclaimed Captain Urquhart. "Don't be like that. They are not all bad."

"Then show me a good one."

"What about Suzanne?" Urquhart asked, indicating the girl who had just left them. "She is quite pretty and very engaging."

"She is fat, and she smells musky."

"Don't you like a woman's smell?"

"Our white women don't smell that way. They have a clean scent about them."

"Black women are more natural. They smell of love and desire."

"You can have them for all I care."

"Oh, I do; and it is wonderful."

Captain Marshall snorted with disgust. In a way he envied Urquhart's facility with women of all races, and his ability to mix in any society wherever he found himself. He was white, an officer and a gentleman; and he abhorred the kind of familiarity that seemed natural between Urquhart and the blacks and mulattos even as he envied the simplicity of that kind of relationship.

"I think you forget your mission," he said truculently.

"And what is that?"

"To hunt down runaway slaves, destroy their camps, obliterate them if necessary."

"Even the good ones?"

"There are no good ones."

"Not even Pharcel?"

"Especially not Pharcel!"

"Why do you hate him so? He did return our officers unharmed."

Captain Urquhart recalled the day, nearly five weeks ago, when the four black soldiers had crept back into the camp late at night without the two white officers who had been sent to lead a reconnaissance of the trace into Pharcel's camp. That shifty-eyed and boastful Napoleon, whom Marshall cultivated so trustingly, had been sent as a guide since he claimed he had single-handedly tracked Pharcel to his lair. The four men had returned gasping with fright, and had given an incoherent account of an ambush by more than ten men armed with spears, clubs and axes who had attacked them right at the entrance to the camp. They had said they had fought hard against those overwhelming numbers, and would most certainly have saved the officers but for a sudden onslaught by about twenty more men. They had continued to fight valiantly and long, but, in the end, they had been forced to retreat and save themselves. The officers had ventured too far ahead of them, and had easily been surrounded and taken away.

Marshall and Urquhart had sent a joint dispatch to the governor about the unfortunate and highly dangerous incident, and the governor had responded with a firm order that they should take action immediately to retrieve the officers and destroy the runaway camp. By the second day after the incident, they were ready to march into the woods when the two officers walked composedly into the encampment. They were unscathed and unmolested except that they had been deprived of their weapons, which they said the runaway chief had kept as a keepsake in token of the cordial friendship which he had enjoyed in their company.

The officers had given a full account of their stay in the camp. They spoke effusively about the order and industry of the men and women as they went about their daily tasks without any overt exercise of authority over them. What was most remarkable, they reported, was the self-sufficiency which was clearly evident in the diversity of the produce and the richness of the surroundings. These runaways had no need to venture out of their camp for their survival as most others were forced to do. These were peaceful people who preferred to be left alone. No sign of animosity had come from them.

As to the situation of the camp, they described it as virtually impregnable, perched as it was on a shelf near the top of a hill on the far side of a deep hollow. The only other approach, they observed, was through a narrow defile that gave onto a thickly wooded slope that stretched for miles down to the coast. The camp was obviously well guarded at all times. There were sentinels hidden in the trees at both entrances. That is how they had come to be caught so easily. They could not be sure, but the men did not carry guns, although the officers had seen discarded pieces of crates which might have contained weapons and ammunition.

The officers were full of praise for Pharcel's decency, and spoke glowingly of the courtesies extended to them. Even though he was a runaway slave, it was difficult not to attribute the highest qualities of civility and gallantry to him. He had treated them with respect and the highest consideration. The officers had not believed at first that they would be permitted to return unharmed. They had been surprised when their escort had brought them right up to the ridge along which was the Carib village, and had shown them a way out of the woods and towards the nearest plantation.

"I find this Pharcel a most intriguing character," Urquhart remarked thoughtfully.

"You give him too much credit," Marshall replied. "He is nothing but an escaped slave, and a vicious one at that."

"Well, not from the reports that we have had," Urquhart argued. "He looks like a decent sort."

"No matter what," Marshall insisted, "I must bring him down."

"That won't be easy," Urquhart chuckled.

"I know how," Marshall said broodingly. "I know just how I will get him when the time comes."

Urquhart looked at him wonderingly. Then he reached for his glass and poured himself more wine. He could not understand what it was about the slave, Pharcel, that stirred such animosity in his friend who was normally so cavalier about his military duties and who preferred to loiter in the drawing rooms of the planters' wives than carry out military raids. Clearly, Pharcel's return of the two officers was itself an overture of peace. Yet here was Marshall, who was usually so spineless in initiating military assaults, wanting so desperately to launch an offensive against a well fortified and highly defensible camp. He had had to use his equal authority as Captain of his own detachment to persuade Marshall to send another dispatch to the governor to inform him of the return of the two officers, and to recommend that the order for an instant assault on the camp should be rescinded.

"There is a reward posted for him dead or alive," Marshall said thoughtfully. "I want him alive."

"Whatever for?" Urquhart asked, a hint of mockery in his voice. "Why not kill him and be done with it?"

"He does not merit the death of a soldier. He must die slowly like the criminal he is."

Marshall's face darkened with resentment.

Urquhart studied him curiously before questioning him further.

"Tell me, my friend, what has he done to you?"

"To me, nothing. But he is the most vile, most dangerous slave at large; and I will get him."

Captain Marshall sat at a small, wooden table set against the wall beneath the sill of an open window. The jalousies were opened wide to let in the bright morning light and the gentle puffs of wind blowing across the wide savannah only a few yards beyond the hedge. He lived in a tiny cottage which he had appropriated from the estate for his personal use. It was a pleasant little house with a verandah running full length at its front; and had previously been occupied by Brent, the overseer, who had been killed recently by Pharcel. Its jalousie windows and doors in every room were always open to the fresh breeze that flowed from the hills at the back, and, at certain times of day, from the open savannah at the front. The window and door shutters were kept latched onto the outer walls, except in stormy weather when they were firmly shut and braced by wooden bars on the inside.

The sitting room where he sat was compact and lightly furnished with rustic, wooden furniture. Besides the square table, there were a straight backed sofa, a few stoutly-built chairs, a coffee table set in the middle of the room and a glass-fronted cabinet against the wall near the sofa. There were two bedrooms sparsely furnished with narrow wooden beds and crudely-built chests of drawers. A small kitchen was erected in the yard a few feet away from where he sat. On the other side of the house and towards the back was a privy no bigger than a sentry box.

Off-duty, he lived alone in the small cottage, attended only by a light-colored woman whom he had hired from the estate house in Geneva. She was big-framed, with a broad face, puffed-up nose and lips that seemed always curved downwards. Her eyes were large and grey, with brown flecks at the irises, and bulged out of her eyelids. Her hair fell around her face and hung below her ears in dull, brown, frizzy curls. She walked with a slow dignity, erect, but with an awkward discordance in the movement of her limbs. It was as if her arms were forever at odds with the rhythm of her legs.

Captain Marshall was very fond of her and never seemed to tire in his pursuit of her favors, though she was never enthusiastic in her responses to his boyish ardor.

The woman came through the door close to the table where the Captain sat. As she came up to him he leaned backwards in his chair and reached for her. She stood quite still beside him while he, seemingly lost in abstraction, stroked her thighs. From her great height she cast down on him a look of utter contempt as his fingers danced along the sturdy columns of her thighs and rose in surreptitious darts further on. He suddenly stopped; dropped his arm as if his actions had been unintentional, and looked up at her with a smile, venal and ingratiating. She resumed her walk across the living room without a further glance at him.

He could not understand what it was about her that had aroused his desire for her. She was robust in build, but not voluptuous; and had that vapid look in her eyes and face that seemed to register no emotion. There was nothing soft or alluring about her looks. Certainly, she was not beautiful or even handsome. But she was submissive. And she was almost white. When he had taken her for the first time, she had simply bent wordlessly to his will; and afterwards she had walked away from him in her silent dignity as if nothing had happened. Yet he continued to be stimulated by her, and every encounter left him more avid than the last.

He knew very little about her since she always kept a cold reserve as far as communication with him was concerned. Thus, he could not have known of the torrid liaison she secretly carried on with a slave who was as black as she was light-colored, and as huge as she was robust. In his presence, her cold dignity and compliant submission were sufficient to clothe her in the vestment of restrictive virtue and inviolable decency. He could not know how much she regarded his puny bursts of adolescent passion with so much contempt and loathing.

As the woman returned across the room he turned to her. She stopped, her eyes closed in patient sufferance, expectantly waiting for another assault.

"Go to the camp and fetch Napoleon" Captain Marshall ordered. "Tell him to come immediately."

The woman nodded, looking relieved as she ambled out of the house. He watched her go, a deep frown darkening his brow. Her unhurried movement sometimes irritated him; but she was efficient in her work, always obliging, stole discretely, and did not complain. He could not ask for more. He wondered why it was he felt so comfortable with her. Normally, he felt awkward and challenged in the presence of black and colored women.

Despite his reputation as a ladies' man in the drawing rooms of white society, where his wit and conversation were known to charm even the most virtuous of wives, he lacked the brashness and curtness of address that seemed to appeal to black and colored females who always seemed nervous and defensive against his superior airs and the suavity of his language. Their defensiveness often seemed like rudeness to him and he had come to avoid intimate contact with them. What he had said to Captain Urquhart about the lack of appeal of black women was not true. His problem was that he could not easily bridge the gap between his innate insecurity and the natural simplicity and earthiness of black women. So he looked upon them with disdain, and kept his distance.

Captain Marshall looked out the window at the bright morning. It was approaching midday and the sun shone brightly on the pale green of the savannah where two horses and a few stray sheep grazed contentedly. Gusts of wind blew through the open window and rattled a few decorative plates hung on the wooden partition above the sofa. On a bare patch of earth near the middle of the savannah, a small eddy had formed in a swirl of dust. It twisted and turned in loops for a short distance before it suddenly died as the wind subsided. A row of mango trees grew on the far side of the savannah, and beyond that was another clearing where the troops were encamped. Through the trees, he could see the outer row of white tents somewhat blurred by the shadow of the trees. On the seaward side, fields of sugarcane spread on a gentle slope that dipped and broke into narrow ravines closer to the shore. In the distance the tall stone chimney of the sugar mill rose out of the cane fields like a giant obelisk.

His mind drifted to his son at Dubique; and he pictured him at a later age playing delightfully on the savannah. He had often gone on short visits to see him, and he had always enjoyed watching him toddle about, his bare rump bouncing on the wooden floor whenever he slipped and fell. When that happened the little toddler would wail loudly. Then his father would swing him about until his cries turned to joyful giggles. That was the only pleasure Captain Marshall got from his visits there. His affection for Georgette had dwindled to an uneasy tolerance.

Since the birth of her baby, Georgette had filled out largely, and had lost the clear and rosy complexion of her girlhood. She had at first tried to entice him again to her embraces, but he had avoided her because he had found her attentions cloying and even repulsive. Georgette could not understand why he had continued to evade any intimate entanglements with her; and she had reproached him for his neglect and inconstancy, but she enjoyed watching him playing with his son on the floor of the wide verandah.

As for Elise, she continued to elude the Captain. She never came out if she knew he was visiting. On the few occasions when they had unexpectedly come face to face, she would give a brief and hasty greeting and hurry away back into her room. He had seen her a few times walking among the trees, head bowed as if in deep and troubled thought; and he had been unable to fathom the true nature of his feelings towards her. He still burned with a fierce longing for her, but deep down he knew it was more a wishing for something that had unaccountably remained unattainable to him. Looking at her so demure and simply elegant in her loose-fitting dress, he could not, even in his wildest fantasies, see her in the arms of a black man. Surely, Georgette had invented the sordid story that she had so bitterly related about seeing her mother and the runaway slave together. It must have been her design to distract his attention away from Elise so that she could win his affection totally. Yet she had appeared to be certain, shocked and disgusted. Then there were those visitations.

He recalled the night when he and Brent had kept watch all night long, patiently waiting for Pharcel to appear. They had watched in vain, and, later, Brent had been killed in the full light of day a short distance from where the Captain had been riding. Then there was that time when Jean and Tom had seen him leaping into the bushes at the rear of the house. They had missed shooting him, but they were certain that it was him. It had to be true. That thought tormented his soul, a torment that could only end with the destruction of the cause. He must capture the slave and kill him slowly.

He looked up and out the window. Napoleon was running across the savannah towards the house. There was no sign of his housekeeper. Marshall could picture her striding leisurely, head high, bosom outthrust, unhurried, and aloof from the world around her. The wind had shifted and blew in a gentle current through the open door of the bedroom. Napoleon entered through the side door and snapped to attention. Captain Marshall motioned him to be at ease; but he remained standing, hardly less rigid than he had been.

"How much do you know Pharcel?" Marshall asked.

"He is a slave who pretends to be a chief."

"But he is. How well do you know him?"

"Not well."

"But you said you tracked him for a whole day and followed him to his hideout."

"I did, but I hardly saw him."

"Would you recognize him if you saw him?" Marshall asked with exasperation.

"I think I would."

"Then this is what I want you to do. You will go to the estate at Dubique, mingle with the slaves as much as you can, and keep a constant watch on the estate house, especially at night. I will speak with the owner to alert him that there are fears of revolt, and let him know that I have sent you as protection against any slave attacks, particularly from the runaway camps."

Napoleon gulped the panic that was rising within him. He did not relish this kind of assignment. If he ever crossed Pharcel's path again, the runaway would kill him.

"If you see Pharcel," Marshall continued, "do not kill him. I want him alive!"

Napoleon turned to go.

"I want you to keep a close watch on the planter's wife. Not too close to call attention to yourself. Keep your distance, but observe. Tell me everything she does, everywhere she goes. Watch her night and day, day and night."

Napoleon perked up his ears, a deep, dark frown on his brow. There was something there. He could sense it. Something intriguing was taking place. He had to know. He had to play his hand carefully. The Captain was not only concerned about Pharcel. He was also concerned about the planter's wife. There must be some connection. The brief contact that he had with Pharcel had shown that the young chief may be presumptuous, but he was clever. His followers accepted him, young and inexperienced as he was, with an unspoken loyalty and respect. He was quite personable, too, with his unusually bright brown complexion and shiny copper hair; a strapping, well-formed youth who exuded a vibrant masculinity that could not fail to stir the concupiscence of any female, white or black. Napoleon's eyes brightened with speculation.

He had known many instances where the social divide between white society and the lowly community of blacks had been breached. This was more common between the white planters and their female slaves, but it was not uncommon to find an irresistible attraction between white women and black or colored males. He had grown up in the city, cleaning the stables of a white official; and he had often witnessed the interaction between some of the white ladies and free black or colored males, mostly rich or educated, who were sometimes admitted to social gatherings.

He had heard many rumors about surreptitious liaisons between white ladies and black gentlemen, and about the questionable paternity of some of the off-spring of white families. He had even been told that some of the white ladies adopted a too stern and vicious attitude towards their black male slaves because they were in strict and self-righteous denial about their own attraction to them.

He himself had never been fortunate to be treated other than with silent contempt, and sometimes with condescension; but some of his friends had spoken of secret happenings with the daughters of their white masters.

The Captain's voice drew him out of his short reverie.

"Bring me the right information and you will be rewarded."

"Yes, Sir."

Napoleon beamed brightly, saluted briskly, and marched out of the cottage. He ran all the way back to the encampment. There was a lot to do before he would depart on his curious mission. More and more he saw exciting possibilities in the task to which he had been assigned.

CHAPTER 20

The day Paulinaire died a deep and somber quiet descended on the land. It was as if a storm had passed, and the world had gone about picking up the pieces of their lives. He died hanging from a gibbet, his entrails flowing from his gaping abdomen and descending to his feet. His friend and agent, Jacques, had been among the throng that had crowded the open field in the southern outskirts of the town; and had been as revolted by the unnecessary butchery as the rest of the curious onlookers.

"He didn't die very well," he told Pharcel afterwards. "He was too much in love with life. Death was no friend to him."

"If he had lived as we have, he would not have been afraid to die," Pharcel replied. "Bala and Sandy were not afraid, neither was Coree Greg."

"Paulinaire was not of the same mettle," Jacques said solemnly. "He was a bold thinker; but not at all a brave man."

"A man who has a passion for power loves life, but he who loves liberty should never be afraid to die." Pharcel looked thoughtfully at Jacques. "Paulinaire lived for power."

Jacques pondered this thought. He had a great admiration for Paulinaire, a man of brilliant intellect and personal dignity, whose eloquence had inspired him and many others to hope for a better life in a world where freedom, justice and equal opportunity was the right of every man and woman. He was a man of outstanding personage who could stand alongside the highest official in the colony and not appear inferior, yet one who could converse with engaging openness with the half-naked and untutored slaves, and reach into their minds and hearts. There would be none other like him. Now there was only Pharcel whose role was still undefined and whose ambitions had not yet flowered to any purpose.

Pharcel had spent many months traveling through the woods during the months that Paulinaire was active among the estates. His camp was secure enough; there was no immediate threat of attack from the militia, nor was there any fear that anyone of his followers would take steps to supplant him in his absence. There was a certain rhythmic order about the daily activities of the men and women that signified peaceful harmony and personal contentment. Furthermore, since the day he had led the small group of refugees from the ruins of Coree Greg's camp, he had never set himself up as chief or commander. The people had followed him willingly, and had looked to him for guidance whenever they felt inclined to seek solutions for difficult problems or whenever some matter requiring adjudication or conciliation arose. Even the many that had recently joined the camp seemed content to move along with its easy tenor of personal independence and consensual leadership. There was no sign of internal conflict or of the emergence of any authority, benign or malevolent, other than himself. He harbored no fears that his absence would in any way open out opportunities for dissention or usurpation of the authority with which he had been so willingly entrusted.

During those months, he visited camps in the East and in the center of the island. There were tracks traversing the island from North to South and from East to West through the forests, and he could travel for miles without coming close to any habitation. Whenever he came to the flat lands at the foot of the great central mountain, he had to hide in the woods until dark because he had learnt to avoid open spaces during daylight. There was always the danger of meeting with estate slaves who would be willing to betray their own kind either for monetary reward or in expectation of manumission for cooperating with their white masters. When night fell he would skirt the boundaries of the estates until he regained the shelter of the deep forest. There he would remain hidden until the morning broke through the mist that always hung over the high mountain, and then he would begin to forge his way through the hidden tracks in the woods.

The approach to Jacco's camp reminded him of the steep though more open steps that ascended to the shelf of land where Bala had built his camp. They were cut into the muddy soil and secured by short lengths of sapling propped tier upon tier right up to the top of the mountain. At the summit, the land flattened to a broad expanse of cultivated gardens, divided in orderly sections by banks of low brush. On the seaward side, the land fell away to rolling hills, giving a magnificent vista of wooded ridges and dark, close gorges extending downwards to the far distant shore. The sound of a rumbling waterfall came faintly from a distance. Other than that, only the cacophonous squawks and screeches of the woodland birds broke the silence. Pharcel felt as secure as if he were in his own camp.

He spent many days there under Jacco's tutelage. The wily old chief, sprightly and game despite his graying hairs, had kept his camp and followers secure for nearly two decades; and few of his people had ever been recaptured. Jacco knew the forest well; was familiar with every track and trace, ridge and valley, ravine and cave from East to West; and could elude any pursuer, and vanish in the woods without a trace. He had come from a small village in Senegal where conditions were sometimes hard; and was accustomed to privation and simple living, especially in times of drought, unseasonable floods, and pestiferous visitations. Here in the forest was bounteous living such as he had never seen, and he asked for nothing more as long as his liberty was not threatened.

Pharcel spent many nights at Jacco's feet, listening to his grave conversation, and chuckling at his occasional twists of caustic humor. Like most of the older chiefs, Jacco was not interested in acquiring weapons from the mulattos; nor did he think that any good would come from an alliance with them in any kind of general insurrection.

"The English are well fortified with guns and a formidable navy," he argued. "They are quite capable of repulsing any frontal attack in the towns and villages. As long as we keep to the woods we are safe."

"Paulinaire thinks the time is ripe for concerted action by the French residents, the mulattos and the slaves and the runaways," Pharcel replied hesitantly. "According to him we are all the oppressed, having a common cause to fight."

"There can never be common cause between blacks and white people, French or English," Jacco said emphatically. "As for the mulattos, have you seen any mule that will condescend to be anything other than a horse?"

"But we can't do it alone," Pharcel protested. "How can we free our brothers and sisters still enslaved on those miserable estates; how will they share in this new world of liberty, fraternity and equality that the French speak about, if we do not join forces with all those who are in sympathy with that cause?"

"The only liberty, fraternity and equality that we are likely to find are out here in the woods," Jacco said harshly. "The English do not have them; neither do the French with all their philosophical hogwash. As for the mulattos, even if they could have them, they would never share them with us. They are a lost race, those mulattos. Mix milk with molasses and what do you get? Mush! It will never be milk or molasses again."

Jacco paused and regarded Pharcel somberly. He looked away and around the camp where men and women, near-naked and care-free, moved about in quiet and uninhibited freedom. His gaze deepened as if drawing into himself visions of another world outside the boundaries of his forest home, a world that was, to him, alien and inimical.

"Do not waste time with Paulinaire," Jacco spoke the name contemptuously. "He is a man of words. Such men wet their pants when real action begins."

He turned again to face Pharcel.

"Those who desire liberty must grasp it themselves," Jacco spoke the words solemnly, as if recalling a wisdom that was established in the beginning of time. "We will welcome those who have gained it; and, here in the forest, we will protect that liberty with our lives."

Pharcel thought of Coree Greg who had done just that to defend the freedom of his followers. He sat for a long while thinking deeply of Jacco's curiously debilitating words, pondering on the dismal future that those words portended. He wondered if that would be his fate, to remain a fugitive forever, waiting to be shot at or inevitably to be killed or captured and ignominiously executed as was done to Bala and Sandy and so many others before. Silently he stood and walked away.

Jacco watched him go, sadly.

For many weeks Paulinaire had been busy among the slaves in the southern districts. Assisted by his colleagues, Jean Louis, Jean-Baptiste, Michael, Paul and Cocque, he visited the slave huts after dark, gathering the slaves around him, and speaking grandly about the glorious feats of Toussaint and his mulatto counterpart, Rigaud, in overturning white rule in San Domingo. The revolution there, he proclaimed, owed its magnificent success to the combined strength of the blacks and the mulattos who together had presented an invincible and irresistible force against colonial France and colonial England. They were not alone in fighting oppression. Even in the all white society of France the poor and downtrodden in Paris had overthrown royalty and the privileged class, and were now in control of their own destiny. Those poor and downtrodden whites, having themselves been the victims of oppression and exploitation for century after century, and having now liberated themselves, were anxious about the plight of the slaves in the colonies; and were ready to support them with arms and men to ensure their freedom.

At first the slaves had listened to him with skepticism and suspicion. Paulinaire's fastidiousness in dress and manners did not go well with the crude simplicity of life in the slave huts. He could not easily suppress his qualms at sharing the primitive hospitality of the slaves, sitting in the open and eating from the blackened pots that were presented to him. Nor could he adjust to the raw sexuality that he found everywhere among them, and he often felt repulsed by any exhibition of unseemly behavior in his presence, and by any overtures made to him either in jest or in welcome by the many women who came to listen to his words. The slaves on their part were distrustful of any man who had not suffered as they had, especially one who cultivated so exactly the air of superiority and apartness that distinguished the white man from themselves. It was Jacques who, in his own simple fashion, gave credence to the validity of Paulinaire's message. Jacques' language was plain and unadorned with flowery sentiments. The message as he conveyed them to the slaves was terse and spoken with simple earnestness: speak together and you will be heard; act together and you will be feared.

Paulinaire had ceased to hope for a general and spontaneous revolt. He was astute enough to understand that the slave communities were too scattered and disjointed, the runaway camps too distant and independent, and the mulatto group too socially and culturally apart to be melded into a workable unit. His more recent strategy was to begin his campaign by fomenting discontent and creating agitation among the slaves, urging them to make more and greater demands so that they would eventually begin to get a sense of their power. When that happened he would use their mass, conscious of its own strength, to gain his ends. By degrees he would have them eating out of his hands. They would be his army, and he their general.

His strategy seemed to have met with some success. At his urging the slaves at Geneva protested against the scant rations that they were given to take to the fields. They would not commence the morning's work until their portions were increased. The overseer was furious, and threatened wholesale flogging and worse if he could identify the ringleaders of this attempt at rebellion. Since he could not, he had to call in the factor, who had grudgingly agreed to increase the day's ration; but he had also promised to deal vigorously with the instigators of the disturbance if there was any further trouble. The word had spread, and, throughout the southern district, slaves had demanded more rations of food and clothing. For a few weeks nothing more had happened to disturb the daily routine on the estates. The slaves had enough to eat, and no one had been punished.

Napoleon had been wandering among the slave huts and around the estate at Dubique for nearly two months, and he had seen or heard nothing of Pharcel. He had watched Elise quietly moving about the house, around the open spaces, and under the trees nearby. He had sometimes seen her sitting with her husband in the dim light that filtered onto the verandah at night before she would sedately rise and disappear indoors, leaving Jean to continue his solitary drinking till late into the night.

Many times he had observed her moving towards the hollow where she took her daily bath, the toddler stumbling at her side. At those times she had that wistful look as if she sought something from the bushes that was never there. Still, he could not reconcile such virtuous living as appeared to be her wont with the scandalous insinuation that Captain Marshall had inadvertently planted in his mind. He could not picture such a chaste woman as she seemed to be at all times, in the arms of a renegade slave. He himself could never hope to come within smiling distance of such a reserved and proper woman. His reports to Captain Marshall had always been the same. Nothing unseemly happened in this dreary place.

Napoleon had spent another uneventful day roaming the slave quarters and sometimes pestering the few pubescent girls who had not yet been drawn to field labor. The night had settled into a warm half light that usually brought the slaves out doors, sitting on their stoops or on logs in neighborly and lethargic conversation. He was about to leave for his nightly vigil around the estate house when he noticed small groups of slaves drifting down towards the shore. He waited until the last of them had passed. Cautiously, he followed them to the open ground where the cane harvest was usually collected in heaps before being transported to the mills at Geneva.

The ground had been cleared, since it was some months before the new cane would be harvested. He crept to the edge of the clearing and hid behind a wagon whose bed slanted down into a thick growth of lemon grass, while its shafts pointed outward to the sky. From there he saw the slaves gathered in a circle, in the middle of which one man sat elevated on a log, and another sat on the warm grass at his feet.

The night was filled with sound, the clacking of crickets, the croaking of frogs and the pounding and splashing of the waves on the stony shore. He strained to listen to the voice of the man sitting elevated above the rest in the center of the circle of slaves. Gradually, below the incessant sounds of the night, he began to distinguish the words that floated across to him; and he was jolted to a fearsome alertness.

"You saw what happened when you asked for more rations," the man was saying. "The power of your collective voice made them listen. You got what you asked for."

There was general assent among the slaves, who nodded and smiled to each other in smug satisfaction.

"That is only the beginning," the man continued. "You now know the power of acting together. As long as you act together no one can be punished, because no single one of you can be held responsible. Tomorrow you must not go to the fields. You will stay in your huts, and demand that you be given more time to work for yourselves. You work six days a week from sunrise to sundown, with very little time to attend to your vegetable gardens. If you have more time to grow what you must eat you will not have to depend on the poor food that the estates give you so grudgingly."

The slaves around the circle looked uncertainly at each other. This was a major step that they were being asked to take. It was one thing to ask for more rations, but to refuse to go to work? That was tantamount to rebellion. A nervous murmuring rose among them, and many fidgeted with fright at the mere thought of outright revolt. They had too often been told what happened to slaves who in any way defied the authority of the white overseers. They had heard that so many had been whipped almost to death for the least infraction. Furthermore, they knew that the militia was always at hand to quell any uprising among them.

Paulinaire rose to his feet, standing erect as he looked down at the frightened faces around him. His graying hair glistened in the shadowy night. He sensed that he had pushed them too far and too fast to the brink of insurrection. He would have to be more circumspect and gentle with them. As he stood leaning slightly forward in the dim light, Napoleon was startled into sudden recognition of the nattily dressed and mild mannered mulatto he had so often seen on the streets and in the taverns in Grandbay. He knew at that instant that it was Paulinaire.

"Do not be afraid," Paulinaire said soothingly to his restive audience. "All the slaves everywhere will be doing the same. They will not work until their demands are met. Right at this moment my associates are in every village in the South urging our brothers to similar action. We will do this together and no one will be hurt. You have my word that this will be so."

For several moments there was complete silence. Paulinaire stood calmly looking about him with an assurance that belied the uncertainty that now enfeebled his spirit. This was the critical moment when he had to be sure he spoke with utmost delicacy, but with strong conviction. If he failed to move them at that moment, then he would lose them forever. A lone voice broke the silence querulously.

"And after that, what then?"

Paulinaire came down from his great height and sat gracefully on the log. There was a long interval during which he appeared lost in his own thoughts. Then he looked boldly at them and spoke with a note of triumph in his voice.

"Then you will have shown the extent of your power," he shouted exultantly. "Then you will be ready for the greater victory that will be ours. After tomorrow, the time will be set for the day of your final liberation. Two weeks from today the French fleet will sail into the Roseau harbor to attack the fortifications there. All along the coast, there will be an uprising of the French inhabitants who are already well supplied with weapons in defiance of the ban which has been placed on them by Governor Orde. That will be the time for our final act to free ourselves from the chains that bind us to the white man and his insufferable greed. The French are our friends. They will set us free just as they have set free the slaves of Martinique and Guadeloupe. There all men live as equals, black, white and mulatto."

The small group of slaves sat breathless as they listened to this electrifying harangue. Paulinaire himself was panting with excitement. He took out his frilled kerchief, mopped his wet brow, and looked up at them again. His voice dropped almost to a whisper.

"You do this tomorrow, and you are on the road to freedom. We are not alone. Besides the French, Pharcel is waiting in the woods with a formidable army. He and his followers are fugitives, but they are well armed. Those who can escape, join them. If you cannot, wait for the day when I send you word. Do not falter. Do not be afraid. Fear never did save anyone. But courage will. And I know you do not lack courage. Remember tomorrow and you will soon be free. I, Paulinaire, tell you so."

A hush came over the crowd. Soon there were excited whispers. An animated group of women began a heated discussion, gesticulating as they forcefully spoke their opinions. A few men crowded around them, and they, too, began raising their voices in strident arguments.

It came first from the women: a subdued humming that rose in rippling waves to rhythmic grunts and whoops, accompanied by energetic out-thrusting of their arms as if in attack or defense. The men soon joined in, and before long the group broke into a stomping, thrusting, growling, snarling, howling, roaring mass of inflamed passion.

Paulinaire breathed a sigh of satisfaction. He knew then that he had won. The rebellion was about to begin.

That same night Napoleon abandoned his lonely watch around the estate house, and trotted the three mile stretch to Geneva to report to Captain Marshall what he had seen and heard. Captain Marshall, even before consulting his colleague Captain Urquhart, sent an urgent dispatch to the Governor, seeking a warrant of arrest. The warrant came the very next day, with notices to be posted for the capture of Paulinaire, dead or alive.

The revolt of the slaves in the southern villages shocked the white community. Planters from all over the island gathered in the capital to urge strong and immediate action against the perpetrators of this act of sedition. Paulinaire and his fellow agitators were condemned out of hand as traitors to the colony. It was said that Grandbay was a hotbed of insurgents that entered freely from the French colonies. Council was urged to take immediate action to quell the revolt before it began to spread to other parts of the island. Since news of a possible French invasion had for some time been circulating among the slaves, they had become restive. It would only take a spark such as was now occurring at Geneva to set a blaze that would consume them all if it was not snuffed out quickly enough.

Paulinaire and his group were held responsible for the ridiculous and totally unacceptable demands that were being made on the already nearly impoverished planters, and must be captured immediately and brought to justice. As for the runaway Pharcel, who was reported to be in league with Paulinaire, he must be taken dead or alive. The authorities should not sit idly by and allow him to roam the forest at will, disrupt the orderly functioning of the estates, and stir dissention and disloyalty among the slaves. If necessary, the planters were prepared to take matters into their own hands as they had done after the massacre at Rosalie.

Within the Council itself there was considerable anger at the defiance which the slaves had shown towards their masters. Such a thing had never been known to occur. It was all the fault of the administration which had been too soft on the slaves, especially in dealing with the runaways. There was great commotion when the planters surrounded the council chamber demanding that Governor Orde take emergency action to put down the disorder in the South. The governor deftly averted the instant imposition of martial law by offering to pay a personal visit to Geneva to investigate the nature of the problem there and to report to the Council immediately afterwards.

The visit of governor Orde to Geneva began with the pomp and ceremony that was usually attendant on the arrival of the King's representative at any place in the colony. The parade ground in the middle of the encampment was resplendent with the colorful uniforms and standards of the two contingents stationed there. Captains Marshall and Urquhart stood beside the governor as platoon after platoon paraded past, giving the martial salute to the distinguished personage who stood there in place of the King. Governor Orde was a slight figure of a man, with intelligent eyes and lofty eyebrows. He looked strangely dwarfed in his white drill uniform and plumed helmet as he stood between the two captains; but when he descended from the platform to inspect the ranks, his personal dignity and the intelligent glow in his face stood out sharply. By the time he came again to stand on the platform, the full authority of his high office was firmly stamped all over him.

A garden party had been hastily arranged for the planter elite in the district to receive the governor. In the warm morning sun, on the spacious grounds of the

Geneva estate house, they all gathered, the women in their moth-balled fineries hastily pressed for use, and the men standing uncomfortably in stiff wrinkled drill suits, rust-spotted cotton and silk shirts and fluffy cravats. Jean and Elise came, he out of a desire to firmly establish his loyalty to the English administration, and she out of boredom and a pressing urge to escape the unbearable confinement of her life on the small estate. The governor seemed charmed by her simplicity and demureness, and spent an inordinate amount of time trying by subtle conversation and probing remarks to uncover the mystery of her smiling reticence. Captain Marshall took an almost proprietary role in introducing Elise to the governor and in his interventions to intercept questions that the governor would have wished to hear answered from Elise's own lips. So much so that, after many such interventions, the governor walked away, his arched eyebrows questioning the too effusive solicitation by his officer on behalf of the modestly attractive French woman and her taciturn husband.

It was not till late evening that the governor met with the slaves. They came and sat in sullen rows on the grounds of the estate house. The governor spoke to them in a soothing, paternalistic voice, saying how concerned he and his Council were at the drastic act of disobedience which they, the slaves, had been led into. He wanted to let them know that he and the Council had their interest at heart, and that he had come to listen to their complaints personally. He also wanted to let them know that there was no truth in what they had been told about a coming French invasion which would give them their freedom.

The British fleet was a formidable one capable of defending the colony against any forces that the French, in their current state of disorder, could send against them; and the French were very well aware of that, and would not dare to attack now or ever. There was also no truth that the French would free the slaves if they were to take control of the colony; and that was not even remotely possible. Those Jacobins in Paris or in nearby Martinique had no intention of doing such a thing. He could assure them that their lot with the English was far better than they would ever be with the French.

The governor spoke to them about the importance of their labor to the success of industry in the colony. Sugar was not as profitable as it used to be, and it required far more effort for the planters to remain in business that ever before. Everyone had to work hard on the estates, the planters no less than the meanest slaves. It was the planters' responsibility to ensure that the estates were properly and profitably run, and to take good and conscientious care of their slaves. It was the duty of the slaves to give the full extent of their labor to their masters. That was the acceptable order of things, and that was what would make these colonies remain viable.

He invited the slaves to come forward with their grievances; and, smiling kindly, he sat and awaited their reaction. The dark rows sitting on the cooling grass with stony faces remained silent. None of them would come forward because none wanted to be identified as leader or spokesman. The heavy weight of the slaves' silence settled on the governor and his attendants, who shifted about in embarrassment as they faced the cold stares of the unmoving mass before them. Somehow they knew that they had been answered, and they understood that the dark silence which had been the only response of the slaves portended no good.

"Get Paulinaire!" was all that the governor said as he walked away in a huff.

The planters refused to make any more concessions to the slaves. The Council met again in emergency session and agreed to impose martial law in the South if the slaves did not return to work immediately. The militia was charged to apprehend Paulinaire and his supporters and bring them to justice without delay. As long as he remained at large, the colony was at grave risk of general insurrection. There was also the greater danger that the runaway chiefs would be drawn into the struggle and begin to harass the planters all over the island. For this reason, Pharcel, being the most active and the best organized among the rest, must be captured or killed immediately.

Meanwhile, Paulinaire, secure in the woods, had quietly sent word that the slaves should return to work; but that they should remain ready for the day when the real revolt would begin. And so it was that after two days of withholding their labor, the slaves rose as usual on the third day and, without any further urging, betook themselves to the fields and began their days work long before the overseers were aware of what they had done. They worked in a glowering silence and at a measured pace. The overseers and drivers cracked their lashes over the defiant backs, but the men and women went calmly on with the day's work as if the threats and the cajolery coming from their tormentors were but the irritating drones of the pesky mosquitoes that hovered in clouds among the stands of sugar cane.

An uneasy calm settled over the southern district. The slaves went to work in gloomy renitence, and bent their muscled backs with deliberate slowness to the task of pulling up the weed among the plants or trimming the thick trash of the dried elongated and serrated leaves that choked the fields of cane before harvesting time. Day after day, the drivers hovered over them in tense watchfulness, and waited for the eruption that they were certain was building up beneath those silent backs.

The militia stood ready. Frequent patrols were sent to the estates, tramping over the wagon tracks and surrounding the fields in menacing order as the slaves bent in quiet and brooding defiance to the rhythm of work that they had spontaneously set for themselves. The drivers fretted, flicking their whips in futile anger. The militiamen looked on helplessly.

At Dubique, Napoleon had been so busy among the slave huts, waiting and watching for more signs of nocturnal gatherings that he had neglected his nightly patrols around the estate house. Thus it was that as he stole in the dark across the open space in front of the house late one night, he glimpsed Elise coming from the deep shadow of the trees just beyond the clearing. She held her skirt high above her knees, rushed breathlessly across the yard, and quickly disappeared into the house.

He ran into the trees from which she had so suddenly emerged, but he found nothing. He thought he heard a slithering sound in the bushes past the trees; and he moved quickly, crouching, towards the sound; but there was only the whisper of the wind in the cane fields, and the cracking and screeching sound of the insects that infested the night. He never mentioned this to Captain Marshall since he was convinced that he had in that crucial time inadvertently missed the long-awaited rendezvous with Pharcel.

Paulinaire was not prepared for the life of discomfort which he found in the woods. He had been to Pharcel's camp, which was well secured and bearable enough for a short stay; but now, he had to be close at hand to receive his messages from the group of French whites on the west coast and from the émigrés from Martinique, whose weapons and supplies were critical for the success of the coming uprising.

He had gone with Jacques to his hideout not far above Geneva, a deep indentation at the base of a hill that was effectively concealed by huge boulders overgrown with matted moss. The boulders themselves were partly hidden by a wide patch of prickly bush which covered a small clearing in the thickly wooded forest. Jacques had managed to cut a path in the thorny bush through which he could crawl to his cavernous retreat.

The place was snug enough and simply furnished. Over the many years since his escape, Jacques had accumulated an assortment of furnishing which, though discordant in quality and style, was quite varied and functional. Somehow, he had been able to assemble and haul to his lair discarded chairs, a three-legged side-board which he propped against the inner wall of the cave, a narrow and scarred mahogany bed with a worn pallet, cracked pieces of chinaware, and sundry unmatched, somewhat tarnished silverware.

Despite its primitive quality, the place had acquired a look of forced respectability; and for the first few days Paulinaire was amused by Jacques pretensions of gracious living. But his habitual fastidiousness soon prevailed over the amused condescension with which he had first accepted the squalid environment. While he had, with insouciant and unabashed presumption, simply taken over the narrow bed, leaving Jacques a thin mat on the bare floor of the cave, and while he could without retching stomach the mess that Jacques culinary skills brought out from the blackened pots that he used for cooking, and while he could abide the hasty and rudimentary daily ablutions that were possible in the absence of clean running water, his mind recoiled at the daily necessity to respond to his other natural functions surrounded only by coarse bush and crawling insects.

In the midst of such discomfort, he became impatient for news of the several events that were to signal the start of the rebellion. He sent Jacques out daily for intelligence concerning the movements of the French fleet and the readiness of the French inhabitants on the western coast. He had Jacques venture out at night to make contact with the few émigrés still at large in Grandbay to keep him posted about the arrival of the much needed support from Martinique. Jacques made frequent journeys to keep Pharcel on the alert for the time of the uprising.

When the intelligence reached Paulinaire that the French fleet of five ships was seen hovering in the northern channel and should be arriving at the capital within two days, he could wait no longer. He dispatched messages post haste to Colihaut, to Martinique and to Pharcel that the rebellion was to start in the South two days hence. The word spread rapidly among the slaves as far northwards as Petit Savanne and as far south as Soufriere and Cachacou.

It began in the early hours of the morning. The night had been dark and still, with a lowering cloud that seemed to blot out the stars. The cloud gave a look of sullen menace to the sky, and hung like a pall over the hills and valleys. Gloomy shadows spread over the fields, and a chill wetness suffused the air. The morning stirred reluctantly as the slaves whispered the signal from hut to hut. They moved in silent haste through the cane fields, through narrow tracks and traces up the steep hillsides, coming from all directions to the plains of Bellevue. They were to assemble there before the sun broke, await the order to rush down the steep downhill track to the Geneva flat, and storm the western side of the field where the militia was encamped. Armed with muskets, machetes, pitchforks, axes and a miscellany of garden tools, they milled about in the dark, unsure where their direction was to come from, and waiting for a voice to command them.

Over on the hill overlooking Geneva, Pharcel waited, his men well armed and eager to use the weapons which they had trained so hard to master. Pharcel and his troop were to attack the northern side of the encampment under cover of the forested hillside, while the invaders from Martinique would close up the southern end. The only avenue of escape left to the beleaguered militia would be towards the East and the stronghold of the small community of the Caribs there. Paulinaire had stationed himself on the bank of the Geneva River where he was to coordinate the attacks.

From the outset it was evident that Paulinaire's plans had come undone. Pharcel had sent Samba to reconnoiter the southern flank of the militia to evaluate the strength of the forces there. He returned with the astounding intelligence that that side was manned by only a score of the French émigrés. The expected contingent from Martinique had not arrived. Pharcel was about to send an urgent dispatch to Paulinaire alerting him to the weak offensive on that side when, in the still grey light of the morning, he saw far out at sea the French fleet under heavy sail on a hasty course towards Martinique. Pharcel swore under his breath an unaccustomed profanity. He knew that such a turn of events spelled disaster. He gripped Samba's arm in panic.

"Go at once," he barked in command. "Tell Paulinaire to halt the charge. Otherwise we are doomed."

It was too late. From the hills to the west came a thunderous roar as of many voices raised in fury. Pharcel's heart sank. He knew then that the battle would be lost. He looked despairingly at the dim shades of the French fleet disappearing in the far distance.

"All is lost," he said, a note sadness in his voice. "It is time to retreat."

Out in the valley on the southern flank, the handful of émigrés looked around in bewilderment. They realized that they could not possibly hold their side of the field with so few men. They heard with rising consternation the pounding roar coming from the western side, a noise as of a disorderly horde in uncontrolled stampede. They bunched together in panic looking desperately around for any sign of the expected reinforcement from Martinique. Seeing only the empty fields around them, they turned their backs and fled along the coast. Before the sun had brightened the morning, they were on their way back across the channel.

The fight was fierce and brutal. In the half light of early dawn the slaves charged upon the encampment. The soldiers were taken completely by surprise, and a few of the outer tents were overrun before the troops could form themselves into orderly ranks to resist the oncoming horde. Facing only one line of attack, they quickly disposed their ranks to surround the disordered mass. The sound of gunfire filled the morning, interspersed by angry roars and yelps and wails of pain and agony. Then it stopped suddenly. A dead calm fell on the trampled field, now littered with several fallen bodies. The slaves had vanished as suddenly as they had come. They went in all directions so that the troops for a while could not be sure where the pursuit should be headed. Three soldiers fell that day and many were wounded. The slaves left only their dead, more than a score of them, lying among the tents.

Paulinaire fled. One of Pharcel's men found him wandering in the woods the next day, and dragged him hastily into the camp. For days the militia combed the surrounding hills from Bellevue to Petit Savanne. They found few stragglers. Most of the slaves had made it safely to the estates from which they had come. They were back in the fields working in sullen silence, their anger still seething in their sweating breasts.

Paulinaire was devastated. For days he sat hunched, shivering in fear and anxiety. When it was safe again to traverse the woods, Pharcel brought him to the coast below the nearby Carib village, and, through the intervention of Kumeni, was able to persuade two of the men of the village to convey him to the northern territory of the Caribs where he could remain in hiding.

What happened there remained a mystery to Pharcel. The Caribs had always been protective of runaway slaves, and harbored them with indifferent tolerance as long as they did not disturb the harmony of their community. Whether it was because of Paulinaire's lofty mien or his distinctive dress and manners, the Caribs became distrustful of him.

He never quite made himself agreeable or even inconspicuous among the community of native indians. But certain it was that he was betrayed. One of the Caribs sold him out for five Johannes.

Lieutenant Governor James Bruce, from his estate at Castle Bruce, had received word about a fugitive among the Caribs, and instantly sent a few of his men to apprehend him. When he saw it was Paulinaire, he sent an urgent overland dispatch to the Governor asking for a formidable contingent of soldiers to escort the fugitive dissident to the justice he so richly deserved. He had always despised Paulinaire for his aristocratic airs and social pretensions; and now he had the man in his grasp, he wanted to be sure he would not escape.

What horrified Pharcel more was not the manner of Paulinaire's execution, but the manner of his dying. Fearful of facing the judgment of his enemies, Paulinaire had begged to be poisoned. His courage had completely dissipated during the days of his trial, and his spirit was already dead by the time he was lifted onto the gibbet.

Pharcel felt alone and betrayed.

CHAPTER 21

"The situation is bad, I tell you," Councilor Winston said. "It is like sitting on a keg of dynamite."

The men had gathered on the little portico on the main street of the town. It was Sunday, and the streets were quiet, almost deserted at this time of day. Only a few stragglers from the late morning mass still strolled leisurely along the main street. It was the time of day when most families gathered at home for a special breakfast of eggnog and the local delicacies usually reserved for Sunday. The small group of friends had gathered after the morning's mass for the customary rounds of punch which Joseph had prepared with particular and meticulous care.

Since the news of Coree Greg's death had reached him, Joseph had become even surlier than before; but he continued to serve his white master and his many associates with a kind of baleful obsequiousness as he moved in and out among them with trays of tidbits and decanters of the planters punch, for the preparation of which he had become universally famous. His ears were always wide open, gathering information, mostly official secrets which he stored in his vast memory. But he had little use now for such valuable intelligence since he no longer had anyone he trusted enough to whom he could pass it. He knew of Pharcel as the stripling who had been favored by his friend, Coree Greg; but he was also aware that Coree Greg had been disturbed by Pharcel's close association with Paulinaire. He did not think he would trust his life in the hands of such a callow youth.

"The planters are very angry about those new levies," McPherson turned an accusatory look at Winston whom they all regarded as the center of authority in the Council.

"The planters are a parsimonious lot," Winston replied. "After all, it is for their own good."

"We all understand," Grove said placatingly. "It is just that we are in such difficult times."

"All times are difficult," McPherson said cynically. "I can't recall any times that were not."

"You shouldn't be complaining," Winston said jestingly. "I've never known you do anything but loll in comfort. Where is that little mulatto tart, by the way? Is she still ensconced in your country house?"

"Where else?" replied McPherson, grinning broadly. "I can't bring her home, can I?"

"I wouldn't put that past you," said Sommerville. "After all, you are the only married bachelor we know."

"Ah, I live my own life, you know that," McPherson laughed self-consciously.

"The planters are only part of the problem," Fagan, the Provost Marshall, took up the lost thread of the conversation. "We have the slaves to contend with. And the runaways are back on the highways and on the estates. They pilfer everything from cattle to provisions."

"This has gone on too long," Stewart grumbled. "We should have eradicated the camps long ago. After Rosalie, I thought we had wiped them out."

"Well, not entirely," Winston explained. "We have Young covering the west coast and the central part of the island, and Urquhart and Marshall in the South. But they seem unable to ferret out the runaways from their forest dens."

"You have to fight fire with fire," Sommerville was already slightly red in the face; and his speech was somewhat slurred. "Or fetch a thief to catch another."

"What do you mean?" Fagan asked, somewhat impatient with Sommerville's obtuse way of conversing.

"Make a pact with Pharcel," Sommerville said smiling. "He seems to be the most moderate and clever. Besides, he didn't support Paulinaire, did he?"

"He was too smart for that," Winston retorted. "He abandoned Paulinaire to his fate."

"Well, he could be our man," Sommerville persisted. "Offer him the right terms."

Winston rubbed his chin thoughtfully.

"You may have a point there," he said speculatively. "You may have something there after all."

Twelve months after the death of Paulinaire, the situation in the colony was still tense. There were the ever-present rumors of war with France which brought about the need for greater government outlays for strengthening the defenses at Fort Shirley and Fort Young. Furthermore, many of the white soldiers had in recent months succumbed to the unhealthy miasma rising from the swamps around Fort Shirley in the north of the island, and it was the general view that the more hardy blacks were better suited for military duty in that area. The Council was forced to approve the hiring of nearly two hundred slaves and the conscription of a number of free blacks for augmenting the forces. All this necessitated increased spending which had to be funded by additional levies on external trade.

The planters, already seriously afflicted by depressed commodity prices, groaned under the added burden so unhappily imposed on them. They also suffered from a shortage of labor due to the conscription of their slaves. Moreover, the rent offered to them was but a pittance which could not compensate for the loss in productivity. They harbored their dissatisfaction quietly, knowing full well the uselessness of making formal complaints to the Council.

Since the Geneva revolt, the slaves had become more restive and truculent. All over the island they joined in silent protest, carrying out their daily tasks with deliberate slowness and with an apathy that could not be broken by the most dreadful threats of flogging and even imprisonment. The women in particular were the more recalcitrant and insolent. They infuriated the overseers and drivers with their songs and chatter, which were usually replete with veiled insults and unflattering innuendoes. Many of them feigned illness and several had taken to drinking potions which brought on temporary fevers and other bodily disorders, so as to escape the daily drudgery in the fields. In this charged atmosphere of silent disobedience and undeclared rebellion, the planters did not know what to do. Harsh punishment was of no avail since it only further depleted the number of those fit for field labor.

The ranks of the runaways swelled as many of the estate slaves slipped away to join them. New camps, smaller than the longer established ones, sprang up in every part of the island under new and lesser chiefs like Zombie and Hall. Once again they began to harass the planters, making frequent raids for food, clothing and even weapons. The highways and the paths through the interior became unsafe as the runaways, emboldened by their increasing numbers and the apparent insecurity of the planters and their white overseers, ventured more boldly out of the woods and towards the coastal villages. The new rebellious spirit set aflame by Paulinaire, and which had spread so rapidly among all the estates, dissuaded any that might otherwise be inclined to do so, from betraying the movements of the runaways. For a time it looked as if the militia had been reduced to impotence, and the runaways could roam wherever they wished with absolute impunity.

To add to the danger in which the colony stood, many of the slaves who had been conscripted to serve in the army and who had been quartered at Fort Shirley, discontented with the brutal treatment by some of their officers and the poor conditions under which they had been forced to live, rose in revolt early one morning. Under the leadership of two black freedmen named Dick and Liverpool, they took control of the gun placements on the ramparts and turned one of the guns against a naval vessel in the harbor. They knew that they vastly outnumbered the white soldiers, and it was their aim to take possession of the Fort and defend it against all outside invaders.

Unfortunately, the gun misfired, and only slight damage was done to the ship. The fight that ensued would have been disastrous for the white soldiers had not reinforcements been quickly rushed from the damaged ship to relieve them. Even so, there were many casualties on both sides. One of the officers had tried to intercept Dick while he was attempting to escape from the guardhouse where he had taken command, and was run through with a bayonet, his body left hanging from a wooden partition like a stuck butterfly. Dick and Liverpool made their escape.

It was in this time of terror and despair that Pharcel emerged as the wooden horse of the colonial administration. Elusive and strangely non-combatant, he was always regarded as a dark horse even by the other chiefs. There was a mystery about him that drew all manner of men to seek his good will and support. The same quality that had drawn Paulinaire to him now seemed to engage the attention of the English officials. They wanted him as an ally.

Captain Urquhart sat on the railing that ran the full length of the front of Captain Marshall's cottage, one leg planted firmly on the ground, the other bent at the knee and resting loosely on the side of a balustrade. His companion, Captain Marshall, stood against the upright post at the corner of the verandah a few paces away from him. A soft wind blew in from the sea and ruffled the dusty leaves of the low hedge that grew around the cottage. Captain Urquhart held in one hand a single sheet of yellow vellum which he raised to his face for the fourth time.

"The instructions are clear," he said to Captain Marshall. "We are to treat with Pharcel."

"What for?"

"We are to offer him a commission."

"Are you mad? Offer a commission to a renegade slave?"

"That is what the Council directs."

"The Council can direct as it pleases, but I will tell you this: the day I see this Pharcel he is a dead slave."

"Look here, Marshall. Whatever your feelings towards this slave, (I do not know what has transpired between you two, nor do I care), we have our orders, and they are to treat with Pharcel."

"He is a runaway; and a vicious one at that. A warrant is still out for his capture, dead or alive."

"The Council's order supersedes this warrant."

"Then I prefer not to have received it. I want him dead!"

Captain Marshall's strident voice was filled with venom, and his eyes were stony with hate. Captain Urquhart regarded him curiously, a worried look on his face. He wondered what it was that had turned his friend with such virulent anger against the runaway. As far as he was concerned, Pharcel was the least dangerous among the other chiefs. He was much more disciplined, and his primary concern seemed to be for the welfare and safety of his men. He never allowed his followers to indulge in petty thievery or in wanton violence against anyone. And he was obviously intelligent.

Captain Urquhart would never forget the way Pharcel had deflected pursuit during the attack on Coree Greg's camp, the sound judgment he had shown in withdrawing from Paulinaire's ill-timed revolt, and the astute way with which he had dealt with the two captured officers who had been brought into his camp. Clearly, the man was brave, cunning, and well endowed with a good survival instinct.

Urquhart knew that for several months Marshall had permanently posted a watch at the small estate at Dubique. He could not understand the reason for this extravagant and extraordinary behavior on his friend's part. As far as he knew, there were only the quiet, despondent-looking French planter and his handsome, though repressed-looking wife, a young daughter who it was rumored had been seduced by Marshall, and a handful of slaves. He did not think the watch could be to protect the daughter; nor did he think the wife could be of much interest to anyone, as attractive as she undoubtedly was; neither could he believe that the small and poorly run estate would be in any danger different from any other.

What was even more mystifying was the choice of Napoleon as guardian and protector of the estate, a man given to much posturing and blathering to boost his own ego. Urquhart had heard rumors of some kind of indecent relationship between the planter's wife and Pharcel, which he felt certain had been put about by Napoleon; and he had promptly dismissed this as wild speculation. Now he began to wonder at the significance and ultimate, unspoken dimensions of this rumor.

"Besides being a runaway, what else is this Pharcel guilty of?"

Marshall fidgeted with embarrassment and evasiveness. His face clouded as he thought of a suitable reply, one which would not put him in a bad light. He could not bring out the truth, and let it be known that he had been bested in love by a mere slave, nor could he admit to a personal vendetta at such a low level which would reflect on his honor as an officer and a gentleman. His mind raced through the circumstances, as he knew them, of Pharcel's escape from Dubique and of his activities in the woods since that time. Except for the murder of his friend Brent, he could find nothing unusual for a slave on the run with which he could accuse Pharcel. Even the circumstances of Brent's death would raise more questions than he was prepared to answer. In panic, his mind began to put together an invention that could at least keep Urquhart's curiosity within bounds, however temporary that should be. To his relief, at that moment his housekeeper came through the door bearing a small tray with two glasses.

Urquhart raised his eyes to the woman as she served him a glass filled with fresh cane juice laced with lemon. He looked in fascination at her big frame and massive haunches, and wondered if there was any truth in what was being said about a romantic attachment between his friend and this unprepossessing amazon. The woman dropped her eyes submissively, but her mouth soured as she turned to serve Marshall.

"You may carry out your orders if you must," Marshall spoke with a note of resignation in his voice. "I will have no part of it. My mission is to have him back in chains or dead."

Urquhart watched the woman go, her great haunches almost filling the doorway. He spoke with amusement to Marshall.

"I find her rather forbidding. How do you suffer her presence every day?"

"Oh, she is good at what she does," Marshall replied, looking somewhat hesitant as if he had left something unspoken.

Urquhart smiled.

"Really?" he asked mischievously.

"She is good at her work."

"Oh, fine!" Urquhart giggled.

"Are you serious about dealing with that runaway?" Marshall was quick to change the subject of their conversation.

"Don't worry," Urquhart spoke in soothing tones, "I will not bother you with such an unwelcome task. I will attend to it myself, and make sure Pharcel keeps out of your way."

The meeting with Pharcel took place in a glade not far from the spot where Cork had attacked him on that dreadful day nearly two years ago. He had been saved then by Jacques' timely intervention. As he came close to the meeting place, Pharcel deployed the men who accompanied him in a circular spread around the glade. He did not emerge from the security of the woods until he was sure that it was safe to do so. He found Captain Urquhart leaning against the trunk of a huge tree that had fallen partly across the open space. There were only two other soldiers with him standing watchfully by his side.

As Pharcel came out of the cover of the trees, Captain Urquhart stood upright, and stepped forward to meet him. The two men stood in the center of the clearing appraising each other, neither saying the first word to commence the discussion. The two other soldiers looked about them nervously as if searching the trees for a threat that they knew was there somewhere close by.

At length, Captain Urquhart spoke, a bright smile flashing across his youthful features.

"At last we meet," he said eagerly. "My name is Frank Urquhart, Captain Urquhart."

Pharcel regarded him curiously, liking the openness of his features, but at the same time cautious about his intentions. He took in Urquhart's neat way of dressing, the healthy glow on his face, and the lack of fastidiousness in his mannerisms. Even Paulinaire had been more demonstrative in speech and manners than the man standing before him. He felt that he could trust him.

Urquhart stood abashed at the silent scrutiny of the brown stalwart with the copper-colored hair and gold-flecked eyes who was standing with so much self-assurance over him. Despite his matted hair and coarse garments, there was a sense of cleanness about Pharcel that gave him a radiant, wholesome look. His face remained inscrutable, although a slight twinkling of his eyes betrayed the natural warmth of his personality.

"I have come with an offer from the Council," Urquhart began carefully.

"What offer?" Pharcel looked querulously at him. "I have asked for nothing."

"The Council has the greatest respect and regard for you and your men," Urquhart said, trying to contain the eagerness in his voice. "It has asked me to make you an offer."

"What offer?" Pharcel repeated the question impatiently.

"It seeks your help."

Pharcel regarded him with astonishment, his eyebrows raised in unspoken appeal.

"The Council has asked me to offer you a commission," Urquhart said brightly.

"To do what?" Pharcel was deliberately brusque, wanting to put the officer at a disadvantage.

Urquhart measured his words carefully. He decided to be as blunt as Pharcel was.

"To clear the woods," he replied simply.

"You ask me to betray my people?"

"Not necessarily."

Pharcel remained silent. He knew well the meaning of what he was asked to do. A shadow fell over his face, and he seemed to draw into himself as he pondered the Captain's words. The English must be hard-pressed to turn to him for help. There must be something there that he could turn to his advantage and for the benefit of his people. It seemed such a long time since the day he had been drawn into Bala's savage gesture of defiance, and he remembered quite well the painful consequences of this adventure. He had followed Paulinaire like a good and fervent disciple, knowing that his dreams of liberty, equality and fraternity could not be attained with the mighty forces aligned against him. Now there were only the timid acts of rebellion carried out daily and hopelessly by the slaves on the estates. As for the other runaway camps, he could not abide the squalidness of their living and the paltry acts of thievery and vandalism that was the sum of their inventiveness and intrepidity. He could not see it clearly, but there could be some promise in the avenue that was being opened out before him for the freedom that was so dear to him.

He turned sharply to Urquhart.

"You have a price on my head."

"No longer, if you are ready to work with us," Urquhart assured him quickly.

"What do I get for doing this?" Pharcel's eyes fixed on the Captain with unwavering challenge.

"Name your terms," Urquhart said eagerly.

Pharcel stood before Major Young, exultant and proud. He held in his hand a certificate of manumission and a grant of 100 acres of land which included the site of his camp. He had also secured agreement that his camp would be let alone as long as it did not harbor any other escapees, and as long as his followers did not engage in attacks or other hostilities against the planters and other white communities. In return, he was to serve as guide to assist the militia in locating the other runaway camps, and to clear the forests of their existence either by suasion or by extermination.

Captain Urquhart and his detachment were to return to Laudat where they would cover the eastern part of the island. Captain Marshall and his troops would remain in the South; but, since Pharcel's camp was the only active group in that area and now exempt from prosecution, there was not much else to be done in that district except to keep surveillance on the coast to contain any threats from insurgents from nearby Martinique. In any case, both Major Young and Captain Urquhart were fully aware of the antagonism that existed between Captain Marshall and Pharcel, an antagonism that would make it impossible for them to cooperate in such a delicate mission. Pharcel was expected to work directly with Major Young whose area spread along the west coast to the interior and northern parts of the island, but he would be available to Urquhart whenever any major assaults were to be carried out on the eastern camps.

His first task was to track down Liverpool and Dick, the two corporals who had led the rebellion at Fort Shirley, and who were now at large in the forest. He was to offer them leniency if they were to return to their Regiment and face a court martial. The Council had been made aware of the appalling conditions under which the black troops had been made to work and the discrimination shown by white officers, both in the assignment of duties and in the distribution of uniforms and daily rations. The court martial would have to take such extenuating circumstances into account, and would no doubt apply light sentences to the two men for desertion, notwithstanding that one white officer had been killed in the scuffle to regain control of the fort. Pharcel thought that this embassy could only bring happy results, and he looked forward with eagerness to conveying it to the two men.

He found them after many days' journey northwards through the forest in a small camp at the foot of the high mountain that overlooked the bay where Fort Shirley was situated. From there, the broad sweep of the coast, curving inwards to form a wide harbor, spread out below. To the south, the land sloped gently, and was covered with dense forest right down to the sea. To the north, a twin-peaked promontory rose from scrubby marshland to the outer end of the bay. Even at that distance, the grey walls of the fort stood out of the harsh vegetation that sprung from the dry and sandy soil, giving a sense of impregnable solidity and isolation. On the broad ramparts of the fort, a battery of guns looked out to sea, its range sweeping the wide distance across the bay.

"So you have become their messenger?" Liverpool asked Pharcel, a note of sarcasm in his voice. He sounded bitter.

"Their emissary, to offer you pardon if you will return." Pharcel sat with them among the few hastily erected huts that made up the camp. "They promise to be lenient."

"What is it they want with you?" Dick looked at Pharcel with open distrust.

"They want you back," Pharcel replied simply.

"But what is it they want with you?" Dick persisted.

Pharcel leaned backwards, his hands spread out behind him on the bare, dry earth, his gaze clouded over with a far away look.

"What they want of me is what I am ready to give to them," he said searching his thoughts for the words that would give true meaning to the deep sentiments that filled his breast. "I have got what I want from them: freedom and a place where the fifty men and women in my camp can live in peace. That is the beginning of a kingdom that will have no end. A people free and separate that will be there long after the planters are gone."

"You believe that?" Liverpool's voice was calm, but he could not disguise the disdain he felt for what he thought was Pharcel's gullibility.

"I believe in what I hold," Pharcel replied confidently. "As for the rest, I have no more faith in the English than you do."

"Then how do you propose to carry out your commission?" Dick asked. He was clearly perplexed by Pharcel's words which seemed so contradictory and rooted in prevarication.

"I have made it clear that I will not betray my people," Pharcel stated simply.

"Then, my friend, you walk on the sharp edge of a sword," Dick said, his voice suddenly sober and concerned. "Your task is impossible."

"It is no task at all," Pharcel smiled knowingly at the deserters. "I will say simply that you refuse."

"May you find the rest of your commission as easy as this one," Liverpool said mockingly.

"Oh, it will be," Pharcel winked happily at the two men. "I will send you word whenever we plan to visit."

They grinned at each other conspiratorially. As they rose from the ground, Dick pulled a pistol from his waistband and pointed it at Pharcel's chest. Pharcel drew back slightly, startled by the sudden gesture. Dick laughed and extended his hand towards Pharcel.

"Take this," he said. "You might need it one day."

Many weeks had passed; and Pharcel had led first one detachment and then another into the woods, but each time they circled the camps they found them deserted. They did manage to capture a few runaways, old men and women who had strayed from the rest, and lost their way among the maze of hills and gullies. Once, they came upon fresh tracks as of many feet in the wet soil close to the stream below where Bala's camp had been, and where Pharcel had leapt over a fall to avoid being caught; the place where the militia had captured Presente. Pharcel recalled how he had hidden below the fall and later followed the stream downwards until he had come close to the clearing where Mabouya had built his camp. The soldiers were intent on following the tracks through the woods, but he urged them to follow him down the stream.

"I know this stream," he told them confidently. "It will lead you straight to Mabouya's camp."

So they followed him over slimy boulders, and through narrow gorges, crawling through patches of prickly wild ferns, and wading across pools of clear water, shivering with cold and fatigue. All day they plunged through dark ravines, sometimes climbing the steep banks to get over high waterfalls, creeping under rotting trunks of giant trees, ever downwards until, long past midday, they suddenly came out in brilliant sunlight where the land flattened and the stream opened out to join the Rosalie River. Pharcel looked about him in bewilderment as if he had come out on the other side of the world.

"We missed it." He looked sheepishly at Captain Urquhart. "We are now down by the sea."

Wearily, the men threw themselves down in the bushes. They grumbled that the day's toil was all for nothing. Pharcel, the very picture of innocent ineptitude, continued to look downcast and mortified. A few of them stared at him with suspicion, and threw accusatory glances at him. Captain Urquhart was annoyed that Pharcel had bungled an expedition which seemed to have had such a promising start, but he contained his vexation, and urged his men to begin the long trek back to their encampment.

"You will not get away with it next time," he said to Pharcel later that evening. "I will keep a closer watch on you."

Major Young had been mistrustful from the start. He had accepted with some skepticism the necessity of employing black troops to man Fort Shirley after yellow fever had decimated the white soldiers there. There was no doubt that they were better able to withstand the humid climate and the mysterious disorders that seemed to rise from the swamp at the base of the fort. For the most part, they were brave men, stalwart soldiers who took great pride in a cherished tradition that they had come from a hardy warrior race. They made good fighting men, formidable in battle, especially when they were led by one of their own. But in temper they were volatile, and in discipline equivocal.

The major was by nature a suspicious man. He held firmly to the philosophy that self interest was the primary motivator in all human actions, and he distrusted anyone who appeared unduly altruistic in his conduct towards other men.

While he could appreciate Pharcel's willingness to cooperate with the colonial authorities in order to gain freedom for himself and some degree of tolerant co-existence for his followers, he could not reconcile the runaway's reputation for valor and cunning with such readiness to betray those like himself who sought freedom from the white man's world, and independence in their own closed communities. He was, therefore, not astonished at Captain Urquhart's report on Pharcel's consistent failure to enable them to spring a surprise attack on the run-away camps. Now that Pharcel was a free man, there was very little that could be done to him except to discipline him as a soldier; and that Major Young would do if he found sufficient cause. Pharcel was a man to be watched.

They had been on the trail of a party of black deserters for many days. Dick and Liverpool were reportedly leading the deserters to join with Jacco in the inac-cessible folds of the forested hills in the interior of the island. The trail had led from the flats below the high mountain in the North, round the base of the mountain through tangled forests, ridges that curled into each other and gorges which ended abruptly at the bottom of sheer precipices. As they gained higher ground, they came to open spaces below the towering trees, cool and uncluttered by the vines and rough vegetation that choked the valleys and gorges. Pharcel had trudged ahead of the troops closely followed by Dado, a corporal of the black reg-iment. Near the edge of the ridge on which they stood, the forest suddenly ended, revealing an open vista of low vegetation that fell gently to a great bowl, in the center of which was a wide lake, its waters cobalt blue and still. Away in the distance, a half circle of hills rose from the edges of the bowl, alternately green and dark where the sides folded into deep gorges. Overhead, the blue of the sky was lightened by puffs of white cloud. It was a wonderful spot to be in. The air was clean with a fresh scent of vibrant vegetation and sun-drenched earth. Parrots fluttered their bright green and vermillion plumage in the branches, and the eerie cooing of mountain doves filled the silence among the trees.

Pharcel stood in wonderment at the beauty of the scene. There was serenity about the airy forest, the gracefully sloping, green hollow, the placid water of the lake, and the shaded surrounding hills that made the presence of uniformed men and weapons an act of violation. For a moment he forgot the utterly distasteful task to which he was bound and the troop of armed soldiers trampling the sacred ground of the primal forest less than a furlong behind him.

A sharp exclamation from Dado jolted him back to awareness. Dado was pointing to the nearer shore of the lake where a group of bare-backed men crouched at the water's edge. The corporal was about to shout his discovery to the oncoming troops when Pharcel whipped out his pistol and shot him full in the chest. Hurriedly, he lifted the stricken man, and brought him deeper among the trees. He dropped him roughly onto the ground, rushed a few paces in the opposite direction, scattering dried leaves and twigs for several yards towards a shallow ditch. He cried out to the troops as they came running through the trees, drawing them away from the open side of the ridge.

"This way!" he shouted, indicating the ditch that curved away into the woods.

The soldiers rushed headlong into the ditch, following its curve until they were lost to view. Major Young stopped beside the fallen soldier and felt his pulse.

"He is dead," he pronounced gravely. The major was clearly perturbed. He looked searchingly at Pharcel. "What happened?"

"They shot him," Pharcel appeared breathless and excited. "As we came around this bend, they were there. Just two of them. They shot him before I could raise the alarm."

The major stood regarding Pharcel for a long time, a dark look clouding his furrowed brow. Pharcel returned his look steadily, and then lowered his eyes to the dead man.

"What do we do with him?" he asked with a look of innocent concern.

"We will go no further," the major said crisply. "Call off the men."

They carried the dead soldier to Fort Shirley and buried him there.

Pharcel was held in the guardhouse until past dinner. Major Young and a young lieutenant came and sat before him.

"Now tell us what really happened," the major said sternly.

Pharcel raised his eyes to him as if suffering a great hurt. He looked reproachfully at the major as if to say his integrity had been unjustly affronted. The major continued to look at him stonily. Pharcel's eyes shifted to the lieutenant with a look of appeal. They met a cold, blank gaze. He knew then that he was up against a full inquisition.

"I told you how it was," he said smoothly to the major. "The men appeared suddenly around the base of the tall tree, and shot the corporal."

"What did they look like?" The major squinted at him, the grey of his eyes as hard as steel.

"Just the two of them. Naked. With a ragged cloth around their middle."

"Where did they go?" The major looked hard at him, suspicion showing clearly on his face.

"Down the ditch," Pharcel replied.

"Did you see them?" the lieutenant's voice was harsh. "Who were they?"

"They disappeared like shadows," Pharcel said, his hand nervously scratching his left temple.

"They must have been shadows," the major said snidely, "because they left no tracks."

"Your pistol was not loaded." The lieutenant leaned backwards in his chair. He looked at Pharcel with unconcealed suspicion.

"You think I killed the corporal?" It was more of a challenge than a question.

"There were no tracks either." The major's gruff voice was full of condemnation.

"Your men were too blind to find them," Pharcel could not disguise the derision in his tone.

"Then why didn't you?" the major asked with exasperation.

"You ordered me to call them off," Pharcel replied.

"Then you lie!" The major shouted the words. He had clearly lost control of the situation.

"Lying is what you white men do best," Pharcel said coolly. He understood the depth of their suspicion and he knew that he would not escape some form of punishment.

"Wait till you feel the sting of the cat o' nine. Then you will know what the white man does best." The major's face reddened with anger and frustration. He rose hurriedly from his seat.

"See that he gets a full score in the morning," he barked to the lieutenant as he stormed out of the guardhouse.

"I am not a slave anymore," Pharcel reminded him boldly. "You forget I am a free man."

"Then you will be flogged as a soldier. It is all the same."

Pharcel awoke in the night to a slight metallic creak at the door of his cell. After his interrogation he had been dragged to a low structure of thick stone walls, the top of which was covered by a grassy mound so that the structure appeared to be subterranean. It had been constructed as bunker for ammunition and weapons, and the top appeared to be part of the natural gradient of the hill against which it stood. Only the stout masonry front showed that the structure was man-made. There were several low grated windows and three doors along its length. The door to the cell through which he had been pushed was only half the height of a man, and he had been forced to bend double to prevent abrasion to his neck and back. Inside, he could barely stand upright.

Two guards had been posted to the door of the cell. As he sat on the cold flag-stones that formed the floor, he could see their legs passing back and forth across the apertures that were the door and window. He sat miserably in his cell watching the incessant procession until he dozed off.

The sound that woke him was no more than a brief scrape of metal. Curious, he crawled to the door and tested it. The metal grate gave before him. He thrust his head through, and glanced fearfully on both sides. The two guards were not there; but, not twenty feet away, a soldier stood solidly, his face towards the sea. Even in the semi-darkness he could make out that the man was black. Pharcel crawled out of the door, and crouched uncertainly against the side of the cell. The soldier remained still, his face firmly set looking outwards to the sea.

Pharcel sidled silently against the wall, and darted quickly across the open space between the bunker and the guardhouse. He squatted noiselessly there for several moments, and then turned to look at the sentinel in the grey light. The man turned briefly towards him, and then hastily turned away, looking intensely at the dark over the sea. Pharcel scuttled quickly in the shadows and round the side of the guardhouse. He slithered across a wide expanse of lawn, mostly in shadow from the light of a pale quarter moon against the trees at its borders.

He kept to the narrow valley between the two hills on which the fort had been built. On one side of him the officers' quarters nestled among the trees on the upper level of a hill. On the other side, the troops' barracks, parade ground, mess and other utility buildings were scattered on the rising ground of the other hill.

The valley was thick with low, coarse brush which tore at his near naked flesh as he plunged through them. He did not know what time of night it was, but he felt the urgency of getting to the other end of the valley into the swamp. He got there at the first light of dawn, and dived heedless into the stagnant water in which sedge and other marsh plants grew in clusters. He waded through the marsh for nearly a quarter of a mile before he stood on firm ground.

The first rosy glow of dawn was just rising at the edge of the sea when he gained the forest a few furlongs up the nearest hill. He struck eastwards away from the trail that they had followed the day before.

CHAPTER 22

The ground beneath his feet was wet, though no rain had fallen for many days. There was the dank smell of decomposing vegetation in the close atmosphere under the thick covering of the branches overhead. That part of the forest always smelled of decay. Very little light came through the closely packed leaves of the giant trees, and the gloom underneath sent a chill to his flesh. Life on the damp floor of the forest was scant. Only a few harmless snakes slithered out of his path, and lizards of a curious muddy color scuttled away rapidly at his approach. Even the birds stayed away from the unnatural stillness that hung over the place. The land there was flat and free of the rocks that were usually strewn about, and his bare feet fell noiselessly on the soggy cushion of rotting leaves and twigs. He was so lost in his thoughts that he was jolted back to awareness by a sudden burst of sunlight.

Just ahead of him the gloom of the forest ended and, through the trees, the green shrubs that grew on the sides of a low hill shone in bright sunlight. He knew then that he would not be far from the ridge that would take him in the direction of his camp. He stepped eagerly into the warm brightness, and began to pick his way through the shrubs to the top of the hill. He was half way up when his attention was arrested by a sound coming from the top. He stopped and crouched low in the cover of the sparse branches around him. The sound came again. It was unmistakably the whine of a dog. He knew that sometimes dogs went astray, and lived for months in the forest until they were found again. At the summit was a track that would take him to the glade where he would find the trace that led directly into his camp. However, that track was often frequented by hunters; so he would have to be careful in his approach to it.

He knew the area well, since he had traversed it back and forth in his many journeys to the eastern coast. The land there was crumpled, forming a maze of ridges that ran one into the other so that a traveler who was not familiar with the tracks and traces that wound and wiggled among them could wander for hours before finding his way out of them. To the unpracticed eye, the ridges looked the same, but Pharcel knew them all. Wherever he stood he could find his bearings, as long as he had sight of the great central peak that rose nearly a mile up to the skies.

He decided to veer right along the side of the hill. Crawling low under the shrubs, he made his way a good distance away from the sound of the dog before he climbed again to meet the track. Near the top of the hill, shrubs gave way to open forest. He found the track among the trees, and stepped cautiously out of the undergrowth onto it. He heard the dog's low growl a short distance away, and the rushing of feet over dry ground. Pharcel bounded onwards down the track. He knew then that he had narrowly escaped an ambuscade. Whoever they were had lain in wait for him, hoping that he would walk straight up the hill onto the track. They were in pursuit, and he had to find a way quickly to shake them off his trail.

Pharcel could hear the dog hard on his heels as he raced down the track. In the distance the sound of pounding feet and excited voices told him that there were many in pursuit and that they were not barefoot Caribs or black hunters. No doubt, it was a party of militiamen on the look out to ambush him as he came out of the black forest. He ran down the full length of the ridge, and then crashed through the bushes onto another. The panting and the baying of the dog seemed closer as he made his way among the shrubs, but the voices seemed to recede further and further away. Springy branches whipped at his face, and his feet became entangled in running vines. He kept onwards until he gained the higher ground of the next ridge.

The chase went on for nearly an hour. At last, he came upon a small stream that ran between two mounds. It was narrow and rocky, and deep pools had formed between huge boulders that were covered with slimy moss. Swiftly, he leapt onto a large boulder on his left, and clambered over it, dived into the pool, and swam a short distance upstream. He gained the other bank near a bend in the stream, and pulled himself up, climbing quickly onto the steep slope.

The dog was rushing back and forth and baying in frustration at the point where he had entered the stream. He knew he had to gain some distance now if he were to elude the troublesome animal. Sprinting onwards for a great distance in the open ground under the trees, he slipped from ridge to ridge. For a while he thought he had succeeded in evading the dog; but then, in the distance, he heard its hard panting as it broke through the bushes and up to the open ground of the forest.

Pharcel plodded on. The shouts of his pursuers echoed across the ridges over which he had come. He was not so worried about them. He was more concerned about the dog whose sharp senses he could not easily elude. Continuing to move from ridge to ridge, always in a circular direction, he suddenly came to a deep fall in the land, a gorge less than fifteen feet across. Twenty feet below him, the same stream that he had crossed further down, swirled and tumbled between giant, moss-green boulders. He stopped and looked desperately around. The gorge was too deep to climb down this side and up the other, and he could not go back. The dog was hard behind him. Towards the side, almost hidden by vines and bushes, he saw a fallen tree trunk that spanned the gorge. It looked as if it had lain there forever. Its branches had fallen off, and its sides seemed to have rotted away and crumbled. It was covered with creepers almost its entire length. He could not be sure whether there was any strength left in its bulk and whether that would be sufficient to bear his weight, but he had no choice. He had to attempt it. The dog was not far off and gaining on him.

He rushed through the rank bushes that grew at the edge of the gorge until he came to the log, hardly aware of the lacerations on his arms, chest and legs. Tentatively, he placed one foot after the other, testing his weight on the fragile bridge. Under his weight, the trunk shifted sideways, but held fast as it settled against a rock. He had to move faster. The dog was already where the trace ended, and would soon pick up his scent through the bushes.

He began, pigeon-toed, to shuffle across the log. Out in the middle, his toe caught in the creepers that covered the rotted bark; and he slipped, almost losing his balance. He glanced at the green boulders twenty feet down, and shuddered. Cautiously he inched across, aware now that the dog was struggling to break through the thick bushes on the other side. As he came within four feet of the other end, the log slipped and rolled sideways. Pharcel stumbled, almost falling over; but, reflexively, his feet shuffled quickly to regain firm purchase on the shifting surface. He steadied himself, remained poised for a moment, crouched, and then leapt over the remaining distance.

From across the gorge, Pharcel saw the dog, one paw resting on the end of the rotting tree trunk. It hesitated as the log seemed to turn over and resettle against the rock. The animal was skittering about and whimpering in fear. Just then a shout broke from the trees, and about six uniformed soldiers stood near the edge of the gorge, looking down and about. Pharcel bolted into the trees. He ran, continuing the circular route until he came to the ridge and the point in the path where the chase had begun. He completed the circle, and then broke into the shrub and headed towards the dank forest from which he had emerged hours earlier. He did not retrace his steps in the direction from which he had traveled earlier in the day, but headed northwards straight into the bowels of the jungle.

He traveled further and further into the interior, sometimes through open forest, sometimes through dense undergrowth, up the sharp incline of wooded hills, and down into dark valleys, damp and dank with rotted leaves. Always there was the sound of rushing water or the rumbling of cascades and waterfalls.

When the sun went down, he lowered himself between the buttresses of a chataignier tree and listened to the night creeping in. He was hungry, and his stomach growled complainingly; but there was nothing to eat. He was in a section of the woods where the ground under the trees was bare and dry. There would be no fruits to eat until he came to the open side of some hill where wild raspberries grew. The darkness settled upon the trees, completely obscuring their towering trunks and the vast canopy of their branches. He gave himself over to sleep even as the thrilling sounds of the tropical night filled the forest.

Pharcel came awake suddenly to a creepy sensation on his exposed belly. He felt a cold dampness and a tingle of movement. The reptile slithered across his abdomen, dragging its great length across his body. He remained still. Judging from the long seconds it took to move over him, the boa must have been over ten feet long. When it finally pulled itself across, Pharcel reached anxiously for his machete; grasped it in readiness, thinking that the snake would return to the warmth of his body, but nothing happened. He stayed awake for what seemed like hours before he finally succumbed again to sleep. It was already bright morning when he awoke. He looked anxiously about, but there was no sign of the boa. There were no other creatures about. Only the cooing sound of wood pigeons and the occasional screech of a hawk disturbed the silence. He rose and stretched himself.

Feeling refreshed, he loped across the dry and open floor of the forest to the next incline. To his left he spotted the central peak, and knew that he was still traveling northwards. He traveled all morning through ever changing ground, now over the open floor of high forest, then through thickets of vines and coarse undergrowth that grew profusely among the trees. He hardly noticed that the forest cover came lower and lower, and the undergrowth denser and denser, until he broke through the trees, and saw before him a vast decline stretching for nearly half a mile. The land opened out in a broad sweep that sloped gradually to an exposed valley. It was covered with wild ferns whose prickly branches formed a thick low cover. Over in the distance the land twisted in a tortured formation of hills and gullies that abutted into each other in an irregular pattern and that finally converged into a hollow at the upper end of the valley. From this hollow clouds of stem rose and remained suspended in a dismal grey mass.

He had never been to this part of the island, but he had heard stories of the devil's cauldron with grey mud that bubbled and emitted sulphurous fumes like the fires of hell. The Caribs whose religion was limited to a simple acknowledgement of good and evil, had spoken of the place as the physical manifestation of the god of evil, Mapouya. To them a visit to that place was a spiritual experience analogous to the shriving of the influence of evil in their lives and in the life of their community.

Pharcel was filled with excitement as he plunged into the thick mass of ferns whose tiny thorns tore into and stung his arms, abdomen and legs. He came out at the lower end of the decline and into a thicket of coarse, stunted trees. There the scent of sulphur was strong in his nostrils as the wind wafted the rising vapor in his direction. It smelled of rotten eggs.

At last he broke through the bramble and stood in a patch of rough grass that surrounded a large sunken bowl from which hot steam rose in swirling clouds. Beyond the margin of grass, the land changed from pale yellow clay to brown scree as it rose to form a ragged edge around the bowl. He walked cautiously through the grass until he came to the rise, and inched his way up the loose sides until he stood over the edge.

The inner walls of the bowl were lined with ash-grey pebbles and pumice. Below that, less than twenty feet down, grayish blue water seethed and bubbled; and geysers spouted high in the steamy air. The far side of the bowl rose steeply to a tall hill, bare of vegetation and covered with rust-brown rocks and shale. At the top where several ridges converged, two streams in beds of yellow clay flowed tumbling into the bowl.

Suddenly, a huge burst of steam rose from the surface of the bubbling water, and spread rapidly around him. For several minutes he remained motionless, completely enveloped in the hot, wet blanket. Everything around him was obscured by the thick, burning vapor, and, for a moment, he was completely disoriented, afraid to move forward or back lest he should turn in the wrong direction and stumble over the edge. As suddenly as it had come, the cloud lifted and drifted away with an easterly wind. He watched the steam wafting over the boiling mass of grey water and onto the eastern hills, and then he slid quickly down the rise to firmer ground. There he stood for a long time in wonderment at the strange phenomenon. So absorbed was he that he did not hear the first yapping of the dog and the faint babble of voices on the slope down which he had struggled through the wild ferns and bramble.

When the sound finally reached him, he turned incredulously towards the slope. He thought he saw the dark, puffed-up face of Napoleon peering down at him above the tangled brush. Startled to desperation, he turned and bolted down a meadow of coarse, thin grass and into the forest beyond. From there the land rose for nearly a mile to a sharp peak and down again through tangled woods.

He fought his way past barriers of vines and over exposed roots that stretched across his path until he broke through to another clearing. To his horror, there before him was another scene of desolation. Below him, the land opened out in a wide basin, bleak and bare and stretching for nearly a quarter of a mile across. Puffs of steam rose from several fumaroles that bubbled and spewed hot water all over its surface. It was a scene infernal in character, but withal beautiful and fascinating, like a morbidly enchanting portrait of Hell, a lunar landscape that was terrible to behold.

On all sides the forest hung in horrified revulsion over the steaming basin where only grey-green mosses and lichen grew in patches. Here and there tufts of yellowed lean grass and ferns struggled for a hold on the rust-brown scree at the edges, among which grayish-brown lizards, slate-colored stoneflies and thick-crusted roaches darted about in desolate purposelessness. No birds, butterflies or other flying insects ventured past the ring of forest trees that seemed to pull backwards from the cauldron of witches' brew. Past the burnt edges, water seethed, simmered, bubbled, boiled, and spouted in streams and pools and geysers that reflected a variety of colors, in green, brown, yellow, pink, orange and a gooey blue-black from the ooze that rose from beneath sulphur encrusted rocks, here and there across the basin. The whooshing sound of geysers, the bubbling of boiling mud, and the overwhelming pungent smell of hot sulphur added to the surreal quality of the scene.

Such was the awe with which Pharcel beheld the obstacle before him that he failed to see the beauty in the wondrous sight. He could hear the baying of the dog and the shouts of his pursuers just a little way behind. Looking around desperately at the land around him, he could find no other way than across the fearful fiery bog. To his right, the forest ended at the edge of a great fissure that dropped in sheer walls hundreds of feet down. To his left, at the further side of the basin, the bare brown side of a vertical cliff stood like a barrier against any further incursion by the spreading devastation.

He rushed down to the edge of the basin and stood on the hot gravel, searching through the vapor that rose from the streams and pools of bubbling mud and water for a way across. He could discern, scattered across the steaming waste, rocks and islands of steamy mud and yellow clay between which thin streams of hot water twisted and turned.

The dog was coming up the incline on the other side of the ridge. He heard Napoleon's booming voice urging it on. Without a backward glance, he stepped onto the first rock near the edge, and leapt forward as he felt the burning sulphur on his naked feet. Onwards he went from rock to rock, from slippery island to slippery island. Out in the middle, he heard a triumphant shout as Napoleon and the dog emerged from the forest cover down to the stony rim of the basin. The dog was running about on the hot stones, barking and whining by turn, keeping well away from the frothing and steaming water. Napoleon urged it on, but still it hesitated, skittering about on the gravel in fear and frustration until Napoleon stepped onto the nearest rock. The dog backed away, but eventually it followed.

Napoleon had entered some yards further down the valley and the route across seemed more direct and faster. There were more rocks on that side, but they got further and further apart nearer to the other side. For a while, he seemed to be gaining on Pharcel. Encouraged, he leapt confidently across from rock to rock, paying little heed to what lay before him. He shouted over his shoulder to the other men, who had just appeared out of the trees, to follow the route he had taken.

Pharcel landed on a patch of yellow, muddy clay. He felt his feet slipping beneath him. Unable to regain his balance, he sprawled onto his back and felt the searing heat of boiling water on his feet. He quickly pulled himself together and crouched in pain as the sulphuric steam soaked into his flesh. Again he heard Napoleon's triumphant roar. Despite the agony he was in, he leapt to his feet, and dashed onto the next patch of mud. Out of the corner of his eyes he saw Napoleon almost abreast of him, looking for a way to narrow the distance between them. He was tempted to abandon caution and make a last desperate dash for the other side, but he quickly restrained himself, and continued to pick his way from rock to rock, and from island to island.

Just twenty yards from the further rim, he heard a loud splash and an agonized, blood curdling shriek of pain. He did not turn to look; but dashed the remaining distance onto the hot, dry stones and into the brush beyond. He knew Napoleon would be dead, cooked in the witch's cauldron.

From the floor of the valley, the land rose so sharply that he had to scramble up its side, grasping onto the trunk of thin trees and gaining support from the roots that projected above the clayey soil. The climb seemed interminable, and he was breathless by the time he gained the top. He stood on a narrow thin edge that dropped immediately and precipitously to the other side. He allowed himself to slide down the decline, grasping onto roots and branches to slow his fall. It was a long way down, but at last the land angled to a gentle gradient, and he was able to pick his way carefully westward.

When he came to the Breakfast River, he veered south over a series of low hills, until he reached the open flats below the high range of mountains that shielded Geneva from the easterly winds. He limped painfully across grassy fields and sedge-filled marshes that brought him at last to the foot of the mountains. His feet were burnt and swollen, and the sulphuric crystals on the rocks, and the saturated mineral richness of the water and mud, had caused his skin to blister and suppurate. He stayed only long enough to form a herbal poultice for his feet before moving onwards to the mountains, on the other side of which was his sanctuary.

CHAPTER 23

He made camp the next day after spending the night in a tight hollow near the top of the high mountain range. A small stream tumbled into a shallow basin at the bottom of the hollow, sending droplets of water over the surrounding shrubs. Feverish and weak with hunger, he drank copiously of the cool, clear water, and found a dry place to rest. He was in agony. His feet were on fire, and the pain from his burnt flesh lanced upwards to his legs and thighs. He slept in snatches, coming awake time and again with the shock of the pain shooting right up to his groin.

He was surprised when he awoke after what seemed like hours to feel the sun on his face. He sat up quickly, and pulled his feet together. They were swollen and numb, and he noticed that the pain was not as intense as it was the day before. He hardly felt any sensation on the soles of his feet, but there were the shooting pains up his legs whenever he placed his weight on one or the other. He knew he ought to get to camp soon or he would perish in the woods.

It was the most agonizing journey that anyone could imagine. When he dragged himself down to the deep valley below his camp, it was late evening and the men and women had already returned to the camp on the higher ground. Pharcel felt safe in the familiar hollow, and was therefore content to crawl under the temporary shelter that they had built to weather the torrent on that fateful day when they had first found the camp site. He could hear the faint voices of his companions coming from above, on the flat summit where he had built his for-midable retreat. The sound of their orderly living comforted him, and he lay there on the bare ground beneath the now rotting straw covering of the shed, feeling a slight pulsing of pain about his ankles. Strangely, he fell into a deep sleep that lasted through the night.

They found him next day still fast asleep, but babbling senselessly and raising his arms in defense as if caught up in a violent nightmare. Carefully, they brought him up the steep incline to the camp above and laid him in his hut. Marie Claire came and took care of him. She removed the ragged and muddy poultice that he had wrapped about his feet, and almost cried out in horror at the sight of his swollen, cracked and oozing feet. The flesh around them was already yellow, as if the blood there had been poisoned by the sulphurous injections into his skin, or as if the malignant minerals in the mud and water of the infernal swamp had seeped into his veins and began their suppurating decay.

She sent Marie Rose to gather a variety of herbs down the hollow and on the sunny side of the slope behind the low ridge that formed the western defense of the camp. Together they prepared a multi-herbal salve which they spread over his feet, legs and thighs. They boiled bird broth and fed him tenderly.

It was nearly two days before he fully regained his senses. The swelling in his feet had subsided, but his flesh was still sore and broken in unhealthy lesions. Now there was less pain but there was the discomfort of not being able to spring from bed and get about his business. The two women forced him to remain in bed, and they continued to dress his wounds, and feed him nutritious broth for many days.

The men and women of the camp came in small groups to see to his welfare and to share with him the latest intelligence coming from all parts of the island. They had almost given up on him when they had heard that he had been taken into custody, and again when they had heard that he had escaped and was fighting his way across the vast forests of the interior. They did not think he could survive the terrors of the forest even if he had succeeded to elude his pursuers and the many bounty hunters who were now all over the woods.

Pharcel learnt with dismay that the militia had cornered Dick and Liverpool right on the doorstep of Congoree's camp and that the two men had fought a deadly fight. Dick had been killed, but Liverpool had fought on until he was severely wounded. He had been taken prisoner together with Gros Bois who was also with them. The militia had gone on to raid several of the newly established camps, and four other chiefs and several of their followers had been captured. He was pleased to learn that his friend and mentor, Jacco, was still at large and defiant.

The news of Liverpool's capture weighed heavily on his mind. Dick had died a hero's death, and so would Liverpool eventually. They were both brave and formidable warriors. But he had witnessed Bala's and Sandy's execution, and he considered the ignominy of being subjected to the white man's justice that was no more than an occasion for mockery and public persecution, and to a death that in its disavowal of personal dignity was an insult to the brave and noble character of the men (albeit they were black men) who had sought to uphold the highest principles of civilized society: love for freedom and personal liberty. He did not wish to witness once again the defamation of the meritorious by the crass designs of the vulgar and uncultured, be they white or mulatto. In his mind, he had already raised Dick and Liverpool to the hall of heroes. Let the white villains do their worst.

He also heard with sadness that Jacques had been captured. Without Paulinaire's constant intrigue, Jacques had lost his *raison d'etre* and had taken to wandering the forested hills above Geneva. In an unwary moment, he had fallen into the hands of a hunting party, who had promptly taken him to Captain Marshall's encampment. Anxious to prove that he was forever vigilant, Marshall had him bound hand and foot like a dangerous subversive, and sent him to the Commandant at the main fort in the capital.

Jacques had strongly disavowed any knowledge of or association with Paulinaire or links with any of the runaway camps. He had declared that from the time of his escape several years ago, he had lived in the nearby woods and came down to the estates every night to feed himself from the gardens and livestock that were so plentiful at Geneva. He had appeared such a pitiful figure that the authorities thought to return him to his former master, but that gentleman had suffered terrible losses in his dealings with the London factors and had perforce to reduce his holdings. Thus it was that Jacques had been put on the auction block and sold to a visiting Frenchman. That same day he had been transported out of the colony to Martinique.

By the end of the week, the soles of Pharcel's feet had healed to a scabrous crust, which gradually peeled away, leaving a delicate membrane that was too sensitive to bear his weight on the rough floor. Marie Rose fashioned for him rough sandals from the fine mesh that fell from the crown of leaves at the top of the coconut trees, to ease his discomfort. The lancing pain up his legs and thighs had abated, and he could move with delicate steps about the house and yard. He was sitting in the shade beneath a calabash tree when a uniformed messenger arrived, escorted by two of his men.

"Captain Marshall commands that you give yourself up within two days, otherwise the wife of the planter at Dubique will be delivered up to the authorities!" The man was brusque in his delivery, but obviously nervous in Pharcel's presence.

"What is the lady charged with?" Pharcel asked with a slight note of mockery.

"Sedition in permitting the traitor Paulinaire to carry on treasonous activities on Dubique estate, harboring and protecting escaped slaves, and consorting with dangerous and rebellious runaways."

It sounded like a well-rehearsed litany.

"But what is all this to me?" Pharcel's face was empty of expression, but there was a slight quickening of his breathing even as he spoke the words.

"She will be brought to justice and hanged as a French traitor if you do not surrender yourself."

"But why should I? I am no longer her slave, nor she my mistress."

"Then I pity her that she has so few friends."

The man's voice betrayed genuine sorrow. Obviously he did not approve of Elise being used as a pawn in the Captain's ruthless ambition to be the one to bring down Pharcel. He did not know the woman well, but she looked harmless enough and pleasant, even if somewhat aloof.

"Where is the woman presently?" Pharcel asked with as much unconcern as he could fabricate.

"Under close guard on the estate. Captain Marshall has given it to her husband that they are under threat and the guardsmen are for their protection."

"How will he prosecute an innocent woman?"

"He does not think she is all that innocent. After all, there was the matter of Paulinaire whom he says was her lover. There is also some rumor, though the Captain never mentions it, that she entertains a runaway slave who visits her at unlikely hours. Such a lovely lady she is. It is hard to believe all this."

"But should she be killed only for scandalous rumors?"

"She will be killed all right. The Council is already alert to those French traitors. It would not take much to condemn her."

"What about her husband? Why is he not implicated and similarly condemned?"

"He is a harmless, drunken fellow. Incapable of intrigue; incapable even of swiving his own slave women, not to mention his own wife."

Pharcel remained silent for a long time. He appeared deep in thought, and one corner of his mouth was turned up in a quiet smile. He looked up at the messenger, a look of puzzlement on his face.

"It is really no concern to me." He spoke at last, feigning a lack of interest in the conversation between him and the soldier. "This is all about white people. You can do what you like with each other. I am only a black man."

"But you can save her!"

"Why should I?"

"She is a woman, an innocent woman."

"Then you save her."

"I am only a corporal."

"Will he really send her to her death?"

"He swears he will; and I believe he will do just that. He looks like a driven man. There is more to this than I can see, but this I know: if he does not get you, she is doomed."

Pharcel regarded the man closely. There was sincerity and genuine concern in everything he spoke. He clearly had little regard for Captain Marshall's humanity or his decency as an officer and a gentleman. Rather, his tone bore a loathing for his superior officer that was barely concealed. The man looked utterly crestfallen as if he had hoped for something miraculous that would save the woman from the danger she was in. He jerked his head upwards suddenly as Pharcel began to speak.

"Tell your Captain I will visit him two days from now. There is a glade formed by a circle of bamboo trees on the ridge overlooking Geneva. I will meet him there four hours after sundown."

The corporal looked at him incredulously. His eyes started in their sockets, and he blubbered incoherently, and stuttered a few words before he could compose himself.

"You mean…. You will save her?"

"Tell the Captain I will be where I said I will be."

The man bowed quickly, and backed away. He did not wait for an escort as he hurriedly raced down the track and over the edge of the deep valley.

Pharcel remained where he was, lost in thought.

All that night, Pharcel's soul was in torment. He agonized over the nature of his relationship with Elise and in what way he could be obligated to her. She was the one who had condemned him to be punished even when she knew that her vicious daughter, Georgette, was the more culpable and that he was merely a victim of her prurient curiosity. Elise was the one who had later assaulted him sexually while he lay in innocent repose in the dark privacy of the arbor, and then abandoned him to an unsatisfied and haunting hunger. She had placed him in great danger, caused him pain and fear so that he had to run away from the relative safety and comfort of the estate and become a fugitive in the perilous woods. In what way then could he be beholden to her so as to give his life for her safety?

Yet he remembered the joy of her giving, the times when she had come to him and opened out the vast ocean of her desire in which his own seemed to stretch and grow to infinite proportions. There was that bond when, in the throes of their passion, their bodies melded in soft, warm, liquid effulgence that seemed more spiritual than physical. Certainly he had found nothing so absorbing, nothing so generously beautiful and complete in any other woman.

Betty had been at first like a sister to him, and her vulnerability had drawn him to her. Theirs had not been a carnal relationship, but a simple fulfillment of an overwhelming need. Theirs was a need which went beyond the pure love of mutually dependent siblings. He had found in her a far greater need for purification of the evil that had blemished her young soul. Their evenings had become so tender; but when he brought her gently to give of herself, she always recoiled at his ardent approaches, and the entry to her soul closed tight against him. He understood that it was an unconscious resistance against the shriving of all the abomination which had been done to her, a shriving which had given her so much pain. In the end, when she unburdened without fear or inhibition the atrocities she had suffered at the hands of the white overseer and his companions, the pain of their union began to ease. He loved her for her vulnerability and for her trusting dependence on his understanding and tenderness. He had succeeded in freeing up her soul before they captured her again. No doubt they would have again destroyed what was left of her.

As for Kumeni, her vast and undemanding submission had brought happiness to him. Hers was a prideful homage given in full subjection that filled a gap in his personal need for self assurance. She treated him with a devotion that was neither possessive nor overbearing as she welcomed him with silent gratitude and let him depart with unexpressed hopefulness. Her nights with him were tempestuous, but wholly submissive. He was never sure what her true emotions were. Yet she was always prepared to give whatever he asked of her.

Which then was love, or even the closest approximation of it? It seemed to him that he had an amalgam of all his emotional and physical needs packaged separately in the three women with whom he had shared his spirit. But somehow, what he had found in Elise was far more intense and profound, even in its physical dimensions, than that in the other two women. As he remembered Jacco's words, he wondered at the irony of his situation. There could be no love, Jacco had said, between white people and black people. Yet here he was with a great big hole in his spirit at the mere thought of living without Elise.

He had survived Betty's capture and deportation, though he had often thought of her susceptible innocence and the day that he had abandoned her when she had needed him most. He could not get rid of his guilt that he had been lost in another woman's arms the day Betty had been caught and abused by the dastardly Brent. But guilt was not love. As for Kumeni, she filled him with the lust of the night, and made his spirit tall with the strength of her devotion. But none of this compared to the unending hunger that gnawed at his soul until he could once again hold the strange white woman in his arms.

His mind drifted to Paulinaire and his doomful prognostications about the future of the blacks and colored if they did not combine in a universal assault against the colonial blight of slavery and racial prejudice. While he had not fully trusted Paulinaire's motive, he had to admit that he was right about many things. The militia had come together to begin a systematic destruction of the several camps around the island. Many of the chiefs had already been killed or taken into captivity. Even the elusive Jacques had at last been taken. It would only be a matter of time before they would take command of the woods and isolate the few remaining chiefs who had the fortitude and the cunning to hold out. But their lives would become even more hazardous and brutal, caged in their own compounds, free but without the liberty they had fought for so dearly.

He awoke next day with a pounding head. He had slept badly. Images raced through his mind as if conjured by a riotous conscience. He had thought again of Betty and tried to shut his inner vision against the picture of her mauled, mutilated and violated. He thought of her lying in the dark of the dusty cellar before she was hauled to the shore to be transported in her torn and smeared dress to the prisons of Roseau. He remembered Presente and her awful cry to him as she was taken out of the bushes to be trussed like an animal and dragged all the way to the city. He never knew what had become of her. And lastly he had thought of the white woman who at first had betrayed him, but who had unexpectedly opened out to him a world of wonder, magnificent joy and surpassing blissfulness such as he had never known could exist.

All day he sat in the shade watching the men and women go by. They had formed their own lives, each as independent as he could possibly be in a small community such as this. He felt humbled that the order of their lives had taken its course and continued unruffled from day to day. He had been their acknowledged leader, but of what relevance was he anymore? Life went on unbroken without him, and this camp would endure many years after he was no more. There was nothing to save here. Rather, it was he who was sheltered by the camp's impregnability. There was nothing here to keep him anymore except his own desire for survival.

If he wanted to save Elise, he was free to do so. But why should he? Why would any man taken from his homeland and enslaved do anything to save the life of one of those who had ultimate responsibility for his abduction and enslavement? What sense did it make for him to sacrifice his life for one of a race that despised and persecuted him? The logic eluded him. But he knew deep down that it was not a matter of logic, and that Elise was not just one of a race that wanted him dead. His heart was heavy and his mind was disturbed. Several times Marie

Rose came to him wanting to relieve him of his misery and to attend to his injured feet; but he waved her away. He stayed there till sundown, hardly paying attention to the meals that were laid beside him. When the night fell he reentered his hut.

Pharcel came out to the open yard next morning as the sun broke through the trees and splashed brilliant rays over the clearing. He stood alone under the calabash tree as bright and radiant as the sun. The men wondered at the sudden change in him, so morose the day before and now so resplendent with energy. The warmth and strength glowing in his countenance drew them to him. They came with jovial greetings, and he responded warmly. When they were all gathered, he spoke calmly to them.

"We have a mission," he said. "We have to save the planter's wife at Dubique"

They did not demur or question.

He told them of his recent adventures with the militia, how he had secured freedom and a grant of land and amnesty for all those in this camp, and how he had used the opportunity while in the employ of Major Young to divert attacks away from the main camps by forewarning the chiefs. He described to them the circumstances that had forced him to kill the too eager black militiaman in order to save Dick, Liverpool and a small party of deserters near a far away, hidden lake; and how he had been taken into custody and imprisoned in an underground cell until one of the guards had left a way open to him. They listened with excitement as he recounted the chase from the dark forest to the terrible valley of fire, and then his painful journey over the hills to the safety of his camp.

Calmly but with intense feeling he told of Captain Marshall and the terrible acts of torture and debasement that he had had done to Betty, the retribution he had exacted in the execution of Brent and Joshua, and the unending, intensifying vendetta between himself and the captain to which there must now be an end. He laid before them the cowardly ultimatum sent by the Captain which had kept him so depressingly low the day before, imaging the Captain as a persecutor of blacks and a hater of innocent women. Then he told them what they must do.

"You will divide yourselves in two groups. A few of you will go to Dubique, to the storehouse by the shore. The rest will go one by one to Geneva as soon as the sun goes down. I will go before you. There are a few things I have to take care of."

He turned confidently to Samba whose face had clouded with uncertainty.

"Samba," he said, "you will lead them down. Give the signal four hours after sundown."

Samba nodded. There was a mystery behind all this which he could not fathom. Instinctively, he felt that there was more to Pharcel's quiet rage than moral objection to the Captain's misdeeds; but he said nothing. If Pharcel commanded, then he would obey.

It was still light when Pharcel left the camp. It had been some time since he last visited the Carib village, and he entered with some uncertainty as to what he would find there and the way he would be received; but nothing had changed, and they received him with their usual indifference. He found Kumeni in a small vegetable garden at the back of her hut, pulling up weeds that grew between patches of manioc, tannia, ochra and roucou plants. She wore only a knee-length, loose skirt. Her long, black, glossy hair swirled about her head and shoulders as she raised her eyes at his approach. Beads of sweat stood out on her full breasts and rounded shoulders. She did not rise, but her face brightened at sight of him.

"I need a boat," he said shortly.

Her face was impassive as she continued to gaze at him, but he could sense some uneasiness in her.

"Tonight." His eyes softened as he took in the look of perplexity on her broad face. "Can you do it?"

She nodded. Her eyes searched his for meaning. He smiled at her questioning eyes.

"Leave it on the beach below."

She nodded again, still looking pleadingly at him.

He came and knelt in front of her, taking her grimy hands in his.

"Thank you," he said softly.

Then he turned and walked away. She watched him turn the corner around the hut. A deep sadness settled on her.

Pharcel hurried through the forest. He had to get to the shore near Dubique before nightfall. He skirted the thin wood above Dubique in a wide arc that took him down a dry gully strewn with crumbly boulders and meager vegetation. He crept down the crusty surface of the gully almost to the shore, and then he scrambled to the top, and crawled along the surface of loose gravel until he was over the crevice where his treasure was stored. It was a perilous maneuver, but he hung over the edge of the cliff, and lowered himself cautiously until his feet rested on a slight projection. He found the crevice a short way to his left, secured the sack around his shoulders, and clawed his way back upwards.

When he came to the beach below the Carib village, the boat was pulled up on the beach, a small canoe, its mast already in place, its sail neatly furled around its spar. There were two oars and a calabash scallop in the stern. He placed the sack in the middle bottom, and quickly gathered fallen coconut fronds to conceal it. The sun was just dipping below the horizon in a blaze of radiant scarlet, yellow and purple when he completed his task. It would soon be dark, and he had to hasten to keep his rendezvous with Captain Marshall.

He did not follow the shorter route along the coast, but kept to the hillsides through the light forest until he came to the cave where Jacques had concealed himself for so many years, just above the bamboo glade. It was a dark night, but clear. Pale light filtered from the canopy of stars. Fireflies flitted and winked their ghostly light among the trees. Pharcel slid between the boulders that hid the entrance to Jacques' cave, and crept silently through the light undergrowth. He found a balata tree overhanging the glade, climbed into its thickly-leaved branches, and waited.

From where he sat he could look down into the bowl circled by the bamboo trees. The dry, golden leaves that rimmed the circle and spread at the bottom emitted a pale glow in the dark. Over the top of the trees he could see the fall of the land to the Geneva valley, and beyond, the glimmer of the sea and the dark line of the horizon. Time moved slowly; and, as he sat among the unmoving branches, his mind drifted to the time when he had lost his innocence. He was not certain when that was. Was it the day that hate was implanted in him when he had been so severely and unjustly flogged? Or was it the time when Elise had engulfed him with a passion that he had found so incredibly wondrous and unspeakably sublime.

The thought of Elise brought him back to reality. He had planned their escape without thinking of her individual sentiment or her personal attachment to her normal life and relationships. He had assumed all along that he could simply ride to her rescue. It was a rash and dangerous assumption, and he was not sure what her reaction would be.

He heard them even before he discerned the faint shadows of their bodies creeping through the bushes under the trees. They came and stood uncertainly near the ring of bamboo. He could not be sure, but nearly a dozen of them crouched near the entrance to the glade.

"Spread out and wait. He should soon be here!" Captain Marshall's whisper cut through the silence.

The men spread out among the bamboo trees. Polished muskets gleamed in the dark.

"When he comes, take him alive if you can. If he tries to escape kill him."

Captain Marshall walked through the gap and entered the glade. He stood there alone, listening to the silence around him, and peering impatiently at the darkness beyond the circle of trees. Time passed, and it seemed they were waiting for eternity. Pharcel rested calmly against the smooth bark of the trunk of the balata tree. The men below were getting restless. They fidgeted in the dark, and slapped at mosquitoes buzzing at their ears. It seemed that hours passed and nothing happened. After a while Pharcel glanced anxiously down the valley.

The night was still and dark. He began to get concerned that his plan had gone awry. Had Samba betrayed him? Were his men intercepted before they could reach their point of rendezvous? Or had Marshall anticipated his move and outwitted him? These questions bothered his mind, and he wondered if the Captain would wait through the night. In panic he felt a creature nibbling at the cord around his waist. It must have been a tree rat. He steeled himself to remain still. The creature nibbled contentedly, and Pharcel could hardly contain an irrepressible urge to brush it away. Just then he heard a shout coming further down the ridge overlooking the valley.

"What is it?" One of the men asked impatiently in a hushed tone.

"There is smoke coming from the valley." The voice came across, tremulous with urgency.

"Tell him to shut up!" Captain Marshall spoke harshly.

Silence returned to the night. Up in the balata tree Pharcel shifted uneasily, trying to dislodge the creature at his waist. The branch shook ever so slightly, but enough to draw eyes to the disturbance.

"There is fire in the valley!" One of the men further away shouted in panic.

Two of the soldiers among the bamboo trees rushed over to the others further down the ridge. Captain Marshall had taken a few steps towards the tree where Pharcel now crouched in readiness, waiting to leap into the bushes if the men approached in a body. The Captain held his pistol firmly, and lifted it to the height of his shoulders. Pharcel held his breath anticipating the explosion.

"Captain! The valley is on fire!" The men had all rushed to the edge of the ridge looking down to the Geneva plain.

Captain Marshall cursed viciously. Reluctantly, he turned and scampered to join his men. Pharcel eased down against the tree trunk at his back. The creature had scuttled away at the noise and bustle below the tree. And then Pharcel saw it. His heart lifted as he looked over the trees and beheld the glow and the rising dark clouds of smoke. He heard Marshall swearing bitterly.

"We've been tricked!" he shouted to the men. "That bloody, black bastard!"

They scampered down the hill to the burning valley.

Pharcel stood for a long time near the edge, looking down at the conflagration that lit up the valley. It was a grand sight. The night below exploded in burning billows of smoke. Sparks shot up to the skies, and spread over the valley like gigantic fireworks. Loud outbursts rent the night as casks of rum and molasses exploded in the rising heat. It seemed the whole works was on fire. Smaller blazes were everywhere about the valley, and arrows of flame shot through the cane fields surrounding the mill.

Pharcel did not linger any longer. He sped down the track towards Dubique, through the fields of cane, and down to the house. The back of the house was surrounded with darkness, but towards the front the dim glow of a distant fire lightened the dark. He could hear frantic voices down the slope near the shore. He stood in the night and listened. No sound came from the house. He edged his way along the side until he came to the front verandah. The light had brightened there, and he could see fiery smoke and sparks rising over the sea. Voices rose and fell, coming from the flat near the shore where the fire raged in the heaps of cane straw that surrounded the storehouse.

Elise and Georgette were alone on the verandah, leaning anxiously towards the noise and the flaming night. Pharcel remained still, wondering what to do next. He could not simply walk in and snatch the woman away in her daughter's presence. But he would if he had to. He was still uncertain what he would do if Elise resisted. Just then he heard the cry of an infant within. Only a faint light came from the interior of the house, though the verandah was bright with the light of the flames that now rose joyfully to the skies. Georgette hesitated, not wanting to leave the fascination of the glowing brightness that spread in widening circles all over the meadow and beyond into the surrounding trees. The cries within grew louder and more insistent. With a gesture of impatience, Georgette turned sharply, and stormed into the house.

Pharcel leapt over the verandah, and wrapped his arms around Elise waist and mouth. She struggled violently in his arms, but he lifted her easily, and staggered down the steps and across the open space to the back of the house. She continued to struggle as he dragged her through the patch of herbs and into the trees. He kept his hand over her mouth until she ceased her struggle. When she rested limply in his arms, he whispered softly to her, and told her of the Captain's threat and the danger she was in. He told her that he had risked all to rescue her. She shook her head in denial, still struggling to get out of his close embrace.

Doubt took hold of Pharcel, and, for a moment, he experienced what it would be like if the world fell below his feet. She was breathing heavily as if in terror. Her bosom rose and fell, and he could feel her short gasps for breath. Suddenly, he felt lost and frightened. He released her, and turned away, poised to fly through the trees. But as quickly, she grasped his arm, and pulled him to her. She laid her head against his beating chest, and cried softly.

Gently, he lifted her in his arms and onto his shoulder. Together they raced up the hill, and did not stop until they reached the flat in the woods.

CHAPTER 24

Black smoke rose to the skies, obliterating the sprinkling of stars. The millhouse was a mass of scarlet and orange flames that rose higher and higher with each new explosion from within the burning interior. The roof had already caved in, leaving the exterior walls standing like an empty shell. The tall chimney at one end, emitted streaks of flames, and rocked precariously with every blast from the exploding casks. The wind carried showers of sparks on its easterly course, and deposited the burning ashes onto the dry trash among the fields of sugar cane.

Less than a quarter of a mile to the west, the estate house had already been burnt down to the ground, and only thin wisps of smoke came from the smoldering remains. Several smaller fires had sprung up among the buildings around the mill, but these had already burnt themselves out. Parts of the fields of cane were also ablaze, and the wind so wafted the flames that they spread, and shot in narrow paths across the fields to surrounding green patches of meadow. What kept the millhouse burning so fiercely were the mountains of casks of rum and the vats of molasses that were stored there.

The militiamen had formed a circle around the mill where, aided by the hordes of villagers, freedmen and slaves who had rushed to the conflagration, they attempted at first to quench the blaze; but, having been constantly repulsed by its growing ferocity, they now simply tried to contain it within the crumbling walls. White men and black men, barebacked and sweat-drenched, sweltered in the infernal heat, the bodies of the black men glistening like polished ebony, the white men's burnt red like boiled lobsters. It was a scene reminiscent of Hell itself, devastation so gigantic and frightening that many stood helpless in shock and desolation.

Captain Marshall rushed about screaming orders and urging his men to intensify their efforts even though he knew that the relay of water buckets could not quell the rage of the fire, but only added to the fierceness of the flames. Several of the men had already succumbed to the steamy heat or had suffered severe burns from the vaporous clouds that spurted in occasional blasts from the exploding casks. Captain Marshall's scarlet tunic stuck to his sweating body, and his wet and tousled hair fell in disorder all about his face and shoulders. The men had told him that his little cottage beyond the fields of cane had burnt to cinders; but he had paid little heed; brushed them aside, and screamed at them to move more quickly with the buckets.

The truth was that he was in desperate confusion. He was certain that this was Pharcel's doing, but he could not understand the purpose of it. Not having any other course of action, he drove his men ruthlessly to more daring assaults on the overpowering flames even though he realized it was futile and senseless to do so. In his mind he knew he had been fooled, but he was baffled how that had come to be. He had no idea where Pharcel could be or why he had retaliated with such desperate and violent action. Somehow the slave had outwitted him, and he did not know what his next move should be.

As he prepared to rush around the circle one more time, he felt a tugging at his sleeve. He brushed the hand aside impatiently, swearing at the men to move faster with the buckets. He came to a halt as the hand pulled him to a standstill. The man was leaning close to his ear shouting words that were lost in the roaring of the flames and the whooshing sounds that came with every new explosion. He thought he heard the word "Dubique" and then "fire". In panic he turned to the man and, frustrated and angry, shouted to him that he should speak louder. His heart sank as he took in the meaning of what the man was saying. Suddenly a light brighter than the flames that filled the night broke into his mind, and he hollered with rage and impotence as he understood the full import of what the man had said.

He broke away from the circle of men, elbowed his way roughly through the crush of villagers, and ran all the way to the encampment, calling from a distance for his horse to be saddled. He fretted, and raged until the stable boy, nervous at the storming impatience, led the horse half saddled to him. The Captain swore at him and fumbled to complete the buckling of the reins and the still loose saddle. Without another word, he swung onto the horse and rode away furiously into the night.

The storehouse was strongly built; and the thick stone walls stoutly resisted the heat of the flames, but the doors and windows had burnt down. All that was left were the blackened frames. The roof was still blazing when Captain Marshall arrived. The heaps of trash around the open space in front of the building had burnt down to a field of hot ashes. The Captain hardly glanced at the burning building and the sweaty dark bodies around it as he took the path that led up to the house. Jean looked in surprise at the haste with which he forced his horse up the steep track, but did not call to him.

The glow of the fire lightened the path, and he urged his horse mercilessly up the steep incline. His heart thundered within his bosom as he thought of the disaster that awaited him at the house. The stratagem that Pharcel had employed now stared him in the face, and he cursed himself for not having anticipated the force of the slave's desperation. Now that he had seen the scale of the destruction at Geneva and the burning storehouse on the shore, there was no doubt in his mind that Pharcel had set the fire at Geneva to draw him away from Dubique, just as he had done with the storehouse to lure his guards away from the house. Now the house was unguarded, and there was no telling what might have happened to Elise and to Georgette and his child.

He could not imagine that a slave could be so possessed with passion that he would go to such lengths to rescue the woman he desired. That was the substance of legend. The Greeks had fought Troy to recover their Helen, but Elise was no Helen. It seemed improbable to him that a simple, homely woman could have been the cause of a conflagration so vast and so terrible. He was breathless with trepidation as he crossed the small meadow to the house.

Georgette was standing on the verandah, holding in her arms the infant, now asleep and swaddled in a thin blanket.

"Where is Elise?" he shouted as he galloped across the meadow.

Georgette, astonished at the anxiety in his voice, looked at him calmly.

"Why, is anything the matter?" she asked, intending to tease him and provoke his impatience.

"Where is she?" There was panic in his voice, and he sat his horse as if prepared to rush precipitately in any direction.

Georgette, not understanding the gravity of his concern, regarded him with amusement, wondering at the cause of his agitation.

"She was here a moment ago," she ventured. "She must have gone down to the fire."

Captain Marshall turned his horse around, and rode down the hill in a heedless gallop. He had paid scant attention to the crowd standing helplessly around the blazing storehouse. He thought he had seen Jean's slender figure among the glowing black faces around the fire, but he had not seen Elise. He could not have missed her elegant figure, usually so calm and poised, among the excited and babbling slaves. She had not been at the house either, though Georgette was certain that she could not have gone very far. If anything untoward had happened at the house, Georgette would have known. His chest tightened with tension as he raced down the hill.

"Where is Elise?" he shouted at the first group he met on the flat near the burning building. They gave him vacant stares, and turned away.

"Where is Elise?" he kept on shouting.

Jean came up to him. His face appeared calm. He had come down to the burning storehouse at the first alarm, but seeing that the flames had already spread through the dry cane trash and engulfed the building, he had given up all hope of saving it. So intense was the heat around the building, no one could come within ten yards of it. He could have organized a relay of buckets, taking water from the nearby stream, but he had quickly realized that such effort would have been wasted. In his typical indifferent way, he had early given up the property as lost. As far as he was concerned, that was merely another item in his long list of failures.

"Elise is up at the house," he said, his voice questioning the reason for the Captain's obvious agitation.

"She is not there," Marshall said.

Jean regarded him closely. He was puzzled as to the reason why the Captain should be so flustered, even alarmed about Elise not being there. She must be somewhere about the house. Why should he be so disturbed anyway?

"Has anybody seen Pharcel?"

A score of eyes turned to the Captain, some widening in fright; but no one answered.

"Has anyone seen Pharcel?" Marshall asked again, his voice charged with vehemence.

A small man emerged from the shadows. He was from a village further north along the coast, and he had been drawn to Dubique by the bright glow that filled the sky for most of the night. He stepped forward.

"I saw someone on the shore sometime before sunset," he said hesitantly. "It might have been him. There was a boat which he was filling with dry coconut fronds."

"How far away?" Marshall demanded.

"Below Petite Savanne," the man replied.

"Damn!" the Captain swore. He dug his heels into the horse's flank and thrashed it to a gallop. They heard the horse's hooves pounding the track along the coast until it faded to near silence.

Jean scratched his head in perplexity. He stood there for a long time, his head bent to his bosom, pondering the Captain's strange behavior and the implicit association of his wife with the runaway slave. Then he quietly left, and walked slowly up the hill to the house.

The grey light of early dawn was just softening the stygian darkness when Pharcel, leading Elise by the hand, came onto the shore. They walked over the wet shingle to the boat, and stood there uncertainly for a few moments. Pharcel had never sailed a canoe. He had no experience with boats. Certainly he had never managed any craft with sails. As a boy, he had sometimes rowed a raft along the coast at Dubique when the sea was at its calmest. Today, huge breakers were rolling in, and he wondered how he could maneuver the delicate craft into such turbulent waters. He had not given thought about the crossing to Martinique. All he had thought about was to escape the shores of Dominica in whatever way he could.

He was in no hurry. Marshall and his men would have their hands full trying to put out the fire at the mill and the buildings and fields around it. Even if the Captain had by now seen through his subterfuge, he doubted if he would leave the greater disaster of the burning mill to come after him. He felt a surge of pride and satisfaction at the thoroughness with which his men had carried out his instructions. He had watched the fire from the hills, and it had already been vast, and spreading fiercely into the sugar cane fields by the time he had left for his descent into Dubique. Marshall and his men would have to work all night to prevent the fire spreading all over Grandbay.

He pre-occupied himself for the moment with removing the coconut fronds from the boat. The bag with the treasure was in the bottom. Carefully, he placed the oars along each side of the canoe where he could quickly grasp them. The sound of the waves was pounding in his ears, and he looked out at them rising and cresting and rolling in balls of foam onto the rocky shore. He was frightened. He guided Elise to the bow of the canoe where he placed her on the bottom with her back to the sea.

He was still uncertain what to do. Looking frightfully at the waves rolling in, he recalled the days when he was just a boy, and how the fishermen of the village, having to launch their canoes into such rough seas, always waited for a calm that came in spells. He had watched for nearly twenty minutes, and he had observed no calming of the waves. He wanted to push off, but he was frightened of the surf that beat so violently on the shore. Though the light had brightened, the waves were no less threatening than they had been in the gloam.

A dark, low cloud hung over the sea. Beyond the crashing waves, the water heaved and fell in deep troughs, and reflected the dismal light that came from the overcast sky. He shuddered as he thought of himself bobbing and plunging directionless in those forbidding depths, and he suddenly turned around and looked with yearning at the more friendly and familiar hills and mountains above him. He would be safer there, he knew, safer than he would be on that restless and threatening sea.

Elise sat in the bow of the boat, looking fearful. Her loose, grey dress was folded over her shapely legs. She wore thin sandals on her feet; her neck and ears were bare of ornaments, and her light hair fell in disorderly strands over her face and around her shoulders. Pharcel watched her sitting there as if in a dream, and he felt himself transported by the magic of the moment. Her lips were parted as if in sudden wonder at herself and what she was about to do. She sensed Pharcel's hesitation and the obvious fear that had filled his eyes. Wanting to get away from the strange situation that she was in, she made as if to rise.

"I can't do it," she said, her voice suddenly tremulous with uncertainty. "I want to go back."

"We can't," Pharcel said firmly. "It is too late. It is too dangerous."

"Take me back," she pleaded. "I won't go any further."

Just then, the sound of pounding hooves broke over the roar of the sea, and through the margin of coconut trees a horseman galloped towards them. He rode like a man possessed, one arm extended like a finger of doom. He held a pistol leveled at the boat. Pharcel looked up in panic. Although it was still too far to recognize the horseman, he was certain it could only be his enemy, the man who had sworn to destroy him.

Captain Marshall rode across the grove, leaping over fallen coconut fronds and scattering the husks of dry nuts that had been left to rot under the trees. He was covered in soot and damp with sweat. His hair clung in wet strands to his forehead. His lips were parted in a snarl as he came abreast of the boat.

Pharcel reached for the stern of the boat, bracing his shoulder to push off into the breakers; but his feet slipped under him, scattering pebbles in a wide arc behind.

"Don't move!" he heard the Captain shout.

Pharcel remained crouched over the boat. His musket was in the bottom, too far for him to grasp. Elise sat in the hollow of the bow, her face pale with shock. She had hardly been aware of the danger she was in. Everything had happened so fast. When she had felt the forceful arms tighten around her mouth and belly she was in terror of death, thinking that the slaves were in revolt again and she was going to be killed. Then the soft, gentle tones of Pharcel's voice had lulled her to a sense of comfort and assurance, and she had followed him still lost in confusion but unafraid. Now that the Captain had broken in upon the enchantment of their adventure, she was filled with guilt, embarrassment and a deep sense of despair.

Captain Marshall had pulled up his horse several paces from the boat, and his approach was deliberately slow and menacing. Pointing his pistol directly at Pharcel, he glowered at him, and spat in disgust at the scene before him. Up to this moment, his mind had refused to accept the possibility that Elise had surrendered her virtue to Pharcel, a slave and a black man; but seeing them together now, she so submissive in the bow of the canoe, and he standing so proud and obviously in control over her, the Captain experienced the kind of revulsion that would overcome him if he watched two worms coupling. The bile rose in his throat as he saw the fear and distress creeping into Elise's eyes. At that moment, he felt only contempt for her.

"Move away from the boat!" he ordered.

Pharcel walked backwards a few paces, keeping his eye on the Captain. He stood erect on the shingles, his bare upper body gleaming brightly in the gathering sunlight. He regarded his enemy with defiance.

Captain Marshall dismounted his horse and stood arrogantly beside the boat. His lips curled in a sardonic smile and his eyes twinkled in triumph.

"Well, Pharcel," he said mockingly, "you are a marvel of stupidity, aren't you? Now you have added abduction to the already enormous burden of your crimes."

Pharcel regarded him coldly. His lips trembled in anger as he stood helpless before the white officer. Fury boiled within him, and he would have leapt like a savage beast at the Captain's smug and mocking face had he not glanced towards Elise and seen the miserable look in her eyes. She looked crestfallen where she sat, and he felt deep sorrow that he had dragged her to this.

"Ah, Elise," Marshall spoke in taunting tones. "Do not be afraid. You are safe now from this savage. I promise you, you will be free from him forever."

Although she had felt shattered and ashamed when the Captain had broken through the trees and stood over them, the sound of the mockery in his voice raised her ire, and she turned to him with a scornful look.

"I do not need your protection." She spoke with as much dignity as she could muster. "There is no need for it. I will find my way back to where I belong."

She raised herself to the gunwales, slung one leg over the side of the boat away from the Captain, and stood hesitantly, the wind from the sea blowing her disheveled hair about her face and wrapping her loose dress around her curvaceous figure. Marshall looked at her appreciatively.

At that moment, his eyes fell on the sack in the bottom of the boat. For a while he regarded the object indifferently, but then he noticed something unusual in the way it bulged towards the bottom, as if something heavy weighed it down. Nonchalantly, he reached into the boat and lifted it. The soft metallic jingle of gold startled him.

"Now what have we here?" he asked, ripping the cord that secured the neck of the sack. Pharcel made a step forward, and the Captain instantly leveled his pistol at his chest. "One more step and you are dead," he snarled.

He dipped his hand in the sack and brought up a handful of coins.

"Why, this is gold," he said incredulously. "A sack full of gold. A veritable treasure!"

He shook the bag, his face beaming with excitement. Pharcel stood resignedly a few feet away. He knew it was hopeless now. He was being held at the point of a pistol. He could either leap away and risk being shot, or submit himself to capture, and hope that he could once again make an escape. Any prospect that he entertained in that regard was dashed by the Captain's next words.

"Well," he said with an evil grin on his dark countenance. "There is no more need to keep you alive. Indeed, there is no more need for either of you. This treasure is worth more than your life, Pharcel; and more than the love of this degraded French trollop."

He fixed his aim on Pharcel's bare chest and grinned with all the malice of his pent-up hate. Pharcel held his breath, waiting for the shock of the bullet. Elise cried out, a loud, wailing cry that resonated over the sound of the surf.

Pharcel felt as if he was suspended in a moment of unreality, somewhere between life and death. He stared at the Captain, unable to comprehend the sudden turn of events. They had come so close to escaping. But for his hesitation in pushing off into the waves, they would have been safely launched into the sea and out of the Captain's reach. Now his life, and evidently that of Elize, hung on the slender thread of his enemy's will. Somehow, he felt totally devoid of emotion, as if death had already taken possession of him. Somewhere in the far recess of his consciousness he heard Elise's voice pleading with the Captain; but he no longer cared.

"No!" she was saying. "You can have it all. Take the gold. Take me. Just let him be."

But the Captain was deaf to her cry. He held the bag of gold in one hand and his pistol, steadily aimed at Pharcel in the other. He laughed triumphantly, a diabolical look carved on his face by the cruel lines about his eyes and lips. He was standing just a few feet away from Pharcel, and he could have killed him quickly. But with deliberate slowness, grinning maliciously at the resigned calm that had fallen on Pharcel's countenance, he lowered the weapon to fix it on his lower abdomen.

"I promised that I would give you a slow and painful death," he spat out harshly, "and you shall have it."

Pharcel's vision brightened and he could sense the slow tightening of the Captain's finger on the well-oiled trigger of the gleaming weapon. The tension held him breathless. It was as if his heart had already stopped beating. Out of the corner of his eye, he saw Elise slip out of the boat, her face dark with purpose. She crouched like an angry lioness about to spring to defend its mate, her arms extended, fingers tensed like drawn claws.

A loud twang came out of the bushes beyond the grove. The sound of gunshot exploded in the air. Pharcel felt no fear; and he felt no pain. The sun shone brightly, coming out of the clouds; and birds were singing in the trees only a few feet away from the shore.

Pharcel's eyes widened with surprise and incomprehension as he saw the Captain's jaw snap open in a painful gasp, eyes widening with consternation, and face twisting with horror and agony. Blood flowed out of his mouth. His arms fell slowly downwards, the pistol and the sack slipping gently from his grasp. For what seemed like minutes, he stood swaying on his feet, an arrow projecting out of his middle. The Captain's eyes bulged out of their sockets and his mouth emitted a sickening gurgle as a stream of blood spurted out between his twisted lips. Pharcel stared unbelieving at the stricken man, not understanding from where his deliverance had come.

He heard a rustle in the bushes beyond the grove of coconut trees. Kumeni strode out into the open. She was naked down to her waist, and wore only a thin cotton skirt and a straw band around her forehead. She came purposefully forward, beckoned to Pharcel to enter the canoe. Pharcel quickly roused himself from the stupor that had taken hold of him, and rushed to Elise who had now collapsed helplessly on the gravel. He helped her into the canoe and followed.

Planting her feet firmly in the gravel, Kumeni pushed the boat into the water. She followed in the foaming wash and deftly leapt into the canoe as it rode over the first wave. The boat lifted on the rolling surf, and crashed into a trough; but by then she had seized the oars, and pulled mightily over the on-coming swell past the breakers and into the furrowing sea. Pharcel sat in the stern, feeling inadequate in this unfamiliar element.

"Can you use the sails?" Pharcel spoke timidly

"Only around the coast," Kumeni replied without much confidence. "Never across the channel"

But as they moved away from the shore towards the open sea, she took hold of the halyard and hoisted the sail. Quickly, she trimmed it, and the tiny vessel was soon skimming over the swells. As the outline of Martinique gained brighter definition, Pharcel relaxed in the stern. He looked with tenderness at Elise who appeared to be still stricken with the shock of their recent crisis.

Kumeni sat on a plank laid across the beam, her legs wide apart as she expertly trimmed the sail to keep the little canoe's bow firmly towards Martinique. Her eyes turned to Pharcel, a placid but longing look on her broad face. She turned at last to the horizon and her eyes went past the white woman sitting listlessly in the bow.

Elise sat at the bow seeing the shoreline of Dominica recede until only the rugged form of the vast complex of hills and mountains rose above the sea. Soon that too got dimmer and dimmer. She felt the little boat skimming over the waves, and herself sinking lower and lower. Waves of agony swept over her abdomen, and her lips tightened in a suppressed cry. Now the world was falling to pieces, and she could not tell the sea from the sky. She felt herself drifting into darkness.

In the stern, Pharcel looked towards her, and saw the agony in her compressed lips and vacant, staring eyes. At first, he thought she was merely frightened; and he was about to call to her when his eyes fell on the widening patch of crimson at her lower abdomen.

"Elise!" he shouted. "Elise! What is it, Elise?"

He rose on his feet, and the boat listed and rocked from side to side, its gunwales almost to the level of the waves. He sat again hurriedly.

Kumeni had turned to look at Elise, and a wash of resignation passed over her face. She had seen the spread of blood, and a chill had crept over her.

"How far?" Pharcel shouted at her. "How much time?"

Kumeni shook her head sadly.

"Not far," she murmured. "Not much time"

CHAPTER 25

On a small plantation near Trois Ilets, the La Pagerie family had lived many years ago among fields of sugar cane. The family had once occupied a modest mansion, but this had been completely destroyed by a hurricane. With insufficient means to restore it, they had been forced to convert a thick-walled mill with a tall chimney at one end, to habitable quarters, dividing the barn-like interior into separate rooms.

Nothing in the ambience of the place or in the particular situation of the nearly impoverished family suggested that one of them would have gained universal pre-eminence as the most renowned woman of the eighteenth century. But the eldest daughter called Josephine, raised among this undistinguished family, and in the squalor of the modified sugar mill, was to become Empress of France, and the leading lady among the royal palaces of Europe.

It must have been the hand of Providence that had brought her to the attention of the son of the then governor of Martinique who took her to France where he married her when she was only sixteen years old. The story of Josephine's life is both tragic and romantic, for not many years after, her husband was executed during the Reign of Terror, and she was once again reduced to the lowest ebb of poverty. But Providence once again intervened, and, in an inexplicable twist of fortune, put her in the way of Emperor Napoleon who fell in love with her, and married her soon after.

Her statue now stands in an open park on the edge of Fort-de-France near the sea. The park is surrounded by rows of royal palms, and within, there are grassy mounds and occasional clumps of trees. At the seaward end, the grey walls of a fort rise like a bulwark against any disturbance to the tranquility of the place. Stone benches are strewn about its periphery, where elegantly dressed patriots sit and rest in the shade of overhanging branches.

She must have been a beautiful woman. The bare arms, slender neck and tall, shapely figure speak of an elegance that was both graceful and alluring. The crowned head now lies in the grass at the base of the statue, having been severed by a disgruntled colored freedman in a fit of rage when it was rumored that it was she who, in 1802, had urged Napoleon to restore slavery to the French colonies, after the slaves had enjoyed a period of freedom that had lasted less than ten years. Napoleon was to divorce her seven years later. The severed neck and the top of the torso had been painted red, with bloody streaks running down the neatly carved bosom to simulate the gory work of the guillotine. Even so, the face on the fallen head shows an expression of gentleness, graciousness and infinite calm, qualities for which Josephine had been universally renowned.

A black man stood with elegant ease near the statue. He was dressed in plain white trousers that clung to his middle and thighs, glossy black boots molded around his calves, and frilled white shirt, partly covered by a maroon jacket, that swept gracefully from his waist to the back of his knees. On his head was a grey top hat very much in the fashion of the times. Despite his robust build, his garments sat on him in immaculate lines, from his broad shoulders to his narrow waist, and down to his muscular thighs.

At the edge of the park, opposite the *Hotel de Ville*, a shiny black and gold-lined carriage stood near the curb. Its coachman, neatly attired, sat upright and attentive in the sun. Now and again he glanced expectantly at the elegant figure standing in the park.

The man standing near the statue of Josephine had found Jacques running errands between merchant warehouses around the dock; and had immediately sought out his master, and offered a handsome payment for him. Jacques had been both surprised and thrilled, and could not believe his good fortune when he was brought to a substantial estate and a gracious mansion at St. Ann, about thirty miles distant from Fort-de-France. He had immediately taken charge of the stables and the rich equipage stored there.

Jacques had been astonished to find Kumeni walking the vast corridors of the mansion with blissful self-possession. She had worn a simple knee-length shift with a bright-colored cord tied around her waist, dyed straw band around her head and soft fawn slippers on her feet.

She had acknowledged Jacques' presence in the mansion, but had ignored him completely after that.

Jacques first major task after he was brought to the plantation was to find a woman slave named Betty who had been deported from the island of Dominica five years before. It was a formidable task. He had asked around the docks; and had even sought help and offered large sums to have a search made of the ships' manifests, where records of slave arrivals about the time when Betty had been transported from Dominica were kept; but he had found no trace of her. He thought that somewhere among the vast plantations that dotted the island, the girl was being held a slave; and he was determined to find her.

Jacques had found Betty nearly a month later in a small village where she was serving as a scullery maid in a poor pension. She was even thinner than she had been when she had left Coree Greg's camp. Her shabby and torn dress hung on her skeletal frame like an over-sized coat on a scarecrow. Jacques had been over-joyed at finding her, and the very next day he returned with a substantial sum to negotiate her purchase.

At the mansion, Betty had quickly regained her gentle, but lively spirit. Every day she walked through the long corridors and splendid halls and bedrooms of the mansion as if in a dream. She walked about with her feet bare, wearing plain loose shifts until she was persuaded to adopt the richer garments that hung in profusion in the large boudoir set aside for the women of the household, and to assay soft sandals on her feet.

Every morning, before the dew was dry, the man walked out of the mansion to a small grove of trees.

Jacques followed him one day, and found him standing, head bowed, in the grove, in the middle of which was a clearing; and in the middle of the clearing a tomb, elegantly appointed with cornices and columns and beautiful carvings. There were no other markings on the tomb, except a name: Elise. Jacques had quietly walked away, leaving the man to his silent retreat.

It was getting close to midday; and the man standing in front of the truncated statue of Empress Josephine shifted impatiently in the shade of the low branches. The leaves above him fluttered in the occasional puffs of wind that blew from the sea. At that time of day, few people walked in the park, preferring to lounge in the many cafes and restaurants that lined the boulevard. These days, it was not an unusual sight to see a black man, in the height of fashion strolling about the town, or sitting on the benches in the park; although black people were still debarred from the better restaurants and clubs. But it was uncommon to find one so obviously self-possessed and yet so doleful.

The man knew very little of the personal history of Josephine; but, at least one day in each week he came faithfully to the park, and stood near her statue in deep reflection. Sometimes he would look intently at the graceful contour of her perfect bust; but most times his eyes would descend to, and linger on the truncated head lying in the grass, as if to draw from its serenity something for which he was in search of everyday of his life.

He was standing lost in his thoughts when Betty, wearing a flowing skirt and flowered blouse, came from a side street just past the *Hotel de Ville*. She carried a shallow basket covered with a colorful cloth. She spoke a few laughing words to Jacques, and then climbed gracefully into the carriage.

Not long after that Kumeni appeared some way along the boulevard. She wore a short, plain skirt and knitted vest open at her breast, and carried a low basket which she placed at the back of the carriage before climbing onto the seat beside Betty.

The man standing near the statue of Josephine raised his head, and, seeing the two women in the carriage, began to walk towards them.

Two men stood under the eave of the closed verandah of the hotel. Low tables with chairs had been placed in the shade on the side walk where the denizens of the town habitually gathered for mid-morning refreshment. Marcel, black and powerfully built with a round head and smiling face, and Charles, of medium stature and rubicund complexion, stood away from the crowd. They were looking curiously at the man that was walking with studied dignity towards the brilliantly accoutered carriage.

"Who is that man?" Charles asked, wistfully taking in his elegant suit and richly appointed carriage.

"That is Pharcel," Marcel informed him. "He is the owner of the plantation at St. Ann."

"He must be very rich," Charles mused, glancing at the two women sitting in the carriage.

"Nobody knows how rich," Marcel laughed intimately. "He is a marvel to everyone. Keeps very much to himself and to his household. They say he is a runaway slave, though he carries a letter of manumission signed by the Governor of Dominica himself."

"There is mystery about him," Charles observed cynically. "He walks with a strange air."

"Yes," agreed Marcel. "He is a tragic figure."

"He is?" Charles' curiosity was aroused.

"As tragic as Josephine out there, with whom he seems to have found such empathy," said Marcel; "but far, far more heroic."

"Well, why don't you tell me about it," suggested Charles.

"It is a long story," Marcel said.

"We have all morning." Charles grinned amiably.

"Well then", said Marcel, "let us find a table, and I will tell you all I know."

The two friends watched curiously as Pharcel entered the carriage.

Jacques flicked his whip over the horses' backs and the carriage moved slowly down the boulevard. They watched it until its glossy brightness disappeared around a corner.

978-0-595-39578-1
0-595-39578-3

Printed in the United States
115161LV00003B/52-75/A